"GIVE 'EM HELL"

HARRY 'S
LIBERATION OF
KOREA

Arthur J. Paone

"GIVE 'EM HELL" HARRY 'S LIBERATION OF KOREA

Arthur J. Paone

BELMAR PUBLICATIONS
ARTHUR J. PAONE
504 – SEVENTEENTH AVENUE
BELMAR, NJ 07719

My labor is humbly dedicated to the memory of Congressman

VITO MARCANTONIO
(1902 - 1954)

"I would be remiss to the things in which I believe if I did not stand up here and state my opinion on this matter. After all, Mr. Chairman, you live only once, and it is best to live one's life with one's conscience than to temporize or accept with silence those things which one believes to be against the interests of one's people and one's nation."

(From his speech on the floor of the US House of Representatives opposing Truman's Korean intervention. 1950 Congressional Record, 9628, June 27, 1950.)

Table of Contents

INTRODUCTION

2003 Edition.
Revised 2013.

Can a legitimate case be made for North Korea's mad scramble to produce nuclear bombs and a missile system capable of delivering them to the United States? When I wrote this sentence in 2003 I was thinking only about North Korea. Now in 2013, with the **seven** million nation of 65 year old Israel (together with the Israeli Lobby in the US) clamoring for the annihilation of the **seventy** million nation of thousand year old Iran, the question has become more universal. One is reminded that in 1953 we had the democratically elected government of Iran undermined and replaced by an accommodating Shah. Like Sigmund Rhee later on in South Korea the Shah became increasingly repressive and hated by his people. But as in South Korea that fact was of little concern to us because the Shah, like Rhee, passed our only test: he was *with* us and *against* the Soviets.

If history is any guide, the answer as to whether a nation needs a nuclear bomb to keep the US from annihilating it, the answer must unfortunately be YES.

The human race has not always moved inexorably forward, gaining knowledge, wisdom and experience and thereby evolving into a better form of *homo sapiens*. We at times have moved forward but at other times have moved backward. Genghis Khan set us back; Galileo moved us a bit forward. Mongol hordes burning down cities and killing millions was certainly a setback for civilization. Martin Luther and the breakup of the "One True Church" was a step forward, ultimately leading to the principle of freedom of, and from, religion enshrined in the US Constitution. President Franklin Delano Roosevelt's sudden death and the accidental ascendance of Harry S. Truman must certainly be viewed, in my opinion, as a setback for civilization.

i

By April of 1945 the delusional Hitler and His Master Race worldview had been crushed, but with much destruction throughout the West; in the East similar if not more destruction accompanied the near end of the Japanese mirage. The Russians, having borne a greater share of the battle against the Nazis, had been left spread over East Europe, victorious -- but hungry, tired and burdened. Only the Americans were still standing -- with continuing massive production from their unscathed factories and great wealth in their treasuries. By default the world looked to America's leader, now the most powerful man on earth, for guidance and help.

As in such historical periods of voids it was a transformative time. What was done now would shape generations to come. Those who were hungry wanted to eat; those whose homes had been destroyed wanted to rebuild; those who had been oppressed wanted freedom; those who had been under foreign yokes wanted to be their own masters; those who had been invaded wanted to forever block the routes of the invaders.
So the Europeans wanted to eat and rebuild; the Chinese wanted to be free of corrupt and exploiting elites; the Russians wanted security along the corridors in Europe that had been used repeatedly to assault them; the Indians, Koreans, Vietnamese, Indochinese and many others wanted independence from their colonial masters -- the Dutch, the English, the French, the Italians.

Many of these dreams and longings were universally shared and could be achieved without conflict with neighbors. Others however would require compromises and balancing. Still others would cause some conflicts that had to be resolved.

If ever history begged for a great person, it was now.

But instead tragedy struck civilization.

On April 12, 1945 Franklin Delano Roosevelt died suddenly at the age of 63. FDR had foreseen much of these Post

War complications and had been preparing for them. He had cajoled the extremely reluctant Churchill to sign declarations suggesting independence for the British colonies. He had insisted that representatives of the most populous nation of the world, China, always be included at the table of world leaders. He used money, material and charm to negotiate and get along with the difficult Russian leader, Joseph Stalin, until reaching a delicate balance of mutual respect and trust. He had set about establishing a world order based on cooperation between the great powers so that all could live in peace and prosperity -- with the particular interests of each such nation taken into full and sensitive consideration.

Into his place came the newly minted Vice President, Harry S. Truman, the erstwhile Senator from Missouri, arriving at this historic pinnacle of power -- without a clue. Having little else to rely on, he willfully made virtues of his weaknesses. Instead of reasoning; he would rely on his "guts." Instead of subtle conciliation; he would "Give 'em Hell." Instead of recognizing and allowing for the complexities facing the world; he would parochially quack what he called the "simple and plain truth." Proudly simple-minded and unrepentant to the end: "I never did give them hell. I just told the truth, and they thought it was hell."(Harry S Truman, Look, Apr. 3, 1956.)

Hence our civilization was set back as we wantonly spent our resources, human and material, on perfecting the arts of destruction as we suffered through an eminently avoidable Cold War; Nuclear Proliferation; the militarization of food and reconstruction aid (The Marshall Plan *Plus* NATO); the Arms Race; Korea; Vietnam; and the endless and dangerous Israeli-Palestinian morass. (On Vietnam, see, e.g., the 1950 article by C. L. Sulzberger, " 'TRUMAN DOCTRINE' HELD SET BY US FOR SOUTHEAST ASIA" for what reads today as a chilling insight into how Truman's pugilism set us on the road to the ignominious and costly meddling in Vietnam. New York Times, May 14, 1950, p. 21.)

On the Palestine question in 1948 Truman found the simple and plain answer quickly. YES, he said to Bernard Baruch and his other Jewish campaign contributors, why not partition Palestine and give about half of it to the Zionists settlers? Another "gut" decision that has plagued us since then. Of course no sensible person just after the Holocaust would have objected to giving the survivors of Hitler's insane extermination program as much refuge as the world could provide. But in opposition to Truman's "Give then Palestine" there certainly must have been specialists in the State Department who were waving their arms and yelling: "Mr. President, please wait. There are already an ancient people living in Palestine."

But the land of Palestine seemed to fit into the President's Bible-based Mid-Western Christian upbringing: the Chosen Land of the Israelites. The fact that he studiously avoided, however, and which has not gone away, was that this particular piece of earth was already occupied, and by a people who could trace their ancestry to a time before the nations of Europe, much less of America, were formed. Yet the President seemed never to have recognized this.

Indeed as I write this revised version, November 21, 2012, Israel is into its 7th day of **again** pulverizing from the air and the sea the 1.7 million defenseless people of Gaza. Talk about unequal matches. So far 139 Gazans have been killed and well over 1,200 wounded; on the other side three Israeli civilians have also been killed. Nothing of any significance on the Israeli side has been damaged but of course the unchallenged Israeli planes and drones in the air, its ships parked in the waters just off Gaza and its tanks sitting on the border are relishing their easy, and *safe*, target practice. Israeli mothers do not react with panic and fear when their children are activated from the reserves: they know that their little ones would just be going for a safe and refreshing "walk in the park" -- after all, whoever got killed, or even hurt, while beating up the practically unarmed Gazans? These were such inspiring and exhilarating "wars."

Each day their defense ministry announces how many hundreds of targets their planes have hit, etc. Like last time in 2008 the Israeli intent seems to be to destroy whatever infrastructure the Gazans still have. I assume that again all the electrical plants in Gaza will be demolished; the minimal drinkable water supply will be severely compromised; what's left of their sewer system from the last attack will be torn up; their police and fire stations blown up again; their factories obliterated. Electricity, drinking water and sewers seem to be the Israeli quarry of choice outside of their "targeted" killings. The fantasy of Gazans wallowing in stinking sewage lifts the Israeli spirits.

I visited Gaza four years ago after the last Israeli bombardment and invasion. Piles of rubble. Now it will probably be worse. The Israelis appear to do this every few years. I suspect it is to test out their new weapons; confirm their intelligence; check out the new US-supplied Iron Dome missile defense system; assassinate a couple hundred people on their endless list of the damned together with any bystanders and finally, but not least, just to amuse themselves. In my view however, the most remarkable testing is that of the human character. The amazing Palestinians just get up again and again and face the world with hope -- something that astounds me.

Most Americans according to polls I hear on the radio are supporting the Israelis. But I doubt most Americans really know what is going on there as it is almost impossible for the average American to get full and accurate reporting from our adamantly pro-Israel Press. For example, how many Americans know that in the 12 months before the assassination of that Hamas leader which set off d this latest flare-up, not **one** Israeli had been killed by a Palestinian; yet the Israelis had killed **65** Palestinians, using one or another excuse in trying to explain away their crimes (http://www.ifamericansknew.org/).

Laws and treaties have no meaning for the Israelis, much less does any notion of fairness or humanity. Truly a monster and

v

lawless state. (See my book: Israel, Our Frankenstein. Belmar, NJ: Belmar Publications, 2010.) Just after out taxpayer financed and US constructed "Iron Dome" had prevented most of the Gazan rockets from landing in Israel and just after the US pathetically joined a grab bag of Pacific Island nations to oppose the overwhelmingly supported Palestinian bid for observer status at the UN, the Israel Government announced that it would build thousands more settlement homes in Palestinian territory, including the vital territory they designated as E-1 which would effectively divide the West Bank and finally make official the end of the already long dead two state option. A "thank you" from our ungrateful Frankenstein expressed by a typically scornful kick in the butt to our President. Proof again that the Israelis control the America government on any issue remotely involving Israel. In reaction to this gross violation of the Geneva Conventions, the United Nations Charter, various other international treaties and UN Resolutions, and probably in violation of restrictive clauses in our own aid and loan guarantee packages to Israel, our Secretary of State could only reiterate the usual American objection, possibly vetted through AIPAC as the maximum allowable "criticism:" *that settlements were counterproductive*, etc., but then nothing else was done, following the pattern of the past 50 years as Israel gobbled up the West Bank.

Of all the many tragic blunders by Truman that have cursed us to this day, I deal with only one of them in this book: the Korean War.

Imagine that you were born in a town in North Korea. Your uncle has been blind for most of his life – the result of an American bomb dropped on his village fifty or so years ago. An aunt is a strange recluse because she doesn't want people to look at her horribly disfigured face – the result of an American napalm attack during that Korean war when as a child she had been tending the fields with her mother. You yourself have been brought up in their house because your parents were killed while riding to town one day in their ox-drawn cart -- their bodies riddled by 50 caliber bullets from an American jet fighter. You don't live in the village you were born in because the Americans burned it down.

Because of that terrible war and the fear that the Americans might do it again, your country has had to maintain such a large army that it cannot afford much else. Yet your leaders had at one point been talking to the Americans about making a settlement so that some guarantee or at least promise could be obtained from them that they would not do it again. The talks were going well. Your leader at the time, Kim Jong IL, gave a lavish and warm welcome to the American Secretary of State, Madeleine Albright, in 2000 and everything was set to welcome the American President Clinton. Finally, after 50 years there would be a treaty that would make everyone feel safer and lessen the need for such a huge Army.

Then all of a sudden just a few months later in 2001 a new President, George Bush, for no apparent reason slams the door in your country's face. On top of that he gratuitously insults and ridicules your leader. This Bush Administration then concocts an "Axis of Evil" which links your country, the Democratic People's Republic of Korea (DPRK), with some other imagined enemies of his, Iraq and Iran – countries with whom you hardly had any contact. Finally, the Americans, step by step, set up Iraq for a turkey shoot, invade that country even though it had made no hostile act against them, kills anyone standing in the way with state of the art weaponry and then occupied that ancient land. Treaties, promises, international law, the United Nations, the outrage of the rest of the world – none of that in the slightest deflected the Americans from their goal to violently change the government of another country.

Nothing could be clearer now to your leaders, and probably to the leaders of a dozen other countries, as to what course they have to take for survival: if they do not want to be occupied by the Americans, they had better hurry up and develop a weapon that will keep the Americans away. The Americans had hated the Soviets but never invaded Russia because the Russians could drop the Bomb on American cities. The same with China. So the DPRK and any other country that wants to remain independent has been made to believe that it must now hurry up and develop its own nuclear bomb and a good delivery system as a deterrent.

Previously the tiny and impoverished Communist state of North Korea, left hanging by the collapse of its Soviet trading partners, had not wanted much. It asked only for a written promise from the United States that it would not attack the DPRK and for some financial aid to feed its people. But the American unilateral subjugation of Iraq and the new Bush Doctrine of Pre-Emptive Strike have given a geometric impetus to nuclear proliferation. The message has sounded around the world – there is a New World Order envisioned by the elite now ruling America. In that new world order only the actual ability to deliver a nuclear bomb to the United States will keep a disfavored country independent. Notwithstanding Washington and Downing Street's theatrical stream of misinformation, Hussein had been bluffing -- he had no Weapons of Mass Destruction, much less any that he could deliver to America. The North Koreans, on the other hand, want to make it clear that they are not bluffing.

Few images better symbolize the harebrained mentality of the people in control of our country in 2002 under Bush than that picture of Deputy Defense Secretary Paul Wolfowitz swaggering in the southern Philippines with a holster strapped to his shoulder (Associated Press Photo in New York Times, June 4, 2002). What intoxicating power! How many others could live out so full the wildest of their childhood fantasies? We have been trying to suppress agrarian guerillas in the southern Philippines since the day we took the islands from the Spanish in 1898. We called the peasant rebels Moros and then Huks, now they are always called some kind of "militant" or "terrorist" group, like the Abu Sayyaf. The Colt .45 Automatic Pistol was specifically designed to be used against the Moro and Huk rebels in close combat. Now comes little Paulie, armed with his own personal pistol to do battle with our ancient enemies. This time we will really put them down.

This is the crowd that Chairman Kim Jong-il had to contend with, and now his son, Kim Jong-un is in no better position. Obama promised -- but has not delivered. We are in the same situation as we were with Bush. Obama until now has made no move to get anywhere near where President Clinton had been when he left office in 2001.

But do the **people** of the DPRK themselves, as opposed to their leaders, have anything to fear from the Americans? Indeed, George W. Bush's stated reason for his loathing of Kim Jong IL is the miserable lot of his people. So what of the little people of Korea, will they accept our generous and gratuitous offer to decapitate their leaders?

Americans do not get any definite images in their minds when they hear their leaders talking about liberating Korea again. We know that with the blood of our young men we saved at least part of Korea from the disease of Communism back in 1950. But exactly what happened during that war does not seem to be part of the American memory.

For Koreans, however, the images of that "liberation" are very vivid – and terrifying. Hundreds of thousands of Koreans, disfigured by American napalm and phosphorous bombs, or living with missing limbs or blind or deaf because of American bombs and mines, have reminded their countrymen each day for the past 60 years what American "liberation" means.

The Koreans had been squabbling among themselves for five years since their release by the Russians and the Americans at the end of World War II. They were trying to reorganize their society and move it from the feudal order of the past. In addition, after 40 years as a colony of Japan there was much that the Koreans had to work out among themselves. On the one hand there were many collaborators who had become wealthy by their cooperation with the Japanese; factory owners and landlords who treated tenants and workers like serfs; on the other hand there were the workers and tenants, now feeling free of the Japanese and demanding a better life.

If left to themselves their country would have gone through some difficult if not bloody growing pains, but then eventually would have taken the shape and character that its people wanted. The people of Korea had no quarrel with the United State, that Great Power, thousands of miles away, which was the only one left standing after World War II. Until the day our planes began the systematic destruction of their country, the Koreans had not killed or wounded a single American. No war had been declared against America. Yet we intervened on one side of this civil conflict, known to us as the Korean War, and brought the type of devastation to this small country that only a Great Power could bring.

During the Korean War the United States intentionally and without apology tried to kill almost every man, woman and child in North Korea, and, with less intention and some apology, did the same to our "allies" in South Korea. Korea became a playground for American Air Power. New and bigger bombs were tested. Faster and more destructive fighter jets were developed. New techniques for destroying large dams, rice crops and cities were introduced. There was no North or South Korea to our Bombers, only "gooks" and targets. The deliberate burning of cities and killing of civilians in North Korea was called "strategic bombing," while the inevitable burning of cities and the killing of civilians in South Korea was called "collateral damage." During testimony on June 15, 1951 before a Senate Committee, one year after the start of the conflict, the General who had commanded the American bomber fleet for the first six months testified that the devastation was universal.

General Rosie O'Donnell:

"*We have, to this date, in the Korean War, dropped* **123,000 tons** *of bombs; and in the entire [WWII] Marianna's campaign . . . throughout almost an entire year*

x

against Japan, **in which 57 major cities were flattened, we only expended 160,000 tons.**"

Chairman Connally.

> *"I am not concerned about* **how many tons** *there were . . . . You can talk about how many tons of missiles you dropped;* **but I am concerned about the results** *of the drops – what did you do?"*

General O'Donnell: *"The results of the tonnage?"*

Chairman Connally. *"Yes."*

General O'Donnell.

> *"I would say that the entire, almost* **the entire Korean Peninsula is just a terrible mess.** *Everything is destroyed. There is nothing standing worthy of the name."*[Emphasis added.]

Senator Connally seemed satisfied with this picture of "the entire Korean Peninsula . . . just a terrible mess" as he asked no more question.

General O'Donnell in 1951 thought that "everything" in Korea had already been destroyed with 123,000 tons of bombs. But the bombing nevertheless continued for another two years. Rubble was being ground into fine dust. Pilots were complaining about the boredom of bombing the same pile of ruins time and time again. By war's end in 1953 we would have dropped over an additional 375,000 tons of bombs.

But are the North Koreans' fears well-grounded? Would the Americans this time do the same thing or even use nuclear weapons against Koreans?

Of course we would. The main reason we did not use atomic bombs in 1950 was a concern about the limited number of

xi

atomic bombs we had and the fear that the Soviets, for whose annihilation we were conserving the A-bombs, might retaliate with atomic bombs of their own. Now of course there are no more Soviets and America's arsenal of doomsday bombs is unlimited. So what would keep the US from nuking the Koreans? One thing, and one thing only – the ability of North Korea to nuke the US or, maybe, one of its allies.

This book is an attempt to explain why the Koreans legitimately fear and deeply distrust the Americans. The source material for my explanation will be American military records and publications. I will use mostly United States Military sources – either official military press releases, testimony of military officers before Congress, official and unofficial biographies of American and Korean military officers, and the reports and manuscripts produced by organizations related to the US Military, like the United State Air Force History and Museums Program. For the sake of transparency I set forth my sources in the text as I use them. I want my evidence and conclusions to be instantly verifiable to any reader, as I know that the conclusions I express above may seem extreme and will be very difficult for many to accept. I hope the extensive use of the exact words used by the actors at the time will convince the reader that there is some basis for my opinions.

The most interesting sources, I believe, are the diaries of some Generals. Many American Generals apparently have kept diaries of their war-time experiences. These diaries were neither official documents nor were they formally sanctioned. In fact, they were frowned upon by the authorities for obvious reasons. The motives for keeping these diaries must have varied. But one can tell that some of these authors, like General Orlando Ward, who commanded the 6th U.S. Infantry Division from October of 1946 to December of 1948 during part of the American Occupation, wanted simply to keep track of his thoughts and to have a discourse with himself, and seems never to have expected his diary to be published. His diary in fact has not been published and can only be found in the archives of the Army's Military History

Institute in Carlisle, Pa. A General like George Stratemeyer, Commander of the Far East Air Force during the first year of the Korean War, on the other hand, seems to be writing to posterity in his diary. But still it is a diary and a lot more frank than the official press releases that he and his staff produced for the obfuscation of the American people.

General Stratemeyer's diary has been edited by William T. Y'Blood, carefully footnoted with very helpful explanations of personalities and events, and published by the USAF in 1999. The General had passed away thirty years earlier in 1969. Nearly all the brackets [ ] in the diary passages I reproduce were inserted as explanations by the editor, William T. Y'Blood. A very few were added by me.

Lieutenant General George E. Stratemeyer headed the Far East Air Force at the beginning of the Korean War but suffered a heart attack in May of 1951. He was replaced by Major General Earle E. Partridge who had commanded, under Stratemeyer, the air force unit based in Tokyo and covering Korea. Since the main source of my book is General Stratemeyer's diary most of my narrative deals with the first year of the war. However, that is when most of the movement and destruction occurred up and down the Korean peninsula, with the war stalemated at about where it started and remained that way till final armistice on July 27, 1953.

George Stratemeyer   Earle Partridge

Another diary I have relied upon, not published and available only in the archives of the Army's Military History Institute, is that of General Earle Partridge. General Partridge as noted commanded the Fifth Air Force under General Stratemeyer during the first year of the Korean War, and then succeeded him when General Stratemeyer became disabled.

I have emphasized words or phrases in the diaries, as well as in passages from books or newspapers by either making the text bold or by putting them into italics. I do this for clarity or to editorialize. Since I do it so often I have not always noted that the emphasis was by me. So unless I note that it was in the original, the emphasis has been added by me.

However, much of this story is contained in the photos of that war. Therefore, I give credit to the privates, corporals, sergeants and captains in the US Army for the photographs they took in Korea. I have named each such individual whenever he is identified on the photos which I have borrowed from the U.S. National Archives. I have also used the photos taken by the airmen of the USAF who took reconnaissance. But unlike the Army, the Air Force did not identify the individual photographers.

I have almost always copied the captions originally supplied by the Army or the Air Force with each photograph. I put the original caption in quotes. So the reader needs to be a little careful about taking some of the captions without a grain of salt. After all, they were written in the heat of battle and many were intended as propaganda to bolster American morale or slant the facts a certain way. For the most part, however, the captions are factual.

CHAPTER I

THE OCCUPATION

"What a mess."
General Orlando Ward, 1946

The American Military occupied Korea below the 38th Parallel from 1945 to the middle of 1948, at which time it was turned over to Sigmund Rhee. This was after an elaborately orchestrated election, supervised by and declared "fair and free " by the UN, had resulted in Rhee's being elected President with nearly 100% of the vote. Rhee also happened to be the only candidate. This was a pattern for successive Rhee reelections until he was finally chased out of Seoul by an angry population in 1960. For most purposes during the period covered by this book, the "UN" in effect meant the US as the UN's finances, policies and operations were controlled by the US.

How the US came to be occupying that portion of Korea below the 38th Parallel is a story studded with accidents, mistakes, chance, greed, arrogance and stupidity. When the Truman Administration had been considering procedures for the surrender of Japan, many decisions had to be made about which Ally would accept the surrender in any particular location, and then get their troops there. The US was the only nation with the ability to make the arrangements. Yet American planners had been caught short by the sudden fall of Japan and they were unprepared for the Japanese surrender in Korea. The Russians were already through Manchuria and heading into Korea while American soldiers were nowhere near. But there were certain elements in the US Government who had targeted one of our own allies, the Soviet Union, as a potential enemy and had begun treating it that way even before the war was over. So, while we were on the one hand helping our British and French allies, and even the Dutch, reintroduce their troops back into their old colonies before the natives got too used to the idea of being their own masters, we were on the other hand also trying to block the Russians from expanding their influence, even in their own backyard.

The idea from the beginning was to deny Korea to the Communists; but with as little expense as possible. This peninsula attached to the land mass of Asia had little value or meaning to us in any way – for military, industrial, natural resources or historic associations, except for Christian missionaries who had built schools and churches here from time to time. Yet the Americans would cause the fateful division of Korea in 1945 not for any strategic reason but primarily to irritate the Russians.

There seems to have been many hands in the mix of rapid decisions that had to be made on management of the complicated Japanese surrender. I believe a significant piece of evidence as to one of those hands that seems to have escaped the historians of the period is a curious memo buried deep within the U.S. Army Military History Institute at Carlisle Barracks, Pa. I came across this surprisingly candid and enlightening document, appropriately marked "TOP SECRET," dated August 11, 1945, among the "H.L. Wolbers Papers" in that Institute. It was written by Edwin W. Pauley and addressed to "The President and The Secretary of State."

Edwin W Pauley, 1945.

Pauley was not just another advisor to President Harry Truman. He was from Indiana, grew up in the South, went to California for his college education and started in the oil business from scratch. During the 1920's and 30's his efforts in the oil fields rewarded him with great wealth and influence. Also in the 30's he began contributing to the Democratic Party and soon became a supporter and close friend of Senator Harry Truman. It was Truman's influence that got FDR in 1941 to appoint Pauley as Lend Lease's manager for the oil being sent to the British and the Soviets. Pauley returned the favor when he, as Treasurer of the Democratic National Committee, and several other individuals, persuaded FDR to drop Henry Wallace in favor of Truman as his Vice Presidential running mate in the 1944 election.

On April 27, 1945, within weeks of FDR's death, the new President appointed Pauley as the American Representative to the Allied Reparations Committee. It was while Pauley was touring the world to determine how much reparations could be extracted from Germany and Japan that he wrote this Top Secret Memo. The following year Truman attempted to promote his friend Pauley into even a greater position of power when he nominated him to be undersecretary of the Navy, with the intent of soon replacing the emotionally deteriorating James Forrestal as Secretary of the Navy. That nomination had to be withdrawn, however, over Truman's fierce and angry resistance, because of issues raised about some murky financial activities by Pauley while Treasurer of the Democratic National Committee as well as the obvious conflict of interest for an oil baron to be in charge of the Navy's vast purchases of oil. Pauley then retreated into the shadows of the White House to join Truman's other cronies in the "Kitchen Cabinet" for the rest of Truman's Presidency, while amassing greater wealth as an oilman. Years later he became a prominent benefactor to the Truman Presidential Library.

His Top Secret memo to Truman and Acheson read in part:

"Conclusions I have reached thru discussions on Reparations and otherwise (I repeat otherwise) lead me to the belief that our forces should occupy quickly as much of the industrial areas of Korea and Manchuria as we can, starting at the southerly tip and progressing northward. I

am assuming all of this will be done at no risk of American lives after organized hostilities have ceased, and occupancy to continue only until satisfactory agreements have been reached between the nations concerned with respect to reparations and territorial rights or other concessions."

(*MacArthur, Pauley and General Wheeler, 1946. Truman Library.*)

It was simple and straightforward advice -- grab as much as we could and then use it to bargain with the Soviets over other things.

The huge industrial facilities and dams developed by the Japanese in Manchuria seemed to be this oilman's primary focus. In the typed memo the words "*Korea and*" are written in by hand, presumably Pauley's, just before the typed word "Manchuria." Was this an afterthought, reflecting Korea's low priority status even with the greediest of Truman's advisors? Was his recommendation political or economic – that is, based on George Kennan's emerging political concept of "containment" of the Soviets or was he merely suggesting we seize as many valuable assets as possible like any looter? In either case it was a very bad

4

omen for FDR's and Vito Marcantonio's vision of Post War cooperation between the US and the Soviet Union.

As the Japanese forces in various parts of the Far East were surrendering, Pauley suggests that we grab and hold onto as much territory as possible, not so much for reparations as for *"otherwise (I repeat otherwise). . ."* and occupy it only for so long as necessary *"until satisfactory agreements have been reached between the nations concerned with respect to reparations and territorial rights or other concessions."* He could not have been envisioning Americans permanently acquiring any part of Manchuria, which of course would be returned to China. Nor could impoverished and mineral-poor Korea, that afterthought, have been his goal for *"territorial rights or other concessions."* In any event, both FDR and Truman had promised "liberation" for this colony of Japan. But the sacred promises of "Liberation" were not as much in Pauley's mind at that point, as was grasping as much of Manchuria and Korea as possible to be used as bargaining chips played in a much bigger game, not yet fully understood but already poisonous, with the Soviets.

Now in the rush of things, the Americans would try to snatch as much land as possible on the borders of Russia -- and hold on to it for *"concessions."* Ironically Pauley's type of thinking had already filtered down to then unknown Colonels Charles Bonesteel and Dean Rusk in an office at the Pentagon. They were assisting in drafting Order Number One which MacArthur would issue to the Japanese after their surrender. Realizing that the Russians could be at the tip of Korea before any Americans could arrive; they took a gamble and drew a line at the 38th Parralel. The goal was to take as much of Korea as possible to deny it to the Russians. Stalin the next day surprised those overreaching land grabbers by agreeing to the draft without objection.

Similar treachery and even more extreme judgments were being expressed at about that very time by Great Britain's Prime Minister, Winston Churchill.

On May 24th Churchill formally instructed in writing his flabbergasted Chiefs of Staff to study the feasibility of an Anglo-American attack on the advancing Soviets in Europe – the ally who has just helped us in defeating Hitler, for the purpose of driving the Soviet troops out of Eastern Europe and back into Russia. Churchill was assuming he could get the Americans involved because he thought he had received a signal from the new President that he was just as belligerent and anti-Soviet as he was. Officials in the Foreign Office and with the Chiefs of Staff were astounded by this apparently irrational request and did their best to bury it on the basis of its impracticality. Britain at that time was bankrupt and its people and military were totally exhausted. It appeared to his advisors that the Old Warrior was beginning to become unhinged. Nevertheless they dutifully went through the motions of putting together a plan of attack, which both Churchill and they called "Operation Unthinkable."

> *"The debate cannot have failed to rouse . . . echoes of 1918-19, when Churchill insisted upon committing to Russia an abortive Allied military expedition designed to reverse the verdict of the 1917 Bolshevik revolution."* (Hastings, Max. Winston's War: Churchill 1940 – 1945. New York: Alfred A. Knopf, 2010.)

His instructions were quickly defanged in a series of deliberately obfuscating and discouraging reports from his Chiefs of Staff. For his part Churchill soon lost interest in this bizarre adventure after realizing that Truman's bellicosity nowhere matched his own (Hastings, Winston's War). The old warmonger Churchill, however, never relented. A few years later the former Prime Minister would travel to America and join Truman in fanning the flames of Anti-Communism with his "Iron Curtain" theatrics.

In September of 1945 about 45,000 men of the war-weary XXIV Division were rushed by General Douglas MacArthur, then stationed in Tokyo and the chief American military commander in the Far East, from Okinawa to Korea to operate as occupation troops (USAFIK – United States Armed Forces in Korea). Three years later when the Occupation officially ended in August of 1948 upon the establishment of the new South Korean Government, the US and President Rhee secretly agreed that the US would control the new Government's military until a final withdrawal of occupation troops. That final withdrawal, 7,000 troops, occurred the following year, at the end of June, 1949, leaving less than 500 American officers and enlisted men as advisors.

There has been a decent amount written in English about the Occupation, with the acknowledged authority being Professor Bruce Cumings. I have adopted his view of the Occupation, though I have read extensively through what original documents General Hodge and his people allowed to survive of their papers in the National Archives. Even with this narrow sampling in the National Archives of their activities, one can see why the Occupation had been a sorry "mess," as one of the Occupation Generals, Orland Ward, routinely characterized it in his diary.

General Ward., Ward Collection: Carlisle Barracks.

I will use the private diary of Major General Orlando Ward (1917 – 1978) (portrait on the left, Courtesy of Orlando Ward Collection, US Army History Institute, Carlisle Barracks) to take a more intimate and frank look at the Occupation, including the role played by General William Dean as Military Governor. I will also utilize, perhaps for the first time in any American book, the testimony of a retired South Korean General, Kim Ik Ruhl, who was a Colonel at the time of the American Occupation. Their stories remained secret during their lives but happily they had made arrangements to assure that their eye-witness accounts would ultimately see the light of day.

General Ward's diary appears to have been a truly personal diary. It is obvious that Ward was using it for his own reflection and as a discipline. It remained private until after his death in 1978 and is now being preserved in the U.S. Army Military History Institute at the Carlisle Barracks in Pennsylvania. Ward's diary entries in my opinion reflected his thinking about events happening at the time as fairly as any writing by a participant could. We find in it his loves and his prejudices, both big and small. To me it rings with the sound of utter honesty, even where one may painfully disagree with his views.

Orlando Ward was born in Missouri, graduated from West Point, chased Pancho Villa in Mexico, fought in WWI and WWII, received his share of medals and could be said to have come from a military family – two uncles were Generals, among other relatives who served as officers in the Army. He was socially and politically what one may describe as conservative, with naturally a strong military and national security viewpoint on public affairs. He retired in 1953 and as noted passed away in 1978.

The contribution that General Orlando Ward makes to history through his diary is contained in both his reflective as well as his off-the-cuff remarks about Korean society at the time, Korean politics, Korean and American personalities active during his stay of duty, the role of communism in Korea, what the Americans ought to have done about Korea and what the effect of the American Occupation was having on Korea. I give heavy weight to the observations of this General who was there at the time and participated in the events.

General Ward commanded the 6th Infantry Division from October of 1946 to December of 1948, several months after the establishment of Rhee's Government. The US had two types of military in Korea during the Occupation – "tactical" troops and "Military Government" troops. Most of the initial 45,000 men of the XXIV Division served as a tactical army, a reserve stationed throughout South Korea for possible use to enforce the Military Government's orders. The rest served as part of the Military Government itself, supervising Korean agencies and departments, including a fledging army ("constabulary") and a large, well-established but very unpopular police force. This Japanese-trained police force, which was retained by the US Military Occupation, we will see later was the cause of much of the turbulence that occurred in South Korea during the Occupation. It was feared and hated by most of the population as having been collaborators of the Japanese. General Hodge's decision to use that police force to control the Korean population was an early watershed error, something along the lines of the American decision to disband the Iraqi Military after the invasion -- sending tens of thousands of angry and armed men into unemployment, and at the same time leaving the weapon depots unguarded. The unreformed and unrepentant Korean police continued to behave as brutally and arbitrarily as they did under the Japanese and consequently, to most Koreans, it seemed that the Americans had just traded places with the Japanese as occupiers.

The American tactical troops and the Military Government troops were each under a different command structure, though ultimately reporting to the Commanding General, John Hodge, and they would periodically run into conflict. As Ward once noted in his diary when he was having a disagreement with the Military Government's officer in Pusan -- it is difficult to manage with two heads. The tactical troops for their part were divided under two commands, one in the northern part of the American zone, headquartered in Seoul; the other covered the southern part and was headquartered in Pusan.

General Ward was in command of the 6th Infantry Division in Pusan. That city was the largest port in Korea and located on the extreme southeast coast of the Korean peninsula. At the same time

Pusan had in effect a local representative of the Military Governor with some troops of his own. In Orlando Ward's diary he would often mention something being done by the Military Government as if he were referring to a foreign entity. In addition, some individual officers would at times be transferred from one unit to the other, as when Colonel Rothwell Brown, under the command of General Ward, was chosen by the Military Governor, General William Dean, to supervise the suppression of disturbances on Cheju-do island in May, 1948.

Generals Ward and Dean knew each other from World War II and from the comments of General Ward in his diary they seemed to like and respect each other. There appeared to be little conflict between them personally.

The troops of Ward's 6th Infantry Division were scattered in small units at different strategic locations throughout the southern part of South Korea. An example of an outpost was the one on the island of Cheju-do. Cheju is about 70 miles off the southwest coast of Korea. The tactical unit on the island, under Ward's command, consisted of a platoon situated in a few buildings on the outskirts of a town. Also on the island but at a different location and taking orders from a different command, was a small detachment of troops representing the Military Government. Ward would be constantly visiting his various outposts trying to maintain discipline and training among the bored Occupation troops and keeping them out of conflict with the local population.

Ward's diary entries indicate much concern about living conditions for his wife and daughter for the time they were with him in Korea. He had set up a comfortable house for them with the usual servants. He deliberately chose a house within walking distance of his offices so that he could walk back and forth from work through the streets of Pusan. He made a point of not only walking through the streets of Pusan but also the surrounding countryside in order to get a better feel for the Korean people. He seems to have been an unusually open and friendly person for an occupying General. We read in his diary how various Koreans would just knock on his door at various times and feel free to open political and social discussions with him and his family. In fact he had regular weekly visits by the same group of individuals, mostly teachers, who would have coffee or drinks with the Wards and exchange information. Never, however, did he forget that he was representing an occupying power and he always took the necessary precautions. His compound was surrounded by a fence and guarded by MP's, who would periodically shoot at moving shadows in the night, though he often remarked about finding the sentries asleep.

Ward was not a civil libertarian and one does not expect that he would be, given the nature of his profession and training. He would readily do things such as run "out of town" political groups which he thought were creating disturbances. For instance, his diary entries for September 16 to September 19, 1947 hint at a running dispute with the Military Government's representative in Pusan, Major Gillett, about a certain political group. Ward had thought that the members of the leftist Labor Party were the cause of some unruliness in Pusan so he advised Gillett to order them to leave Pusan or go to jail. Apparently Gillett kept resisting up to the point Ward felt he had to call the Commander General Hodge's office in Seoul to get Ward's orders enforced by Gillett. Subsequently the group of Labor Party members, according to an amused entry in Ward's diary, finally *"formed up – with band and took off, no police in evidence. Looks as if their flurry is over. . . ."*

But Ward's "running them out of town" was actually an example of using a "light touch" compared to the mass arrests and incarcerations based only on "suspicions" and "associations" or the assassinations of suspected subversives then being conducted by the Korean police under authority of the US Military Government.

General John Hodge had come into Korea as head of the occupying U.S. forces and the only instructions he seemed to have had from MacArthur were to keep the Koreans in the South from uniting with the Koreans in the North, regardless of family ties or the pull of history. The North was under Russian occupation and therefore "communistic." At all costs Hodge felt his primary duty was to keep the poison of communism from spreading to the South. Ward would later confide to a reporter that the US was in South Korea for the sole purpose of denying it to the Soviets. When the reporter later quoted him, without attribution, Hodge sent around an angry letter to his commanders reminding them to be cautious about what they said to reporters. Ward was amused and commented approvingly in his diary on the reporter's article.

But managing an Occupation under such circumstances was an extremely difficult task, particularly for a person like General Hodge, who had served valiantly in World War II and was selected to oversee the occupation of Korea only because his Division was the closest, in Okinawa, at the time of the Japanese surrender. Hodge was totally unequipped to deal with a populace which wanted *immediate* independence as they thought had been promised to them and many of whom also wanted radical reforms in their society. In addition it was a populace which was deeply disappointed and in fact enraged that the Allies had decided to partition their county and occupy it with two different armies. The Allies, though having promised independence, now thought that a temporary five year trusteeship of a divided country would be necessary to prepare the Koreans for the job of governing themselves. The problem was that the Koreans didn't think so. There therefore were tremendous pent-up hopes for freedom, self-government, the immediate unification of Korea, better labor conditions and better pay, land distribution, retribution against the wealthy collaborators, and so on. General Hodge for his part was simply unable to see or understand what these passions and hopes were all about. In his view any groups or persons showing interest in even a shadow of reform, much less radical change, were considered troublemakers, were lumped together and assumed to be communist agitators or their stooges. He and his boss, General McArthur, were as one in this way of thinking.

MacArthur in one of his first memos on the Occupation to George Marshall, then the Secretary of Defense, summarized the reports he had himself received from General Hodge, beginning his summaries as follows:

> *"The general situation in southern Korea at present is compared to a powder keg ready to explode upon application of a spark. The splitting of Korea into two parts for occupation by force of nations operating under widely divergent policies and with no common command is an impossible situation."* (*Top Secret Report from Commander in Chief Armed Forces, Tokyo* [MacArthur] *to WARCOS* [George Marshall], Sept. 18, 1945. Online doc at the Truman Library & Museum website.)

MacArthur also sent along to Marshall Hodge's complaint about the "bad" behavior of the American reporters who first arrived on the scene in Korea. They had, according to Hodge, promptly sympathized with the leftist Koreans and even encouraged them in their mistaken belief that liberation meant real freedom, independence and unification immediately.

As opposed to those agitators who were seeking reform of their society Hodge and McArthur straightaway attached themselves to the anti-"commy" side of the population, which included primarily the landowners, wealthy merchants and the missionary-educated Koreans who conveniently could speak English. Many of these wealthy merchants and landlords were extremely unpopular with the general population as they had often collaborated with the Japanese. Hodge added to this circle of "anti-commies" the Koreans who were fleeing from the Russians in the north in the hundreds of thousands. Many of those fleeing were wealthy landowners who had had their land confiscated by the Russian Occupiers and redistributed to their tenants; likewise owners of factories and other industries that had been nationalized by the Communists; still others were simply fleeing the early looting and pillaging of the first Russian soldiers to arrive. The US Ambassador to South Korea, John Muccio, would later characterize these refugees from the North as "generally people of some means." *("Substance of Statements Made at Wake Island Conference."* Truman Library and Museum, online.)

Finally, thinking that they could use them as figureheads, MacArthur and Hodge brought back a number of aged exiles who all shared a very right wing philosophy, people like Sigmund (Syngman) Rhee, who had set himself up in the US for the past 40 years during the Japanese occupation as the representative of the Korean Provisional Government in exile; Kim Koo, the President of that Provisional Government but who was located in Shanghai, China, also for 40 years; and Kim Kiusik (Kusic), also a Korean leader exiled in China. These men had been away from Korea so long that ordinary Koreans found it difficult to understand their speech. They and their large coteries duly arrived in Korea on US transports. No sooner were they there, however, when Hodge started to learn to his regret that these men, though very conservative and even extremely right wing, were fiercely independent; had their own agendas and were well beyond his ability to manipulate.

The resulting mix led the Korean society that was under American Occupation into extreme polarization of right and left, the "Rightist" and the "Leftist", as they called themselves and each other, with nobody allowed in between. Yet the Right and the Left had one great passion in common -- the **unification** of Korea. They were not the ones who drew a line along the 38th parallel separating families and communities. None of the Koreans had asked to be put under the control of one Great Power in the North and a different one in the South. For that reason both the Right and the Left were always angry at the American General Hodge, who seemed to embody a major obstacle to unification.

14

Consequently Hodge spent most of his time while in Korea unsuccessfully trying to suppress the nationalists, both Right and Left, who wanted unification, as well as the reformists who wanted widespread changes in society, including changes in labor conditions and land distribution, which he quickly branded as "commies."

Ill-advisedly he chose as his main tools for maintaining "law and order," which in effect meant the suppression of these nationalists and leftist reformers, two readily available groups. One was the well-organized squads of youths created from the families of the wealthy merchants, landowners and others fleeing from the north. The second was the unpopular Japanese-trained police force. From the day he stepped ashore in Korea in 1945 to the day he left in August of 1948, leaving the country in the dictatorial hands of Sigmund Rhee, General Hodge, with the right wing Koreans he had adopted as his allies and enforcers, was chasing around and suppressing innumerable newspapers, political parties and uprisings of one sort or another. The estimates of people who were killed for political reasons during the Occupation naturally vary widely, as the only ones with the ability to count, the American Occupiers, were not counting. But undoubtedly many tens of thousands were killed. Just on Cheju-do, as we will see, the "pacification" claimed the lives of 60,000 Koreans, mostly villagers and peasants.

However, the lot of the Korean people in the South did not get any better after Hodge left the country in August of 1948 in the hands of the autocratic Sigmund Rhee, with whom he himself by that time had also been squabbling.

"Dr. Syngman Rhee, President of the new Korean Government, and General of the Army Douglas MacArthur, Supreme Commander Allied Powers, following the arrival of the Korean President at Haneda Air Base, Tokyo, Japan. Mr. MacArthur and other high ranking military and civilian officials are also on hand to greet Dr. Rhee. While in Japan, Dr. Rhee will discuss the repatriation of Koreans residing in Japan."
19 October 1948   US Army Signal Corps Photo (Kaye)

Even hawkish officials in the Defense and State Department who were pursuing the policy of using Korea to "contain" Russia or to "teach it a lesson," thought that their chosen agent, Rhee, was often irrational and dictatorial. They were disturbed by his widespread use of mass arrests and torture of both left and right opponents, the shutting down of any opposition newspaper and the arrests of even right wing members of the Assembly that opposed him. In their view he had in effect created a police state.

While the American government tried to keep this unhappy reality away from the public, the fact that Korea under Rhee in 1949 and 1950, well before the war, was not only non-democratic but was in fact a police state was widely known (e.g., article by Walter Sullivan with headlines: POLICE BRUTALITY IN KOREA ASSAILED: **Torture, Wholesale Executions of Reds**

16

Held Driving People into Arms of Communists, February 1, 1950, <u>New York Times</u>. This article was quoted by Vito Marcantonio during the February 7, 1950 House debate on aid to Korea.)

CHAPTER II

MAKING MATTERS WORSE

". . . a stupid and fruitless endeavor."
General Orlando Ward, October 19, 1948

Korea had been a colony of Japan for 40 years. Like all colonialist the Japanese used it solely for their own profit, structuring the economy, the educational system, the food system, etc.., for the benefit of the home country. Koreans were given very little authority in running their own land. In addition, much of the school system and other such institutions were segregated between the Koreans and the large number of Japanese colonists who emigrated to the important cities of Korea. As was the case in other Japanese colonies, all the top civilian administrators of the government as well as the administrators of the big businesses, factories, hospitals, court system, etc., were ethnic Japanese, either born in Korea or emigrated from Japan. At the end of WWII there were several hundred thousand Japanese in Korea either as troops, or as managers of industry, the courts, and the police system or just as ordinary residents.

Stalin had promised FDR and Churchill, and then later Truman and Atlee (Yalta and Potsdam), that once Germany was defeated the Soviet Union would turn some of its forces to the East and help the Allies against Japan. Russia made this commitment even though it was then engaged in a fierce death struggle with the Nazis. Stalin's promise was greeted with much relief by the Americans who anticipated a difficult struggle with the Japanese in the Far East. True to their word, the Russians did exactly what they had promised when Germany had finally been defeated. Stalin had estimated that it would take about three months to march his troops and their equipment from the Western Front across thousands of miles to the Eastern Front. That is precisely the time it actually

18

took. Russia had not been at war with Japan at the time had made his promise, but he now declared war, in accordance with his agreement with the US and Britain, and by early August his troops were moving into Manchuria and Korea in support of the Allies.

As it happened this was just at the time the US had dropped the Atom Bombs on Japan, accelerating the Japanese surrender and making a highly dreaded invasion of Japan unnecessary. Consequently some in the US Government, who had always viewed Communist Russia with Churchillian suspicion and even hostility, immediately regretted that the US had earlier begged the Russians to come in. Now, morphing from poor to rich cousins, they became worried that the Russians, with the imminent collapse of Japan, would move in and take a lot of territory. One such territory which they jealously fretted about was the peninsular of Korea, notwithstanding that it was on the border of Russia, had a long history of relations with it and was mineral-poor.

When the Japanese Governor-General in Korea, General Noboyuki Able, commanding 375,000 troops, realized that he would have to surrender and saw the Russians advancing into Korea, he assumed that the surrender of the entire peninsular of Korea would be to the Russians. As a result he desperately rushed to set up a native body of Koreans to act as a government. He intended this body to behave as a figurehead and assist him in dealing with the Russians. He hoped that it would help keep order during the surrender process and protect the lives and property of the hundreds of thousands stranded Japanese, soldiers and civilians. The person finally selected by General Able to lead this figurehead government, after Abe had been turned down by his first choices, Korean collaborators who now feared for their lives, was a long time Korean nationalist who as a job had represented the Singer Sewing Machine company in Korea but had no connection with the various Korean exile groups. This individual was Lyuh Woon Hong (Woon Kong Lyuh or Yo Wun Hyung). (Lyuh was assassinated on a street in Seoul two years later and his family always accused the by-then American favorite, Sigmund Rhee, as behind the assassination.)

To General Able's surprise and discomfit, the figurehead body under Lyuh quickly took on a life of its own as it became swelled with the nationalists and political prisoners Able had just released from the jails in anticipation of the surrender. To everyone's wonder this Lyuh and his allies promptly set up a peninsula-wide administrative structure to govern Korea. This should not have been such a surprise as the Korean nationalists had been waiting and fighting for this day of true independence for 40 years – their time had come. They selected Seoul as their headquarters and declared themselves the **"People's Republic"** in early September. This Lyuh organization was described in a United Press report as a "provisional Korean commission representing all classes and all political parties" (PM, September 12, 1945).

General Hodge and the XXIVth Division finally arrived in early September; a full month after the Russians had taken the Japanese surrender in the north of Korea. The Soviet troops, though totally unopposed, had dutifully halted at the 38th parallel in full compliance with the agreed General Order Number One issued by MacArthur as Allied Commander in the Far East.

The meeting of American and Russian troops at the 38th parallel produced many images of "what could have been." This early friendliness between the Allied troops was widespread, as American reporters who journeyed up to the Russian occupation headquarters would report (New York Times, September 15, 1945). But thanks to Truman and some of his Generals, including MacArthur and Hodge, it was not to last.

The American Military occupied Korea below the 38th Parallel from 1945 to the middle of 1948, at which time it was turned over to Sigmund Rhee. This was after an elaborately orchestrated election, supervised by and declared "fair and free" by the UN, had resulted in Rhee, the only candidate, being elected President with nearly 100% of the vote – a pattern that was to persist until Rhee was finally chased out of Seoul by an angry population in 1960. For most purposes during this period of time the "UN" meant the "US" as its finances, policies and operations were controlled by the US.

As the saying goes, everything that could go wrong went wrong from the very beginning of the American "liberation" of Korea. A curse of some sort that has come down to this very day, over 65 years later and through numerous Administrations, Republican and Democratic. No one seems able to come up with a solution -- as intractable as our relations with Cuba since the Kennedys and with Palestine since, again, Truman.

The Koreans had expected Liberation! as promised repeatedly by the Allies since the Cairo Declaration of 1943. Instead two Korean civilians were killed by Japanese policemen as a crowd of workers attempted to greet the Americans landing in Jinsen. Then General Hodge further stupefies the Koreans by telling them not only that they are not politically mature enough to govern themselves just yet, but that they were to remain under the capable hands of our surrendering enemy -- reinstating the hated colonial Japanese administration intact. The Governor, General Noboyuki Abe, and the Police Director, Tadao Nishihiro – who had just killed the two Korean civilians for trying to greet the Americans, may have been as surprised as the Koreans. It was a colossal blunder and headlined in one US newspaper as "flabbergasting" (PM, September 11, 1945).

Rev. Monsignor Edward J. Flanaghan and Lt. Gen John Hodge, 1947

Was this simply an innocent blunder by Hodge, a brave warrior but inexperienced in the complications of an occupation for which he no instructions from the unprepared State Department? Or was it MacArthur's honest mistake, after all he had retained the Japanese administrators in Japan to enforce his orders -- though of course Korea was not Japan. It did not help the image of the Americans when at the same time the Russians were promptly expelling not only the Japanese from government and industrial posts in their occupied area, but also the Korean collaborations who were just as hated by the populations. In addition, the Russians were finding no shortage of Koreans to run the Russian zone. There had been thousands of Koreans living across the border in Manchuria and parts of Russia who had fled the Japanese occupation. Many of them, including soldiers who had fought in the Russian Army, returned with the Russian occupation troops. Ironically, the collaborators and their allies being turned out of their positions by the Russians would trek south and find a warm welcome in the American zone, gaining positions of prominence in Hodge's advisory committees. The children of these refugees from the Russian zone would in turn form the basis of Nazi-like youth groups, financed in large part by the US, who were to terrorize the population in the south in the coming years as "anti-communist" shock troops.

General Hodge's subsequent behavior indicated that these initial steps were not just innocent mistakes but part of a deliberate policy. Though like the Russians he had found Lyuh's organization, the People's Republic, managing things efficiently, he discarded it while the Russians utilized it. Hodge somehow had convinced himself from the very start that these native Koreans and their organizations were not just Korean nationalists but were communist agents of the Russians in the north. A bizarre conclusion that is hard to explain.

Perhaps it was someone in the US Government who fed him this line of thinking, but it was something he apparently sincerely believed. In testimony to a UN Commission sent to Korea three years later to supervise the election in May of 1948, he seriously testified that Lyuh's People's Republic, which had been created at the urging of Japanese General Able just before the Americans arrived in 1945, *"dates back to many years of preparedness for the situation in which the Soviets were active."* He seemed to have discovered somewhere that the year 1925 was an important date with regard to communism in Korea. Hodge even went to the trouble of personally browbeating his unit's historians until they produced an anti-communist diatribe which he passed off to visitors as a political history of Korea. Every group from the US that visited the American Military Government in Korea during his tour there would receive the same sermon. Korea was crawling with communists, and they date back to 1925, etc..

Hodge himself revealed in his own words the motivation, racism, prejudices and ignorance that drove him as the head of the Military Government. Before that same Commission he testified:

> *When we came into South Korea, we found an existence here of poverty, plus disease, plus communist-led **people's committees in full sway and fairly well in control**. . . . We found here a decadent nation **without the slightest concept of political life** as the free nations of the world know it. These people had no concept of the responsibilities inherent in the basic freedoms.*

All of this would have been news to the thousands of Koreans who had died fighting the Japanese for independence, or to the thousands whom he had found, contrary to his own characterizations, "fairly well in control" of the country when he arrived.

Hodge had found a native government in operation, with administrators down to the village level. To the astonishment of the Koreans, however, who thought they were being liberated from the Japanese, Hodge retained the Japanese Governor, General Abe, and asked him to continue running the country with his Japanese troops, though under Hodge's overall command. That was OK with General MacArthur who had done the same thing in Japan. The difference here of course was that the Korean population considered the Japanese as foreign occupiers. At the same time Hodge set about dismantling and discrediting the People's Republic that had been formed by the Koreans themselves and which was already effectively running the country. A disaster, of course, from the very beginning.

24

Hodge got an immediate lesson about the newly freed Koreans when thousands promptly took to the streets throughout Korea south of the 38th parallel to demand that General Abe and his Japanese troops be removed. Washington reacted quickly and ordered MacArthur and Hodge to replace the General and his troops. Aside from that incident, however, Hodge was on his own. What was happening in Korea was for the most part of little interest to the US Press. And that was not good.

It is no surprise that even after he left Korea and was stationed as the Commanding General of the Third Army at Fort McPherson, his "commy" obsession followed him. General Albert E. Brown had served with General Hodge during the Korean Occupation. In response to the now retired Brown's request for comments on the draft of General Brown's proposed memoirs, Hodge had this to say in a letter to him on January 24, 1951:

> *There has never been any question but that the Communists had gone all out in establishing the People's Republic, in South as well as North Korea, in the month available to them after the Japanese had quit until we arrived 8 September for occupation. This was a long time, well planned operation, starting in the mid-twenties, with the Communists operating under the guise of patriots in the underground against the Japs. . . .* ***Flatly stated, one of our early missions was to break down this Communist government outside of any directives and without benefit of backing by the Joint Chiefs of Staff or the State Department*** (emphasis added). (Albert E. Brown Papers, Box 3, U.S. Army Military Institute, Carlisle Barracks.)

This is an illuminating admission. Somehow this American General *on his own* had decided that his main job was to dismantle a native governmental structure that was at least functioning, feeding the people and keeping law and order, because he

25

suspected they were communists disguised as patriots. Hodge had never step foot in Korea before so it must be assumed that whatever he knew of the local situation at that point he had just learned from his "interpreters," the missionary-educated wealthy Koreans, or from General Abe and his officers, whom he was supposedly uprooting. He proudly tells Brown that he did this without orders and without any "backing" from State or Defense.

General Ward with Col., later General, Chae. Korea, 1948
(Courtesy of Orlando Ward Collection, US Army History Institute, Carlisle Barracks.)

It took General Orlando Ward, on the other hand, only a month after arriving in Korea to come to a dramatically different opinion. Even during his orientation meeting with General Hodge and MacArthur's staff in Tokyo he thought that the Americans were over-simplifying things. He was told that Korea was full of strikes by workers, riots and shootings against the police.

>*"Good briefing but gave impression that we had taught the Japs how to strike as well as the Koreans. And that we were blaming the communists for the results"* (October 17, 1946).

26

Four weeks later he attended a meeting in Seoul called by General Hodge with various Occupation officers as well as some people from the State Department. With some sarcasm he noted in his diary: *"Hodge gave history of our **interference** and its success. . . ."* Then he quite firmly and simply, with ominous prescience, further noted for posterity:

> *"Success here is impossible. To pull out gracefully is the best solution"* (November 19, 1946).

Ward immediately also disliked the way the Military Government was using the Japanese-trained and hated police for controlling the population. *"We are backing police in their strong arm policies . . . ."* (October 28, 1946).

Even before Ward's arrival in Korea, however, there had been intelligence reports of disturbing behavior by the Korean police force under Hodge's Military Government. As early as December, 1945, US Counterintelligence Corps officers were sending to Washington reports of Korean police using extreme brutality. One such report describes police mercilessly beating and perhaps even killing children who were holding a peaceful demonstration for unification with the North while US Military Troops stood by and watched in apparent approval.

> *All the policemen as if at a given signal rushed in and began beating the students with sticks, clubs, rifle butts, or anything they had. Firing broke out . . . and the policemen kept after the students . . . small boys and girls were beaten just as mercilessly as were the older boys and girls . . . . A number of the Military Government troops were on the street during this whole incident.* (File No. 59-P-42, 19 Dec. 1945, RG 338, Box 26, Folder: "Historical Journal," N.A.).

Yet to General Hodge the Japanese trained Korean police were a godsend. He denied that they were the tools of the wealthy merchants and landowners and the Rightist parties. To that UN Commission which was supervising the 1948 election in Korea he stated:

> *The charges against the police belonging to this or that political group cannot be sustained. . . . [On] the whole they have been loyal to the interim government* [meaning, to him] *and have followed through in the maintenance of law and order to the best of their ability. . . . I hear from some sources that South Korea is a **police state**. I would like to point out that South Korea is an **occupied area**. It is at present operated under the direction of the military. The police force is charged with maintenance of law and order and, in addition, the observation for subversive activity aimed at upsetting the peace and security of the area.*

This again would have been news to the Koreans, who had been promised liberation by the Allies, not occupation. No one, apparently, had told that to Hodge. It was unfortunate for the Koreans and for history that they had found themselves, through pure accident, in the control of a General who could barely contain his disgust and disdain for "these people." On the other hand, any of a number of other Generals at that time would have probably behaved the same way, particularly if they were getting encouragement from some people in Washington.

During General Ward's tour he also became uneasy with the heavy hand used by the Military Government and the various American and Korean intelligence agents it employed. Particularly poor was the handling by the Military Government of local disturbances and the blind support it gave to the brutal police.

Army photographers have helpfully, though not intentionally, preserved for us some of the police behavior that General Ward and the Counterintelligence officers had found so disturbing. The captions in these pictures as written by the US Army, however, give no hint of disapproval. It seemed that at that time and place anything was allowed so long as the victims were carefully labeled as "communists."

In March of 1948, for example, the Military Government organized a large gathering in Seoul Stadium to celebrate a Korean holiday, ironically, the **1919** *Korean Declaration of Independence* from the Japanese. In addition, at the celebration General Hodge was to announce that the UN would hold an election in the Spring to establish an independent Korean Government in the South.

Many people in the occupied zone, not just the communists, objected to an election that would take place only in the South. Both the Right and the Left wanted elections to be held throughout both the North and the South so that the resulting Korean Government would be of a unified Korea. Many felt that a separate election in the South would further divide the country and maybe even encourage the Russians to set up a separate nation in the North (which eventually did happen). The Russians would not agree to elections supervised by the UN which they felt was under US control and could not be trusted to be honest. In addition, the South had a greater population and if manipulated by the Americans and the Rightists, would determine the outcome of the elections -- surely resulting in a government on its border in the hands of the US and hostile to the Soviets.

These are some pictures taken during Hodge's announcement at Seoul Stadium that the US would urge the UN to hold elections in South Korea.

"Lt. General John H. Hodge, CG, USAFIK, reads an address to the estimated eighty thousand Koreans that Jammed Seoul Stadium this morning to commemorate the Korean Declaration of Independence from the Japanese in 1919. Gen Hodge informed the people of the US proposal to the UN for a free election in Korea this Spring."   1 March 1948

"Korean Police break up a small group of young rioters during the celebration of the Korean Declaration of Independence from Japan in 1919. The day, normally one of violence, was surprisingly quiet and orderly, due to the well-disciplined Korean Police Force."   1 March 1948   US Army Signal Corps   (Cramer)

30

"Another communist agitator is led from the crowd by Police after an attempt to break up the mass meeting of an estimated eighty thousand Rightists in Seoul Stadium. The small group of communists formed a football flying wedge scattering communist leaflets as they pushed their way through the crowd." 1 March 1948　　　　　US Army Signal Corps (Cramer)

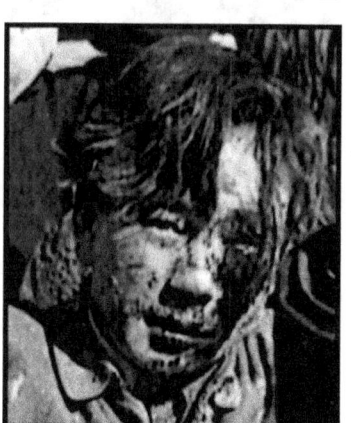
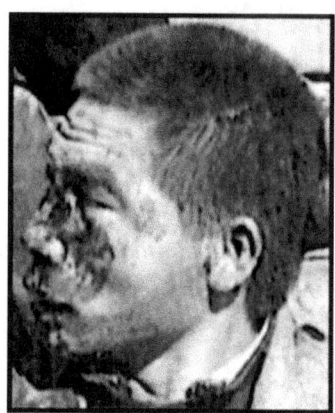

"*Korean Communists awaiting search after being forcibly removed from Seoul Stadium this morning. An estimated eighty thousand Rightists gathered to commemorate the Korean Declaration of Independence from Japan in 1919 when a small group of Communists started running through the crowd in a football wedge formation, scattering Communist leaflets. They were apprehended by Korean Police and taken off for further questioning.*"
1 March 1948   US Army Signal Corps (Buerkle)

If we can give the caption writers some credibility, these poor souls, who had simply been distributing leaflets to the crowd in the Stadium, and who already looked pretty beat up, were now going to be *searched and questioned* by the Korean police. Imagine what they looked like after the more intimate encounter of searching and questioning, assuming that they were still alive.

In an attempt to keep his own troops from being entangled in this type of bestial behavior, General Ward wrote a letter to his commanders on November 3, 1946 (The Ward Papers, Box 5, U.S. Army Military History Institute, Carlisle Barracks):

> *"I feel that our* [tactical] *troops are a reserve and that they should not ordinarily be used singly or in pairs to lend an air of authority to the local police. By their presence in an area and by patrol visits to the police stations, they will lend sufficient authority to the local police. They do not take over the local police duties unless the situation demands.*
>
> *"When on duty if they observe any act of cruelty, revenge or the unnecessary use of force on the part of local police, it is essential that they, at the appropriate time, (when the police will not lose face) remonstrate with the police. By so doing and by friendly talks with the local authorities they will gradually indoctrinate them with methods which will attain results without raising the ire of the populace through the misuse of their authority. Certainly our objective is to reach a time when local police can walk the streets singly at night with impunity."*

This letter of instructions also indirectly discloses the condition of Korean society at the time and the futility of our meddling. US troops were actually needed to **guard the local police** from the population – the local police who had been trained and utilized by the Japanese to keep the population suppressed. An impossible mission. A time-bomb.

On February 15, 1947 General Ward commented in his diary on some news reports he had been reading.

> *"GCM* [Secretary of Defense, George C. Marshall] *says cut in budget will cause withdrawal of troops from Korea. . . . – So what?* **We are making a mess of . . .** [Korea] *and had better get out."*

In September his attitude had not changed. He had gone up to Seoul at the request of General Hodge who was touring with Under Secretary of the Army William F. Draper, whom Ward had known personally. Draper had wanted to speak with Ward. Ward reports in his diary what he had to say to Draper:

> *"What a mess. . . . Had good talk with him. I think it is get out with as much face saving as possible. . . ."* (September 23, 1947).

William H. Draper, Jr. had worked for many years with James Forrestal, then the Secretary of the Navy, at the financial firm of Dillon, Read & Co. Later in life in an oral history interview for the Truman Library Draper spoke of his great admiration for the Truman Presidency, except for one thing. Truman should have followed MacArthur's advice to do what was necessary to "win" the war in Korea. "We fought the Korean War with one hand behind our backs."

Ward was so disgusted with the way the Occupation was being handled that by May of 1948 he was even telling friends that *"the Japs did better"* (May 16, 1948 conversation with the Gunbys).

General Orlando Ward's conviction that it was a mistake to continue having the US military in Korea deepened the longer he was there.

"To me KOREA is a STRATEGIC HAZARD rather than a STRATEGIC ASSET. We have not enough to save the people of the world and attempt to do so will so lower our potential as to make us subject to eventual debility – degeneration and disaster. There are too many in authority who do not analyze facts before acting – who do not measure the cloth with which they have to work. Our present policy is building southern Korea so as to be ripe for over running by the Soviet dominated North Korea. In other words, to no avail." (May 9, 1947)

The fundamental military principle that Korea was a strategic hazard, primarily because our Military knew we could not be effective in any war on the Asian mainland, was echoed again and again by Generals and diplomats at later Congressional hearings as I will note below.

Ward also never could understand Hodge's insistence that every disturbance was always communist inspired. He saw economics as moving the people in Korea, not ideology.

"More I see of . . . Koreans the more I think they are not much concerned about anything but their next meal. They are independent" (March 9, 1947).

The General often commented on how the people from the State Department as well as his military colleagues were always able to find a *"Communist behind many bushes"* (September 10, 1948). He marveled, tongue in check, how there could have been revolutions in South America in the 1850's and yet there were no Communists around then. He found that Hodge *"will not listen to anything not assumed to be communist in origin. He may be right to a certain extent. G2's [Intelligence] are prone to report fancies rather than fact."* (May 9, 1948). At one point after noting that "Brown exaggerates" -- I am not sure which Brown this refers to – he puts in quotes the following:

> *" 'That perennial bogy man of all generations of reactionaries, a conspiracy of agitators subsidized by foreigners' "* (March 8, 1948).

After the 1948 US inspired elections in South Korea, which as feared split up the country permanently because the Russians then followed the example and set up a separate state in the North, the South Koreans established a constitution and other elements of government. Ward's dry but telling observations:

> *"Korean Constitution a dictatorship. What they want"* (July 15, 1948)

> *"[I]t will only end in Rich getting richer – Poor no better and enmity against us when we stop giving. Fruitless – stupid endeavor to give a few lucrative jobs." (November 7, 1948).*

As Ward was preparing to leave Korea, he went to a ceremonial dinner in Seoul on November 16th. He met the Rhees again and told himself in his diary that night that the Rhees were "tottering" and wanted the US to stay in Korea only to keep them in office.

The XXIV's G-2 (intelligence) file contains a record of an interview on December 4, 1948 with Chang, Taik-Sang, Minister of Foreign Affairs in the new Rhee government:

> *"Chang spoke very frankly as he is inclined to do with those Americans he knows well. . . . Chang* [said] *the Government of the Republic of Korea was getting farther removed from the people it governs every day. . . .*[it] *is floating around in the air like a fairy castle. . .* **The President [Rhee] has no respect whatsoever for rules and regulations** *and good governmental procedure. He will establish a rule today and forget he ever thought of it tomorrow. I hear about the decisions my office should be making when I read the newspapers. The President flies into an* **insane rage** *every time I attempt to obtain additional information on these decisions he has made which pertain to* [my] *Ministry of Foreign Affairs."* (Thomas Herren Papers, U.S. Army Military Institute, Carlisle Barracks). [Emphasis added.]

Among his last entries while still in Korea, Ward summarized his feelings about the US Occupation of Korea:

> *"We are on a stupid and fruitless endeavor which will cost much and produce little or no good to us, to the Koreans and to the world"* (October 19, 1948).

General Ward, whose 57th birthday was on November 4, 1948, very much wanted to stay on active duty. As it became clear that the military mission in Korea was winding down, he speculated on a number of active duty assignments he would like, only to see them go to others. At one point he was being considered as a replacement for Hodge, but it went to John Coulter. Then he was hoping to take over the 8th Army, but it went to Walton Walker, the unfortunate General whom we will meet during the ensuing war. Ward was obviously out of step with "the Program" of the day as his diary comments make clear. It was not accidental that when the powers-that-be wanted to quickly and brutally put down a disturbance on the island of Cheju which was in his jurisdiction, they took one of his men, who was with The Program, to do the job and then kept Ward out of the loop for the most part. His feelings must have been well known throughout the Army and the Army was just not going to give him a significant active duty placement. Though he insisted in his diary that he would rather retire than agree to an assignment that would just put him "on the shelf" (October 25, 1948), he ultimately agreed to do just that.

In his last diary notations for 1948, Ward seemed resigned to his an assignment to the Historical Section in DC, though he still struggled with the idea of just retiring. He also harbored a dream:

> *"I am for retiring. Have been for some time. No I am going to write a **true** history as it did **actually** happen until they fire me . . . ."* (December 3, 1948).

Later, when the Korean War started in 1950 and Truman decided to intervene, General Ward, then heading the Army's Historical unit in Washington, commented in his diary that it was probably the only thing Truman could do. But by February, 1951 when everyone was calling Korea a "disaster," he lamented Truman's sudden reversal of policy. In a letter to Senator James Kem, a very conservative Republican Senator, he responded to a number of issues raised by the Senator. Senator Kem had asked Ward to comment on the following observation of Kem's:

> "Any policy which forces us to fight the Reds, as we are fighting them in Korea now – across an ocean, within walking distance of their masses of reserves, on terms of battle in which they are forever superior – cannot be anything but what it has turned out to be in Korea; a bloody entanglement, to use Walter Lippmann's phrase."

Ward's response was:

> *"There is an old saying to the effect 'do not get*
> *involved in the land mass of Asia.' It still holds. Korea, to*
> *me, is an example of where we had made a carefully*
> *thought out decision and then reversed it without careful*
> *consideration of the long-range outcome"* (Orlando Ward
> Papers, "Correspondence, Speeches," Box 6, U.S. Army
> Military Institute, Carlisle Barracks).

Orlando Ward, however, remained a supporter, a "disciple,"
as he described himself, of General MacArthur and expressed
annoyance in his diaries with the critical Congressional testimony
of Generals Marshall and Bradley after MacArthur's removal. But
unlike General Stratemeyer, who thought that MacArthur walked
on water, he had a more realistic appreciation of the old General's
limitations.

CHAPTER III

CHEJU 4.3

"Scorched earth tactics are not allowed . . . .
General Dean's conscience and humanity would punish
him some day."
General Kim Ik Ruhl

The people of Korea remember April 3, 1948 simply as "Cheju 4.3."

Cheju (now also called Jeju, a popular resort and honeymoon destination) is an island about 70 miles off the southwest coast of Korea. Near the end of the official American Occupation there began an uprising which resulted during the next year in the wholesale slaughter of villagers and the burning down of their homes.

The population of Cheju-do ("do" meaning "island") was at that time approximately 300,000. The death toll for the islanders during the year-long suppression campaign, conducted at first directly by the American Military Government, using primarily the Korean national police force, the developing Korean Army and right wing youth groups, and then carried on by the Rhee Government with the same forces but still under the overall direction of American advisors, was estimated at between 30,000 to 60,000 -- 10 to 20% of the population. An additional 40,000 islanders escaped to Japan. Seventy percent of the villages had been burned down and 100,000 people, more than one-third of the survivors on the island, had been herded into guarded villages on the coast. Sixty-five thousand more people were homeless. (Paper presented by Professor Bruce Cumings, University of Chicago, at the 50th Anniversary Conference of the April 3, 1948 Chejudo Rebellion, Tokyo, March 14, 1998 as reprinted, November 15, 2002, http://www.kimsoft.com/1997/cheju98.htm).

Information about the uprising that began on April 3, 1948 and the subsequent massacres has been mostly suppressed during the almost 50 years of subsequent dictatorships and junta governments that were supported by successive American Administrations. In the past few years, however, survivors have begun to tell their story of an indigenous disturbance falsely labeled "communistic" and crushed with brutal force by the Korean national police and army under American supervision (see, e.g., <u>New York Times</u>, article by Howard W. French: "South Koreans Seek Truth about '48 Massacre," October 24, 2001; <u>Paper</u> presented by Professor Bruce Cumings, cited above).

Today those who want to recall the event comment on the re-invention of Cheju Island as a resort with most of the best properties owned by the individuals and relatives of the police and youth groups who had confiscated the land from the "communists."

"Aerial view of only US military installation on Cheju Island. Compound of the 59ᵗʰ MG Co. The Military Government of this island of approximately one hundred and seventy miles circumference is administered by thirty-six officers and men." 1 May 1948, Army Signal Corps Mootz.

41

While I will continue to use General Ward's diary to get some candid contemporary insights into this unhappy affair, I will primarily be relying on the eye-witness account of one of the Korean military participants, testimony that has come to light only recently.

Kim Ik Ruhl was the commander of the newborn 9th Regiment of the Korean constabulary, or army, stationed on Cheju-do Island in 1948 during the uprising. He was a Colonel at the time. The constabulary force was in its infancy and did not even have modern weapons. The Americans had been extremely reluctant to distribute M-1 rifles, grenades or other modern weapons to the yet unstable and untrained men in the constabulary. So the constabulary carried for the most part old Japanese rifles, usually without ammunition. In contrast the US had supplied modern carbines to the police forces who had been trained by the Japanese and whom the Americans relied upon for maintaining "law and order."

Colonel Kim later served bravely and with distinction in the South Korean Army during the ensuing Korean War and ultimately retired as a Lieutenant General. He passed away in December, 1988.

Among his papers left behind was a manuscript with the title: The Truth About Cheju 4.3. He asked his heirs to have it published after his death so that the truth about that massacre would be told. However, they could not get it published because under the type of American approved governments Korea had until 1993, this controversial book would have brought danger to anyone connected with it. This gentleman had lived for forty years with a secret he could not safely disclose. It was too dangerous in Korea during his lifetime under the American approved dictatorships to speak truthfully about what had happened. But his manuscript has finally seen the light of day and it is not flattering to the US authorities in charge at that time, including the Military Governor, William Dean.

I have utilized the translation of General Kim's manuscript as it appears [2002] on the Korean Web Weekly, http://www.kimsoft.com/1997/43kim11.htm. General Kim's manuscript is also attached as an appendix to the five volume "4.3 Speaks" series by Chemin Ilbo, Volume 2, pp. 270-357, ISBN 89-7924-006-6, Seoul Publication Service, Seoul, Korea. The Library of Congress Control Number is 95473292 (Call No. DS917.55 .A14 1995 Korea).

The circumstances of how Kim's book finally got published would be enough to bestow on it an aura of authenticity and accuracy. However, I have found some totally independent sources which corroborate Kim's narrative as well. Several diary entries of General Ward contain facts which coincide with General Kim's account, including Ward's entry for April 29, 1948 relating to his trip with Military Governor General Dean to Cheju-do Island. That is around the time that Colonel Kim says Dean had come to the island with a group of Korean leaders and met with Colonel Kim and his American advisor, Colonel Mansfield. Further corroboration of Kim's story comes from the US Army itself. There is an Army Signal Corps. film called "May Day" which was filmed on Cheju-do from April 30th to May 5th. The film features the Military Governor General Dean on an inspection trip to Cheju-do and actually depicts the cast of attendees at a meeting with Dean in early May that is independently described by General Kim in his long hidden manuscript ("May Day," NARA 023451, CR # 111 ADC 7114). This little gem of a film was found in the National Archives by Professor John Merrill who mentions it in his 1989 book: Korea: The Peninsular Origins of the War.

The following are pictures taken from "May Day" which show General Dean arriving on the island sometime between April 29 and May 5th, along with the individuals which Colonel Kim identifies in his manuscript as having attended a meeting with him. Professor Merrill describes the film as a propaganda film. It apparently was intended to demonstrate how the National Police and Korean Constabulary, under American guidance, rescue

43

besieged islanders from some rebels. It must also serve as proof, however unwittingly, that we were ultimately responsible for the 60,000 islanders killed during the next year in the suppression campaign, perhaps including some of those depicted in this propaganda film.

General Dean with:
Army Commander Gen. Song Ho Chang   *and Civil Affairs*
                                          Minister Ahn Jae Hong

Col. Kim Ik Ruhl greeting
Dean and *Ahn Jae Hong*

Dean entering jeep on Cheju-do

armyrev1.mov

armyrev1.mov

Islanders who may or may not have survived during the suppressionof the next 12 months.

According to General Kim, the islanders historically disliked the mainland Koreans 70 miles away, as he and nearly all of the constabulary were. So the islanders kept their distance from the soldiers stationed there as well as the national police, who were also mainlanders. The isolated people of the island even spoke a dialect which mainlanders had a hard time understanding.

"*CHEJU-DO MOUNTIES – The Korean constabulary, either mounted or afoot, have proved their efficiency and reliability through working with the US Military Government. These mounted police are stationed at Cheju-do, Korea, as evidence by the Korean woman carrying her burden by shoulder straps.*" 21 May 1948 USAF Office of Public Relations

The only thing approaching an ideology that Kim noticed among the islanders was that they considered the Americans merely to have replaced the Japanese as occupiers. Any Korean working with the Americans was as despised as those who had worked for the Japanese. The basic cause of the uprising, according to Kim, had nothing to do with ideology or communism, but was economic at its heart.

Kim knew from personal observation and information from some of his men who were natives of the island what the basic causes were of the subsequent uprising. The islanders had had a long tradition of trading with Japan and China, skirting the regulations and custom duties attempted to be imposed from all sides. In effect they had created a free port, and deeply resented any intrusion from the mainlanders. But a number of mainlander policemen and recently imported Northwest Youth members were

48

trying to muscle in on the smugglers. Some of the police were simply stealing from the smugglers, while others would kidnap family members and torture them in jail until their families agreed to sharing the business.

General Kim's description, written in the '80's and long after he retired, of the island's *de facto* "free-port" economy and the constant attempts by the police to rip off the unregulated traders is amazingly corroborated in almost every detail by a Confidential Memo dated 9 December 1946 from the Military Government's own Department of Public Information. (Record Group 338, Box 26, Folder "Footnotes." N.A..) The Memo's authors likewise described the tradition of smuggling and the tension between the islanders and the thieving police from the mainland. Kim's observations are further corroborated by General Orlando Ward in a number of his diary entries as will be seen.

In addition, Lieutenant Colonel Lawrence A. Nelson, a Special Investigator out of Occupation Headquarters had been reporting for months about the friction between the mainland police and the islanders. He blamed the Rightist Governor from the mainland for incidents of police brutality and his labeling of anyone opposing him as "leftist." In a report to General John Hodge dated November 22, 1947 Nelson recommended the removal of that local Korean Governor because, among other things, *"terrorism and beatings have been traced to the Governor."* He warned that *"the condition* [on the island] *is becoming dangerous."*

General Hodge and the US Military Governor, Dean, upon receiving Colonel Nelson's earlier reports, at first asked him for more documentation. They gave as their reason for delaying any action on his recommendation was that they could not just remove a governor appointed by the Korean Advisory Council – though they routinely did so.

This stalling went on for months into late 1947 and early 1948. Then when Colonel Nelson made his final report, still recommending drastic administrative in governing the island and the removal of the governor, Dean simply rejected his main recommendations. It was getting close to the showcase UN supervised elections and nobody wanted to rock the boat. Shortly thereafter the riots started. (R.G. 228, Box 83, Folder: "Cheju-do Political Situation." N.A..)

"Seated in the front row of the mass meeting held for the delegates of the United Nations Temporary Commission on Korea, in the Seoul Stadium, are, l. to r., Major General Albert E. Brown, Assistant CG, USAFIK; Major General W.F. Dean, US Military Governor of Korea; and Lieutenant General John R. Hodge, CG, USAFIK. They are among the 20,000 persons who have gathered there."
14 January 1948   US Army Signal Corps (Mootz)

Clearly the real situation on Cheju-do had been widely understood within the Military Government from almost the beginning of the Occupation. There was a simmering economic and turf conflict between the islanders and the mainlanders that needed very little provocation to ignite. That spark occurred on April 3, 1948 with the discovery by the islanders of the badly tortured body of one of their own who had been in the custody of the police. As Ward noted in his diary on April 5th, *". . . Cheju do on a rampage."*

When the uprising started the Military Government, that is, General John Hodge as Commanding General, and his subordinate, General William Dean as Military Governor, sent in massive national police reinforcements from the mainland. The Americans at this stage of the Occupation were trying to extricate themselves from Korea without losing face and felt that they could not afford any bad publicity. They had been making elaborate preparations for a showcase "free" election in this "test case" for democracy on the doorstep of Red Russian. Kim wrote that *the US commanders and the police chiefs believed that once the suppression campaign started, 2 – 3 days would be enough to wipe out the rebels."*

That did not happen. The police tactics of indiscriminate arrests, killings and burnings only succeeded in spreading the rebellion until it encompassed most of the island. Colonel Kim, who was in charge of the small Constabulary force on the island but was taking orders from the Military Government's officers, tried desperately in those early days to work out a settlement. He met repeatedly with the islanders and the police, but could reach no agreement. He ascribed the failure of negotiations primarily to sabotage by the mainlander police and the Northwest Youth groups working with the police.

After the uprising had gone on for a month the Military Governor, William Dean, came down for a meeting with Kim and Colonel Mansfield, the US advisor to Kim's Regiment. Dean had decided that the police were not up to the task and wanted the Korean Constabulary, the 9th Regiment under 28-year old Colonel Kim, to take over the job of suppression.

From General Orlando Ward's diary entries of April 29, 1948:

> *Breakfast with Bill Dean. Off at 8:00 A.M.* [to Cheju-do]. *. . . . Looks as if Police are reaping benefits of miss treatment of natives. 6 police killed. 60 islanders. No witnesses brought in alive. Thumbs wired together. Hung by heels. Shot sans trial. Resent mainlanders. Flew over island. Reminded me of Chasing Villa. Action they contemplate will be fruitless. Trouble should be cured at source. . . . Assistant G2* [Intelligence] *– hunted for and found communist backing. 90% local and justified resentment."*

Some days before General Dean arrived for the conference, Colonel Kim received a mysterious order from his advisor, Colonel Mansfield. He was to go to the office of the Cheju branch of the US CIC, counterintelligence, and meet with an unnamed American. Kim followed orders and went over to the CIC. This individual, according to Kim, refused to identify himself but said he was a political adviser to General Dean.

The unidentified American told Kim that the only way to stop the rebellion fast was to use the kind of drastic methods that the Japanese had used in Korea and throughout their empire to deal with indigenous guerilla forces. This was called "scorched earth" tactics -- basically burning down any village that the rebels might use for sanctuary or assistance and killing any villagers who resisted or who actually aided the rebels. Kim was asked to utilize these tactics and help the US during this high-publicity election time.

Kim was appalled by the idea. He told the American that there was just no way he would do that to his own people. The American offered various amounts of money, reached $100,000.00, which Kim refused, and then asked in exasperation how much it would take for Kim to do it. He also guaranteed safe passage for

Kim, his family and relatives to the United States. He even showed Kim magazine pictures of the kind of life Kim and his family would have in comfortable suburban areas of the United States. Kim thought the whole thing was disgusting and he steadfastly refused.

Colonel Mansfield had told Kim that the rebellion on the island was coming at a very bad time for the United States. The US was trying to get the UN to supervise elections in the south to set up a separate government and the insurrection would be used by the Soviets against the US. *"Washington instructed Gen. Dean to settle the rebellion at once."* In addition, Mansfield told him, it was important for international reasons that the communists be blamed for instigating the rebellion.

General Dean came down to the island again, according to Kim's account, on May 5th and had with him several people, including the Korean National Police Chief, Cho Byong Ok; Civil Affairs Minister Ahn Jae Hong; Army Commander Gen. Song Ho Chang; the local Police Commissioner; the local governor and some others. Dean was also accompanied by his interpreter, a Christian minister also with the name Kim. At the meeting Colonel Kim explained that the insurrection had been caused by police greed and brutality and its attempt to strong-arm the smugglers. The police's "scorched earth" tactics had only enraged the islanders and spread the rebellion. Kim laid out a plan which would end the insurrection without further bloodshed.

The Police Chief, Cho Byong Ok and Colonel Kim Ik Ruhl got into a very heated argument about this, with the Police Chief accusing Kim of being a communist and with Kim punching the Police Chief. According to Kim General Dean left in a hurry and was very upset by the whole thing.

Without any warning the next day a Lt. Col Park Jin Gyon showed up at Colonel Kim's office. Kim knew Park and his reputation as an officer in the dreaded Japanese Kwantung Army.

Park had spent 5 years with the Japanese Military in its Manchurian counter-guerilla operations and also served with the Japanese on Cheju Island. Park brought an order from Colonel Mansfield which replaced Kim with Park, making Kim Park's advisor. Park thereupon instructed Kim that they were going to suppress the insurrection by a wide- scale use of the scorched earth method, burning down villages thought to be sympathetic to the rebels and herding the inhabitants to guarded settlements on the coast.

Kim refused to do this and eventually was reassigned off the island. Later on Kim would be arrested for investigation of involvement in a military mutiny at the city of Yosu, but he was able to elude his American and Korean enemies to go on to serve faithfully for many years in the Korean Army.

It was Kim's opinion that General Dean had issued secret "scorch earth" orders to Park because Dean knew that Park would carry them out, while Kim would not.

> *"Washington told Gen. Dean to settle up the Cheju issue promptly and he urgently needed a Korean yes-man to command the 9th Regiment."*

The US at that time was trying to showcase the little "democracy" it had created in the Far East right under the Soviets' nose. The "UN supervised elections" were only a month away and the Americans had been on a wild and vigorous campaign to make everything "look good."

From his grave Kim sent a curse:

> *"Scorched earth tactics are not allowed even in war situations and any commander who uses them are deemed criminals and punishable as such. Ordering or condoning scorched earth tactics in peacetime in a territory under his command is a serious matter if the outside world*

discovered the truth. Even if not convicted as a war criminal and punished, General Dean's conscience and humanity would punish him some day."

From General Ward's diary entry of April 30, 1948:

"Dinner with IG [Inspector General] group at JRH [General Hodge]. . . . All 'commy' complex."

General Ward, May 6, 1948:

"Chief [General Hodge] called from Seoul. . . . It is amazing how we were able to have . . . revolutions in SA and other places sans 'communist agitation.'"

General Ward, May 9, 1948:

The article in the <u>New Yorker</u> dated 1859 indicated that there could be strife at the Poles sans COMMUNISTIC instigation. We could years ago have revolutions in SA just for a revolution. I must remember that 'you can tell a general but you can't tell him much.' JRH [General Hodge] is a good example of that. He will not listen to anything not assumed to be communist in origin. He may be right to a certain extent. G2's [Intelligence unit] are prone to report fancies rather than fact. They are much like News Reporters who incidentally have in many cases confused liberty and license when they come to the truth.

General Ward, May 24, 1948:

". . . . JHR [Hodge] has 'communistic' [Red conspiracy complex] as has Rothwell Brown. . . ."

55

Ward had a feeling that General Dean would ask for Colonel Rothwell Brown who was serving under Ward, to deal with the uprisings in Cheju-do. *"McF and I bet Dean would ask for him. He did."* (May 18, 1948.)

General Orlando Ward awarding a decoration to Colonel Rothwell Brown in the Spring of 1948, before Brown was reassigned by General Dean to supervise the suppression onCheju-do. (Courtesy Orlando Ward Collection, US Army Military Institute, Carlisle Barracks).

Rothwell Brown had been a protégé of Ward's and had in fact been assigned to Korea at General Ward's request. After Brown was chosen by Dean on May 18, 1948 to take over the supervision of the United States tactical troops in Cheju-do, Ward saw Brown off at the Pusan airport. Part of Brown's orders in his new assignment was to report directly to Dean, thus taking Cheju-do, in Ward's bailiwick, out of Ward's jurisdiction, at least for the purpose of dealing with the uprising, and by-passing General Ward even with reports. General Ward did not seem to resent this, but he was worried that Dean and Brown were going down the wrong path. After seeing him off at the airport, Ward noted in his diary on May 18th:

> *"Met Brown at air port. He is creating situation in his mind on Cheju-do which he will fit into"*

The next day, even though Cheju-do and Brown had just been removed from his jurisdiction, General Ward nevertheless wrote Brown a letter with a little gentle advice:

> *"I am sorry you are leaving the Division, and certainly wish you the best of luck in your new assignment. I am glad that they have assigned you in charge of Cheju Do, and I am sure that from here on out the place will quiet down considerably.*
>
> ***I have one caution, which may or may not be pertinent, but I cannot help but remember there have been times in the past when disturbances and revolutions of tremendous size were held in South America and other places without Communistic instigation.*** *That doesn't mean there are not some on Cheju. On the other hand,* ***I do feel that the main trouble is that engendered by hatred of the police.*** *These disturbances will continue until this irritation has been removed by replacing those in whom the populace have no confidence, and by demonstrating the proper attitude."* [Emphasis added.]

However, Ward's gentle and even deferential efforts to point Brown and Dean in the right direction were fruitless. In a few weeks Brown supposedly had gotten to the bottom of it all and was able to make a report to General Hodge on the cause of the uprising. In his July 1, 1948 Report to Hodge and Dean, Brown relates that he had *"approximately 5,000 inhabitants of Cheju-do"* rounded up and **"interrogated" by the South Korean police**. These are the very police who were hated by the populace and which, according to Ward as well as many scholars who have researched the subject, was the cause of the uprisings. The normal form of "interrogation" by these Japanese-trained police routinely involved torture. It was one of these torture deaths that had sparked the uprising in the first place.

Sure enough, as Ward thought he would and as Hodge and Dean must have wanted, Rothwell Brown concluded from the information gained by these interrogations that all the troubles had been instigated by communist organizers *"sent in from the mainland."* He found that:

> *"at the height of the rioting, it is estimated that the People's Democratic Army* [the rebels] *had a strength of approximately 4,000 officers and men.* **Less than 10% of this force was equipped with rifles**, *the balance being armed with Japanese* **swords and native made spears**. *The* **Women's Auxiliary** *of the South Korean Labor Party was also established and very complete lists of* **membership have been uncovered.**"

Rothwell Brown's report to Hodge was what Hodge and Dean had wanted to hear. But they must have wondered about some of his numbers and hoped that nobody was going to examine Brown's Report too carefully, as his numbers seemed somewhat incredible. Indeed, sixty years later parts of Brown's Report are almost amusing. If we are to believe the Colonel the Communists must have been Christ-like in their ability to multiply loaves and fishes.

> *"It is estimated that* **not over six** *trained agitators and organizes were sent in from the outside. . . that an additional* **five to seven hundred** *sympathizers, with some real understanding of Communism and its purposes, joined these six specialized organizers. . . . It is estimated that between* **sixty and seventy thousand** *people on the Island actually joined the South Korean Labor Party. However, it has been quite apparent that a large majority . . . had no real understanding . . . or desire to join the Communistic movement.* **They were, for the main part, ignorant,**

uneducated farmers and fishermen *whose livelihood had been profoundly disturbed by the war* [World War II]. . . . *"*

The foolishness of Brown's Report, the cruelty of the resulting "scorched earth" program that perhaps killed as many as 60,000 of these islanders, and an unconscious damning of himself and all the others who took part in the suppression is unintentionally revealed by one of the reasons he gives for the difficulty of putting down the revolt:

> *"Blood ties . . . link most of the families on the island and make it extremely difficult to obtain information."*

Imagine what the hated police, the cause of the trouble, did to those poor prisoners, already recalcitrant and unwilling subjects, to extract incriminating information about their own relatives.

Far-fetched on its face as is Brown's finding that an island-wide uprising by seventy thousand inhabitants had been started by **six** outside communist agitators; even more so was his story that the well organized and efficient Communists, though they had carefully planned this rebellion over a period of time, nevertheless were only able to find rifles for 10% of the rebels, with the rest carrying *"Japanese swords and native made spears"* against the American-armed police.

"Two confessed murderers captured on Cheju Island during the reign of terror currently in progress." 1 May 1948 US Army Signal Corps. (Mootz)

The day after he wrote his Report, July 2nd, Colonel Brown finally responded to Ward's cautionary letter of May 19th:

"I am inclosing a copy of my report on the activities in Cheju-Do in the hope that it may be of interest to you. I realize that there have been many differences of opinion as to the causes of the rioting on the island. I hope that my report will give some clarity to the picture as it existed there. ***One thing is absolutely certain – that the island was organized as a Communist base. The evidence was irrefutable once we really began to dig into the matter.*** *Police brutality and inefficient government were but incidental to the Communist designs on this island."* (Both letters and the Report in Box 3, Rothwell Brown Papers, U.S. Army Military History Institute, Carlisle Barracks.)

The disturbances on Cheju were not completely put down for another year, and at a horrendous cost to the local population. Ward noted in his diary on October 2, 1948:

> *"Police killing on Cheju."*

On October 11, he wrote:

> *"NWest Youth being used on Cheju do as in a Korean CIC* [Intelligence]. *Bad Judgment by Col. Voss. . . . ."*

An example of the brutality with which the uprising was suppressed is contained in one of the Army's Confidential G-2 (Intelligence) Periodic Reports (3 March 1949, Record Group 338, Box 32, Folder: "History of USAFIK." N.A.). The G-2 Report first quoted from a Korean Army's dispatch on the continuing disturbances on Cheju-do:

> [From the Korean Army dispatch] *" 'On 20 February, 76 rebels from TODU-RI were executed by the MIN BO DAN (People Protective Corps* [i.e., Northwest Youth] *), **who used spears** in the performance of these executions. Five women and numerous children of middle school age were included in the group. National Police and KUNKI DAI (Korean Army Military Police) supervised the operation.' "*

After relating this information from the Korean Army, G-2 then commented on it:

> *"Four members of KMAG* [American Officers in the United States Korea Military Advisory Group] *witnessed, by chance, the execution of 38 rebels and counted 38 already dead when they arrived. Previous reports have indicated that rebels were being executed by Armed Forces personnel, before a firing squad. This is the*

61

first report of a mass execution being conducted by the
MIN BO DAN [i.e. the Northwest Youth]. "

What is one to make of this?

General Ward had thought it was *"bad judgment"* for
Colonel Voss to be using the Northwest Youth gangs in Cheju do.
We are at this time in complete control of the Korean Army and
the National Police. We were in control of their arms and Rhee had
agreed that we would continue to run the Korean Military until the
end of 1949, that's what the KMAG was there for. Our orders to
the Korean Military usually were conveyed by the officers of the
KMAG.

Are we expected to believe that four of these US officers
unexpectedly found themselves at that exact location on the island,
just stumbling on this official execution *"by chance"*? Further, that
these KMAG officers, who were in control of the Korean Military,
could do nothing but meekly count 38 dead upon their arrival and
then stand around to watch and count as the Northwest Youth
goons continued to slaughter 38 more men, women and *"numerous
children"* with bamboo spears? One has to imagine the time it took
to kill the additional 38 people with spears. Imagine the screaming
and crying that went on, particularly from the mothers watching
their children being killed. Yet we are told that the Americans were
accidental and innocent bystanders. If this horrific story survived
the "cleansing' process and found its way into the National
Archives for me to read in 2002, then I am afraid it must be just the
"tip of the iceberg."

The US Ambassador to Korea, John Muccio, casually
reported on the brutality with which the uprising was being put
down. From a Confidential Memo he wrote on April 9, 1949 to
Secretary of State Dean Acheson, he remarks:

> *"Photographs of operations on Cheju indicate*
> *unusual sadistic propensities on the part of both*

*Government and guerrilla forces. Signal atrocities have
been reported, indicating mass massacre of village
populations, including women and children, accompanied
by widespread looting and arson. In some cases the Army
has been guilty of revenge operations against guerrillas
which have brought down vengeance on unarmed villagers."*

But Muccio does not even hint that the US, though it still
controlled the Korean Military, legally by secret treaty and in fact
because every riffle and bullet was paid for by US taxpayers, that
we did anything to stop the mass murders, lootings and burnings.
Instead he used the results of the suppression as an example of the
new Korean Government's effectiveness. The Ambassador's April
9, 1949 report to Dean Acheson continued:

> *"Defense Minister Sihn Sung Mo is now on Cheju
> Island at the express request of President Rhee, with orders
> to remain until guerillas have been wiped out and order
> restored . . . .*
>
> *It is clear from the nature of the propaganda
> emanating from Soviet-controlled radio that Cheju Island
> has been chosen as the spot for a **major Soviet effort** to
> sow confusion and terror in southern Korea . . . .With such
> conditions deep in the rear area of the Republic, President
> Rhee has been forced to take the decision to stamp out
> unrest and insecurity . . . . It seems obvious that Soviet
> agents are being filtered into Cheju without great
> difficulty . . . ."*

Recall that Colonel Rothwell Brown had been sent in by Military
Governor William Dean a **year** earlier with essentially the same
mandate "to *stamp out unrest and insecurity*"; that according to Brown
what Muccio was now calling a "**major** Soviet effort" was started by
only *"six trained agitators"* and that most of the rebels, who were *"for
the main part, ignorant, uneducated farmers and fishermen"* were
primarily *"armed with Japanese swords and*

63

native made spears"; that Colonel Voss had been using the Northwest Youth gangs to slaughter the natives to General Ward's disapproval; and that by this point most of the island was in ruins already, nearly all of its 300,000 inhabitants had been either killed, corralled into what amounted to concentration camps, made homeless or had fled the island.

But Muccio's audience for these fabrications that were intended to make the "tottering" Rhee look like a resolute leader was actually the US Congress, whose members for the most part seemed as ignorant of what was going on in Korea as the proverbial "man in the moon".

At the time of Muccio's report Truman's bill to continue military and economic aid to Korea was being considered by Congress. On June 20, 1949 the House Committee on Foreign Affairs was holding a hearing on a bill to provide $150,000,000 in economic aid to South Korea. One Congressman at the hearing raised the question of whether the money was being poured down a "rat hole;" whether Korea in any even had any chance of surviving as a nation. Congressman Fulton further asked if the Korean Army was "dependable."

The answers to these questions came from the Administration's Edgar A. Johnson, Director of the Korean Aid Program in the Economic Cooperation Administration. Johnson had spent years in Korea and had just returned from there. He knew better but here he presented the tortured fiction compiled by the State Department for consumption by Congress. As proof that the Korean Army was reliable and that Rhee was in control of the situation, he cited the year-long uprising on Cheju Island

> *"where a great number of misguided villagers had been persuaded to follow the Communist cause. . . .*

> *"The test* [for Rhee's Government] *came. . . on the island of Cheju where the Communist forces had*

64

withdrawn into the interior. , , , It was the first test of the Korean Army to overcome those forces. I was last on the island of Cheju in March of 1949 and the campaign was substantially finished. The Korean Army had drawn a tighter and tighter perimeter. . . . The campaign took until the spring of 1949. However, that was successfully accomplished."

CHAPTER IV

THE "FAIR AND FREE" ELECTIONS

One of the reasons General Hodge was so anxious to put a quick end to the April 4th disturbances on Cheju-do was the upcoming American instigated May 10th elections in his zone. Both the Russians and the Americans had been calling for elections in Korea and the unification of the two zones into one nation, something that the Koreans passionately wanted. However neither of the big powers intended to give up its influence over Korea, or at least its part.

The United Nations, under American influence, had proposed an election throughout Korea. But this proposal had been rejected by the Russians who feared that the Americans would manipulate the vote in their zone, which was larger than that in the Russian zone (22,000,000 versus 9,000,000), and thereby control the resulting government. Instead the Russians called for a conference on April 14th in Pyongyang and invited leaders from the North and the South where the Koreans by themselves could begin working out a plan for unification.

Hodge is quoted in an article in the New York Times, which "newspaper of record" incidentally had reported nothing on the revolt in Cheju-do, much less its actual causes, as calling the proposed conference just " '*another effort to deceive the good people of South Korea*' ."(New York Times, Richard J.H. Johnston, "Hodge Sees Plot in Korean Parley," April 7, 1948, p. 14.) According to the Times article Hodge said *that only Communists, fellow travelers and others opposed to United Nations sponsored elections had been asked to the conference.* Yet the article also points out that Kim Koo and Kimm Kiusic, whom it describes as

66

"disaffected Rightists" had planned on going to the conference from the South. Though Hodge now dismissed them as having *"no mandate to speak for the people of South Korea,"* recall that these were two of the three leaders of the exiled Korean Provisional Government whom Hodge had brought back from China and whom he hoped would act as his figureheads. He had more luck with the third exile he had brought back, Syngman Rhee, who vigorously supported the May 10th election for reasons we will see below.

Richard J.H. Johnston's byline was on many of the New York Times articles appearing at the time relating to Korea, and it appears that the US Military Government could always count on his reporting its version of the facts. In a subsequent article after the elections, Johnston describes Rhee's program for his government as *"representative democracy based on universal suffrage patterned closely after the American system."* (New York Times, May 16, 1948, Part IV, p. 5.)

In the pre-election April 7th article Hodge is further quoted as saying:

> *"It is absolutely essential that every man and woman over twenty-one years of age go to a place of registry immediately and register. They must go to the polling places on elections day* [May 10] *and vote for their own representatives . . . ."*

Hodge actually had good reason to be confident that the Koreans would overwhelmingly go to their "place of registry" and register to vote, and then vote on the appointed day. To a Korean in the American zone, you would register and you would vote, or you would risk not eating. This was guaranteed by the fact that under American Occupation there was always the unsettling worry for Koreans of where they were going to get tomorrow's ration of rice. The period of the American Occupation was marred by chronic rice shortages in a rice-rich country, one of the many things grossly mismanaged by the Military Government. Under the

American plan each Korean was given a "ration card" for his or her rice. This card was kept at an office run by people appointed by the Military Government with the assistance of those Right Wing advisors, such as Rhee, that Hodge had surrounded himself with. It was at **this same office** that one also had to go to register. The Military Government people, therefore, who were holding your ration card, would know whether you registered or not. Likewise for the election, whether you voted. Hence the 90 to 99% turnouts.

As it happened the Soviets postponed the conference so neither Koo nor Kiusic attended, though Kiusic and his entourage had make it to the site of the conference in the North. Meanwhile Hodge was able to issue a statement that because more than 90% of eligible voters had registered which

> "[it] *shows an overwhelming expression by the Korean people of their desire to vote in a democratic election . . . . and discredits those vociferous self-appointed leaders of the dissident minority elements who have joined with Communist elements in opposing or boycotting the elections."*

In addition, Military Governor Dean on April 20, 1948 had deputized none other than the right wing Northwest Youth goons to work under the police as "voluntary policemen" to help maintain a "free atmosphere" for the 1948 UN supervised elections. Ambassador John Muccio later explained why the Americans were using these young goons whom they had trained.

> "*The Mission has done a great job training the young Koreans. They have pushed aside the old Chinese and Japanese trained Koreans. There is no hope in the old Koreans, but in the young ones there is great hope."* (Wake Island Conference.)

These tough right wing youths, standing "guard" at each of the polls, were probably redundant to the American efforts to elect

Rhee and put on a good "election" show for the world. Both the *"dissident Rightists"* Koo and Kiusic as well as the Leftists boycotted the election because they felt it would result in permanently divided Korea. As a result Rhee was the only major candidate for President.

As if having only one candidate on the ballot was not enough, the Military Government made sure that the Koreans knew who to vote for. Below is a 1948 Korean election poster that has been preserved in the US National Archives. The archivist identifies it as a poster featuring President Rhee and General Douglas MacArthur (MacArthur has a flower wreath draped over him as he waves to the crowd; Rhee standing next to him) and that Rhee's party was *"the political party the US supported in the election."*

Photos taken by American soldiers during the election were intended to demonstrate a "free and fair" election but today they would suggest something else. One can see the Northwest goons in their threatening poses around the polling places. Then there are the obviously staged capture of "communists" who were supposedly trying to disrupt the election. One US Embassy official attributed the relatively peaceful election to the presence of strong young men from the Northwest Group as volunteers at each polling place.

"Ch'unch'on, Korea Koreans line up in front of one of the many polling booths in Ch'unch'on, Korea about 20 miles south of the 38th parallel to cast their ballots in the first free election in the history of Korea. Lines started to form over an hour before the polls opened and **perfect order was maintained by voluntary police."**

10 May 1948   US Army Signal Corps (Mootz)

71

"SEOUL, KOREA"
"Korean Police check superficial wounds suffered by election official when five communist raiders attacked the polling place where he was working today. The Official was struck by fragmentation of a hand grenade thrown by one of the raiders. Korean policemen closed in, killing one of the raiders and capturing the other four." 10 May 1950 US Army (Evans)

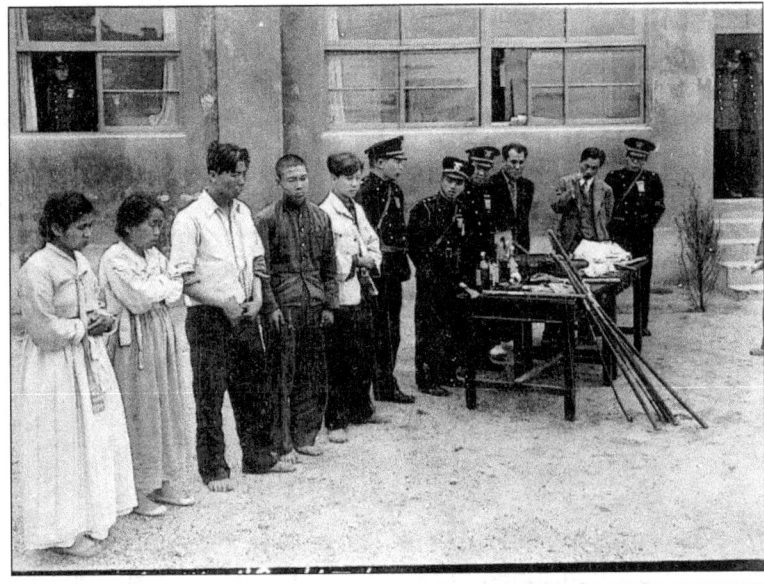

"Five Communist agitators captured in a surprise raid by Korean Police this morning. This group, including two women, were apparently bent on destroying every police box in the city of Seoul. They had in their possession explosives tagged for each individual police station. The woman as extreme left is the wife of the attempted assassin of Police Chief Chang, Tak San, who is now serving a life sentence in the penitentiary. This was another of the many foiled plots on the part of Communist agitators to break up the UN supervised elections in Korea." 10 May 1950　　US Army (Evans)

Observers in the State Department in February, 1948, three months **before** the elections, were predicting an almost 100% voter turnout and almost a 100% vote for Rhee's supporters. Again, this was easy to predict as there was in effect only one major candidate running and the election process would be in the hands of Rhee's supporters. The union leaders and left-wing leaders who would have opposed Rhee were in jail or had gone underground for fear of arrests or assassination. The moderate wing as well as the most prominent right-wing opponents of Rhee were boycotting the election as they objected to the consequent permanent division of Korea.

Notwithstanding all of this, there were still scattered voters who did not vote for Rhee. Even though the left, moderates and some of the right had boycotted the election, and no communist party was allowed even to exist as such, Richard J.H. Johnston of the New York Times somehow was able to utilize the results of this election to come up with an estimate of Communists support in South Korea. He simply counted **every** vote that was **not** for Rhee as a vote by a **Communist**.

"[T]*he elections were in effect a vital test of Communist strength here. If nothing else, they proved that Communist strength lay somewhere below 5 per cent of South Korean political power.*" (New York Times, May 16, 1948, Part IV, page 5.)

During the hearings in Congress a year later for economic aid to Korea mentioned previously, supporters frequently cited the "free" elections "supervised" by the UN as proof the South Korea was a democratic country worthy of support. When asked if the US Military had taken any position with respect to candidates, the answer was "absolutely not, the US was neutral."

CHAPTER V

CIVIL WAR IN KOREA

On Sunday June 25, 1950 Major General Earle Partridge
was in his headquarters in Tokyo. He was acting as the
Commander of the Far East Air Force (FEAF) in the temporary
absence of his Commander, Lieutenant General George
Stratemeyer, who happened to be in Washington for meetings.

From Major General Earle Partridge's Sunday, 25 June
1950 [Tokyo time] diary entry:

> *Returned to learn of invasion of South Korea by
> North Korea Army. ... 374th [Troop Carrier Wing] and 8th*
> [Fighter-Bomber Wing] *were alerted to implement FAF*
> [Fifth Air Force, located in Japan] *Ops Plan #4.* [Plan for
> evacuation of U.S. civilians and military personnel from
> Korea.] *. . . .War officially declared by North Koreans 1100.
> Conference at my house about 1900. ... White* [Lt. Col.
> John M. White, Jr. FEAF A-2] *expressed view that U.S.
> would abandon South Korea to Reds. I disagree. This line
> of action is unthinkable and I await with interest the policy
> of the U.S. JCS.*

The next day the US military began an evacuation of American
civilians through Seoul and Pusan, though President Syngman
Rhee and his government had already abandoned Seoul the night
before. Ambassador Muccio had tried in vain to talk Rhee from
fleeing, arguing that his military had enough weapons and men to
put up a defense of Seoul. Muccio in a report to Washington
described Rhee as incoherent and his statements "repetitious, half-
formed and disconnected." (FRUS, 7; 142.) The requisitioned
ships carrying the evacuees were escorted by Air Force planes. The

planes ran into no hostile action except for two North Korean jets that briefly "bounced off" an American jet but then quickly retreated to above the 38th parallel.

Major General Earle Partridge's diary entry, Monday, 26 June 1950:

> *General Almond* [Major General Edward M. Almond, MacArthur's deputy chief of staff] *called to relay information which he had just received from Colonel Wright* [Col. W.H.S. Wright, acting chief of Korean Military Advisory Group, KMAG] *in Korea. He stated that one of our Mustangs had jettisoned two tanks in the Seoul area and that one of these struck and killed six Koreans.*
>
> *The General was disturbed that our aircraft were avoiding combat rather than engaging and destroying the North Korean airplanes. He directed me to take the necessary action to insure that our AF patrols maintain an aggressive attitude in the accomplishment of their mission* [that is, escorting the ships evacuating civilians]. *General Almond was especially caustic regarding the failure of one of our F-82 pilots to shoot down a Yak* [North Korean fighter airplane] *which flew over Inchon anchorage. The F-82 was 'bounced' but not shot at. Pilot of '82 ducked into the low cloud and when he came out seconds later, Yak had disappeared.*

Early the next morning, Tuesday, June 27th, General Partridge, complying with General Arnold's wishes, issued from his headquarters in Tokyo instructions to his pilots taking off from American bases in Japan to *"use aggressive action in the event that hostile aircraft interfere or attempt to interfere with FAF mission* [of evacuation] *or acts in an unfriendly manner to South Korea forces or our own."*

General Partridge, Tuesday, 27 June 1950:

A redline [very important message from senior official requiring prompt and special handling] *from General Vandenberg* [Hoyt S. Vandenberg, Chief of Staff, USAF] *requested further data as to why our F-82 pilot avoided combat over Inchon yesterday. . . .*

"I was again called to the Dai Ichi Building [building in Tokyo where General Douglas MacArthur and the American Occupation authorities were headquartered] *for a teleconference with Washington. Present were Generals MacArthur* [Commander in Chief Far East, CINCFE]*, Almond, Hickey* [Major General Doyle O. Hickey, Deputy Chief of Staff, Far East Command, "FEC"]*, Beiderlinden, Willoughby* [Major General Charles Willoughby, headed FEC G-2, Intelligence]*, Wright and Eberle, and Admiral Joy* [Vice Admiral C. Turner Joy, Commander Naval Forces, Far East].

*"The teleconference directed a **major reversal** of policy on the part of the US Government. CINCFE*

[General Mac Arthur] *was directed to employ such naval and Air Forces as were at his disposal to bolster the SK* [South Korean] *forces and restore the territorial integrity of that nation. . . .*

"CINCFE turned to me and directed immediate action . . . The general was almost jubilant at the end of the conference.

"He outlined the far-reaching results which will be achieved if the air effort can be made effective tonight and tomorrow. He stressed again and

77

*again the necessity of hitting the North Korean
forces in the next 36 hours with every resource at
our disposal, carrying the action through the night
if this is possible. He expressed the firm conviction
that vigorous action by the FAF [Fifth Air Force –
the unit under Partridge's command and stationed
in Japan] would result in driving the North Korean
forces back into their territory in disorder. . . .*

According to General Partridge, the old General was
"jubilant" that Washington had reversed its long and carefully
crafted policy on Korea, which MacArthur himself had helped to
shape, and decided instead for war on the mainland of Asia.
MacArthur was 72 by this time and only a retirement from his
Emperor-like status in the Far East had been looming ahead for
him.

MacArthur, like Partridge and many others, was surprised
by the American Government's wholesale reversal of policy. The
Army had been trying from day one of the Korean Occupation in
1945 to **get out**. It considered Korea to be of no strategic
importance to the US and it was risky to have troops on such a
vulnerable peninsula, and on the borders of Russia and China. If
war with Russia started any American troops on the peninsula
would be slaughtered. It was entirely unnecessary from a military
point of view to have anyone in Korea itself, as the United States
Air Force could neutralize Korea flying from its bases in Japan and
Okinawa and thereby keep it from being used by the Russians.
Mac Arthur was asked by the Joint Chiefs in 1947 for his opinion
on Korea and he strongly advocated a pullout of the 45,000
Occupation troops then stationed in Korea. In addition, he advised
that no commitments be given to the Koreans, as their country
would be indefensible in a war with Russia or China.

Secretary of the Navy, James Forrestal, wrote of a Cabinet
lunch attended by President Truman on September 29, 1947. He
recorded in his diary that:

"Secretary [of State] *Marshall said that he was giving close study to the question of getting out of Korea, that to many of his people in the State Department it seemed that the Russian offer to withdraw provided we did might be an opportunity. Harriman raised the question of whether we could get out without loss of face. That Marshall said, was the aspect of the question to which he was giving most serious thought.* (Forrestal, James. <u>Diaries</u>. Ed. Walter Millis. New York: Viking Press, 1951. 321 – 322.)

After the US failed to take advantage of the Soviet offer of mutual withdrawal, the Soviets nevertheless unilaterally withdrew its troops from North Korea the following year, 1948. The American then had no choice and itself withdrew its troops at the end of 1949.

By late 1949, according to James F. Schnabel, an Army intelligence officer who served in the Far East and later wrote an official history of the Korean War, the American intelligence community assumed that there was going to be a civil war between North and South Korea by the next summer and that the North would conquer the South. In the intelligence briefing he received when he reported to duty in Tokyo, he was told about this conclusion and *"the point was not emphasized particularly and the fact seemed to be accepted as regrettable but inevitable."*

The Russians had pulled out their occupation troops from North Korea in 1948 and the US had been looking a little "colonial" in keeping its troops there. However, there was an element in Congress and in the State Department that wanted to keep any piece of real estate in the world away from the Communists. These groups' motives were varied – containment of Communism at any cost, twitching Russia's nose by creating a "test case for democracy" on the borders of Red Russia and Red China, or as Congressman Eaton (Charles A. Eaton, R. NJ), stated during a June 16, 1949 hearing of the House Committee on Foreign Affairs:

*"We have 1 ½ billion **brown people** in the Orient.*

*"They are for the first time conscious of their nationhood and their passion to be free. **That is a revolution** of tremendous world importance in itself.*

"There are two dominant forces in the world, the United States and Russia. Russia is making tremendous progress in the Orient. She has practically taken over China and proposes eventually to take over Japan. Now, how are we going to meet that?

*"**Are we going to meet it with a mailed fist** and an iron will or are we going to meet it with classifications and soft words? We might just as well spit in the face of a hurricane as to try that. . . .*

*"**What is the decision of the U.S. Government? Are we going to stand up** and notify Russia and the world that we are there in the Orient, we are going to stay there, and we are not going to permit the Orient to come under the **control of slavery** if it is possible to prevent it."*

Congressman Eaton was the ranking or highest Republican on the Foreign Affairs Committee. The Committee was conducting a hearing on the Korean Aid Act of 1949, a bill introduced by the Administration proposing $150,000,000 in economic aid to Korea. James Webb, Under Secretary of State, was one of the principal Administration's witnesses but he preferred to have George Kennan answer most of the questions *"since I am very new at this business."* He introduced Kennan as having just *"been nominated by the President as Counselor of the Department, and who is our senior professional Foreign Service officer in the Department. He is the head of our Policy Planning staff. . . ."*

80

Congressman Eaton asked them the following question:

*"Do you think we should stay in Korea and make that **a clinic demonstration of our principles of civilization**?"*

George Kennan on behalf of the Administration responded:

> *"**By armed force, no**, sir, because I do not think that is the answer, and I think there would be a real danger that if we were to do it we might make fools of ourselves and give the Korean Communists and the Russians a perfectly gratuitous little triumph . . .*

> *"If one of the things we are afraid of is that Communist political sentiment might sweep down there, Communist penetration and Communist domination of the local political movements, that would happen with our troops there, and there is no worse position for our troops than to find themselves suddenly engulfed in a sea of adverse political sentiment.*

> *"It is a question of **defense by the southern Korean Government** -- what we call the legitimate Government of Korea, **against Koreans from the North. I do not think our forces should be mixed in that.** The Russians would love to see that situation come about and they would sit back there and laugh their heads off if we got our forces engaged with any Koreans at all, and there would be a strong temptation, then, on the part of the people in southern Korea . . . to laugh a little too, because they all, I think, like to see occasionally things happen to outsiders and the forces of the big, white powers there. . . ".*

This was the set policy of the Truman Administration, and it had been developed after careful study. The United States considered this tip of the mainland of Asia as the worst possible place to have a showdown with Russia. It had no intention of

81

allowing itself to be dragged into a conflict on this indefensible peninsula. Secretary Webb told the Congressmen that even having just 7,000 troops in Korea, the remaining occupational troops, down from 45,000 at the beginning of the occupation in 1945, would have a detrimental effect on the government and people of South Korea in that it might create the false impression that the troops would be there to fight when in fact America was determined that its troops were *"**not going to engage in a Korean civil war.**"*

The Administration was requesting this $150,000,000 in economic aid in addition to the arming and training of the South Koreans for their self defense. As to objections to the claims that South Korea was a police state under the authoritarian Sigmund Rhee which we had put in power, Mr. Kennan replied:

> *We realize that people are not lily-white anywhere and throughout the Far East you are going to get a great deal of seaminess, a great deal of cruelty, a great deal of intolerance and a great deal of inexperience in these groups. . . .*

> *If we can keep these people at least independent and where they have possibilities for a long term maturity of political institutions under their own steam . . .*

> **I understand there is a possibility of civil war in Korea. . . . I would not recommend our getting our forces involved in there.** *As I say, I can think of nothing that would please the Kremlin better than to see us get into a military row with a lot of Koreans. . . .*

At the same hearing the representatives of the Joint Chiefs of Staff laboriously tried to explain to the Congressmen and Congresswomen, some of whom thought that it would be nice to have a *"foothold"* in Asia on the doorstep of Russia and China,

82

why Korea was of little importance to the United States and why the United States should not get trapped into any fighting there.

Congresswoman Douglas (Helen Gahagan Douglas, D. Ca.) asked: "If the Army were to say, 'Well, it is not safe to give up Korea and we are going to stay for another year,' what would be the psychological effect, not only in Korea, but throughout the rest of that part of the world?"

Major General Charles L. Bolte, Director, Plans and Operations Division, Department of the Army, on behalf of the Military Establishment answered:

> *"I am afraid that it would create a delusion on the part of the Koreans. Instead of their doing the building of their own forces, which we have been sponsoring, they might have an unfounded hope that the tactical units that we would have there, if we kept them there additionally, would become involved in case of an advance from North Korea, or even a Russian advance, and* **we certainly would not want our tactical units involved in combat on the Korean Peninsula.**"

Congressman Judd (Walter H. Judd, R., Minn.) was a Christian Minister who had served in China in the tradition of a long line of Protestant missionaries from the United States. Judd, as a charter member of what was known as the China Lobby possessed a wildly unrealistic conviction about our ability to control the outcome of the civil war in China between Mao and Chiang. His feelings were passionate, bordering on psychotic. He often heatedly sparred with Congressman Vito Marcantonio on the floor of the House over this issue He wanted to know:

> *"Are our naval and air forces in Japan going to be disturbed by the Russians getting a big base there at Pusan* [South Korea]?"

General Bolte: *"I think General MacArthur would be disturbed but he would prefer not to be involved tactically on the Korean Peninsula."*

Mr. Judd: *"He would prefer to lose that base to the Russians rather than fight there himself?"*

General Bolte: *"Yes."*

Later, Congressman Lodge (John Davis Lodge, R. Conn.)asked:

"Why do we want to get out [of Korea]?"

Mr. Kennan:

"Because it is an exposed, unsound military position, *one that is doing no good, and we are anxious to get rid of positions of that sort."*

The next day at the hearing some Congressmen kept on insisting that it would be dangerous to American interests in Japan to withdraw the remaining occupation troops from Korea. Congressmen Vorys (John M. Vorys, R. Ohio) observed:

"I was told by a man who returned from Japan, Monday, who asked me what we were doing in Japan, that Japan was entirely indefensible from a military standpoint if the Communists took over the mainland. Would you care to comment on that statement or rumor?"

After a discussion "off the record," General Bolte replied for the US Military:

"I would not agree with that. Very definitely we intend, in the last analysis, if it came to a showdown,

to hold on to Japan, Okinawa, and other islands in the Japanese archipelago. . . . "

Congresswoman Bolton (Frances P. Bolton, R. Ohio) inquired:

"The Army feels Japan is a very tenable spot, even if the airfields and so on in Korea become the property of the Soviets?"

After another discussion "off the record" General Bolte answered:

"That is so, Mrs. Bolton."

Mrs. Bolton persisted: *"Where do you get your confidence?"*

General Bolte responded:

"I am familiar with our plans and we feel our bases are not only adequate but better."

Congresswoman Bolton:

"The Communists can move down the cost to Sumatra and Ceylon and so forth? They can keep right on going without having to trouble themselves with inner China."

General Bolte:

"We have arrangements with the Philippine Republic and have certain forces, air forces, in the Philippines by agreement. . . . We have other bases: Guam and Saipan, in the Pacific."

85

Congressman John Lodge from Connecticut just could not let the issue go away. He could not understand how the Military could say that it was not worth trying to keep the harbor of Pusan in South Korea (though his next question disclosed that he did not even know where it was).

Mr. Lodge:

"*General, as another Navy man, I would be very much interested in having your comment as to the importance of the harbor of Pusan; whether you feel that the loss of that harbor, being, as I understand it, **just a few miles away from the island of Honshu**, would be serious to our position in Japan?*"

General Bolte:

"*The only disadvantage in not holding on to the Korean Peninsula is that it does not deny the use of the Korean Peninsula to Soviet and Communist forces.*"

Mr. Lodge:

"*Do you mean there is no positive disadvantage in our losing that port?*"

General Bolte:
"*No, we are perfectly satisfied with what we have.*"

Congressman Judd seemed to continue having a difficult time in our simply eliminating any part of Korea as important militarily to the US:

"*We were told the other day that it [Pusan] is the best natural harbor in all of Northeast Asia.*"

General Bolte:

"It is a very fine natural harbor but our air bases are well within range of any of those points, sufficiently to deny them the use of it."

Nevertheless certain hawkish members of Congress still were not happy with comments of the Generals from the Army, though the Generals had said they represented the Joint Chiefs of Staff. So Congressman Lodge asked for someone else to testify. *"It just occurred to me, General, and this is in no way meant as a reflection on you, but in order for this committee to pass in a responsible manner on this very important subject I thought it might be well to have naval testimony on this whole affair."*

Accordingly and without protest the very next day Rear Admiral Edmund T. Woolridge, Assistant Chief of Naval Operations, Department of the Navy, appeared on behalf of the Navy and Admiral Louis E. Denfeld, Chief of Naval Operations.

Congresswoman Bolton:

"I understand there is a harbor in Korea."

Admiral Wooldridge: *"Yes, there is. There is Pusan on the Southeast, and Inchon in the west central."*

Mrs. Bolton: *"Is it a good harbor?"*

Admiral Wooldridge:

"A relatively good harbor and relatively small"

Mrs. Bolton: *"Would you be sorry to lose it?"*

Admiral Wooldridge: *"*

If I may answer that indirectly, we would be sorry to see any harbor in the world go under Communist

87

domination. But as far as the Navy having any desire to hold that for use in case of war is concerned, no, because it is too far advanced. It is projected too far into the enemy or potential enemy zone."

Mrs. Bolton: *"Is the same thing true, General Hamilton, in the manner of an airfield in Korea?"*

Brigadier General Paul M. Hamilton, Chief of Policy Division, Directorate of Plans and Operations, Headquarters of the U.S. Air Force, Representing General Hoyt Vandenberg:

"There is an airfield but there are no airfields which are considered to be of any tactical value. . . . The air activity [of the US] in the case of hostilities in Korea, would more than likely be coming from bases further back, and any enemy activity [would be coming] *from out of Korea. It is too hard to try and hold. It is the same trouble the Navy has. The base is too advanced into enemy territory."*

Later on Congressman Judd posed this question:

"It has been testified that Pusan in our hands would not be of great value to us. Would it be of great value to the Russians and a detriment to us if it were in their hands?"

This was one of Congressman Judd's pet types of rhetoric. He was a Christian Minister who had served in China in the tradition of a long line of Protestant missionaries from the United States. He had passionate feelings about our obligations to keep China from the communists and to support Chiang Kai-shek. If someone would prove that the United States did not need a piece of territory for its own security, he would try to arrive at the opposite conclusion by suggesting that nevertheless it was just as important to keep it out of the hands of an enemy. It was a very dangerous and belligerent zero-sum game.

88

Admiral Wooldridge, however, easily avoided the trap:

> *"I think possibly it would be **as untenable to them as it would be to us** because looking at the map you can see it is within range of our air operations from Okinawa and Japan."*

The same issue was gone over again and again. Some of the armchair generals and admirals in Congress were reluctant to accept the reality that we should not or could not fight over every inch of ground in the world against Communism.

Mr. Fulton (James G. Fulton, R. Pa.):

> *"Is there any reason for having a forward strongpoint that would keep under airpower cover a certain area up in Russia, such as oilfields and industries?"*

Admiral Wooldridge:

> *"I would say the degree of effort to hold a place there*[Korea] *militarily would be all out of proportion to the dividends that you would obtain from it."*

General Hamilton: *"I subscribe entirely to that answer."*

One of the mightiest hawks and China Lobby enthusiasts in Congress was John Davis Lodge, Republican of Connecticut, who seems, from his following comments, to have also envisioned himself as a military strategist.

> *"Let us assume that virtually the whole of China collapses and that is followed by Indochina, Indonesia, Siam, Malaya, and Burma. At that point I think you will agree that our position in Japan is threatened. Our position in the Philippines and Okinawa is seriously threatened. If we find ourselves in a war would there be no*

89

*appreciable difference between having to make an
amphibious landing on the continent from Japan, which
would be our base. I assume, for combined operation, and
having a toehold in southern Korea, which is, alter all on
the continent and which we could treat as a beachhead,
from which to deploy our forces in a combined operation?
That is a question addressed to all three of you gentlemen."*

The response from the Military came from Brigadier
General Thomas S. Timberman, Chief of Operations Group, Plans
and Operations Division, Office of the Chief of Staff, Department
of the Army:

> *"First: A base in Korea would **not be a tenable base**,
> as compared with that in the Japanese archipelago. Second:
> Any plans to reenter the [Asian] continent would no doubt
> **bypass Korea.**"*

Mr. Lodge: *"Even if we held Korea?"*

General Timberman: *"Even though we held Korea, yes."*

Mr. Lodge:

> *"Even if we held Korea, which is, as I understand it,
> **90 miles from the island of Honshu** [Japan], it is in the
> present plan – and if this is top secret do not reply to it,
> please – it would not be the present plan to use southern
> Korea as a beachhead, through which to place our troops
> and for the Navy to keep pushing in more from Japan and
> from the United States."*

General Timberman:

> *"From the Army point of view, any reentry on the
> continent would **bypass and not use Korea**."*

90

Mr. Lodge:

> *"In other words,* [as if plain English were not sufficient] *on thehypothesis that I have indicated there would be virtually no strategic disadvantage to our having no toehold at all on the continent of Asia?"*

General Timberman: *"It would be a very, very minor disadvantage."*

Yet the Members of Congress went on, as if their denseness had no end, or just that they for some reason pretended not to understand. This group of hawks did not like to hear what they were hearing, and they were temporarily set back. The remaining 7,000 tactical troops were pulled out at the end of June, 1949. But next year these same hawks who just could not take "no" for an answer were the happiest crowd around when President Truman, like someone just arriving from the planet Mars, using only his "gut" as a guide and to show the world that he was a "tough guy," surprised everybody by throwing everything over the cliff.

Mr. Fulton:

> *"Why would it not be possible to continue to negotiate with them* [the Rhee Government of South Korea] *and keep a base there? For example, an air base or a navy base or something like that? . . ."*

General Hamilton:

> *"As far as the air forces are concerned, I do not think it is a question of why it will not be possible. I think it probably would be possible but there is no desire to incur the responsibility for it. There is no commensurate advantage."*

91

Mr. Fulton:

"Even though that extends the circumference of your air cover above Peiping and Mukden?"

General Hamilton:

*"Unless you wanted to go into the creation of very much larger air facilities than are there now, there **is nothing to be gained by moving forward bases into the Korean Peninsula** from where we could operate at the present moment."*

Mr. Fulton: *"Even though you could cover the whole way there?"*

General Hamilton: *"I know the con's heavily outweigh the pro's in any such undertaking."*

Mr. Fulton: *"I will have to take your word on that."*

Each committee member seemed to want to feel and touch the same issue to be assured.

Mr. Smith (Lawrence H. Smith, R. Wis.):

"I have asked you from a military standpoint how will this [proposed $150,000,000 economic] *aid program* [to Korea] *increase our security. . . ."*

General Timberman:

*"**The geography of Korea** – that is, the land itself – **is of no great importance strategically, to our military position in the Far East**. . . ."*

Mr. Smith:

> *"It seems you have just admitted that from a military standpoint it does not involve us?"*

General Timberman: *"No, it does not."*

The General then tried to summarize again one of the danger of leaving **any** tactical troops in Korea.

> *"If we left troops in Korea we would be giving false hopes to those people because **I do not think anyone would suggest we enter into combat with the northern Korean forces.**"*

The following week Secretary of State Dean Acheson appeared before the Committee and testified in support of the economic aid bill for Korea.

Secretary Acheson:

> *"The Korean problem is one upon which we must act. . . . If you do not do it, you are absolutely certain that the whole situation in Korea will collapse and Korea will fall into the Communist area. If you dodo this, there is a chance that it will not. We cannot tell you that Korea is going to stand up and under all pressures. We would not be honest at all if we told you that, but there is a good fighting chance that the Koreans can take care of themselves.*

> ***"I believe we cannot possibly guarantee the southern Koreans their independence by American military power. That is a very bad strategic position for us to be in. It is a commitment which we should not undertake. . . ."*** (Emphasis added.)

This is the Secretary of State in June of 1949 presumably speaking on behalf of the President with respect to American Policy on Korea. It is a repetition of what his under-secretaries had testified to and it was the policy as developed by the Government after years of study and incorporated into national policy papers.

These Committee hearings in June of 1949 were in "Executive" session and theoretically secret. The transcripts were not officially made available to the public until the mid-'70's. However the gist of Acheson's and the other witnesses' testimony was incorporated in majority and minority reports on the bill (House Report 962, Part 1, July 1, 1949, Part 2, July 26, 1949, 81st Cong. 1st Sess.) which in turn was repeated in the newspapers (for example, New York Times, July 2, 1949: "VOTE AID OR KOREA WILL FALL IN 3 MONTHS, ACHESON SAYS").

In 1949 Mao's forces had pushed Chiang Kai-shek and most of his fighters into the sea and were preparing to go after the last piece of Chinese territory, Formosa. Because the island of Formosa was so heavily armed Mao would need the assistance of an air force and navy, of which he had neither. So Mao had been gingerly approaching Stalin for air and naval assistance. Stalin had not supported Mao's revolution up to this point, and in fact had been making treaties and arrangements with Chiang Kai-shek. Yet while preparing to take over Formosa, the Chinese also had their hands full in consolidating their control over the newly acquired land mass and in reconstructing a country laid waste by decades of civil war and incompetent and corrupt administration by Chiang Kai-shek.

At the same time in 1949, the leader of North Korea, Kim Il Sung, was anxious to finish the Korean revolution and consolidate all of Korea under his rule. Now that the Chinese Communist had taken all of China, except Formosa, or Taiwan, it was his turn. So he also approached Stalin with requests for military aid.

94

In response to Mao's requests, Stalin encouraged him to believe that he would get air assistance from Russia to take control of Formosa, in large measure to make up for the lack of Soviet support for Mao over the many years of civil war in China. Like Tito in Yugoslavia, Mao had fought and won his long civil war without much help from Stalin. Stalin therefore was being solicitous with the victorious Chinese leader. He did not need another independent and contrary Communist leader in the world along the lines of Tito.

However, as for Kim's entreaties for help in unifying Korea by force, Stalin firmly turned him down during their discussions in 1949. It was too dangerous in that the Americans might intervene. Stalin's foreign policy was dominated by extreme caution and the overriding principle of avoiding war with the Americans – whom he knew would not hesitate to use atom bombs to devastate Russia. (Chinese and Soviet documents and memoirs surfacing in recent decades have given us a clear understanding of how and why the Korean War started. I have relied heavily on what I believe is the most comprehensive treatment of the subject which utilizes those documents, Professor Richard C. Thornton's Odd Man Out: Truman, Stalin, Mao and the Origins of the Korean War. Washington, D.C.: Brassey's, 2000.)

But some months later the situation was dramatically clarified for everybody. Now Stalin, Mao and Kim Il Sung did not need any kind of intelligence service to determine exactly the American policy toward Korea. They did not need the warren of traitors and communists which right-wing politicians like Senator Joe McCarthy were claiming had infested the State Department. Because if they were not able to determine that policy from access to Congressional hearings or to the secret planning, discussions and policy papers issued by the Defense and State Departments and the National Security Agency, they could have found out the same thing by reading the newspapers.

Secretary of State Dean Acheson wanted to make sure that Stalin and Mao knew that we did not intend to intervene in Korea if there were a civil war there. Acheson at the time was trying, though primarily with words, to entice Mao from Stalin by this and other strategies. Therefore he decided to go public in a big way so there would be no misunderstanding about American policy on Korea and Formosa – as if setting it in stone. Hence in a speech on January 12, 1950 to the National Press Club in Washington DC, he pretty much told the world that the US would maintain a hands-off approach to both Formosa and South Korea, no matter what happened in those localities.

Some historians theorize that Acheson was trying to separate Mao from Stalin, encouraging another Tito, by offering pieces of territory in Asia to China – the "wedge" theory. This theory was widely speculated on at the time, as for example, in articles by the New York Times foreign correspondent, C.L. Sulzberger (March 3, 1950).

Many also argued that the most rational approach to the China matter at that time would have been to do what other countries of the world were doing and advocating, even our close British allies, that is, to recognize the Communist regime as the legitimate government of China, give it the "China seat" in the UN and go about building normal trade relations with her. To my way of thinking, this would have been the right thing to do, but it was not done until two wars later, millions of dead and wasted decades. In January of 1950 Truman and Acheson felt it would be politically dangerous if they went much beyond publicly offering to stay out of China's backyard. For the purpose of conveying this message, Acheson was not embarrassed in his National Press Club speech to hijack temporarily the language of the Left:

> "Let's come now to the matters which Asia has in common. . . . One of these factors is a revulsion against the acceptance of misery and poverty as the normal condition of life. Throughout all of this vast area, you have that

fundamental revolutionary aspect in mind and belief.
*The other common aspect that they have is the **revulsion
against foreign domination**. Whether that foreign
domination takes the form of colonialism or whether it
takes the form of imperialism, they are through with it.
They have had enough of it, and they want no more. . . .*

     *"**The symbol of these concepts has become
nationalism**. National independence has become the
symbol both of **freedom from foreign domination** and
freedom from the tyranny of poverty and misery. . . .*

     *"Resignation is no longer the typical emotion of
Asia. It has given way to hope, to a sense of effort, and in
many cases, to a real sense of anger. . . . [M]uch of the
bewilderment which has seized the minds of many of us
about recent developments in China comes from a **failure
to understand this basic revolutionary force** which is loose
in Asia . . ."*

These words could have been written by the leading leftist
political leader at that time, Congressman Vito Marcantonio of
East Harlem. One could hear the Marcantonio tones in the speech
and could envision his giving it in the well of Congress or on the
stage at a mass anti-war rally in Madison Square Garden – which
as we will see, he subsequently did.

Much of Acheson's speech was in defense of the Truman
Administration policy on China against the China Lobby in
Congress. The Administration had been under constant attack from
right-wing Republicans, including periodic calls for Acheson's
removal, for the "loss" of China to Communism -- as if the utter
corruption (for example, a good portion of American aid wound up
invested in US real estate by Chiang and his cohorts), tyranny and
incompetence of Chiang Kai-shek had nothing to do with it and as if
the US had not already poured over $3,000,000,000 down the drain in
support of Chiang. But Acheson was also trying to reach

out to Mao and the language of the Left respecting the revolutionary fervor stirring in the Far East was useful.

In light of America's subsequent slaughter of millions in Korea and its almost identical and incredible repetition in Vietnam just 10 or 15 years later to suppress indigenous national revolutions, some of Acheson's language is chilling in its intentional deceit.

> *"Our real interest is in those people as people. . . .It is important to take this attitude not as a mere negative reaction to communism but as the most positive affirmation of the most affirmative truth that we hold, which is the dignity and right of every nation, of every people, and of every individual to develop in their own way, making their own mistakes, reaching their own triumphs but acting under their own responsibility. . . ."*

The speech, as noted, has been interpreted as essentially a desperate attempt to keep Mao from joining up with Stalin – an abortive, short-lived and faint-hearted attempt to drive a wedge between China and Russia. He did not know it at the time, but it was much too late. The billions of dollars and years of military support we had given Chiang Kai-shek had long ago convinced Mao to "lean" toward Stalin as the more likely person who would help in gaining Formosa and reconstructing China. Russia also had troops in Manchuria and Mongolia and interests in railroads and ports in China that had been recently confirmed in treaties with Chiang Kai-shek when he had been in control. To expect China to turn its back on Russia at this point in time was foolhardy.

The Americans had just finished a messy military occupation in Korea where tens of thousands of people had been killed because they were suspected of being revolutionaries. Everyone seemed to acknowledge the Occupation as a failure. General Douglas MacArthur commented at the Wake Conference on October 15, 1950: "*All occupations are failures.*" The person making a transcript of the meeting noted: "*The President nodded in agreement.*" Then we turned the country over to a near-insane autocrat. One by one this dictator would kill off his opponents, old and young, Right and Left. The leftist leader, Lyuh, who had headed the short-lived People's Republic in 1945 after the surrender of Japan had already been assassinated in 1947, with Rhee being the prime suspect. Even Rhee's ancient right-wing comrade from decades of exile, Kim Koo, was assassinated in July, 1949. When Koo's assistant asked for an independent investigation of the killing, he was arrested by Rhee's military police that were now making mass summary arrests without warrants. When a major Korean newspaper also suggested that there be an investigation into Koo's assassination, it was closed down and its chief editor arrested. Without the slightest qualms Rhee would later order the execution of tens of thousands of political prisoners at the start of the Korean War.

The deceit at the top of the American Government was pervasive, even among the deceivers. Truman at this time was secretly giving his approval, without even Acheson knowing, to a CIA plan to destabilize the leftist government of Guatemala. This was being done for the benefit of the United Fruit Company which was having labor problems there – a course of action resulting in decades of violence in Guatemala and the deaths of hundreds of thousands (U.S. Department of State, Office of the Historian: "Foreign Relations, Guatemala, 1952-1954," July 7, 2003 <http://www.state.gov/r/pa/ho/frus/ike/guat/20195.htm>; Stephen Kinzer gave excepts of the recently declassified Guatemala papers in New York Times, July 6, 2003).

Also at the same time America was shipping arms and other support to the French to suppress the nationalists in Indo-China and keep what was left of the French colonial empire. Ho Chi Minh himself seems to have been taken in by the American hypocrisy as he would actually write letters directly to President Truman requesting help in his people's quest for liberty against the French, in the spirit of the American Revolution. But headlines in American newspapers were already categorizing the attempt to suppress Ho Chi Minh as hopeless: "VIET NAM FIGHTING IS ENDLESS, COSTLY," Tillman Durdin, New York Times, March 3, 1950 – though the editors of the Times were urging Truman at the same time to help the French against the "communists" in Vietnam as part of the overall policy of "containment." The Times was *with* the program and even cheering it on.

At Wake everyone expressed disappointment with the lack of fighting spirit being shown by France, evidencing little sympathy for a people who had suffered the devastation of a war on their land and four years of Nazi Occupation. Admiral Radford almost mocked the war-weary French as he explained to the Wake group how they had come by Hawaii, where he was in charge for the US, with ships on their way to the war in Indochina, and they were according to the Admiral obviously dragging their feet. He joked that if he had invited them he was sure they would have stayed in Hawaii for six months. The President noted that they had been **working on the French** *"for years without success"* and that *"[i]f the French Prime Minister comes to see me, he is going to hear some very plain talk. I am going to talk cold turkey to him. If you don't want him to hear that kind of talk, you had better keep him away from me."*

Just plain talk from a plain and simple man -- the exact opposite of what the world needed at that time. The pugilist we called our President at the time warned his aides that he would strike unless someone held him back. The President of the most powerful nation on earth was going to *"talk cold turkey"* to coerce the reluctant French to do battle with the communist revolutionaries in Vietnam. Later when the French finally withdrew notwithstanding our boundless financial and military support, we disdainfully took up the "burden" only to be completely defeated ourselves -- with 58,000 Americans killed and over 2 million Vietnam civilians dead as a result of our efforts to "liberate" yet another country in the Far East. Now Vietnam is a prosperous Communist country doing much business with the United States and the rest of the world. While in Korea where we

100

only "half-lost" or "half-won", the peninsular continues to be bitterly divided into pro and anti whomever.

The part of the National Press Club speech that day, however, which has received the most attention was where Acheson announced what areas of the Pacific America considered vital to its security. *"They are essential parts of the defensive perimeter of the Pacific, and they must and will be held."* Then he drew a line, something easy to comprehend and which would eliminate any tragic misunderstandings:

> *"This defensive perimeter runs along the Aleutians to Japan and then goes to the Ryukyus* [Okinawa]. . . . [and then] *to the Philippine Islands. . .*

> *"So far as the military security of other areas in the Pacific is concerned, it must be clear that no person can guarantee these areas against military attack. . . ."*

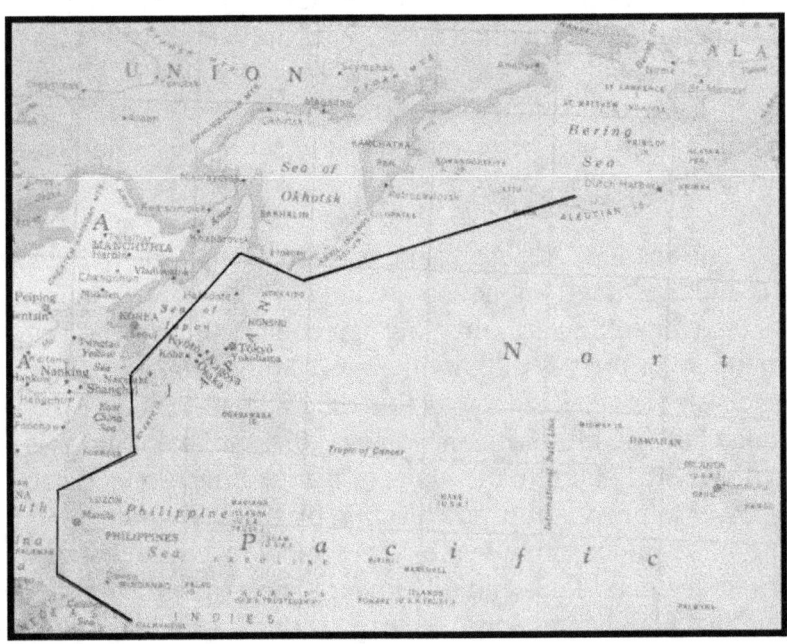

101

To anyone living in the Pacific area it certainly was vitally important what this Superpower considered to be its bailiwick. One would not want to cross that line intentionally, and one had to be grateful to this American who had made things simple and just drew a clear line on a map that even the blind, deaf and dumb could comprehend.

If you lived in Korea, the message was loud and clear, almost deafening, as Rhee's violent reaction the next day made clear -- the Americans had just said that Korea was not of vital concern to them, the Koreans were on their own militarily. That precisely reflected Acheson's testimony to Congress six months earlier – seeking to help Korea with economic aid but making clear that we had no intention of getting involved in a civil war *"with a lot of Koreans."*

The doctrine was further enshrined in a National Security Paper used by all senior officials for their guidance. Indeed the defensive perimeter that Acheson drew that day was the same as what General MacArthur had already publicly described. The Russian troops had been withdrawn from occupation of North Korea in 1948; the United States troops had followed in 1949; now the Koreans were on their own and had to settle their affairs among themselves. Likewise for Formosa.

Those areas, Acheson said, would have to look to their own efforts and the "international community" if they were attacked, not to the United States. Directing someone to the "international community" or the UN at that time was like sending a thirsty man to the desert for water. Since its founding just after WWII, the UN had done nothing militarily and was toothless in that regard, particularly since all five members of the Security Council had the veto power to prevent unwanted action by the UN – the compromise device employed by its creators to assure its birth. In reality the United States and the Soviet Union were the only powers that could "guaranty" security. If the US said it could not, then you were on your own.

Interestedly, when war broke out a few months later and Truman decided that the US would intervene, he was careful immediately to instruct Acheson to cloak the US action with a sham UN cover. Almost as if they had discussed this scenario beforehand.

Indeed Professor Thornton argues that Truman and Acheson had for some time been setting up South Korea as bait to instigate just enough of a confrontation with China to help him sell to Congress his enormously expensive worldwide military containment program as set forth in the still unsigned NSC 68 sitting in a draw in his office. This baiting included keeping the South Korean military just weak enough to invite an invasion from the North Koreans and then provoking China into the war by sending MacArthur up to China's Manchurian border at the Yalu River, but not beyond so as not to incite a general war with China and the Soviets.

I have much respect for Professor Thornton, a noted scholar and teacher of history and international affairs who has written widely on China and the international political scene, but I must disagree. Thornton's theory or speculation infuses President Truman with a subtle intellect and the patience of a long term strategic thinker. Unfortunately the US was not being led by such a person; but by a simple minded individual who prided himself on plain talk and his ability to cut through the maze of complicated facts by simply checking with his instincts and his guts.

Secretary of State Acheson had already put in place the mechanism for the US to stay out of the Korean conflict everyone expected without losing any "face." In December, 1949 he had instructed Ambassador John Muccio to have President Rhee, in the case of a major military attack across the 38th Parallel, to appeal to the *United Nations* -- not to the United States. The UN, Acheson instructed Muccio, had already "anticipated the possibility of a major military conflict in Korea" and had all the appropriate bodies

103

in place to deal with it. (See Confidential Memo No. 83, Acheson to Muccio, December 14, 1949; FRUS, 1949, Vol. VII, p. 1108).

This of course was just more "make believe" as Acheson well knew that no effective action from the UN could be expected because of the Soviet's veto power on the Security Council. But as it turned out when the war actually started in June of 1950, the Soviets did not appear at the Security Council's meetings on Korea as they had been boycotting the UN for its failure to recognize Mao's Government. Fortuitously, then, Truman thus was able to use the Security Council to cover the American Government's unilateral intervention. But even if the Soviets had not been boycotting the Security Council at the time, Truman and Acheson would still have been able to make use of the UN for cover by bypassing the Security Council and going to the General Assembly, thoroughly controlled by the US, as they in fact did later on when the Russians had returned to the Security Council.

Soviet and Chines documents disclose that it was soon after this speech that Stalin began to change his advice to Kim Il Sung. He no longer would veto Kim's passion to reunite Korea and he agreed to give him arms and military advisors. But Stalin remained cautious. He warned Kim that if his plans for a swift conquest of the South did not work out and he ran into trouble, that he could expect no help from Russian troops. Russia had no intention of risking war with the United States. If he needed help, he would have to turn to China. So Stalin based his tentative approval to Kim's plans upon Kim's getting Mao to agree to them as well.

Mao, for his part, had wanted Stalin's help in taking Formosa so he was inclined to support projects approved by Stalin. In addition, he felt indebted to the Koreans for the thousands of ethnic Korean soldiers who fought with the Communists in China's civil war and against Japan. For these reasons Mao could not very well say "no" to Kim. When Kim later visited Mao and described to him what he claimed, with some disingenuousness, was Stalin's "enthusiastic" approval for Kim's project, Mao could only nod a reluctant approval. Even then he told Kim that China was in no position to be of any material help. Kim assured Mao that he did not need any more help than what Stalin was providing. Contemporary participants have told us that Mao was never shown Kim's battle plans, which had been drawn up by the Russian military advisors, nor the date of the attack. Mao was still piling up men and equipment for an invasion of Formosa when Kim attacked South Korea and ultimately put a halt to Mao's own plans. (See Thornton, Odd Man Out.)

Congress, shortly after Acheson's January, 1950, National Press Club speech, got on board by at first rejecting and then grudgingly approving some economic aid to Korea. The Congressional debate which the Russians, Koreans and Chinese could have read in the US Press, confirmed that the Americans thought Korea was important symbolically, but certainly did not warrant any military action on our part.

As mentioned above, the Truman Administration had sent over to Congress in the Spring of 1949 an "urgent" request for $150,000,000 for Korean economic aid – much of which involved the purchase of American products like cotton, fertilizer and oil and then paying American shippers to transport them to Korea. It requested action as soon as possible as the Government of Korea would not last three more months without the economic assistance from the United States. The House Armed Services Committee held the June hearings quoted above and approved the request in a hotly divided vote in July, 1949. But the full House itself took no action on this "urgent" matter until the following January, almost a year after the Truman Administration had first sent the bill over. That in itself would tell any observer that Korea was not important to the United States.

When the 1949 Aid Bill was finally debated in Congress the week following Acheson's National Press Club speech, much of the testimony from the House Armed Services' "Executive" hearings the previous June was repeated or paraphrased by the debating Members of Congress. Then the House **defeated** the Bill, by one vote (192-191).

Congressman Christian A. Herter, R. Mass., summarized the testimony of the Generals, Admirals and State Department officials from that June hearing:

> *"Testimony will be given here . . . that **Korea is militarily untenable, that under none of our defense plans as such could we consider trying to hold Korea in** the event of aggressive action north of the thirty-eighth parallel by either Communist trained Korean troops* or by Russian troops."

Congressman Vorys:

> *"In this legislation there is no direct benefit to our military security; our troops are out; the Soviets can come into south Korea whenever they wish.. . . . Why, therefore, do we go forward with this program **which does not involve our military security**, which does not help solve our own economic problems and will not solve Korea's economic problems . . . ."*

Congressman Chiperfield (Robert B. Chiperfield, R. Ill):

> *"This proposed action would be **putting money down a rat hole**. If the island of Formosa, located over 100 miles from the mainland of China, cannot be defended against aggression as contended by Secretary of State Dean Acheson, how much less could South Korea be defended being the tail end of the peninsula, with guerrilla activities in North Korea and Communist control in Manchuria?*

> *As we pointed out in our minority report:*

106

'Korea is hopelessly outflanked by the adjacent land mass of China, and the peninsula has no connecting link with any friendly continental power. Every ton of supplies contemplated to be furnished under the terms of this legislation must be transported vast distances. . . .'

"The testimony before our committee disclosed that Korea was not considered as vital to our security program . . . ."

Congressman Lemke (William Lemke, R., N.D.):

"Are we going to withdraw? Are we going to throw another nation to communistic Russia? That is the whole question. Or are we going to call a halt and take a stand for the people who still believe in peace and not in aggression. . . ."

*"We were told by the highest officials in Korea that **if we would let them alone they could reunite their country** that we so cruelly divided and that belonged to them. **Of course there is civil war** between these two factions. The Communists go over in nightly raids of the South Koreans; but the South Koreans have 22,000,000 people and the North have only 9,000,000. The South Koreans can take care of themselves unless Russia steps in."*

Congressman Burnside (D., West Virginia):

*" **Korea is the only Christian country** in Asia.* [actually it was essentially a Confucian and Buddhist society, and had been that for at least a thousand years, only about 10% Christian; though Sigmund Rhee and many of the wealthy class were missionary-educated and were at least nominal

107

Christians]. *All the Christians here certainly should think about endeavoring to the best of their ability to maintain the only Christian country in Asia."*

Congressman Jackson (Donald L. Jackson, R. Calif):

> *"South Korea is hopelessly outflanked on the west by the adjacent land mass of China, and that the entire line along the thirty-eighth parallel is open to full-scale and unrestricted warfare at any time.*
>
> *"South Korea lies 7,000 miles west of San Francisco. . . . Vladivostok 500 miles to the north. It is quite obvious that in any economic or political challenge to supply contesting forces in the north and the south, that we would be at a decided disadvantage as represented by the difference between 500 and 7,000 miles.*

> *"The third of the arrows, and perhaps the one most important from the Soviet standpoint, is the one which indicates the direction of and the distance to the Russian industrial area east of the Urals. **It is inconceivable to many of us that the Communists would countenance the maintenance of such a threat to their productive capacity. . . . but if anything is likely or certain in this world today it would appear to be the eventual engulfment of South Korea by the rampant forces of communism. . . .***

> *"South Korea is no Japan, no Okinawa, no Philippines. Not one word of military testimony is on the record indicating the essential nature of the peninsula in the plans for the national defense. To the contrary, it has been state time and again that*

108

*from the military standpoint **South Korea is
indefensible and tactically isolated. . . .***"*

On this first go-around in the House the Bill was actually
defeated by the margin of one vote. It was the first time the
Truman Administration was defeated in a request for money which
it claimed was essential in the fight against Communist expansion.
Newsweek described Dr. John Myun Chang, South Korea's
ambassador to the US, as stumbling out of the House gallery after
the vote *"pale and shaken."* The same article also ridiculed Vito
Marcantonio for what it claimed was his celebrating the defeat of
the bill with Adam Clayton Powell. *"We did it,"* Newsweek quoted
what Marcantonio supposedly said to Powell in the Speaker's
lobby, *"our two votes killed the bill."*

The White House immediately got to work. With a promise
of about an additional $10,000,000 for Chiang Kai-shek added to
the Korean Bill, it got the one-issue China Lobby Members to vote
for the Bill on a second vote taken on February 9, 1950. It now
passed, 240 - 134.

During debate on this second go-around it was
Congressman Vito Marcantonio who best described the evolving
world of the Far East. This was not the first time he had to
admonish his colleagues that we should stay out of China and not
interfere in its internal battles. As far back as 1935 he had objected
to a budget proposal for the continued maintenance of six
American naval ships on the Yangtze River for the "protection of
Americans in the Yangtze Valley between Chungking and
Shanghai." He said that if missionaries and businessmen wanted to
go to China for their own reasons, spiritual or for financial profit,
then they should take their own risks and not depend on US
taxpayers to send our ships to protect them. An Admiral had
testified at a hearing on the funding that the area was infested with
"Communism and banditry." But Marcantonio contended that we
should not be in the business of keeping the people of China from
Communism or revolution (April 24, 1935).

Now 15 years later in this extemporaneous speech on the floor of the House he suggested what in the long run would have been the healthiest perspective if we could have adopted it as a national policy:

"We have spent more than $3,000,000,000 since VJ-day to save Chiang Kai-shek when Chiang Kai-shek was on the mainland of China. . . . Now it is proposed that, with $10,000,000 at most, we may save Chiang Kai-shek on the island of Formosa. **It**

seems to me that we fail to realize the real causes for our failure. *We failed to save Chiang Kai-shek because the people of China,* **people everywhere in Asia, are throwing off the shackles of foreign control, exploitation, and tyranny**, *and are establishing for themselves, through* **their own native revolutions**, *if you please, their own governments.* **I say that this Congress has failed to recognize fundamental principles; that the people of China are entitled to their revolution** *just as much as the people of the United States were entitled to their revolution back in 1776.*

110

"What has been the result? The people of China have established their revolution and are now consolidating it. We are not going to halt it. **We are not going to stop it either with hydrogen bombs** *or with the $10,000,000 to Chiang Kai-shek on the island of Formosa. The corrupt, tyrannical government of Chiang Kai-shek is something of the past. It is finished. It has been done in by the people of China. We in the United States must not forget what history has taught us, that* **never has the defense of tyranny and corruption anywhere in the world been in the interest of the people of the United States.** *We here are continuing the defense of tyranny and corruption by going to the aid of Chiang Kai-shek. In doing so we continue to ally ourselves with a crooked Fascist dictator against 400,000,000 Chinese people, their nation, and their friends all over Asia.*

"What I have said about China is equally applicable to [Korea]. *We have heard* **talk about the defense of democracy in Korea.** *We are told that this $60,000,000 must be used for the rulers of South Korea in the defense of democracy. First of all, what is the situation with respect to the people of Korea? I wish the Members of this House, before voting on this so called Korean aid bill, would read both volumes I and II of report of the United Nations Commission on Korea. . . .* **[Y]ou can well recognize that you cannot just go into a country, draw a line, and divide the country in two;** *the United Nations recognized it, and they recognized that what the people of North and South Korea wanted was independence and a unified nation."*

111

Marcantonio then recounted for his Congressional colleagues stories from the newspapers about Sigmund Rhee's authoritarian rule: the wholesale arrests of opponents, both right and left, wildly branding them all as Communists; the overflowing jails; the arrests of even right-wing opposition leaders in the Assembly; the assassination of political and social leaders; the constant social, political and economic turmoil in South Korea. Marcantonio continued:

> *"So that the story of South Korea is a repetition of Chiang Kai-shek's tyranny in China. It is the story of tyranny, it is the story of corruption, it is the story of suppressing the national aspirations of the people for a united and independent country.*
>
> *We tried to help this tyranny in China. We failed. We are now repeating the same interference in Korea. We are going to fail there too. . . ."*

State Department papers made public decades later show that what Congressman Vito Marcantonio was saying in Congress about the situation in Korea was exactly what the experts in the State Department were discussing among themselves in private. For example, the following comments are taken from a confidential policy discussion held at the State Department among the officials responsible for our political policy in Korea (Confidential Memorandum of Conversation by the Officer in Charge of Korean Affairs (Niles W. Bond), dated March 15, 1950, FRUS, 1950, Vol. VII, pp. 30 -33):

> *"Dr. Bunce . . . was most anxious to discuss . . . the difficulty which the American Mission in Korea was encountering in dealing effectively with President Rhee and his personal entourage. . . . The Mission was seriously concerned about the increasing tendency on the part of*

112

President Rhee toward a personal authoritarian type of government backed by police support."

The Memo recounts Bunce's description of Rhee's "somewhat equivocal" (diplomatic language for "corrupt") conduct in the sale of 100,000 tons of rice to Japan. Further, Bunce was concerned that Rhee *"had continued to by-pass the provisions of the Constitution . . . ."* He also thought that if things continued as they were *"that the coming elections in Korea would be dominated by the police and youth groups."* (That of course would be just the same as we have seen had happened two years earlier.)

Bond, the Officer in Charge of Korean Affairs, also noted that his superior, W. Walton Butterworth, the Officer in Charge of the Far East desk, commented that in Korea there was *"no such thing as 'normal democratic processes.' "*

Edward W. Doherty in the Office of Northeast Asian Affairs, was also quoted by Bond as saying in this meeting that

> *"if the present trend continued very long, the time might come when the lesser of two evils would be to cut loose* [from Korea] *and run the risk of incurring such* [loss of face] *consequences."*

So while all of Truman's experts on Korea and the Far East understood that there was *"no such thing as 'normal democratic processes' "* in Rhee's South Korea, the President was at the same time pushing Congress to authorize $150,000,000 to help save this *"test case of democracy."* Deception and lying to the American people indeed was Truman's deliberate policy on this matter.

Bond's Confidential Memo further carefully recorded the agreement among all the participants of the need for:

> *"relatively optimistic statements for Congressional consumption in connection with consideration of Korea aid*

113

bills, . . . the time had not yet come when all of the circumstances of the situation, as they were being discussed at this meeting, should be made available to Congress."

That time for full and honest disclosure did not come for decades.

The author of this Confidential Memo, Niles W. Bond, who was a long time State Department official and was at that time in charge of the Korean Desk, gave an oral history interview for the Truman Library on December 28, 1973. He recounted how the Pentagon had kept insisting that they get out of Korea because it was an untenable position, and that the US had no long term strategic interest in Korea. While the State Department, according to Bond, tacitly agreed with that assessment, it nevertheless kept delaying the departure for political and "face saving" reasons.

Events, however, moved faster than anybody and would not wait for the truth to be disclosed. Just a little over three months later, on June 25th, when the long anticipated civil war in Korea did indeed break out, President Truman, like some Martian having just landed on our planet, disregarding our Generals, our Admirals and our experts, and consulting only his own entrails decided to reverse course.

He now, on his own, would spend America's wealth and send Americans to die and to kill six million people for the supposed purpose of saving a country, which we would utterly

114

devastate in any event, where there was *"no such thing as normal democratic processers."* Indeed, the buck did stop there, though millions would soon wish that he had passed it on.

The issues confronting the President of the United States at that point in history were complicated and needed an intelligent, delicate and subtle leader. FDR had been carefully nurturing a post-war world order based on cooperation with the Soviet Union. But upon FDR's death Harry Truman from Missouri popped up in the Presidency with an atavistic anti-communism that would lead us into an unnecessary and wasteful decades - long "Cold War." Civilization was taking a step backward.

Years later, in a November 16, 1959 interview, a typically unrepentant Truman ruminated on his momentous decision on going to war in Korea:

> *"In the long run, the **jump** decision that I made in the beginning was usually the right one. . . . [You] **immediately** make a decision when things are put up to you, and **you don't want to tell anybody** that you've made the decision. . . . [I]n the long run, if **you're** heart's right and you know the history and the background of these things it'll be right. . . . You'll find nine times in ten the decision **off the cuff**, in the long run, is the correct one. . . . When Dean Acheson called me in Independence and told me that the North Koreans had invaded South Korea and asked me what to do, I said, **Get the United Nations agreement** that we're going to prevent that from happening."*

Under Secretary of State James Webb had met Truman the day of his return to Washington from Independence, Mo., on June 26, 1950:

> *"As soon as the doors of the car were closed . . . the President immediately stated that . . . this was a challenge that we must meet. I think his words were something like this: '**By God, I'm going to let them have it.**' . . . . I*

115

> *intervened and said "Mr. President we have done a great deal of work with all concerned . . . and **I think you should hear these carefully worked out recommendations before making up your mind** as to any action to be taken.' The President in effect said, 'Well O.K. of course but you know how I feel.'"*

Webb's words of caution, his advice to the President to listen first to the counsel of those who had "*done a great deal of work*", were lost on this "tough guy."

To today's ears Truman's immediate instructions to Acheson to "Get the **United Nations** agreement" sounds like a strange thing to have said. This is the President of the United States giving instructions to the Secretary of State regarding a matter of war and peace. Shouldn't he have been instructing Acheson to get in touch with the **US Congress** which of course had the only Constitutional authority to declare war? Or should Acheson at least have been instructed to call the Cabinet together for consultations? Or even the entire National Security Council? After all this was American blood he was about to spill and American wealth he was about to pillage. Shouldn't Americans other than Little Harry have something to say about this? No, it was "Get the United Nations."

If we look at the situation in June of 1950, however, we can readily see why Truman went to the UN for speedy approval of his actions instead of to his own country. At that moment he could not predict, as it happened, that the American people and, in particular, the US Congress, would wholeheartedly approve of our intervening in a civil war in the Far East. However he did know that he had the UN in his hip pocket. Most of the 60 members of the UN at that time were recipients of one kind or another of American assistance, military or financial. The nations of Europe were exhausted and bankrupt. America's massive post WWII foreign aid program had made sure that any vote in the UN would go Truman's way.

In 1949 foreign aid amounted to a staggering 2.9% of US Gross Domestic Product, without even counting military assistance. (In 2010 the percentage was 0.03%.) For a variety of national self-interest reasons -- to stimulate the world economy so as to sell more American goods; to buy friends to "contain" communism; to assure the vitality of the free market that benefited the American economy; etc., the American Government had launched the Truman Doctrine for Greece and Turkey; the Marshall Plan for Western Europe; the Point Four Program for selected other countries in Latin America and the Near and Far East; and a number of other bilateral programs that resulted in making most members of the UN beholden in some degree to the US. These nations therefore would be very reluctant to cross their benefactor. It was much easier for Truman to get France, Italy, Greece, Iran, Turkey, Israel, Pakistan, Great Britain, etc. to approve Truman's war plans than the Senators or Members of the House from Alabama, New York and California.

Even the President's unilateral "gut" decision to fight was covered over with sham consultations held in Blair House (then serving as the White House) during the first days of the crisis when the main decisions were made. He did not call the full Cabinet to Blair House for consultations; nor the full National Security Council. Even they would present obstacles with some of their more independent members. Instead Acheson and Truman selected fourteen men for the meetings at Blair House, confident that they could prod this group into covering Truman's instinctive decision with a patina of rational deliberation.

Photo credits:
General Douglas MacArthur, Hanada Air Base, Tokyo, Japan. US Army Signal Corps. Photographer Kay. 19 October 1948.

Vito Marcantonio. Photo appears in I Vote My Conscience, Ed. Annette T. Rubinstein and Associates, The Vito Marcantonio Memorial, 1956, reprinted by the Calandra Institute, 2002. The photo also appears in the book by Professor Gerald Meyer, Vito Marcantonio, State University of New York Press, 1989.

President Harry S. Truman. US Army Signal Corps, AFB in Hawaii, on his trip to see General Douglas MacArthur on Wake Island during the Korean War.   14 October 1950.

CHAPTER VI

THE AMERICANS ARE COMING!

From the diary entry of General Partridge, Tuesday, 27 June 1950:

> *"During the course of the evening, General Almond called to give me a very rough time indeed regarding the failure of the AF to drop a single bomb in Korea yesterday. During the course of the teleconference, I had been so incautious as to predict that we would have a B-26 [light bombers] mission operating against the North Korean forces before dark.*

"This mission did come off but smaller than had [been] anticipated because most of the B-26 aircraft were engaged in escort activities. The small force of five airplanes which finally took off were aborted due to bad weather; in addition to that, the strikes that were scheduled to continue through the night were scattered because of the bad weather.

*"General Almond took a dim view of the entire proceeding and said so in no uncertain terms, particularly when he discovered that the forecast for this morning's weather was bad. He repeated again and again that in order to save the South Korean forces and their government from collapse, it is mandatory that we take some visible action in support. He wanted bombs put on the ground in that narrow corridor between the 38th [parallel] and Seoul, employing any means and **without any accuracy. . . ."***

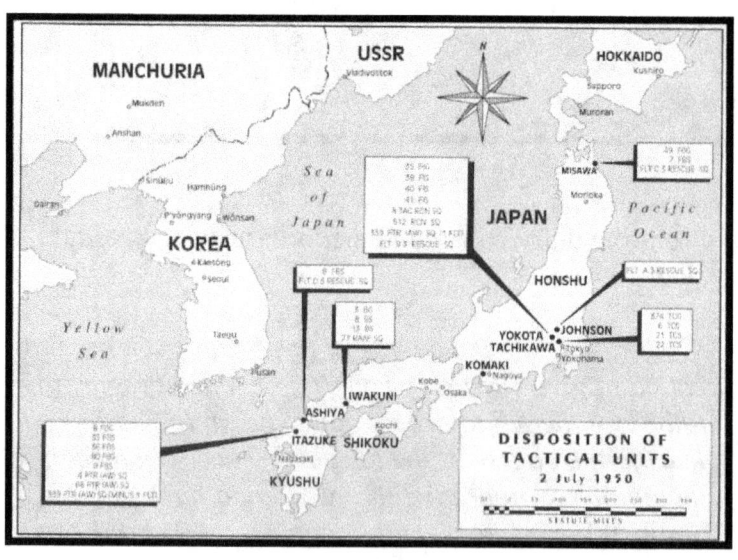

Location of the Fifth Air Force's bases (Map 3 from Y'Blood's <u>Stratemeyer</u>.)

Partridge did the best he could. On the morning of the 28th he sent out from airports in Japan two flights of 12 light bombers, B-26's, to sweep along the 38th parallel for the purpose of strafing and rocketing "targets of opportunity." In the afternoon four heavier bombers, B-29 "Superfortresses," the World War II workhorses which each carried a bomb load of 20,000 pounds, were launched in pairs of two. One pair roamed

> *"the road and rail lines between Seoul and Kapyong and the other* [pair] *covered similar arteries between Seoul and Uijongbu* [both towns in South Korea]. *Each bomber crew toggled out bombs **against anything that looked to be worth a bomb.** It was a strange employment for the strategic bombers* [which are designed to fly at high altitudes and drop bombs against large targets], *but General MacArthur had called for a maximum show of force"* (Robert Futrell, USAF Military Historian, The USAF In Korea).

According to another USAF publication, Steadfast and Courageous: FEAF Bomber Command and the Air War in Korea:

"Some thirty tons of bombs were dropped in this fashion."

From General Stratemeyer's diary, *25 June 1950*:

>*"Enroute back to Tokyo after two weeks' temporary duty to Washington, D.C. and landed at Hickam [AFB in Honolulu] when the news reached me that North Korea had declared war on South Korea . . . . to take not only South Korea but the rest of the world by surprise. Field intelligence had broken down somewhere and FEC had no forewarned knowledge of the massing of the estimated 200,000 troops nor their intent to cross the Parallel. Upon receipt of news of the **civil war**, I changed my plans to return direct to Tokyo via Wake instead of Okinawa."*

"Lt. General George Stratemeyer, r, being welcomed back to Haneda Air Base just south of Tokyo by Maj. General Earle Partridge, L, who had acted as Commander of the FEAF in the temporary absence of Stratemeyer.
"Also in attendance, center l to r, Maj. Gen. Victor Bertrandias and Brigadier Gen Edward White." June 27, 1950 OPI, DOD

More in accordance with their design and mission, though stretching their fuel capacity, several sorties of F-80 and F-82 fighter aircraft flew from Japan to the battlefront to strafe what they thought were the North Korean lines. Both the B-26 light bombers and the F-80 and F-82 jet fighters were to make an "extreme effort" to hit *"moving traffic"* among other targets of opportunity in the area between the 38th Parallel and the front lines, now well south of Seoul.

The next day, the 29th, Partridge was able to launch eight Superfortresses (B-29's) (sometime during 1950 the Superfortresse's "heavy" designation was changed to "medium" because of the introduction of the even heavier class of B-36 bombers). The eight B-29's now broke off into two sets of four, one set dropping bombs on Kimpo airfield outside Seoul which the South Koreans had so recently abandoned. The other four each dropped its 20,000 pounds of bombs on the main railroad station in Seoul, only a few days before, the Capital of South Korea.

The unlucky inhabitants of Seoul, as well as the city itself, suddenly had their status changed, by no act of their own, from *"friendly"* to *"enemy."* Not a good thing when the air was dominated by angry American planes. The Kimpo airport and Seoul were repeatedly bombed by the US almost every day for the next three months. General Stratemeyer's diary, Saturday, 15 July 1950: *"Directive issued and received from General MacArthur through General Almond to hit Kimpo airport and the marshaling yards at Seoul today, using B-29's. . . ."* Stratemeyer, Monday, 17 July 1950: *". . .* [sending General Mac Arthur] *a set of pictures showing the destructive effect of the FEAF Bomber Command strike yesterday on Seoul – 1,504 x five hundred pound bombs were dropped – or 376 tons."*

On the 30th of June nearly all the B-29's that were now ready for combat were loaded up with fragmentation bombs to attack the Air Force's first target actually in North Korea, the airfield at Wonsan. However, at the last minute the bombers were redirected to give emergency assistance to the battlefront in South Korea – they were ordered to give tactical support to the collapsing South Korean Army. The B-29's, designed to fly at altitudes of 15,000 to 20,000 feet flew from Kadena in Okinawa (a 10 hour round trip) and struck *"what appeared to be troop formations on the approaches to the bridges, with no real knowledge of the results"* (USAF, Steadfast).

Stratemeyer, Tuesday, 4 July 1950:

> *". . . received word that inadvertently, portion of the South Korean line was strafed by my planes inflicting some damage to that portion of the line."*

Unfortunately this urgency to hit something, just anything, and the fact that the Air Force's equipment makeup in the early days of the war was not ideal for close ground support, resulted in killing as many South Korean soldiers as North Korean ones. *"Friendly fire"* terrorized both friend and foe alike. Bombers were sent out with no more instructions than to hit whatever targets looked good from the air. Fighters strafed anything moving on the roads. Tons of bombs were dropped with no clue as to where they were going. A show had to be put on.

This indiscriminate bombing was made worse by the simple fact that all the bombing was being done in South Korea, the area we were supposed to be saving. Truman's advisers were not unaware of the political risks. Clark Clifford, a close adviser who had earlier left the Administration to return to private law practice, wrote a short note on June 29, 1950, to Truman in which he said:

> *"I am concerned about the present order which limits our aid to that area south of the 38ᵗʰ parallel. I understand the reason for such order but I am distressed that, in bombing towns and cities in South Korea, **we are bombing friendly people and friendly areas.**"*

Here we have a civilian observer, a close friend and advisor to Truman, who in the very first days of the war understood immediately what was all wrong about this: **"we are bombing friendly people and friendly areas."** Why were we killing our own friends? – so that we could **"draw the line"** against Communism? This refrain sounded quite heroic in the halls of Congress. But what were the Koreans in Seoul thinking about that heroic line just before being exterminated by US bombs.

Everything was being done by the seat of the pants. The wheel was being reinvented as there had been no plans for American involvement in a Korean civil war. MacArthur and the Generals at the teleconferences with Washington during the first few days of the invasion were not the only ones surprised by Truman's decision to go to war. The notion of Americans fighting in Korea had been so completely rejected as unsound by US military planners that the only plans ever made for Korea were for evacuation of American nationals in case of a conflict. So everything else after Truman's orders to go to war had to be created from scratch.

It wasn't just that the South Koreans had not been equipped with modern weapons nor properly trained, but the American soldiers themselves were unprepared, physically and mentally, for conflict. The first American ground troops suddenly thrown into battle to stop the advancing North Koreans had been on easy occupation duty in Japan. In addition, they were not properly equipped. For example, their 2.36 inch rocket launchers, the old World War II bazookas, could not penetrate the new heavy T34 Russian tanks being used by the North Koreans. Heavy artillery and tanks up to the task were not in Japan. On the other hand, the North Korean soldiers spearheading the drive were mostly hardened veterans from the wars in China – many thousands of exiled Korean guerillas had fought with the Chinese almost simultaneously against the occupying Japanese and against the Nationalists of Chiang Kai-shek.

So when the unprepared and ill-equipped Americans were fed piecemeal into the battle, it only resulted in a slaughter and a rout -- and the ones being slaughtered were the Americans because the South Korean Army and the South Korean police were busy fleeing south or killing political prisoners on the orders of the faster fleeing Sigmund Rhee. While the police would not stand and fight the northerners, they had enough time and ammunition to open the jails and execute the men and women who were about to be freed by the northerners – executions that they would later blame on the Communists.

After his turn as Military Governor in Korea General William Dean had been reassigned to Japan as commanding general of the 24th Infantry Division, part of the 8th Army stationed as occupation troops in Japan. Presumably because of his recent familiarity with Korea he had been picked by MacArthur in early July, 1950, to head the American forces being rushed in from Japan piecemeal to stop the North Korean advance, or at least to stop the South Korean retreat.

About 400 riflemen from the 24th Infantry Division were the first Americans sent in on July 1st under Lieutenant Colonel Charles B. Smith, forming the "Smith Task Force." Dean, the 24th Commanding Officer, followed the next day and was to make contact with Brigadier General John H. Church at Taejon after joining up with his men. Church himself had gone to Korea a couple days earlier on a fact finding mission that was changed mid-stream to a military mission when Truman ordered the troops in.

Taejon was familiar territory to Dean. Describing his attempt to identify Taejon from the air as he attempted to land, he noted that *"I had been over this area several times in 1948 and 1949"* during his tour as Military Governor. The first thing he noticed on landing was that South Korean civilians were thronging the roads heading south, and "unfortunately thousands and thousands of national police officers and some military also were marching south, apparently making no effort to stand and fight." The police force that had been under Dean's command and had so brutally suppressed all opposition to the Military Government and then to the succeeding right wing Rhee regime, now was running away from any real fight by the "thousands and thousands." The Dean who wrote this in his 1954 book wanted us to know that.

Dean found the South Korean headquarters already operating under its third chief of staff since June 25th, Lee Bum Suk, and was *"torn by internal strife, with everyone shouting 'Communist' at one another. . . ."* The first Chief of Staff while retreating south had blown up a bridge over the Han River just south of Seoul as soon as he got over it, even though the bridge was packed with other retreating South Korean soldiers and evacuating civilians. The second Chief of Staff had gone over to the other side.

The first battles engaged in by the Americans were in the Osan, Chonan and Taejon area. With scorn Dean explains how his whole left flank, after he had retreated from P'yongta'ek, was

> *"defended only by some dubious forces known as the **Northwest Youth Group** – five hundred or a thousand dissident, non-Communist North Koreans who had been armed by the South Korean government but were not part of the regular Army. Other people had considerable confidence in them, but I did not share it – and the fact is, North Koreans harried our flank on that side from then on. There is no doubt that those Northwest Youths were blood-thirsty people who hated the Communists, but they did us very little good."*

Dean certainly knew about how "blood-thirsty" these goons were. He had made his own use of them while he was Military Governor – for various tasks, including as deputized "police" to help supervise the 1948 elections. Recall also that General Orlando Ward thought it was a mistake for the Military Government, then

127

under the Commanding General John Hodge and his the Military Governor, General Dean, to deputize the Northwest Youths to help put down the uprisings on Cheju-do. But Dean and the authoritarian Rhee government that followed wanted the services of Northwest Youths precisely because they were so "blood-thirsty" and cruel. They rampaged through Cheju-do for almost a year until they had killed anyone opposing the Rhee government and then took their land, settled down and today their descendants own and run the prosperous resorts on Cheju-do.

But now, on the ground in 1950 and facing an armed opponent, Dean had no use for these "blood-thirsty" toughs who had helped him out on Cheju-do and during the 1948 elections of which he was so proud. As regular soldiers he was let down by them.

It was outside of Taejon that Dean got separated from his men while fighting and began a month-long odyssey in trying to reach his lines again. The hills and villages he traveled through were all of course in South Korea and he had only recently been the Military Governor of this country. The people here were part of the South Korea which we had come to defend. They should certainly have been friendly to their benefactors. Yet Dean found barely two people who would help him with food during that month. Quite the opposite, everyone seemed to behave as an enemy.

He soon was avoiding all the villages because groups of people, armed mostly with bamboo spears, from almost every village he came across began to chase him. Entire villages were organizing themselves to capture him. "*I was afraid to go down to the villages.*" He became particularly angry at the little boys who seemed to be making a party of trying to capture him. He had to run from a number of these groups.

Aside from the risk of being captured, his biggest concern was getting food. Since he had to avoid the villages, he travelled

128

through the mountains, where he seemed to have relearned what he must have know before:

> "*Up here in the mountain area I seldom found a house standing – the result of the South Korean government's prewar* [Rhee's pre-1950 handiwork] *campaign against the guerrillas, which had consisted largely of burning the house of anyone the constabulary or police even suspected of harboring or cooperating with guerrillas.*"

What Dean does not mention is that the police and constabulary had used the same methods for him while he was Military Governor.

He also had to avoid the South Korean men and women who were working on repairing roads and railroads that had been bombed by the Americans.

> "*During the day I could see that the Communists already had organized the whole area. Labor had been impressed all over the place. Men worked in big gangs, mostly on the roads; and old Japanese or Russian rifles and burp guns had been given to a few youths in each town. These kids were swelled up with the importance of their jobs as home guards and just itching for a chance to fire those weapons. I couldn't take any more risks.*"

He therefore early on learned to travel only at night through the countryside to avoid the people Truman had decided needed our help to avoid slavery. He was finally captured somewhere near Yongdam after hours of hiding in bushes while the local women did their washing in the river. He had been spotted by a woman whom he thought had paid no attention to him. The locals, the people he had just recently governed and whom he was sent in to save, then turned him over to the North Korean Army, the "Inmun

129

Gun." He remained a captive until the Armistice in 1953. We will see more of him later as he had much to say about his captivity.

As quoted above Lt. General Stratemeyer as soon as he learned of the fighting had no hesitancy in calling it a **civil war** among the Koreans. By its very terms it suggests a fight between brothers -- and something everybody else ought to stay out of. During the testimony before the House Committee on Foreign Affairs in 1949, parts of which I quoted above, a number of witnesses confidently predicted not only a civil war within one to three years of the US Occupation troop withdrawal in 1949, but also that the Communists in North Korea would sweep through South Korea. That was exactly what happened. Why anyone was surprised is a mystery to this day. At any rate, I must note Stratemeyer's immediate description of the event as a "civil war." This is the type of war and in Korea that the military had repeatedly stated was likely to occur and which the US must stay out of at all costs. It would be unsound and hopeless to fight in Korea, 7,000 miles from the American West Coast, on the borders of China and Russia and in a confusing fight among a "*whole lot of Koreans.*"

Yet here we were, sending ultimately 35,000 young American men to their deaths because Truman wanted to prove that he could be as tough against the Communists as his Republican hecklers. The <u>Washington Post</u> the day before the outbreak of hostilities carried a U.P. story reporting that the

> "*Eastern States Republicans today . . . cheered Senator Joseph R. McCarthy (R. Wis.) for his free-swinging campaign against the State Department. . . . Republicans from 17 states and the District of Columbia . . . apparently gave McCarthy a green light for his campaign to prove the State Department is infested with Communists. Representative Leonard Hall (N.Y.) had a good word for McCarthy. Hall is chairman of the Republican Congressional Campaign Committee. 'McCarthy hit the*

*Administration where it hurts,' he told the Republicans,
'and the brickbats and headlines have been flying ever
since.' "*

In any event, Truman's decision to go to war received almost universal acclaim in the United States. For years Truman had been bashing Communism and the imagined threat of Russian imperialism. He had generated a few false war scares at the most effective times for either passage of some legislation or to improve his Party's election chances. He had given official approval to the Red witch-hunt when he unleashed the specter of disloyalty in high places with his Loyalty Review Board. He, with the help of J. Edgar Hoover, had out right- winged the right-wing in the quest for communists, traitors, and homosexuals in the State Department and everywhere else in America. Even Congressmen were not immune to the witch-hunt, judging by the secret and extensive surveillance by the FBI of dissenting political figures, including Congressman Vito Marcantonio.

But by 1950 the train was getting away from Truman and he needed to get back into the conductor's seat. Instead of being viewed as the tough boss man fighting the cancerous spread of Communism in America and the world, as he was hoping to be because of his "loyalty" programs, his enemies were making him a target for being "soft" on Communists. The Korean War was the ideal vehicle for Truman and his allies to get back up to the head of the line. It hit the right chord, at the right time. Finally, that demon Stalin was going to get his due.

Truman's gambit seemed at first to work. When his aggressive message announcing that he had authorized MacArthur to use the Air Force and the Navy against the North Koreans was read to Congress, many of his erstwhile most bitter critics rose to their feet to join in the cheering. "ALMOST UNANIMOUS APPROVAL IS VOICED IN CONGRESS BY BOTH SIDES – HOUSE CHEERS," (New York Times, June 28, 1950). "A BLOW FOR PEACE," (New York

131

Herald Tribune, June 28, 1950). "SAVING KOREA," (Washington Post, June 27, 1950).

In Congress the leaders of each House read aloud the President's statement that he had ordered MacArthur in Tokyo to use the navy and the air force at his disposal to halt the invasion. It was greeted with enthusiasm and relief – and war cries. *"I rise to congratulate the administration upon the entry of abdominal fortitude in the far-eastern policy,"* declared Representative Hugh D. Scott, Jr., Republican of Pennsylvania. *"I am glad to see that guts have finally received their proper recognition . . ."*

The New York Times reported in its June 28, 1950 edition:

> *"Senator William F. Knowland, Republican of California, who has been a frequent critic of Administration Far Eastern policy, was the first to take the floor in support of the President's announcement. . . . He was followed by Senator Leverett Saltonstall, Republican of Massachusetts. . . . . Senator H. Alexander Smith, Republican of New Jersey, said the action was in line with the responsibilities of the United States to carry out our obligation. . . . Senator Henry Cabot Lodge Jr., Republican of Massachusetts, expressed the hope that President Truman 'will not shrink from using the Army if the best military judgment indicates that that is the effective course to take'. . . . "*

The policy reversal did lead to some chortling by Republicans: "U/S/ FAR EAST POLICY REVERSED BY TRUMAN'S ORDER FOR ACTION: STAND OF HERBERT HOOVER, MACARTHUR, TAFT AND OTHER REPUBLICAN SENATORS SEEN AS UPHELD (New York Herald Tribune, June 28, 1950). But Truman's "bold" move for a short time did succeed in "sterilizing" his Republican hecklers.

The newspapers, however, did point out that not everybody got up and cheered.

> *"The most outspoken objection to the Chief Executive's course was expressed by Representative Vito Marcantonio, American Labor Party of New York, who charged that Mr. Truman had usurped the powers of Congress by declaring war against North Korea. . . ."*
> (Harold B. Hinton, <u>New York Times</u>, June 28, 1950)

From the Congressional Record of June 27, 1950 we read that after the President's message was read and House Members began, one after another, to almost shout approval for the President's aggressiveness, Vito Marcantonio spoiled the party when he quietly gave his own opinion on the President's communication. His speech, delivered to a hostile and belligerent House, is perhaps the finest words that an American representative could have used at that time both in its dignified sadness and brilliant foresight.

> *"The words I am using do not adequately describe* **the disastrous consequences this course will have** *on the people of the United States unless checked by the people themselves.*
>
> *"I refer specifically to these words the majority leader read from the President's statement: 'In these circumstances I have ordered United States air and sea forces to give the Korean Government troops cover and support.'*
>
> *"Then again the President is quoted: 'Accordingly I have ordered the Seventh Fleet to prevent any attack on Formosa.'*
>
> *"This means the utilization of Americans in our Armed Forces in* **two civil wars**, *one that is taking place in Korea and one that is well nigh completed*

133

in China. **For all purposes, we were at war with the government and people of Korea,** and we might as well face it, the moment these words were enunciated.

"I would be remiss to the things in which I believe if I did not stand up here and state my  *opinion on this matter. After all, Mr. Chairman, you live only once, and it is best to live one's life with one's conscience than to temporize or accept with silence those things which one believes to be against the interests of one's people and one's nation.*

. . . .

"I know we are going to have and we have been having a lot of war drum beating. The beating of the war drums has been such that they may drown out reason. But I think it is time, before it is too late, that we pause and take inventory of what has happened in Asia.

"We have been warned time and time again and all signs in Asia have been pointed to what? That the people of Asia, the people of China, have been seeking national liberation. . . .

"I remember the words I said here on February 7 about Korea. I stated in the well of this House that the defense of tyranny was never in the best interests of the people of the United States. I pointed out the similarity between the rottenness that existed in the Chiang Kai-shek government and

134

that existing in the South Korean Government – the imprisonment of 40,000 people; the harsh exploitation of the people, the feeling of unrest, and the contempt for the rulers of South Korea on the part of the general masses of the people. **It was a government imposed on the people of Korea by force of arms, a police state***; and I stated at that time that that Government could not long endure, that it would be wiped out by the will of the people of Korea.*

"I also said at that time that **you cannot take a nation and draw a line through it and divide it and split into two countries a nation which is an ethnic unity, a people united culturally and racially over centuries.** *But we tried to do it. . . . The tyrannical rulers of South Korea continued to deny this legitimate aspiration of the people, ruthlessly suppressed every endeavor on the part of the people to achieve this objective and thus created an irrepressible conflict.*

135

*"Here now we are sending American aviators to lay down their lives, sending American sailors to lay down their lives, **and who knows how soon it will be before our infantry will be sent to lay down their lives to defend, aid and abet tyranny** and perpetrate aggression against the Korean people who strive for a united and independent nation.*

"Now you may want this action. I do not. I know that the American people will not want this action when they think it over, and I know that they will thrust through this terrible dark cloud of war that has been descending on them. Oh, yes, you can indulge in

*attacks on communism. You can keep on making impassioned pleas for the destruction of communism, but I tell you that **the issue in China, in Asia, in Korea and in Viet Nam is the right of these peoples to self-determination**, to a government of their own, to independence and national unity.*

*"Remember one thing: A bomb was dropped on Hiroshima. It had terrible consequences, but it did not frighten the people of China and it did not frighten the people of Korea. For again, **these people despite the terror of the atom bomb have refused to abandon their efforts for national liberation. They will no more abandon this objective than the American people did during our Revolution**. . . .*

"War is not inevitable; there are alternatives, but this declaration on the part of President Truman is an acceptance of the doctrine of the inevitability of war. I stand here and challenge that doctrine. I say that the ingenuity of Americans and people all over the world challenge this doctrine.

These words of dissent pushed some parts of the House into an angry mood and Members began verbally attacking Marcantonio.

Congressman Abraham A. Ribicoff, D. Conn.:

"If we were to follow his [Marcantonio] *advice this Nation would gradually surrender nation after nation to Soviet imperialism. The Gentleman from New York says that the action of the President will lead to disaster. I contend that any other action by the President of the United*

137

*States would lead to disaster. . . . **[Marcantonio] talks as if this were an action by Korean patriots**; this is action by pawns of Soviet imperialism. . . . 'Peace through strength' should be the slogan of the United States. We should not continue to back away time and time again because Russia seeks to make a move. . . ."*

Congressman Hays of Ohio:

"The gentleman from New York [Marcantonio] either with deliberate intent or through ignorance, sees fit to defend upon this floor time and time again the naked acts of aggression against various free governments of this world which are directed and dictated from Moscow. . . .

*He talks today about the nations of Asia determining for themselves which sort of government they are going to have. I wonder who he thinks he is kidding? You know and I know that the march of Red communism across China was not dictated by the Chinese people, it was dictated by the Kremlin, it was financed by the Kremlin, and the armies which march across China were armed by the Kremlin. This invasion from North Korea against South Korea is not the will of the Korean people. It is directed by a bunch of gangsters who have been sent in from Russia or Manchuria . . . **If we sit idly by and allow them to do it, they will subject the free nations of the world one by one to a state of slavery**. . . ."*

But the next speaker, the conservative Republican from Pennsylvania, James G. Fulton, to his everlasting credit tried to call a halt to these attacks on Marcantonio:

"In the House today this is a time of high feeling and critical decision, and we people who want to see the right course taken by the United States must feel sure that those who disagree with us have the right to speak. Instead

138

of criticizing and instead of aiming bellicose words at one man in this House, we ought to be reassured that the advocates of a certain point of view have the right to stand up here and say it. . . . Each of us, if we are fair in this House, must restrain ourselves from name calling, must settle ourselves down and say to the gentleman from New York [Marcantonio] **'You keep on speaking because no matter whether we disagree with you, you certainly speak honestly' and I might even say this afternoon under the temper of certain portions of this House, 'and bravely.' . . . .''**

Fulton's admonition may have slowed down the name-calling in the House, but the Press picked it up with a vengeance. On June 30th the New York Times editors had this to say under the headline: "VITO PASSES THE TEST:"

> *"The Communist attack on Southern Korea has provided another one of those tests to which Moscow subjects it followers . . . the hard core of the faithful remains undisturbed, and prominent among them is the present Representative in Congress of the 18th District – Vito Marcantonio. He attacked President Truman from the floor of the House, then took his stand with convicted Communists in Madison Square Garden and denounced American aid to Korea as 'Operation Desperation by Wall Street and the imperialists.'*

> *"Marcantonio has passed Moscow's test. He has shown that he will defend Russia against the United States, against the interests of true peace and justice, against the facts and the dictates of common sense. He has earned the confidence of the Politburo and lost any last shred of respect which his fellow-countrymen might have felt for him. He has always been a nuisance; now he has passed beyond that stage. The sooner he is deprived of his Congressional soapbox, the better."*

The <u>Washington Post</u> on June 29th under the editorial headline: "COMPANY THEY KEEP" tried to ridicule Marcantonio by saying that he and the very conservative <u>Chicago Tribune</u> were now bedfellows with the Communists in their similar claim that the President had 'usurped the powers of Congress by declaring war without its consent.'

The following month when Marcantonio was the lone vote against a military assistance bill (361-1), the <u>Daily Mirror</u> (New York) under the editorial headline "STILL THE SAME STOOGE" stated: *"The best stooge Stalin ever had in the U.S. Congress has come through again in familiar fashion. . . ."*

Marcantonio did not just debate the issues on the floor of the House. He took to the radio, street corners and rallies with his ideas as well -- he would organize meetings and attempt to persuade in every way he could. Two days after the House debate he is one of the speakers at a Madison Square Garden rally, along with Paul Robeson, the opera singer and civil rights crusader who just had his passport lifted by the State Department, Gus Hall, the recently convicted leader of the US Communist Party and Ring Lardner, one of the "Hollywood Ten" convicted of contempt of Congress for refusal to "name names" at a hearing of the House Unamerican Activities Committee and soon to go to jail. Under the headline: "PROTEST RALLY AT GARDEN HITS U.S. KOREAN AID: 9,000 HEAR MARCANTONIO, ROBESON, CONVICTED RED TERM IT A WAR PLOT," the <u>New York Herald Tribune</u> quotes Paul Robeson as saying that the American intervention

> *"is the culmination of a wicked and shameful policy which our government has ruthless pursued with respect to Colonial peoples."*

These were formative times. Truman and other atavistic forces were setting the mold and running over the Marcantonio/Robeson voices. A back-page article in the

140

<u>Washington Post</u> of Wednesday, June 28, 1950, contained this seemingly ordinary story about a place most people never heard of : "INDO-CHINA LOOKS UPON U.S. ACTION IN KOREA AS PATTERN IN EVENT OF RED INVASION THERE."

> *"Hanoi, Indo-China. June 27 (AP).* **United States action in the Korean crisis is looked upon in Indo-China as a pattern of future American action in the event this country is invaded by Chinese Communist. . . ."**

Whoever this reporter was quoting certainly got that right. Though as it turned out, there was no Chinese Communist invasion of Vietnam, just an American one.

CHAPTER VII

SITTING STRAW DUCKS

A *wujingak* type of thatched-roof house.
Hanoak, Photo by Suh, Jai-Sik

    Korea in 1950 had several major cities, some large towns, but most people lived in villages that their families had lived in for many hundreds of years. The Koreans had accepted the concept of Buddha from China before the time of Christ and reshaped in as they made Buddhism the basis of their culture. During the Chosen Dynasty in the 14th Century they likewise accepted the teaching of Confucius from China and reshaped it as well as it became the official Korean way of life for the duration of the Chosen Dynasty into the 20th Century. Under the influence of Confucianism the family dominated life, and the patriarch led the family. Villages were composed of extended families related to each other and presided over by the patriarch of the head family.

The faculty members of several Korean universities who teach housing and interior design have written a very instructive book called <u>Hanoak: Traditional Korean Homes</u>. There are eight names listed as authors, the first two being Choi, Jae-Soon and Chun, Jin-Hee and was published in 1999 by the publishing house of Hollym International Corp. with locations in Elizabeth, NJ and Seoul, Korea. They have a web site that includes a listing of their books on Korea in English (http://www.hollym.com). <u>Hanoak</u> is easy to read and follow, partly due I am sure to the fine translations by Maija Rhee Devine. I have taken from this book much of the information I use here in this part of the Chapter on Korean culture and the structure of their homes, including some excellent photographs taken by Suh, Jai-Sik.

According to <u>Hanoak,</u> a census of 1933 listed about 7,800 tribal villages with 30 or more families; 3,000 with 50 or more, 1,200 with 70 or more and 400 with 100 or more families. The design of the villages was based on the Confucian concept of family and leadership by the head family. So the major house belonged to the patriarch of the head family, immediate relatives had choice sites nearby, and so on. As noted, villages expanded by the number of related families attached to them. This is an important fact to understand if we are to comprehend the depth of the damage caused by uprooting even one of these villages.

Nagganupsong, a traditional village.
"Typical layout of a cluster of thatched roof houses whose roof lines harmonize with the shapes of the surrounding hills." Hanoak, Photo by Suh, Jai-sik

As would be expected, the size and quality of homes depended on the class of the family, though the Government in the Chosen Dynasty had various regulations to guard against ostentatious and lavish structures in accordance with Confucian principles. For our purposes it is only necessary to note that the materials used were primarily wood, straw, mud and in the finer homes, tiles. The commoner lived in a home with wooden floors, mud walls and a thatch roof. The upper classes had walls of logs or carved wood and roofs of tile.

All the living accommodations reflected the philosophy of Confucius, with more space and prominence always given to the head family in a town or village, and to the patriarch of that leading family and to the eldest son. Among the commoners the same Confucian family principles were followed but of course with less material and space. But the authority and order was the same, with respect shown to elders and to ancestors.

"The exterior view . . . of a kiyok or bent or L-shaped house."
Photo by Suh, Jai-sik in <u>Hanoak</u>

"A beautifully constructed and decorated upper class house."

<u>Hanoak</u>. Photo by Suh, Jai-Sik.

According to Confucian principles, the men and the women kept separate quarters in those houses where people could afford to do so, usually only in upper class houses. In the women's quarters were the kitchens and gardens. In the men's quarters were the studies. The first son often had his study right next to the father's study.

"The courtyard of the women's quarters of the Chunghyo-dong. Landscaped in the middle with trees and flowers, the courtyard elicited a sense of comfort and security. The kitchen, where women folk spent most of their time." <u>Hanoak</u>   Photo by Suh, Jai-Sik.

Variations in temperature accounted for much of the differences in type of construction. In the farther north with the colder winters and heavier snow, much thought had to be given to study walls and roofs not only for insulation but also to withstand the weight of the snow. The roofs may have been thatched and the walls made of mud or logs, but they were layered and constructed

146

in one area to emphasize warmth and in the southern areas to take advantage of the breezes.

> *"The exterior view . . . of a tubangjip (log house) typical of Ullung island. The sturdy log walls withstood heavy snow falls. Secondary wudegi walls were constructed all around the house to prevent blockage of passageways between buildings by snow accumulation."* Hanoak. Photo by Suh, Jai-Sik.

In the towns and cities the homes were clustered close together as the towns and cities grew over hundreds of years. Straw, thatched roof and wood were the primary materials for residential buildings in villages, towns and cities.

To measure the devastation to Korea that the War brought, I have tried to obtain photographs of Korean society just before 1950. Of course the best photos would have been the reconnaissance photos taken by US planes. One reads the daily mission reports in the National Archives of the reconnaissance flights and realizes that we took the perfect before-and-after pictures, as the photographers had first to photograph the target for the pilots and then photograph after the bombing to let the pilots know what was the effect of their missions. For some reason I found a number of the "after" photographs among the Air Force photos given to the National Archives, but somewhere along the line the "before" photos lost their way or I just did not look in the right places.

The mission reports from the reconnaissance flights, incidentally, make interesting reading. The photo interpreters seemed satisfied when they did not see a soul on a city street, meaning that the citizens were fearful enough of the sound of even only one oncoming reconnaissance plane that they had run for cover. But from time to time you can hear their annoyance when they remark on people "nonchalantly" walking in the streets or riding a vehicle notwithstanding the threatening sound of their plane.

At any rate I did find some photographs from the 1920's and 1930's in Volume I and Volume II of an historical pictorial series generously lent to me by the librarian in the Korean Cultural Service located on the 6th floor at 460 Park Avenue, New York. The Cultural Service appears to be related to the South Korean Consulate located across the hall. The photographs in the rest of this Chapter come from those two volumes in the Korean Cultural Service library. The identification of the cities or buildings and any quotations I use as captions are taken from the English portion of the descriptions accompanying the photographs in these volumes.

CHINNAMPO, *city view.*

KUNSAN

City Views.

149

HAMHUNG
Association of Financial Unions building.

Association of Financial Unions bulding, Hamgyŏngnamdo province.

District Court

Hamhŭng district court.

Products Exposition Hall

150

PYONGYANG
*Public Citizens
Hall.*

PYONGYANG   *Railroad Hotel*

PYONGYANG   *District Court of Appeals*

WONSAN *Bank of Development branch* (top). *City view* (middle). *Train Station* (bottom).

"*Pongmyong Pavilion of Kaechon primary school . . . built three hundred years ago.*"

Students and teachers.

153

HOERYONG *"Walled border* [with China] *city. Far behind runs the Tuman River."*

CHONJU in the 1920's

South Gate, CHONJU

Mokp'o

木浦

시가지 남쪽에서 바라본 목포항 Mokp'o streets commanding a view of Mokp'o port.

목포 시가지의 한국인 거리(1920년대)

MOKPO scenes.

I show you these scenes of Korean towns and cities, because I want you to understand that this was what in 1950 we reduced to ashes. And for what?

156

CHAPTER VIII

COOKING KOREANS

"The strategy employed by bombardiers of the 452nd Light Bomb Wing when one of their B-26's placed a napalm bomb dead center in this enemy supply dump in Korea was based on getting an assist from 'mother nature'. Fierce winds sweeping over the flat terrain soon had the entire concentration blazing. Fighters and light bombers of the US Far East Air Forces have given the napalm treatment to thousands of tons of vital enemy supplies and equipment far to the rear area, in a program of interdiction to prevent their being put to use on the front lines."
January, 1951 Official USAF (caption to a photo).

Stratemeyer, Friday, 7 July 1950:

"*Complimented by General Almond, Chief of Staff, GHO, FEC, on our news release as of today which started out –* "Far East Air Forces has now completed 1,100 sorties. . . .

"*General Dean called from Korea and gave me four targets over which he wanted air support. Apparently as has been shown by tests, our bazookas can not penetrate the Soviet Tank. . . . General Dean's targets were all mostly on arteries – rail, ferry crossing and the road between P'yongta'ek and Osan. . . .*[Location of first contact between American troops and the North Korean forces, about 49 miles south of Seoul.]

157

*"Weather unfavorable; two F-80's lost; missions directed against factories in the North, bridges, convoys, and troop movements. F-82 on an 'intruder mission' **in the Inch'on area** [the South Korean port city near Seoul] **dropped one napalm bomb**; results believed by pilot to be good. . . ."*

An "intruder mission," as this F-82 was on, is usually a flight behind enemy lines at night intended to harass the enemy. Inchon at this point was already behind enemy lines. This is Stratemeyer's first mention of napalm in the war, but the next day he also refers to the "first use" of napalm, this time by 2 F-51's.

Stratemeyer, Saturday, 8 July 1950:

The first use of napalm brought about these results (I have been urging its use now for about a week): 2 F-51s on a bombing and strafing mission report using 1x 6 napalm and destroyed: 4 small tanks, 5 trucks with 35 ft. trailers. Four vehicles exploded – other equipment damaged by 50 cal. fire."

Stratemeyer, Wednesday, 19 July 1950:

Asked my Operations for a report on napalm usage.

According to the official USAF Historian Robert Futrell, General Stratemeyer from early in the Korean conflict insisted on the wide use of napalm. He had seen the effectiveness of napalm in World War II and wanted it used. In the beginning of the war the requirement that the pilots fly low to drop the tanks of napalm caused problems because of faulty fusing and mixtures. In addition, the preparation of the napalm mixture and its attachment to the planes added heavy burdens to the already overworked ground crews. Hence the crews and pilots initially resisted the frequent use of napalm.

However, after some experimentation the fighter-bombers became adept at utilizing napalm. The 8th Fighter-Bomber Group called napalm '*the most effective weapon yet introduced.*" A 110-gallon napalm bomb would spread over an area about 275 feet long and 80 feet wise, according to Futrell, and burning with a 1500 degree flash would normally devastate the area.

> "*Napalm was also considered as an effective weapon against dug-in troops, vehicles, **and village targets**"* (Futrell).

"Village targets," from what we have seen above, of course were ideal burning objects. A 110-gallon tank dropped in the middle of a village would instantly ignite a hellish fire, 275 feet by 80 feet, which would swiftly spread from one thatch and wood house to the next– quickly consuming the village before anyone could leave. Later in the conflict tanks four times as large and filled with napalm were being utilized by the Air Force.

A napalm bomb is one type of incendiary bomb. The idea is not just to cause a fire, but to have a sticky and burning substance spread around, attach to as much as possible and be nearly impossible to put out before the substance itself disintegrates. Gilbert Dreyfus explains that the napalm is a gel substance obtained from the salts of aluminum, palmitic or other fatty acids, and naphthenic acids. This jelly is added to tanks of gasoline. *"These acids give a viscous consistency to gasoline so that an incendiary jelly results."* (Dreyfus.)

The flaming blob splashes on people and objects and cannot be extinguished. The most frequently used container for napalm was one containing nearly 500 liters of gasoline, jellied by an addition of napalm varying from six to thirteen percent. *"Napalm acts not only by burning but has an equally devastating effect which consists of a complicated process whereby shock, absorption of oxygen from the air, smoke and noxious gases become lethal."* (Dreyfus.)

Many of those killed by a napalm bomb are killed by carbon monoxide poisoning. Taking shelter during a napalm attack is useless, as the shelters have their oxygen sucked out by the napalm and asphyxiation results. Indeed the Air Force soon perfected the technique of sending in a bomber first with general purpose bombs or explosives which was intended to get people to seek shelter. Then the napalm fires would asphyxiate them in their supposedly safe shelters. So the two main causes of death by napalm are by fire and by asphyxiation. The napalm burns on a human are distinguishable from ordinary burns "*by the fact that they are covered with viscous black magma resembling tar. The depth of the burn is always considerable*" (Dreyfus). Shock and infection are some of the other causes of death. And in napalm burns, Dreyfus continues,

> "*a final element is of great importance: this is the gravity of facial burning. Eye burns can lead to loss of one or both eyes. Nasal and ear passages involved develop extended suppuration and necrosis which abscess with unbearable pain to the patient. The face becomes hideous with psychological trauma of formidable proportions.*"

"LIQUID FIRE – This dramatic picture shows how enemy supply build-up area and warehouses look after a strike by Fifth Air Force B-26 "Invader" bombers of the 452nd Bomb Wing (Light). When aerial reconnaissance showed that a landing

160

*along the river near Hanchon in North Korea contained
stockpiles of supplies, B-26's laden with napalm, rockets and .50
caliber ammunition, were soon off to the attack. Brisk winds
fanned the flames into every nook of these thatch-topped
huts. . . ."* US FEAF May, 1951

When this raging fire finishes its work there will be nothing left of
this "built-up area," a euphemism used by military caption writers
for a residential and business complex of buildings.

The best chance for survival according to Dreyfus is
evacuation immediately and comprehensive treatment in a medical
facility at the level of a general hospital. Needless to say, the
victims of American napalm bombing in Korea for the most part
did not have access to any effective treatment.

These buildings are described in the Air Force caption as *"an enemy supply concentration."* Looks to me, an amateur of course, more like a residential neighborhood. Besides, would the enemy store military supplies in thatch roofed huts? That fire will now spread and turn to ashes everything in the neighborhood.

The Fifth Air Force, Partridge's group, naturally often expressed pride in its widespread use of napalm, as its boss Stratemeyer had been encouraging. On October 12, 1950 it issued a press release that included five pictures from a test demonstration of how destructive napalm was. The press release stated in part:

"The fighters and light bombers recently have doubled the use of napalm explosives in ground support. As much as 13,714 gallons have been dropped in a single day. Four types are used -- gas jell, incendiary powder, napalm tank and napalm-white phosphorous bombs.

"One 100-pound bomb covers a pear-shaped area about 275 feet long and 80 feet wide. Dropped at a minimum altitude, napalms are ignited by the sparking of the tank on hard surface, by fuse grenades or by fighter aircraft., Upon ignition, the bombs burn at 1500 degrees heat and usually devastate the area covered."

There are no reports that the North Koreans or the Chinese, who entered the war later, ever used incendiary or napalm bombs. This may be because they did not have any or that in any event they could not deliver them as the Americans controlled the air for the most part from day one. It could also mean, and most probably, that they were not interested in incinerating their own people.

Usually the American bombers could fly with no fear of encountering enemy planes, though this changed somewhat later in the war when Chinese and Russian pilots manning MIG-15's challenged the Americans in the area just south of the Yalu that became as known "MIG Alley." But for most of the war and over all of Korea, American bombers were free to roam and use the Most efficient methods of destruction.

"FIERY INFERNO"

"Thatch-topped huts harboring supplies of food, lubricants and ammunition aided the destructive power of napalm, as the entire enemy supply concentration is turned into a fiery mass. . . ."

April 12, 1951
Official USAF Photo

Another description of a napalm bomb, this one given by the Federation of American Scientists Military Analysis Network on its website, is that it is a mixture of **benzene** (21%), **gasoline**

(33%), and **polystyrene** (46%). Neither benzene nor gasoline can be extinguished with water, gasoline floats on water and is of course dangerous if inhaled or swallowed. Polystyrene *"is the white, tough plastic that is used to make cups, plates . . . It dissolves easily in acetone and benzene, but not in gasoline. . . . Heated polystyrene softens at about 185 F.. . . In air, polystyrene melts and burns with a yellow, sooty flame"* (FAS Military Analysis Network).

Stratemeyer's faith in the effectiveness of napalm to cause terror and destruction was borne out by interrogation of prisoners taken during the war. An Air force photo caption reads:

> *"Most Feared Weapon -- Prisoner interrogation has determined that napalm bombs are the most feared of all weapons used by the US Far East Air Forces in Korea. Shown is the blast from one of these fire bombs as it begins to envelop a building used as a military barracks by the Communists. The jellied gasoline covers the building and is forced through open windows and doors by the blast. In the upper left of the picture can be seen flames from the first of two napalm tanks dropped by B-26 light bombers on a village used by the enemy in Korea to shelter troops and store supplies."* USAF January 1951

CHAPTER IX

THE ROAD TO HELL . . .

The North Korean Army quickly rolled over the South Korean defenses at the 38th Parallel on June 25th. Kim Il Sung, the North Korean leader, had been a famous Korean nationalist who at first fought as a guerilla against the Japanese occupiers of his homeland. He had operated out of Manchuria until he had to flee because the Japanese Army was getting close to capturing him. He went to Siberia where he found Communist Russia ready to support him and the Korean cause of independence from Japan. He was trained by the Soviets and joined their Army.

When the Soviets declared war against Japan in compliance with their promises to the Americans and the British, and marched into Manchuria and Korea, they had wisely brought Kim Il Sung and other ethnic Koreans like him back to Korea. Soviet Russia's Siberia had served for 40 years as a safe haven for Korean nationalists escaping the Japanese colonialists. In addition, thousands of Koreans were in turn born in Siberia. These political exiles and their children therefore served as a natural connection between the Soviet Union and Korea. That is one of the reasons the Soviets had an easy time of it during their occupation of North Korea. The clueless Americans, on the other hand, had nothing like them among their entourage when they came to occupy Korea, and in fact eventually gathered together as their constituency elements from the opposite end of the spectrum, those wealthy landlords, merchants and bureaucrats who had collaborated with the Japanese occupiers.

The core of Kim's troops were Korean veterans like himself from the Soviet Army and, to a greater extent, ethnic Korean veterans of the Chinese Communist Armies who had

165

fought first the Japanese and then the Chinese Nationalists. According to the account in The U.S. Army Center of Military History (website: http://www.history.army.mil/html/about/overview.html) he had 135,000 men in 8 full divisions, each including a regiment of artillery; 2 divisions at half strength; 2 separate regiments; an armored brigade with 120 Soviet T34 medium tanks; and 5 border constabulary brigades (United States Military Institute, American Military History, The Korean War).

The South Korean Army (ROK), in opposition, had 95,000 men, no tanks and eighty nine 105-mm howitzers. More significantly, while some of its officers had experience with the Japanese Army, very few of its soldiers had seen combat. In addition they had been poorly trained by a lackadaisical 500 man American Advisory Group which in turn had a low priority in Washington.

The idea from the beginning had been to deny Korea to the Communists but with as little expense as possible. This peninsula, attached to the land mass of Asia, had little value or meaning to us in any way -- for military, industrial, natural resources or historic connections. The Americans had caused the division of Korea in 1945 not for any strategic reason but primarily to irritate the Russians who of course had an immense historical and physical interest in this bordering country.

Though the nascent "containment" hawks in Washington were delighted that Stalin, by agreeing to the proposed Order No. 1 issued by MacArthur and halting his troops at the 38th Parrallel, had allowed them to occupy part of Korea, they were nevertheless unwilling to invest much else in it. The bottom line was that Korea was of no military value to the US. This was an economic and strategic policy subsequently enshrined in a National Security Paper – documents used as guiding principles for all governmental agencies.

In addition, while the Americans wanted to aggravate the Russians and try to make fools of them on their own doorstep, they did not want anyone getting them into a war. This later led to a constant tussle with Sigmund Rhee who just would not behave as the compliant figurehead General Hodge had hoped he would. The missionary-educated Sigmund Rhee, who had been out of the country for decades and was already in his seventies, and his coalition of wealthy landlords, industrialists and other Japanese collaborators, frightened the Americans with his constant and almost irrational talk of *invading* North Korea and uniting the country by force. Consequently the weapons given to Rhee -- M-1's, vehicles, artillery, -- were purely of a defensive nature. No air force, no navy, no tanks. When John Muccio, the Ambassador to South Korea, tried to lobby inn Washington for some airplanes for Rhee's government, he was referred to the terms of the relevant National Security Paper strictly limiting weapons to defense. Get that changed, he was told, and you will get your planes.

The groups in the American Occupation Zone that had been armed with these limited weapons (the **constabulary** or army; the Japanese trained **police** force; and the anti-communist **youth groups** recruited from refugees from the north) had found them sufficient to set up what was essentially a police state for the benefit of Rhee and his allies. But in a real war, as this was going to be, they were no match for the northerners. So when the attack came, the veteran and well-armed northerners marched freely down the peninsula.

Aside from being better armed and trained, there was another important reason why the North Korean Army marched so freely down the country. As they moved into South Korea they were greeted by a **friendly** population, many of whom were even relatives. POW General Dean later gave witness to the fact that the northerners were being readily accepted by the populace in the South, even with enthusiasm.

167

In turn the northerners were not laying waste to the countryside as they moved down; they were not looting and raping or indiscriminately slaughtering their brothers; they were not burning down the towns and villages as they moved through them. It was not the practice of the North Korean Army, nor had it the ability, to open up its way by first laying down a path of devastation. No planes from the North firebombed the cities in the South. No armada of aircraft and warships from the North bombarded the cities into wildernesses. As the early battle between the northerners and the southerners ensued, it was clear that neither side had the plans nor the firepower nor the desire to burn down every one of their own cities, towns and villages when they confronted each other. That would be left to the American liberation.

At this point if they had been left alone, as most observers had thought they would be, as American policy in its own National Security papers had assume they would be, and as Congressman Marcantonio had pleaded, the country would have been unified in a few weeks with an infinitesimal amount of bloodshed and destruction compared to what was to happen. Instead, Truman's surprising intervention inevitably led to transforming the Korean into a wasteland as the Americans for the next three years unloaded onto the entire peninsula a massive tonnage of explosives, napalm, phosphorous and other incendiary bombs.

With the most powerful nation in the world now in the war, what would have been a neighborhood disturbance resulting in scratches to the brawlers, evolved into a nightmare of destruction and slaughter.

As I was revising and reviewing this section of my book today, November 19, 2012, I took some time out to read the news on the internet. I was staggered by an article in the Washington Post. The Americans are finally withdrawing from Afghanistan and taking their hellish firepower with them. In the article there are a series of photos showing how the Afghanistan Army has substituted **donkeys** to transport their supplies in place of the American helicopters they had just so recently relied on.

This newly reconfigured system of minimalist death and destruction now being delivered by donkey convoys must have been greeted by **both** sides of this internal conflict with much relief – as it was in lieu of the mighty destruction wrecked by the ferocious American helicopters with their deadly and sophisticated missiles. One is forced to wonder from this scene and its comparison to what happened when the US intervened in the civil war in Korea over 60 years earlier: Is it really impossible for humans to learn from their mistakes, over and over again?

In the beginning it was the retreat *south* by the Americans and the South Koreans to the defensive beachhead around the port of Pusan at the extreme end of Korea, that regrettably required the destruction of South Korean towns, villages and cities so as to deny them to the advancing enemy. Later it would be the American advance *north* that again regrettably required our firepower to blast away the enemy in front of us. Never mind that the blasting would not only kill enemy troops, but also many of the civilians caught in the middle and would destroy their homes, factories, hospitals, churches, stores, farms, animals, sewer systems, water systems, electrical systems and everything else it took to live.

The little difference that there was in our approach to our "allies" south of the latitudinal line of the 38th parallel and to our "enemies" just north of it is illustrated by a comment in one of General Stratemeyer's diary entries, Wednesday, 19 July 1950:

> "... Had a conference with General MacArthur at 1815 hours and talked from the following notes: ... Bombing will be **visual** if possible; by **radar** if not. The weather over the immediate battlefront [which at that time was still in South Korea] is predicted 'poor' for tomorrow (20 July); however, one bomb group medium will be given targets in the area between the 37th and 38th Parallels [that is, over South Korean cities and towns] and will attack if possible. I propose for air strikes tomorrow (20 July) to use one bomb group medium on the airfield and supply dump of bombs and fuel at (#1) P'yongang, (#3) Onjon-ni, (#5) Mirim-ni. **Visual** if possible; by **radar** if not, and one bomb group medium on the airfield and supply of bombs and fuel at -------- [in original]. Our reconnaissance pictures show that there are great supplies of fuel, bombs and other types of supplies just adjacent to these airdromes. Because of weather, we might have to do radar bombing; however, **these airdromes are in North Korea and if all bombs do not hit target area, it should be of no concern**"

Killing civilians in the **North** because of highly inaccurate bombing by **radar** in bad weather "*should be of no concern.*" While killing civilians in the **South**, on the other hand, was "*regrettable.*" The difference was semantic. The killing was the same.

Note how the General specifies whether the bombing was *visual* or by *radar*. His orders were to try visual if possible, which would mean less collateral damage, but if not, then do it by radar. Nearly all the bombs dropped on Korea in those days would be what we now call "dumb bombs" – bombs without any guidance, just aimed from the plane, taking wind and velocity and height and weather and visibility into consideration. There were experiments with guidance systems, such as the Razon and the Tarzon bombs, but these primitive versions of guided missiles were just as, if not more, inaccurate as radar bombing.

Even with the best of weather and in day time with visual bombing, dumb bombs would be anywhere from 10 to 800 feet off their mark – up to two and a half football fields away. So if you were bombing, let's say, the Verrazano Bridge between Brooklyn and Staten Island from 16,000 feet, a number of your bombs would have to hit and wipe out the residential neighborhoods of Bay Ridge and Bensonhurst in Brooklyn and a good deal of Staten Island near the Bridge. Or taking out the Brooklyn Bridge in the same manner would wipe out half of Manhattan. That was with *visual* bombing. With *radar* – the off-target rate would be even higher.

Nevertheless, there still was a significance difference between *visual* bombing and *radar* bombing. If the bombs are to hit the airfields and supply dumps only, and not the rest of the adjacent city or town, then it would be better to be able at least *to see* the airfield. So it would obviously be better to fly lower and actually see the targets. If you did not care whether the bombs hit only their target, then you could fly high over the clouds, using radar and only hope that most of your bombs hit the target. But if they did kill+ civilians, since, as Stratemeyer notes, it is in North Korea, "*it should be of no concern.*" The higher the bombers flew, and the B-29's usually flew at 15,000 to 20,000 feet, sometimes as high as 25,000 feet, the less accuracy there was. Likewise in poor weather or at night, accuracy suffered. The less accurate the bombing, the more destruction to the civilian population and their homes.

There is an Air Force picture of a bridge being bombed in Korea which I believe may prove my point.. In this picture there apparently are bombs exploding on their target, the bridge. But look to your left, way up the river, and it seems there is a dark cloud suggesting an explosion. Why would the pilots bomb way upstream in the river if they were targeting the bridge? So that must be an errant bomb. In this case it just went upstream into the river, but during what seems must have been numerous previous bombings it is not hard to imagine that a lot of bombs exploded on the land on either side of the bridge -- residential? commercial? industrial? I don't know, but I would wager they were not the targets.

The caption on the photo reads as follows:

"79636 A.C. Thousands of man hours were required to repair this bridge in Korea, knocked out by planes of the U.S. Far East Air Forces. As it nears a semblance of useful condition, more destruction is on the way in the form of para-demolition bombs dropped from B-26s of the Fifth Air Force's 452nd Light Bomb Wing. March 1951 PLEASE CREDIT: 'Official US Air Force Photo.' "

The bridge is under a lot of black smoke, but then there is also black smoke way to the left on what looks like a residential landscape. Also take a look on the land on either side of the bridge -- a desert of bombed out craters and impossible to recognize what was there before.

In any event, from the damage done ultimately to South Korea, it would seem that General Stratemeyer's attempt at making a distinction between North Korean civilians and South Korean civilians did not help the South Koreans very much.

By August 3rd of 1950, within weeks of the initial assault, the Americans were quickly building up their forces and ground

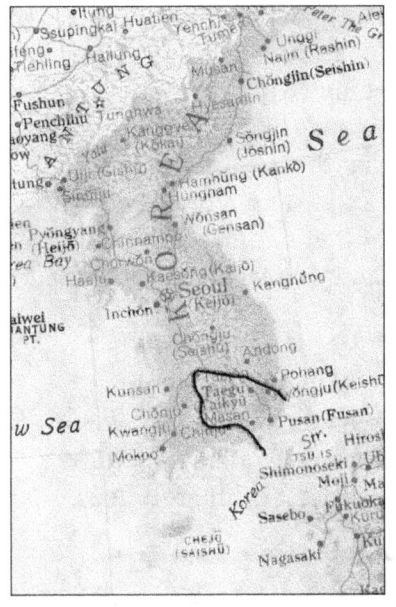

weapons – marines were pouring in; they now had 3.3-inch "super-bazookas" that could finally penetrate the Soviet T34 tanks; and had the equal or better Sherman and 45-ton Pershing tanks. But they and the South Koreans were still in retreat. They were leaving their positions on the banks of the narrow Kum River and consolidating to what they hoped would be a strong natural barrier on the south side of the broader Naktong River. The ultimate defense perimeter for the Americans and South Koreans had shrunken down to a 150 mile semi-circle around the port of Pusan on the southeast tip of Korea. As the Americans withdrew to that tiny perimeter they destroyed the towns and villages they were abandoning. These towns and its inhabitants, of course, were in South Korea.

8A/FEC-50-6239 12 Aug 50 "South Koreans evacuate their homes, as the 25th Inf Div takes over their town . . ."
12 August 1950
PFC Weidner US Army

The Army photographers and its photo caption writers did their best to soften the images of war. But in fact there was no disguising that we were the ones driving Koreans from the homes and villages that they had developed over a thousand years. Then we **burned them down** so that the advancing North Koreans could not make any use of them. The Russians would later charge in the UN, to the derision of the US Delegate, that those villagers who refused to evacuate during the American and South Korean retreat had been executed. We have no records of that in our National Archives. But what we do have tells, perhaps inadvertently, more than some of us may want to know.

For example, the photo above relates to a village being evacuated by the 25th Infantry Division. Was the evacuation voluntary? If we zoom in on that photo we see what appears to be an American soldier marching along in the midst of the refugees.

Was he there just to keep them company?

"A South Korean village burns as a result of an ammunition dump explosion in the Shinjumuk section, Korea, where US troops are supporting the 1st ROK Div in action against the North Korean invaders."

26 August 1950
Sgt. Stewart
US Army

Everybody walked, except the Generals.

"General J. Lawton Collins, Chief of Staff, US Army; Lt. Gen. Walton H. Walker, CG, Ground Forces in Korea; and Maj. Gen. William B. Kean, Jr. CG, 25th Inf. Div., L/R, leave the 25th Infantry Division Command Post at Masan in a jeep." 23 August 1950 Signal Corps Photo (Buckle)

"The defense perimeter . . . was marked by flaming towns and villages, from Chinju on the south to Yongdok on the east coast 80 miles north of Pusan . . . Latest to fall was flaming Kumchon, 35 miles northwest of Taegu, South Korean provisional capital [which is] *60 miles northwest of Pusan. . . ."* (Washington Post, August 3, 1950).

The same Washington Post article continued:

"Correspondent O.H.P. King, with ground forces in the area, said air strikes set Chinju ablaze and fired the neighboring village of Sachon in a five-hour raid. . . . The withdrawal was 'orderly and planned.' . . .Aircraft continued to give heavy, close support to the ground forces. They flew more than 500 tactical sorties Wednesday with their major effort thrown into the Chinju sector. The southern coastal towns of Mokpo and Yosu were hard hit with naval gunfire as well as aerial rockets and cannon fire. British and South Korean naval craft shelled Mokpo. American destroyers hit Yosu."

Before the American retreat, Yosu, Mokpo, Chinju, Sachon and Kumchon, with their neighboring towns and villages, were functioning South Korean communities. These were the "little brown people" that Truman had said he was liberating. Now they were "**military targets**" because the enemy might use them. Who was responsible for this carnage? The North Koreans who had been moving swiftly down the peninsula to the cheers of the populace, never burning down even one home? Or the Americans who were executing a "strategic retreat" to save themselves?

On August 1st MacArthur's Command issued Official Release 180 which read in part:

"Fifth Air Force and R.A.A.F. [Australian] *fighters, flying about 259 sorties close to the battle line, hit vehicles, buildings and railroad rolling stock at Namwon,*

181

Hwanggan, Yosu, Sunchon, Hadong, Yongdong, Kochang, Chirye, Chonju, Yechon and Andong [again, all friendly South Korean towns we had come to "liberate"]. . . ."

Official Release 176 from MacArthur's Headquarters issued the day before had announced:

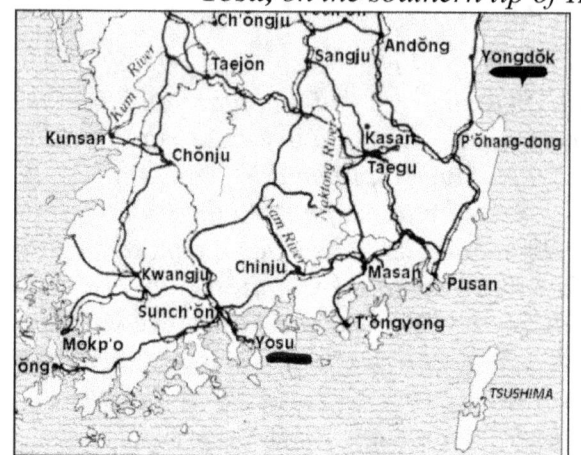

*"**Yosu,** on the southern tip of Korea, was attacked on Monday by F-82 twin Mustang fighter pilots, who strafed marshaling yards and set fire to warehouses and storage dumps with rocket and machine-gun fire. . . . The light B-26 Invaders used rockets to set fire to warehouses north of the Kum River and supply trucks moving on the road south of Seoul."*

The <u>Washington Post</u> reported on the 2nd of August:

*"**Naval Forces Pound Yongdok** -- An American observation pilot cruising over the Yongdok [South Korea] front Tuesday reported that North Koreans had fallen back to positions 1500 yards north of the ruined port. Troop concentrations within range of shore fire took a heavy toll of North Korean troops.*

"Yongdok has been pounded repeatedly by allied naval forces cruising close offshore for deadly, high velocity bombardment runs."

182

On the 4th the <u>Post</u> reported:

> "... *In the only other major ground action Thursday, South Korean troops of the Third Division re-occupied the battered east coast port of Yongdok, 80 miles north of Pusan, to reestablish it as the eastern anchor of the defenders.*
>
> *Yongdok has been heavily shelled by United States and British cruisers and destroyers. The warships sent six and eight-inch shells into the North Korean Fourth Division as it pulled back. ...*"

The most detailed public accounts available in English of the Americans destroying a city as they abandoned it in a retreat are two articles by reporters who flew over Kumchon while it was being destroyed, perhaps in the same observation plane. One reporter, W. H. Lawrence, wrote for the <u>New York Times</u>, while the other, Hal Boyle, writing for the Associated Press, had his article published in the <u>Washington Post,</u> both on August 3, 1950.

Lawrence's article is headlined: "KUMCHON ABLAZE, AIR VIEW REVEALS – WRITER FLYING ALONG THE FRONT SEES EARTH SCORCHED AS U.S. TROOPS NARROW PERIMETER." Lawrence reported:

> *"Kumchon is in flames below us, abandoned by United States forces withdrawing in the direction of the Naktong River line. The Eight Army pulled out of Kumchon and a number of Korean villages today, not as a result of enemy pressure but to take up new positions on a new defense line. . .* **The Americans are pursuing a scorched earth policy** *as they withdraw,* **leveling villages** *to the ground so that the enemy cannot take advantage of houses or other buildings to camouflage his tanks, supplies and*

183

*vehicles from the attacking United State Air Force in the
daylight hours. . .* [emphasis added] .

> *"When the First Cavalry Division quit Kumchon it
> did a thorough destruction job. As we flew over the city . . .
> we could see a score or more fires burning. . . . Dense
> clouds of smoke rolled up, blotting out for minutes at a time
> the bright blood-red sun, about to set behind the city."*

Lawrence explained that there was no contact between the
retreating G.I.'s and the advancing North Koreans. The Army was
pulling back its northern and western lines to behind the Naktong
River where they would dig in and wait for reinforcements from
the Marines then landing at Pusan. He relates how the plane he was
in then flew south and west of Taegu, still held by the Americans
and South Koreans, for a quick run behind the enemy lines.

> *"Below us, Hyopchon, which the Americans lost two days
> ago, was aflame and American fighters were active in the
> general area."*

The reporter further tells his readers that during this flight
over the destruction and devastation of this South Korean city he
was able to listen with earphones to some of the conversations
between American pilots and ground control officers. He *got a
momentary but impressive account of **the field day that the Air
Force was enjoying** against the enemy on a bright sunshiny day"*
[emphasis added].

From some of that conversation:

> *"Pilot to ground control: 'There's a town on that Y
> in the road which we'll have to hit again. . . .'*

> *"Pilot to ground control: 'We got those gooks (a
> G.I. nickname for North Koreans* [Lawrence's explanation])
> *crossing the river. I'd guess there were fifty to 100 of them
> crossing from north to south headed toward Chirye.' "*

184

Hal Boyle, writing for the Associated Press, took a somewhat different tone in describing the same scene of desolation. His headline in the <u>Washington Post</u> was: "KUMCHON IS A HADES AS YANKS WITHDRAW"

*"Leaping towers of orange flame are burning out the heart of ancient Kumchon tonight as . . . American troops pull out. . . . [I]t is like having a **bleacher seat in hell** to see it from a plane circling at 500 feet. The entire western waterfront is burning – about 500 yards or more of solid flame and billowing black smoke.*

"The red and orange tongues lick skyward at least 100 feet. In the northeast quarter of the city another area erupts like a vast furnace door suddenly opened. . . .

"There is dust, discomfort, danger and death below. But if an artist could paint the scene from this height he could make war look beautiful – if you thought only in terms of color and not of wasted effort and broken bodies. . . .

"The American withdrawal is a fighting one. They are mad because gook guerillas even dared to raid their command post before dawn.

"On the hillside, phosphorous artillery shells burst like gigantic powder puffs. Three nearby villages have joined in the concert of flame. Through the thickening smoke a blood-red sun shines a bloody farewell to a bloody day. . . . It shines like a beacon to Dante's Hades – a red sun lighting a red victory. . . ."

185

"Kumchon is only another of the many [South Korean] *cities that have fallen to the Communists in the last few days* [and therefore destroyed by the Americans]. . . . *From Kumchon in an 80-mile arc sweeping southward to Chinju on the south coast the battle line could be followed by a string of flaming villages.*" [Emphasis added].

Stratemeyer, 3 August 1950:

"One F-51 believed hit by small arms ground fire; crashed near Kumchon."

The American withdrawal to the east banks of the Naktong River was considered a success as it was done without the North Koreans realizing what was happening. There was little contact between the forces and so losses were light for the Americans and South Koreans. In addition, only burnt out rubble was left for the North Koreans.

"United States fighter planes strafed the west banks of the Naktong River today, scattering Communist soldiers who were moving toward that United States defense line with carts. . . . Eight Navy Corsairs bombed and rocketed villages west of the river. They left them in flames." [emphasis added] (Washington Post, August 5, 1950).

"Although the retreat has again shrunk the defense perimeter, . . . the invaders got [only] *further acres of scorched South Korean territory, and plans and intelligence officers regard the withdrawal as a successful and profitable maneuver* (New York Times, August 4, 1950). *"* [Emphasis added]

186

Stratemeyer, Friday, 4 August 1950:

> *"Headquarters' Advance* [the 5th Air Force
> headquarters in Korea with Generals Partridge and
> Timberlake] *evacuating Taegu for Pusan."*

But the retreat had already suddenly ended. Taegu, about
65 miles from Pusan, on the perimeter defense line around Pusan,
never fell to the enemy. Partridge decided to keep part of his staff
at Taegu and the 8th Army Headquarters under General Walker
also stayed at Taegu until September, as did Rhee, his government
and US Ambassador Muccio. The North Koreans by this time were
becoming exhausted and the pounding by the US Air Force on
their very long supply lines was having an effect. At the same time
the Americans were building up strength. While the American and
South Korean troops on the ground could not feel it yet, the turning
point had been reached.

But this was no comfort to the population of South Korea.
During the next month while the Americans built up their forces
within the Pusan perimeter, a defensive holding action resulted in
the destruction of even more friendly towns.

Official Release 358 issued September 1st:

> *"Fighters and light bombers flew all day, then
> others in their groups took over operations and flew all last
> night.*

> *"One flight of F-80's rocketed and strafed military
> installations in a town near Pohang* [South Korea] *last
> night, setting fire to warehouses and other building
> occupied by the Communists. The town was Yonggadong.
> Fourteen separate fires were counted by the pilots as they
> left. . . .*

"Light invader bombers late yesterday attacked North Korean headquarters in Kumchon, about twenty-seven miles northwest of Taegu.

"It was a high altitude mission [meaning, more likely to be inaccurate] *but the bombs made a good pattern on the target,' said First Lieut. . . ."*

On September the 1st the <u>New York Times</u> reported that *"the enemy had captured the town of Kigye -- now also a mass of ruins –and had been driving on Pohang. . . ."* On the 2nd one of its reporters recounted the fate of another **South Korean** town from which the Americans had retreated and that of its inhabitants, now suddenly morphed into the "enemy":

From a ridge to the east of Haman, air force and marine fighters could be seen swarming on Haman first with rockets, then with bombs and finally strafing the foe inside. At one period there were eleven Corsairs over Haman taking turns inflicting punishment on the enemy inside the town. Huge clouds of white and black smoke billowed up from the burning town. . . .

When there was any lull in the air cover United States artillery opened up with round after round into the town itself.

The <u>Washington Post</u> on September 6th reported:

*Sixteen miles to the northeast of Kyongju, fallen **Pohang** was reported afire from a American B-26 bomb raid. The Reds Tuesday night seized Pohang, second only to Pusan as a port of supply. . . . Pilots reported Pohang was in flames."*

188

(Scene from Pohang.) (August 23, 1950. US Army, Lt. Winslow)

On September 7th it told of the end of yet another South Korean town :

> *"Twenty-three miles southwest of Taegu, the town of Changnyong was described by Associated Press correspondent Don Huth as a fire-gutted battleground."*

And so it went during the long retreat, town after town – the Americans destroying the very same Korean towns *south* of the 38th Parallel that we had come to save from slavery.

CHAPTER X

CAUGHT

"BEHIND ENEMY LINES"

By the end of August, 1950, most of the country that we claimed to be rescuing from the menace of communism was now "behind enemy lines" or "behind the bomb line."

It was not healthy to be "behind enemy lines" or "behind the bomb line." ANYTHING beyond that line was considered to be of **military** value to the enemy and therefore was fair game for strafing with 50 mm machine guns and rockets or bombing with GP (general purpose explosives) or napalm – day or night.

The Bomb Line was the temporary line drawn by the military commanders between friendly and enemy forces for the purposes of bombing. Everything on the enemy side could be bombed, but only targets that had been identified and approved or under the direction of a controller could be bombed on the friendly side. Behind the Bomb Line the targets that might be of military use to the enemy, at first, included all roads and bridges, ports and airports, warehouses, factories of every sort, power plants, large stores of rice and other foods.

Then the definition of legitimate targets began to expand exponentially. Now anything that the enemy "could" use to hide troops, weapons, etc., was a proper target. So the list included schools, hospitals, churches. Eventually just any house or building behind enemy lines and anything just *moving* behind enemy lines was fair game.

Even ranks of refugees trudging along roads were included as legitimate military targets. Retired Air Force Major Alton A. Pendleton piloted an F-80 jet fighter with the 49th Fighter Wing stationed at Taegu during the Korean War. In his 1998 autobiography, <u>Three O'Clock High</u>, almost 50 years later, he reports that because *"enemy soldiers would get inside a refugee column and move down the road in broad daylight"* **the fighters had standing *"orders to strike the entire column.*** *The pilots did not like it, but most of us followed orders"* (Chapter I: "MIG ALLEY," 21 August 2003 http://www.onr.com/user/dtg/Chapter 1 htm)

The pilots carried rockets and 50 caliber "API" (armor piercing incendiary) bullets for strafing and they would dutifully mow down the refugees -- men, women and children -- though Major Pendleton noted that some of the pilots *"silently objected to this and put their ordnance to the side of the refugee column."* Since everyone knew that these protesting pilots, if they wanted to, could hit a single individual while flying at 500 mph, their fellow pilots would "tease" them on these occasions for being such bad shots (Pendleton, Chapter I).

191

Official Release 188 (August 2, 1950) from
MacArthur Headquarters in Tokyo:

*Fifth Air Force B-29's flew an increased
number of night intruder missions aimed at North
Korean troop and supply movements being carried
out under the cover of darkness. Night flying B-26's
bombed and* **strafed bridges and highways in the
Seoul area and south***. A marshaling yard at*
Ansong *was bombed and* **vehicular targets were hit
at Seoul, Yosu and Taejon***. Possible damage was
inflicted on a bridge in the Seoul area.*

Daylight B-26 missions were flown to
Mokpo *where the* **dock area** *was bombed and* **left
burning***, as well as to* **Seoul** *and* **Taejon***. The light*

bombers attacked four hangars at Taejon now believed to be serving as repair shops.

*Fifth Air Force F-80 jets and F-51's were joined by RoyalAustralian Air Force Mustangs in flying more than 400 armed reconnaissance and close support sorties **behind the North Korean lines.***

*The fighters kept up a **constant stream of attacks**, including some night operations aimed at troop concentrations, vehicles and other military objectives.*

*Assigned target areas ranged from **Yongdok and Yonghae** on the east coast to **Mokpo** in the southwest. At the latter city F-80's brought their rockets to bear on the marshalling yard, railroad station and **a factory** causing fires and extensive damage.*

*F-80's also claimed a **power plant** at **Kunsan**. . . . Fifth Air Force F-51's fired a **power station** and supply dump at **Chinju** and a **power plant** at **Yongdok**. Bridges were bombed or rocketed at **Yonghae, Kochang** and **Chinju**, and the marshalling yards at **Sunchon** were strafed and bombed. **Dock installation at Yosu were strafed and left burning**. . . .*

Each of these cities and towns were in an area we had forcibly carved out of the peninsula, called a "democracy" by the name of South Korea and declared worthy of shedding American blood to save them from communist "slavery." Now we were reducing them to dust.

193

The South Korean port city of Mokpo was now in enemy hands so it was being systematically destroyed. Here is a scenic view of Mokpo in the 1920's, which must have seemed like the "good old days" to the inhabitants of Mokpo, even though it had been under hash Japanese colonial rule:

시가지 남쪽에서 바라본 목포항 Mokp'o streets commanding a view of Mokp'o port.

목포 시가지의 한국인 거리(1920년대)

(The Korean Cultural Service Library.)

Suffering the same fate from the liberating Americans was Mokpo's sister port city Kunsan. Again, this city had been better off under the Japanese, at least it was allowed to exist. Again, from the Korean Cultural Service Library we can find scenic views of Kunsan in the 20's under Japanese rule:

194

195

The targets in these towns and cities of necessity were located next door to where people lived – people who had only days before had been living in freedom under the "democratic" government of our ally, South Korea. Now we were blowing up their factories and power plants, and collaterally, their homes.

Since daylight travel was especially hazardous to the North Koreans, most of their movement was at night. US aircraft, therefore, would strafe the roads during the night, in addition to the daylight flights. As the resourceful northerners were using foot power, carts and oxen to drive the Americans off the peninsula, "anything" that moved on the roads were legitimate "military" targets. Jets screaming down from the skis could not be expected to make any fine distinctions between a northern in uniform or a southern civilian. The figure in the field could be sowing seeds for wheat, or he could be a guerilla sowing the seeds of revolution. Since oxen could be used for pulling a cart full of troops, as well as a cart full of hay – they could be blasted.

196

With most of Korea behind enemy lines and the United States Air Force free to roam the entire peninsula without fear of the non-existent North Korean Air Force, every man, woman and child moving in Korea outside the 150 mile safety zone of the Pusan perimeter was now in jeopardy from the American planes. Not surprisingly, Pusan was inundated with refugees fleeing "communism" and seeking "democracy and freedom" – and incidentally safety from the endless and terrifying attacks of American planes.

From the diary entry of General Earle Partridge, 16 December 1950:

> *"During recent days we have been carrying out attacks beyond the bomb line on any activities which might have military significance. For example, **we have been attacking all males** who are carrying arms or **who are moving** about in a manner which indicates that they are potential enemy."*

One has to ask whether a pilot going 500 miles an hour could tell the difference between a male and a female, a boy or a man, a young male from an old male. Moreover, how could the pilot determine at that flashing speed that the individual is carrying something that might be a weapon – could it be a walking stick, could it be a rake? Or how does a streaming fighter determine in a second's time that the person is "moving in a manner" that indicates he is a "potential enemy?" This verbiage of course was absurd. The fact was that *anything* alive shot at. Beyond our "Bomb Line" anything that moved could be bombed or strafed -- and it was.

198

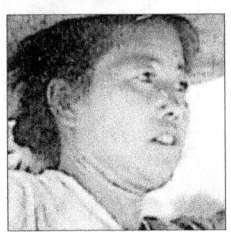

"Refugees fleeing from Combat area, near Taegu."
20 August 50   US Army   Capt. Scheiber

Partridge admits in his diary that he had learned through "friendly sources" that some of the bombing or strafing victims had been South Koreans or that they were *entirely innocent.* But he also noted that there was nothing he could do about that.

> *"This is a matter of extreme regret, but I do not know how to direct selective attacks without giving the enemy sanctuary over a wide area."*

What the honest General, I believe, was trying to tell posterity, without saying so, was that they were shooting at and trying to kill anything that moved on the other side of the bomb line:

"We are attacking any transportation and carts, animals capable of acting as beasts of burden. . . . ."

In this passage of his diary he describes another such ambiguous incident. It was an attack near Yonan in South Korean territory west of Kaesong.

It was reported by an ECA [Economic Cooperation Agency – an American government agency giving aid to the South Koreans] *official that several of our aircraft worked over some South Koreans who were collecting peat. Extensive damage was done, many people and animals killed, and 30,000 bags of peat destroyed.*

He told himself, however, that his conscience was clear because:

"*This Air Force was operating within its instructions. The . . . attack was made **outside of the bomb line**."*

ANYTHING beyond the bomb line was a legitimate target, absolving all blame or shame.

One of the cities mentioned frequently in the Official Releases as a target of our planes was on the western perimeter of the Pusan defensive line. The towns and cities on the perimeter were especially brutalized during the summer months of 1950.

"Fighter-bombers of the Fifth Air Force were busily plastering Chinju on 2 and 3 August and achieving excellent results as shown by this photograph." Department of Defense Photo

Bridges and roads were being constantly bombarded to make them unusable to the advancing northerners; but somehow the northerners kept coming. One of their key assets in furthering their swift advance was the local South Korean population. According to POW General William F. Dean, the local population in the south quite readily agreed to form endless work gangs to repair the roads and bridges for the northerners that were being destroyed by the Americans. General Dean, awarded the Congressional Medal of Honor and an impeccable source, made this important observation while an involuntary eyewitness "behind enemy lines" for three years as a North Korean captive (Dean, William F. General Dean's Story, London, England: Greenwood Press, 1973).

These thousands of workers, who happen to have lived south of the 38th parallel and therefore theoretically were the ones we had come to save from slavery, of necessity became primary targets for the American planes.

The planes, however, could not be everywhere all the time. In addition, at the distant sound of their jets or engines, the south Korean workers would drop their shovels and flee into the woods, leaving only the old and slow-footed of the workers as trgets for the F-51's and F-80's with their machine guns and napalm. This too was annoying to the Americans until they devised a method of dealing with these industrious and hardworking South Korean crews that were disappearing upon their approach. The answer was the "delayed action" bomb.

The fuse on a bomb could be adjusted to trigger an explosion at a predetermined detonation time – from instantaneous to up to 144 hours. In addition, the B-29 armaments specialists could rig the fuse so that any attempt by the North Koreans to defuse one of these unexploded bombs waiting to do their damage would trigger the bomb's explosion (Lt. Col. George A. Larson, U.S. Air Force (ret.), Military.com). Early in the conflict, therefore, the United State Air Force began mixing into its bomb loads a number of bombs with delayed action fuses. Roads would be bombed and cratered. After the planes had safely gone, the work crews would come out to repair the damage. Then an hour later, or 12 hours later or the next day or days later, the crew would be blown to pieces by the time-bomb.

Official Release 554, 15 October 1950:

> *"Twenty-six B-29's attacked seventy-eight different targets with generally excellent results. . . . Delayed-action bombs will further hinder any use of the rail and highway system."*

US Navy Historians marvel at the persistence and ingenuity of the Korean men and women, those who happen to be north of the 38th parallel as well as those south of it, who would repeatedly rebuild bridges as fast as the Americans could destroy them. James A. Field, Jr. in Chapter 10 of the Department of the Navy's <u>History of United States Naval Operations: Korea</u> originally published in 1962 tells a story about these workers and about the use of delayed-action bombs in an attempt to defeat them.

On March 2, 1951 a vital and vulnerable link in a rail line was discovered. A bridge was sighted in North Korea eight miles southwest of the town of Kilchu. The rail line was hidden for long stretches in long tunnels burrowed through the hills but for a brief period it would come into view to pass over a deep gully on a single track line on top of a six-span bridge, 650 feet long and 60 feet high. It was a perfect target. "The tunnels," according to Field's account, *"made it difficult to bypass; its height made it difficult to repair."*

The bridge was attacked by Navy Corsairs on March 2nd but they were only able to damage one of the approaches. Navy Lieutenant Commander Harold G. Carlson, leading his Corsairs from the *Princeton* in two attacks, ultimately succeeded on March 7th in dropping one of the six spans, damaging a second and shifting two more out of line. The Admiral in command of the Task Force christened the valley in honor of Commander Carlson, thereafter to be known in Naval history as "Carlson's Valley."

But here is where the story gets it fame. On the 14th of March the Americans were surprised by an examination of routine reconnaissance photos to discover that workers had made *"rough but effective repairs in the form of wooden cribbing, built up [60 feet] to replace the missing spans."*

So a 4th Strike was made the next day, knocking down all the new construction and dropping another span. Yet within two days pilots saw large piles of wooden ties assembled in the gully in readiness for rebuilding.

> *"The extraordinary persistence of this engineering effort, paralleled at all important broken bridges, . . . demonstrated the availability of repair crew and materials. . . ."*

Admiral Ofsite was getting tired of repeatedly sending his Corsairs to destroy the same bridge so he appealed to the Air Force. On March 15th

> *"Admiral Ofsite recommended . . . that Bomber Command be asked to inhibit repair activity by **seeding the gully with long-delay bombs**. . . . On the 24th a B-29 was sent out with a bomb load fused for long and varying delays, and three days later the effort was repeated."*

Incredibly, even with these unpleasant surprises for the men and women working on the bridge,

> *"the enemy continued to press the work with great determination. . . . By the 30th, cribbing of the four central spans and the northern approach had been completed,*

204

*transverse members had been installed, and only the rails
were lacking."*

Admiral Ofsite then sent off Strikes 5 and 6 which now destroyed
everything, *"leaving only the concrete piers."*

The Koreans finally abandoned reconstruction of that 60
foot high bridge. But it seems that they had not totally given up.
Later photos revealed to the Americans, according to Field's
official Naval History account, that the labor force had begun to
construct a four mile circuitous bypass, including eight new short
and low bridges. So the Navy's Corsairs began attacking these new
bridges. However after repeated attacks followed by repeated
rebuilding, it was the Navy that gave up.

*"The new simplicity of repair made the site no longer an
attractive one"* for the Corsairs.

Admiral Ofsite's Task Force then turned their attention
southward to the area of Songjin and through the months of April,
May and June *"the same sequence of destruction, cribbing,
destruction, and bypassing would take place"* (Field, History of
United States Naval Operations: Korea, Chapter 10, Part 2, 1962,
Department of the Navy – Naval Historical Center, Washington,
D.C. edited 2000 for Online Publication, July 4, 2003
<http://www.history.navy.mil/books/field/ch10b.htm>).

CHAPTER XI

SEOUL --

BEYOND THE BOMB LINE

Seoul, Korea's largest city with an estimated population in 1950 of 1,400,000 and until weeks earlier the capital of the country we had come to save, had quickly fallen "behind enemy lines." It was Korea's major city, had important industries, highways, bridges, power plants and other forms of modern infrastructure. Consequently it and its surrounding towns and villages became a major bombing target. Daily attacks were scheduled from the first day of the war and grew in intensity, rising to a crescendo with the assault on September 15th at Inchon, the seaport serving Seoul.

Stratemeyer, Saturday, 15 July 1950:

> *"Directive issued and received from General MacArthur through General Almond to hit Kimpo airport and the marshalling yards at Seoul today, using B-29's. . . ."*

Stratemeyer, Monday, 17 July 1950:

> *"Signed a letter to General MacArthur . . . with a set of pictures showing the destructive effect of the FEAF Bomber Command strike yesterday on Seoul – 1,504 x five hundred pound bombs were dropped – or 376 tons."*

Stratemeyer, Thursday, 3 August 1950:

> *"Called to General MacArthur's office at 1900 hours. Those present were: (other than CINCFE and myself) Almond, Wright, and Weyland. We discussed with him a signal* [message] *which he had received from General*

206

*Walker telling him that a pilot had reported several convoys going south toward Seoul and three trains moving south toward Seoul. In the discussion, CINCFE reiterated that he wanted **a line cut across Korea**, north of Seoul, to stop all communications moving south. Of course, I was delighted to receive that direction as we had preached that doctrine since the B-29s arrived."*

Stratemeyer already had prepared his list of targets for an "**interdiction**" line which ran along a belt between the 37th and 38th parallels (Note by the editor, Y'Blood, to Stratemeyer's August 3 entry, citing Futrell). There was to be nothing but devastation along that belt. The goal was that nothing was to pass through that interdiction line. Communication targets in that belt were to be targeted and bombed heavily and repeatedly. This "interdiction" line, this "no man's' land which was to be laid waste, again was in South Korea and occupied by the people we had come to rescue from communism.

Stratemeyer, Friday, 11 August 1950:

Sent following memo to O'Donnell [Major General Emmett "Rosie" O'Donnell, Jr., Bomber Commander]:
The Bomber Command has been plugging away at the west railroad bridge at Seoul from 28 June to date, and it still stands. . . . Apparently 500, 1000 and 2000 pound bombs are ineffective. There are larger bombs available for the destruction of this target at Okinawa. . . . I still want it taken out and urge that it be a continuing target for the FEAF Bomber Command until it is destroyed.

That railroad bridge was finally destroyed on August 20th after nine B-29's dropped 54 more tons of bombs on it in one day while at the same time 37 Corsairs and Skyraiders from the Navy had a go at it.

The Far East Air Force Reconnaissance Branch's Report No. 56 dated July 24, 1950 reported that "*NO DAMAGE*" was done by previous bombing raids to the railroad yard at Taejong, an important transportation hub in south central Korea, well south of Seoul. The railroad yard is describe in the Report as "2,100' long, 11 tracks wide." That would seem like a pretty big target -- but the bombs repeatedly missed. Similar reports were made for targets in Seoul and other cities. The erring bombs presumably landed on unintended areas near the targets. Nearly all the targets were within the cities being attacked, their power plants, factories, roads and railroad yards. If the bombs were missing those targets, what, and who, were they blowing up?

Yet it was not just bridges and roads in and around Seoul, Taejong, and other South Korean cities that were considered legitimate targets. Every conceivable object that might be of assistance to the occupying North Koreans was bombed, apparently without regard to the residents of Seoul – either for their lives or their means of living.

Mission Review Report No. 56 just quoted (National Archives, Record Group 341), for instance, lists the usual suspects as targets – airfields, power plants, electric company buildings, machine manufacturing plants, bridges, railroad tracts, railroad years, transformer stations, "possible" military barracks, "probable" ammunitions storage areas, shipyards, port areas. But this July 24, 1950 Report No. 56 also lists as bombing targets at least 12 sites, described only by their latitude and longitude coordinates, as "*Unidentified industry*." These were targets bombed repeatedly so long as the Americans were not in occupation of those cities, at least from June 30th to September 20th. Any building where people could work, any place where anything could be manufactured, baby carriages to hair brushes, was bombarded, and presumably with the same degree of accuracy and "collateral damage" as noted.

208

"A group of South Korean children, left homeless by the destruction of Seoul, wander through the City streets in search for food."
29 Oct 1950, Cpl. Ronald L. Hancock

"Korean women and children search the rubble of Seoul for anything that can be used or burned as fuel."
1 Nov 1950 Capt. F. L. Scheiber   US Army

The FEAF's Reconnaissance Branch was responsible for daily photographing of potential targets as well as determining what damage resulted after a bombing raid on specified targets. Its reports in the Nation Archives (Record Group 341) contain a mass of detail (though no photographs).

Numerous targets were listed for bombing, and were described by their longitude and latitude coordinates, in the Seoul area almost every day from late June to its recapture in late September. Each specified target was given its own target number. The same target numbers and their related coordinates are listed day after day until Air Force examiners were satisfied with the damage done.

For example, the Ryuzan Railroad shops and yards, Target No. 43, with coordinates 37:31:45 N, 126:57:45E, is listed as having "*No Damage*" after one particular raid from the photos examined on July 3, 1950. The same Target No. 43 is listed again from photos examined on July 11 but again a report of "*No Damage*" is given. However for July 24th Report the Ryuzan shops and yards are finally reported with "*extensive damage to shops*" and that "*all tracks leaving yard on North end cut at or near choke point.*" But the Report also states that the reconnaissance photos also show that "*repairs under way.*" Finally the July 26th report for Target No. 43 reads simply: "*severely damaged.*" One target took almost a month of bombing, but finally it earned the satisfactory stage of "*severely damaged.*"

Electrical resources for the enemy, now in Seoul, and incidentally for the 1,400,000 residents as well, were high priority targets. Two thermal electric power plants in the Seoul vicinity with coordinates of 37:33:00 N, 126:54:00E and 36:18:45N, 127:26:30E (Targets Nos. R6.92 and R6.159) are listed for bombing on July 23rd and July 20th respectively.

Another goal was to eliminate communication facilities for the enemy in Seoul, and of course for everyone else. Photographs of bomb damage to Target No. R6.122 with coordinates 37:31:15N, 126:58:15E, are periodically reported on, including on July 23, July 24, July 26, August 5th and August 21st. This Target No. R6.122, is described in the July 24th report as a "*Radio transmitter station*" consisting of "*four towers, 1,800' between outside towers. One probable transmitter building. Three minor buildings.*"

It appears to me from my reading of the reports that whatever "interesting" building the photo interpreters could not identify was nevertheless classified as a legitimate military target by merely labeling it as "unidentified."

For instance, Mission Review Report No. 56 dated July 24, 1950, lists the usual suspects as targets in and around the Seoul: – airfields, power plants, electric company buildings, machine manufacturing plants, bridges, railroad tracks, railroad yards, transformer stations, "*possible*" military barracks, "*probable*" ammunition storage area, shipyards and the entire port area. But it also lists at least 12 other targets, described only by their latitude and longitude coordinates, as "Unidentified industry." It appears that any building, anywhere in the Seoul, where people could work; any place where anything could be manufactured, was attacked. No ambiguous building escaped. The result as to "collateral damage" was predictable.

So many people were killed in the American bombings of Seoul during that period that children became parents overnight to their little sisters and brothers. This photo was taken by the US Army after only the first 'liberation" of Seoul.

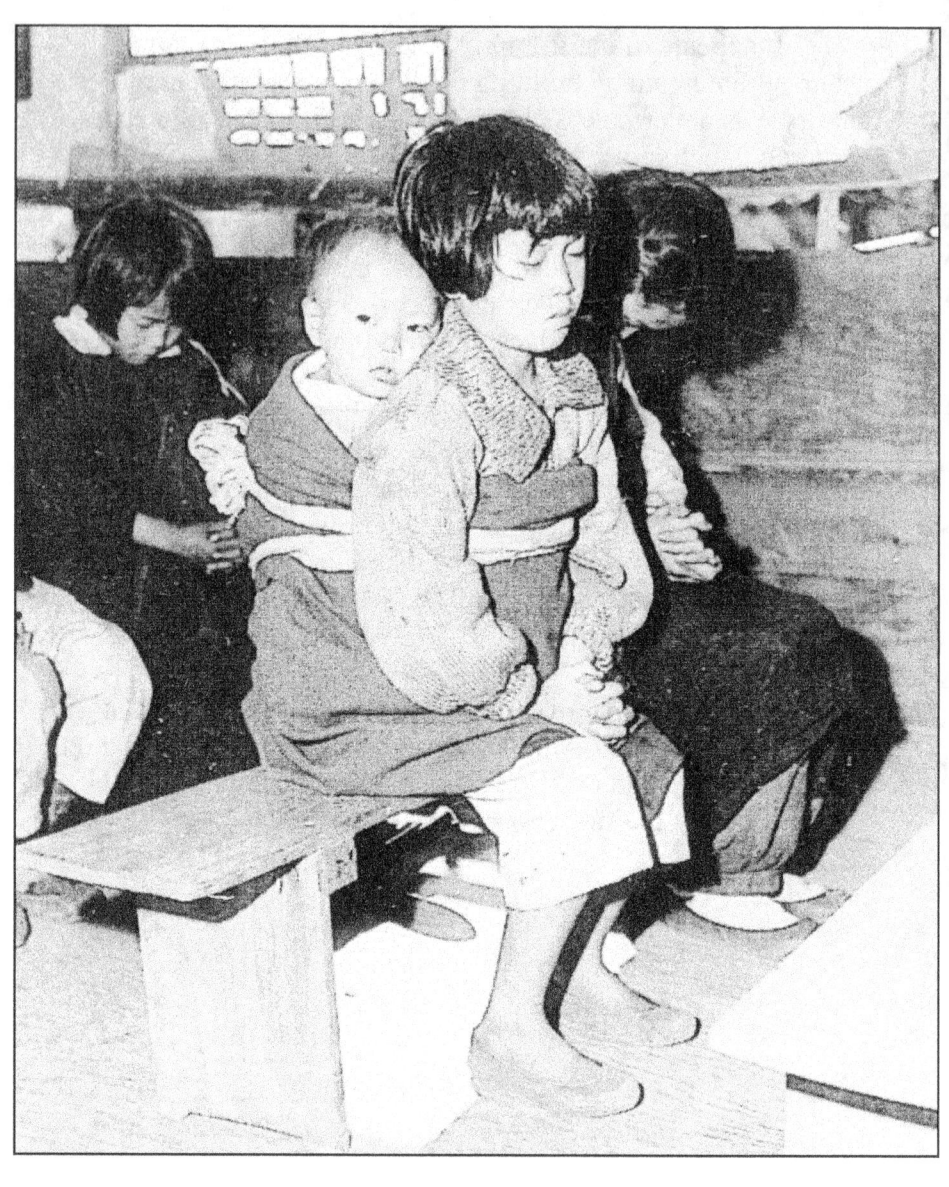

"South Korean children attend worship services in damage church near Seoul. . . ."
US Army Photo by Cpl. Ronald L. Hancock 29 Oct 50

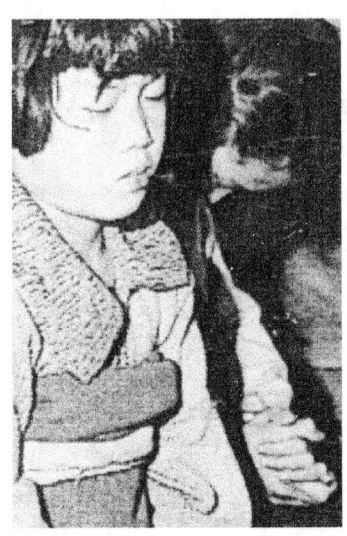

Though this type of bombing and strafing went on through August and into September, the people of the Seoul area had *seen nothing yet*, as they say. MacArthur's brilliant amphibious landing with 260 ships well behind enemy lines at Inchon, the port just northwest of Seoul, set the stage for an as yet unseen demonstration of destructive power.

Stratemeyer, 15 September 1950:

> *"0630 hours Marines debark Inchon.*
> *"0900 hours general offensive, EUSAK"* [Eighth United States Army in Korea, then under General Walton Walker].

Official Release 442 from MacArthur's Headquarters, Friday, 15 September, 1950:

> *American and British cruisers and destroyers plus carrier aircraft brought the war home the past two days to the Communist-held* **Inchon-Seoul area. The bombardment of the area under the direction of Rear Admiral John M. Higgins, U.S. Navy, was the preliminary blow. . .A**

213

> *furious forty-five minute bombardment by cruisers*
> *and destroyers . . . at the crack of dawn this*
> *morning carried on until the Marine amphibious*
> *group cracked the beach. . . .*
> *For two days preceding the landing the cruiser,*
> *aircraft carrier and destroyer forces had been*
> *pummeling practically every section of the Inchon*
> *area. . . .*

This hellish devastation, of course, was being unleashed on the populace of the Seoul area, the capital of the nation we were liberating. Who would be left to welcome the liberators?

The bombardment was so successful that the landing met little resistance according to General MacArthur who observed the landing from a ship offshore. The only enemy reaction noted by reporters were "principally of small arms fire."

The next day when the newly liberated residents of Inchon, a city of 250,000 people before the American liberation, returned to their city, they found

> *"two-thirds of the buildings destroyed and many*
> *friends and relatives dead. The city still was smoldering*
> *from the impact of the bombardment"* (New York Herald
> Tribune, September 17, 1950).

Reporters interviewed Korean Rear Admiral Sohn Wun Il, Chief of the tiny South Korean sea forces. He estimated that two-thirds of Inchon *"was destroyed mostly by shelling."* The Tribune's report gave the official explanation of why two-thirds of the rescued town had been destroyed while liberating it:

> *"American and British naval forces tried to*
> *concentrate on Red gun positions* ***but the guns were all***
> ***over*** *the hilly peninsula on which the city is built."*

214

Korean Admiral Sohn's marine brigade was mopping up in Inchon and had the job of *"distinguishing friend from foe,"* no easy task in a civil war. He told reporters that the residents of the city had unfortunately just returned yesterday from an earlier evacuation and walked right into the American and British bombardment, so that *"many were killed."* Yet, Rhee's Admiral insisted *"the people seem happy. . . . They are glad to see the Communists driven out"* (New York Herald Tribune, September 17, 1950).

YA/FEC-50-20889.

As Admiral Sohn and his South Korean troops went about *"distinguishing friend from foe"* there began a series of curious "discoveries" that would repeat themselves again and again in the cities and towns that the Americans and South Koreans were once more "liberating." Scores and scores of men, woman and children were found to have been executed, many buried in mass graves. So began the endless pictures appearing in US newspapers of the "atrocities" supposedly committed by the North Koreans either in their advance or retreat. American Army photographers readily accepted the word of the South Korean officers that the civilians had been murdered by Northern soldiers, and so they wrote their captions.

A writer for the Associated Press had more to say on Admiral Sohn Wun Il's comment that *"the people are happy"* about the American liberation of their now "blackened and badly torn" city.

215

"The people certainly do not look happy. If they are glad the war has finally passed them by, they do not show it. . . . Today they were going about the sad business of trying to live in the midst of great devastation, to bury their dead, get a bowl of rice to eat. . . .

"The people were not so much as glancing at the [US] marines and sailors pouring through. . . . A woman sitting on the edge of a stone pier, motionless as the stones themselves, stared out across the harbor. It was littered with junks and half-sunken small craft. Perhaps one of them had been hers. Her eyes never shifted and her head never moved.

"A Korean boy – he looked about 14 years old – made his way painfully down the street, holding his right leg stiff and straight. A blood-stained bandage was wrapped round his knee. . . .

*"A truckload of prisoners passed. **The captives wore white clothing, not uniforms.** They stood in the truck, packed tight and holding their hands over their heads. . .*"* (Associated Press, <u>New York Times</u>, September 17, 1950).

Note that the Associated Press reporter indicated that the prisoners, packed tight in the truck, wore **civilian clothes**, not military uniforms. It is unlikely, of course, that the North Korean Army, caught by surprise, would have had its troops switched out of their uniforms and dress as civilians. This was the beginning of the South Korean Army's and police's *"distinguishing friend from foe"* in recaptured territory, a rather swift process that in all probability led to a similarly swift death for these suspected foes, and then perhaps their bodies pictured as examples of yet more North Korean "atrocities."

This was the first large city recaptured by the Americans. The intrepid but fervently anti-communist reporter Marguerite Higgins was on the scene with the Marines and reported that the North Korean Army during their 10 week occupation *"appears to have been well behaved as individuals"* (New York Herald Tribune, September 18, 1950).

Indeed, the former Inchon mayor's reinstatement by Major General Oliver P. Smith, commanding the First Marine Division, indicated that the Northerners had not harmed the local officials in captured South Korean cities. This Rhee government official, Pyo Yng Moon, had naturally been arrested by the northerners when they captured the city months earlier. Yet he was found safe and sound, having been "released last Friday after the Marines landed" (AP, Washington Post, September 20, 1950).

From Official Release 451, 17 September 1950:

> *"With the liberation of Inchon from Communist rule now accomplished, elements of ROK forces have been charged with the preservation of its internal law and order and with the restoration of its constituted civil government."*

Rhee's troops, *"charged* [by MacArthur] *with the preservation of . . . law and order,"* now began another of their

217

many roundups of persons suspected of collaborating with the Northerners. Estimates of civilians executed by Rhee after the recapture of South Koreans cities ranged all over the map as no serious attempt was made to keep track. The Americans, Australians and British were not conducting the executions, but, except for one group of Australians noted in a press report, they were not stopping them either.

The Americans marched through Inchon and on to Seoul, 25 miles to the east, preceded every step of the way as usual by a continuous and rolling destructive bombardment.

> *"Carrier-based Navy planes concentrated their 315 strikes in the Inchon-Seoul-Kimpo area in close support of the advancing marine forces. Navy dive bombers dropped 246 tons of incendiary and fragmentation bombs, 120 jellied gasoline bombs and fired almost 1,000 five-inch rockets"* (<u>New York Herald Tribune</u>, September 17, 1950).

The Navy reported the next day on the armaments used in what it actually called its "precision" bombing of Inchon by planes from its carrier force at sea:

> *"In three days . . . the planes dropped 246 tons of incendiary and fragmentation bombs, 120 napalm bombs and 979 rockets."*

The US newspapers merely repeated this characterization of the bombing as *"precision"* bombing (for example, <u>New York Times</u>, September 17, 1950, p. 3). One would think that it was obvious that the term *"precision bombing"* in 1950 was an oxymoron, certainly if 246 tons of napalm and incendiary bombs were dropped that wiped out two-thirds of a city.

The Americans went on in a few days to take over Seoul with little resistance and behind a rolling mass of explosives and napalm.

"

"*HOUSING SITUATION IN SEOUL*" [Both photos.]
"*Makeshift houses like the ones pictured here are used by the families in Seoul, South Korea, who were left homeless during heavy fighting between US Troops and the North Korean Forces in that City.*" US Army Photo   Cpt. Ronald L. Hancock   31 Oct 50

"*Thousands of Leathernecks spanned the* [Han] *River on their way to liberate the former South Korean capital city. . .* [T]*he guns of United Nations cruisers loosed a terrific aerial bombardment which wiped out the 200 Reds prior to the morning crossing. Low-flying planes covered the Marines as they reached the east bank and began pushing toward Seoul.*" <u>Washington Post</u>, September 20, 1950).

"DAMAGED CHURCH NEAR SEOUL"

"Small Church near Seoul, damaged during heavy fighting by US troops against the North Korean forces in that area. . . ."

29 Oct 1950
Cpl. Ronald L. Hancock
US Army

As it turned out, this second *"liberation"* was short-lived. Some months later the Americans and the Rhee government again had to evacuate Seoul, this time to the advancing Chinese. But then shortly thereafter the American and South Korean armies took it back again. James Field, writing for the US Naval Historical Center, commented about this repeated *"liberation"* of Seoul:

> *"Seoul . . . on the 15th [March, 1951] was reoccupied without a fight. But two conquests and two liberations had taken a frightful toll, and hardly a tenth of the city's original population still skulked amid the ruins."*

CHAPTER XII

CLEARING A SAFE PATH
THROUGH SOUTH KOREA . . .
AGAIN !

On September 15, 1950 the Americans launched a general offensive along the Pusan line at the southern tip of Korea to coincide with the amphibious invasion at Inchon. The northerners had essentially expended themselves by this time and the Americans probably could have broken out of the Pusan perimeter without the assault at Inchon. But that assault seemed to have caught the northerners unprepared, with no reserves, and threatened to entrap their army which was well south around Pusan. They had not deployed any serious forces in their rear nor near the area of Seoul-Inchon. The North Koreans therefore began immediately to pull out some of their troops on the Pusan perimeter to go north again – either to battle the invaders or at least to escape any envelopment. But there were still battles and resistance in many sectors along the Pusan perimeter.

As at Inchon, the path for the advancing American Eighth Army now breaking out of the Pusan perimeter was leveled with as much firepower as the unchallenged US Air Force and the US Naval forces could unleash. Again, all of the destruction was visited on the people in South Korea.

> *"The Communist line of retreat was following the route of conquest it took during July and August. The road back led over 'Heartbreak Highway.' The paved roadway runs 90 miles south of Seoul across the Kum River to the*

*devastated town of Taejon, then turns eastward for 53 miles
to cross the Naktong River at Waegwan and enter Taegu"*
(Washington Post, September 20, 1950).

Futrell in his Official United States Air Force History tells
of the use of delayed action bombs and napalm bombs during this
particular advance:

> *"Roads to the northeast of Seoul were mined by B-
> 29's with delayed action bombs set to explode at night.
> Pilots on surveillance were briefed to seek their own choke-
> points on roads, where a bomb blast would crater the
> roadway or bring down a landslide. . . . On the 2d Division
> front on 17 September, Fifth Air Force fighters dropped
> 210 x 110-gallon napalm tanks, killing an estimated 1,200
> enemy troops as they attempted to retreat across the
> Naktong. Other fighters saturated with napalm the 'Walled
> City' of Yongchon, the strong fortification resisting the
> Eighth Army advance eight miles north of Taegu, and left it
> ablaze."*

From the New York Herald Tribune, September 17, 1950:

> *"Ever-increasing numbers of American war planes
> kept pace with the mounting United Nations offensive
> yesterday and rained fiery destruction on North Korean
> Communist front-line troops, supplies and rear bases."*

At this time of course the *"Communist front-line"* was
arrayed along a semicircle of South Korean cities, towns, villages
and farms.

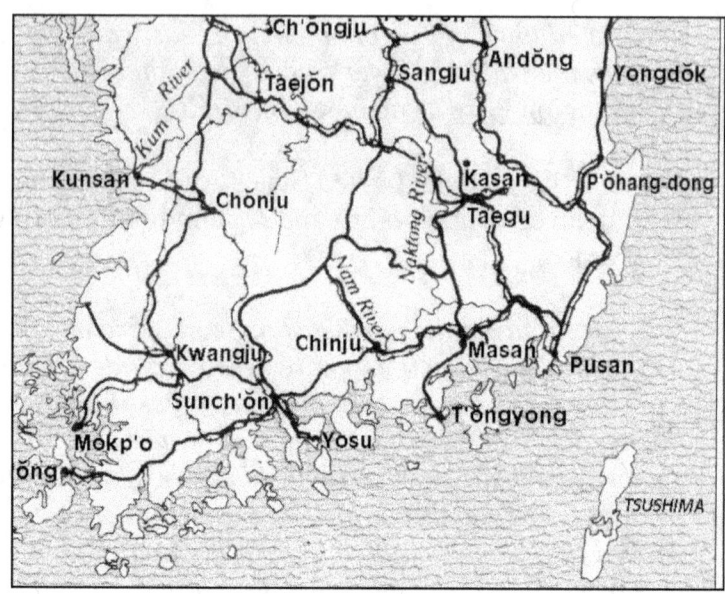

Official Release 445, September 16, 1950:

> *"United States Far East Air Forces planes were loaded this morning with bombs, rockets, napalm and 50-caliber machine-gun ammunition for heavy strikes in South Korea in air support of United Nations ground forces. . . . United States Air Force planes concentrated along the battle line in the southeastern sector of Korea to keep the Communists pinned down. More than 400 sorties of all types were flown"*

Official Releases 451 and 449, September 17, 1950:

> *"Light bombers picked up where they left off the night before and damaged or destroyed Communist vehicles, warehouses and other military targets in a thirty-mile circle around Taejon. . . . At Taejon a formation of B-29's dropped bombs on the marshalling yards, warehouses and storage area. Large explosions and fires followed direct hits. . . . Flying in close-support operations . . .*

224

planes of the Fifth Air Force . . . attacked . . . buildings housing enemy forces all along the immediate battlefront. . . . Target areas included Tabu, Angang, Yosu, Chongyang, Pohang, Kumchon, Uiryong, Sachon, Hamchang and Sangju [South Korea]"

Release from Eighth Army Headquarters, September 17, 1950:

"On the northwest corner of the United Nations line, enemy strong points in the Walled City of Kasan and in the hills east of Waegwan impeded the progress of friendly troops"

New York Times, September 18, 1950:

"The hardest fighting still prevailed along the front of the United States First Cavalry Division, in front of the Naktong River crossing at Waegwan, and along the road north from the advanced headquarters at Taegu to Tabu. At Waegwan, the main Taegu-Seoul highway makes its river crossing, and this would be the most direct route for troops from the perimeter to join hands with the invasion force to the north. . . . The enemy still held the Walled City on Mount Kasan – bastion of this region. . . ."

Official Release 461 issued September 19, 1950:

"United States Fifth Air Force fighters were off at first light this morning for Korea and another assault on retreating Communist troops as a follow-up[to] yesterday's banner results. . . . B-29 Superforts . . . carried out a special type of mission by saturating a two-square mile area west of the Naktong River. . . . [40] B-29's dropped 1,600 500-pound general purpose bombs that were fused to explode instantaneously."

Stratemeyer, Tuesday 19 September 1950:

> *"Sent redline to Vandenberg: 'Add the word* ***'beautiful''*** *to the several words already coined by ground forces in Korea to describe FEAF air efforts. Latest word – 'beautiful' was used by Major General Hobart Gay, First Cav. Commander, in describing B-29 tactical strike on Communist positions west of Waegwan on Monday, September 18, when 1600 bombs were dropped on a 2 square mile area just in front of U.N. positions.' "*

Washington Post, September 21, 1950:

> *"The United States Twenty-fourth Division recaptured burned-out Waegwan. . . ."*

On the 20th Stratemeyer wrote:

> *"Partridge . . . had information that 3,800 dead were found by the ground forces in the walled city* [Kasan] *and that it is our opinion that our 60-tank napalm attack on 17 September did that job."*

Official Release 457:

> *"B-26 light bombers, F-80 jet fighter-bombers and F-81 fighters bombed, rocketed and strafed large concentrations of troops, causing a rout in at least one sector. Liberally bombing the area with napalm, scores of positions were made untenable and results for the day were reported as excellent by Air Force forward controllers all along the battle front."*

Official Release 458:
> *"During a four-hour period yesterday morning the U.S.S. Missouri pounded more than*

226

*300 tons of high explosive into the **Pohang** [South Korea] area. . . . Making effective use of shore fire-control spotting, the Mighty Mo pin-pointed her targets, enabling ROK ground forces to cross a bridge over the Hyongsan River standing up."*

The <u>Washington Post</u> reported that the

*"South Korean Third Division troops sent patrols into **Pohang**, the battered east coast port. **The 16-inch guns of the U.S.S. Missouri, the mightiest warship in the world, blasted the way"*** (September 20, 1950).

Just a few weeks earlier this unfortunate South Korean city had experienced Americans going the other way and burning up their **rear**. *"Fallen Pohang was reported afire from American B-26 bomb raids. . . . Pilots reported Pohang was in flames. . . ."* (<u>Washington Post</u>, September 7, 1950) Now Pohang was in **front** of the Americans, now advancing, and got even harsher treatment.

Japanese travel books in the '30's referred to Pohang as a *"pretty port city."* But now there was simply no Pohang.

"Scene of Pohang, on the east coast of Korea, after artillery duel and air strikes."

Photo by Lt. Winslow
US Army Photo

Am I suggesting that we should not have made the path for our troops as safe as possible? That instead of the 33,000 killed, we should have risked fighting man- to-man, so to speak, and suffered the hundreds of thousands of military casualties incurred by the other side, much less the millions of civilians that were to die.

No, not at all. Once we committed to the war, we had an obligation to minimize the loss of Americans.

But this wholesale slaughter was a **foreseeable consequence** of inserting a nation like the US with all of its firepower into a growing-up struggle between brothers. Instead of at the **thousands** of Koreans killed in a local civil war; thanks to our intervention there were **millions** and millions dead. A leader should have seen what entering into this conflict would have meant. Our Military understood it and that is why they had been against it. Vito Marcantonio had seen what would happen, and pleaded for us to stay out of it. Why couldn't Truman see this?

CHAPTER XIII

"PRECISION" BOMBING

". . .bombing was so accurate as to do little damage to civilian installations . . ."
Futrell, USAF Military Historian

The difference in destruction wrought by our bombs between the area south of the 38th parallel and that north of the 38th was primarily semantic. A town burned down south of the 38th was as much a heap of ashes as one burned north of it. But the one in the south was "regrettably" burned only incidentally or as "collateral damage" – the enemy was somehow using it so it had to be destroyed, or it was in the way for some other "military" reason. On the other hand, a town in the north was targeted to be burned down simply because it was above that line drawn by Dean Rusk late one night back in 1945.

The people in the towns on either side of the parallel may have looked the same; spoke the same language; may have been related and may have been part of the same culture for a thousand or more years. But the Dean Rusk Line had made those humans south of it the ones we were saving; while at the same time magically made those north of it into demons. Our propaganda made quite dramatic distinctions between the innocent *"little brown people"* we were saving and the demons we were destroying -- though in fact we may have destroyed as many on one side of the line as on the other. To our diplomats and military planners, the killing of civilians in the south by our bombing was regrettable, but the killing of those north of the line was of *"no concern."* The G.I. on the ground or the pilot in the cockpit was at least being honest in reflecting real American policy when he referred to all Koreans as "gooks."

The destruction of the cities, towns, and villages north of the 38th parallel was intentional from the beginning. The killing of the civilians was a military goal to destroy the morale on the "other" side. Taken from them also were their means of livelihood, their factories, farms, vehicles, animals. Then every form of mechanism they may have had for modern life – electric power plants, sewers, telephone lines, dams, irrigation canals.

Those people who could not be killed directly with explosives, or burned to death with napalm or other incendiaries were starved to death. Stratemeyer and Partridge struggled over the task of bursting the Hwachon Reservoir just north of the 38th parallel. Reservoirs of course not only provided water power for electricity, but controlled water for irrigation of the rice crops. Blowing up a dam not only cut off electricity, but it flooded the crops and villages.

Stratemeyer took a flight over the huge Hwachon Reservoir on January 16, 1951 and again realized the *"uselessness of normal bombing"* to destroy the dam and flood the fields. Stratemeyer had made a special request to the Strategic Air Command in the US to make a special B-36 run from the US, carrying larger bombs than they had in Korea, to blow up the dams. General LeMay, however, reluctantly had to decline the request as they just could not afford to use the scarce B-36's in this way. The new heavy bombers were earmarked for Soviet targets in case of World War III.

Partridge at the same time was on the alert for any new war tools that would help blow up the dams. On March 1st he sent an excited memo to Stratemeyer asking for more information on General Vandenberg's casual remark made to General Ridgeway at a meeting that there were new types of bombs being developed in the US that would be capable of destroying the Hwachon Dam.

The Far East Air Force had one B-29 Bomber Group when the Korean civil war started. Soon two other groups from the already stretched Strategic Air Command were lent to the FEAF.

Truman and the Joint Chiefs from 1945 had been shaping the military around the atomic bomb. With the Bomb, the theory was, one could reduce most of the rest of the military. But even the carriers of this weapon, structured to be able to deliver as great destruction on the Soviet Union as possible, was limited. So when the call came to General Curtis LeMay to divert two of his bomber groups to a tiny location in Asia, he considered it a nuisance and a distraction. But he applied the same strategic bombing philosophy to this defenseless country as he had developed for the Soviet Union – immediate and massive destruction.

The North Korea air force, such as it was, had been obliterated in the early days of the war. Stratemeyer noted in his diary entry of July 10, 1950: "*FEAF aircraft have held air superiority from the first and enemy activity has all but disappeared.*" For the first year at least, when most of the destruction was accomplished, the US Air Force had no significant opposition in the air. B-29's which would normally drop their loads from as high as 22,000 to 30,000 feet to avoid enemy ground fire or flak, in Korea were usually able to fly at 15,000 to 22,000 feet, select the angle best suited for their purposes and bomb at their leisure, generally without fear of serious flak from the ground or attacks from the air. The population of North Korea, designated by the Dean Rusk Line as the "enemy," was totally defenseless.

When he was called upon to assist in the Korean civil war, Le May saw no reason why the US should not just continue where it had left off in World War II, the massive firebombing of enemy cities. He had orchestrated the burning of Tokyo and numerous other Japanese cities. Now the cities, villages and towns in Korea, with their wooden and thatched homes and buildings, close together streets and lack of fire-fighting abilities, would make perfect targets. That the Koreans, unlike the Japanese and Germans, had not declared war against the US or killed a single one of our soldiers, did not make any difference to LeMay. An enemy was an enemy.

"We slipped a little idea under the door up there in the Pentagon. . . . Maybe if we turned SAC loose, not with atomic weapons but with some incendiaries, against four or five towns in North Korea, this will convince them we mean business and maybe it'll stop it" (Le May as quoted in a 1972 interview in Thomas Coffey's 1986 biography, <u>Iron Eagle : The Turbulent Life of General Curtis LeMay</u>. New York: Crown, 1986).

Le May related to his interviewers how the cautious politicians at the time had rejected his idea of a fast, unannounced and devastating blow to knock out the North Koreans. Yet in the end, Le May observed, the same result had obtained.

"So we go on and we don't do it, and [we] *let the war go on.* **Over a period of three and a half or four years . . . we did burn down every town in North Korea and every town in South Korea.** *. . . And what? Killed off 20 percent of the Korean population."*

The total, north and south, Korean population in 1950 was 30,000,000. So by Le May's estimate, we had killed off 6,000,000 Koreans.

Le May's theory was that an early overkill would in the long run save lives on both sides as it would end the war quickly. His biographer, however, like many others, thought that such a strategy would have more likely brought China into the war earlier or even have set off World War III. However, neither the North Koreans nor, later in the war, the Chinese, were intimidated or stopped by the massive bombing ultimately employed by LeMay's B-29's -- just as Congressman Vito Marcantonio had predicted.

General Stratemeyer understood from the beginning that any kind of bombing of industrial areas would result in civilian deaths. Initially he had struggled with the bombing in the cities. He even suggested to MacArthur that for public relations purposes

232

before the large scale strategic bombings commenced that some warning be given to the population.

Stratemeyer, Tuesday, 4 July 1950:

"Just received information, Vandenberg to Stratemeyer, that Major General Rosie O'Donnell as bomber commander, and the 22d and 92d Bomb Groups, were proceeding to Far East Command . . . . Vandenberg wishes ... that all targets back of immediate battlefront within North Korea be taken out."

Emmett "Rosie" O'Donnell, Jr.

Stratemeyer, Tuesday, 11 July 1950:

"1830 hours an appointment with CINCFE: following items are those I will discuss with him. . . .

*I have issued direct orders to him (General O'Donnell) that no urban area targets will be attacked except on direct orders from you through me. 8. **Again, since our first strike targets are bound to kill and wound civilians,** I recommend that an announcement be made by you urging them to vacate all urban centers that are close to military targets; namely, railroad centers, airfields, heavy industry locations, harbors and sub bases, and POL [petroleum, oil, and lubricants] storage facilities and refineries."*

So the mass bombing of industrial sites commenced.

233

Stratemeyer's comment, however, on his having issued "direct orders" to O'Donnell that he could bomb urban areas only if specifically authorized by MacArthur and Stratemeyer suggests that Stratemeyer, at this early stage of the war at least, was wary of the flamboyant Rosie O'Donnell, Jr.

l/r: Generals Edward H. White, Emmett 'Rosie' O'Donnell, Jr., Raymond C. Maude and Francis L. Ankenbrandt. 23 July 1950 USAF.

Major General Emmett "Rosie" O'Donnell, one of Le May's protégés and likewise a veteran of the firebombing of Japanese cities, would later describe his recommendations when he went out to Korea. His testimony on June 25, 1951, during the hearings held by Congress to review Truman's dismissal of MacArthur, would suggest that he wanted to use atomic bombs on North Korea from the very beginning:

> *"It was my intention and hope, not having any instructions, that we would be able to get out there and to cash in on our psychological advantage in having gotten into the theater and into the war so fast, by putting a very severe blow on the North Koreans, with advanced warning, perhaps, telling them that they had gone too far in what we all recognized as being a case of aggression, and General MacArthur would go top side to make a statement, and we now have at our command **a weapon** that can really dish out some severe destruction, and let us go to work on **burning five major cities in North Korea to the ground,***

and to destroy completely every 1 of about 18 major strategic targets."

The Congressional hearing record made public is full of "[Deleted.]" notations, so it is difficult to get the full picture of what these Generals at the MacArthur hearings were presenting to Congress at the time. But in the O'Donnell testimony that was not deleted, he spoke of using **"a weapon"** of great destruction. That would suggest that he wanted to drop an atomic bomb on each of the five major North Korean cities. At any rate, according to his testimony, a few months later when the Chinese entered the war, he was one of those publicly and expressly advocating use of the atomic bombs

Le May and O'Donnell had suggested a massive strategic attack with B-29's on North Korean cities as soon as O'Donnell and his B-29's were sent out to Korea in July 1950. However, as O'Donnell testified in 1951, General Stratemeyer, under whom he was working, needed them first and foremost to help the retreating troops on the front line. Stratemeyer, according to O'Donnell:

> *"told us it would not be possible to carry out an attack such as that at that time, the reason being that our hard-pressed ground forces were in a very bad state, indeed, and that every weapon at the command of the theater commander must, and properly should be, used in support of the ground forces."*

In any event, O'Donnell and his bombers encountered no enemy air action during the six months he was out in Korea *"worthy of the name."* The casualty rate for the B-29 Bomber men and equipment, he testified, was equal to what they would have had during a training mission in the States.

Chairman Russell [Richard B. Russell, D., Georgia Senator, Chairman of theSenate Committee on Armed Services]:

235

"Now you stated that you could not burn the cities there, that you hoped to burn out all these cities. As I understood you intended to give them notice you had better get out of the war or we will burn your cities?"

General O'Donnell. *"I thought that would take care of the humane aspects of the problem. . . ."*

Chairman Russell. *"What decision was made at that suggestion of yours?"*

General O'Donnell. *"We were not at that time permitted to do it."*

Chairman Russell. *"Was that for lack of adequate number of planes or was it some matter of policy?"*

General O'Donnell. *"I think it was an overriding political or diplomatic consideration, sir. I don't know. I am the bomber commander out there and I got the word from General Stratemeyer who said 'No,' not at this time.*
. . ..
Senator Bridges [Styles Bridges, R., N.H.]: *"General O'Donnell, you spoke earlier in your testimony of cities or towns that you were prohibited from bombing or attacking. Were those towns and cities, some of them, within the area of North Korea?"*

General O'Donnell: *"All of them were, sir."*

Senator Bridges: *"About what period did that include; what time?"*

General O'Donnell: *"Well, this was initially when we first got out there we were instructed not to use incendiary bombs, not to burn down the cities, but there were no compunctions on the part of our commanders to bomb*

236

legitimate military targets within those cities with high explosives. . . . "

Senator Stennis [John C. Stennis, D. MS]: *"Early in your testimony this morning you said that the O'Donnell plan had 18 major strategic targets . . . and then you had five primary spots of some*
kind".

General O'Donnell: *"The main cities were Pyongyang, first, the capital, Seishin,Rashin, Wonsan, and Chinnampo. . . . I could have done that in 10 days flat . . ."*

Senator Stennis: ***"Now, as a matter of fact, Northern Korea has been virtually destroyed, hasn't it? Those cities have been virtually destroyed."***

General O'Donnell: ***"Oh, yes; we did it all later anyhow."***

*"Billowy columns of smoke and flames erupt violently from target following a bombing raid over **Chinnampo**, Korea, by B-29's of 92nd Bomb Group."* 31 August 1950 USAF Photo

While everything that could be destroyed in North Korea from airplanes was destroyed by the US by the end of the Korean War, there was much talk, especially in the beginning, about "pinpoint" and "precision" bombing. In addition, the US did in fact drop millions of propaganda leaflets in North Korea warning the citizens to get away from military targets as they were to be bombed.

But even an amateur analysis of the "military" targets in North Korea from the very beginning of the war would show that massive civilian casualties were to be expected, and most probably intended. This, after all, was the goal of "strategic" bombing – terror -- to break the enemy's spirit. The various locations of the targets in each city were so spread out and the nature of bombing from 20,000 feet at that time, often through clouds and guided by radar only, meant that a fairly good number of bombs would go beyond their targets, say, docks or warehouses, and hit residential areas. In fact, of course, that is what happened. Then later in the war even the pretenses of warnings and avoiding civilian casualties were dropped as entire cities and villages in North Korea were declared to be "military targets" and burnt down with napalm without prior warning.

Futrell, the official USAF military historian, makes a valiant attempt to seem righteous on this issue, but his own scholarly honesty in the rest of his work defeats this attempt. He makes *pro-forma* defensive statements in his study like:

> "To the end of the Korean war FEAF would be bound by a rule which was finally stated in this language: 'Every effort will be made to attack military targets only, and to avoid needless civilian casualties.'"

And again:

> "The FEAF Bomber Command strategic air attacks destroyed none but legitimate military targets in North

*Korea, and **the bombing was so accurate as to do little damage to civilian installations near the industrial plants.***"

Yet as early in the war as October 17, 1950, when the following photograph of Wonsan was taken by USAF reconnaissance, it would be difficult to tell whether there was "*little damage to civilian installations near the industrial plants,*" as Futrell's statement claims. There simply was very little of anything standing, whether industrial or civilian. In addition, "military targets" already included hotels, churches and banks. What buildings could be more civilian? The Air Force caption writers usually tried to give some military justification for what otherwise seem like grim mass killings of the civilian population.

Bombed out Wonsan

If there was any question as to whether civilian targets were hit directly, the USAF reconnaissance photographers removed any doubts for us. What could be more civilian than banks, churches, schools, etc. In its enthusiasm in 1950 to tell the world how much damage it could do, the USAF I believe has told posterity more than it wanted to.

"Wreckage of hotel caused by bomb damage, Wonsan, Korea" 23 October 1950   USAF Photo

"This destruction of a hotel near marshalling yards in Wonsan, Korea, is the result of bombing by B-29 'Superforts' of the U.S. Far East Air Force." 23 October 1950 USAF Photo

Beds can be seen in the debris. And perhaps these two civilians are searching for the bodies of relatives in the hotel's wreckage.

241

"*Fifth Air Force light bombers closed this No. Korean bank one Saturday afternoon.*

All that remained standing after the air strike were these three safes. Money that would have aided Communist troops went up in flames following the napalm bombing and general 'working over' delivered by hard-hitting 452nd Bomb Wing B-26's."

"B26 MAKES DIRECT HIT ON PRIORITY STRUCTURE NEAR WONAN HARBOR. Immediate explosion from a direct hit made by a B-26 Invader light bomber on a **church** *containing high explosives for the Communists, is shown in this photo the second after the 452nd Light Bomb Wing's plane had dropped its bombs directly on target. Wonsan harbor . . . ."*
US Air Force Photo   March, 1951

243

Hotels, banks, churches – direct hits. For a supposedly godless Communist country the Air Force found a lot of churches just in Wonsan that warranted targeting.

Official Release 196, August 4, 1950:

> "On the east coast of Korea, a *large North Korean supply center, the town of Chukdandong, was set afire by naval bombardment in what an air spotter described as 'a **beautiful job.**' An American destroyer pounded **175 rounds of ammunition <u>into the town</u>**. "(Emphasis added.)

USAF historian Futrell makes his own comments about avoiding *"needless civilian casualties,"* if indeed they are his and not an obligatory USAF official insertion, appear absurd as he proceeds meticulously to describe carpet bombings, the burning down of cities with incendiaries, the tonnage of explosives dropped on locations and the like. Further, he does not hesitate to pass on to us such information about a US attack on Wonsan as

> *"a U.S. State Department representative reported about **two-thirds of the city's dwellings destroyed**, virtually all of its industry gone, and its **population reduced** from about 150,000 to not over 20,000."*

Even with all that destruction, however, the Joint Chiefs of Staff still were not satisfied that enough damage was being done to the infrastructure of North Korea. They thought MacArthur was using the strategic bombing B-29's too much for tactical or troop support instead of what they were better suited for, high altitude "strategic", that is carpet, bombing of cities. They therefore "advised" him that "mass air operations against industrial targets in North Korea were 'highly desirable'" (Futrell). This illustrates what General Rosie O'Donnell in his Congressional testimony did not make clear when he told the Senators that he was not initially allowed to use incendiaries. While initially restrained from the use of incendiaries (which restraint was soon lifted in any event), most

244

of the other elements of SAC's plan that he had taken with him to Korea were adopted. Specifically the concept of "area" or "mass" bombing of the industrial targets in the major North Korea cities.

Since the cities were not that large and the targeted industries in each city were close to each other, the number of raids required to destroy the targets could be reduced by bombing the whole "area," and not just the specific target. "Area" or "mass" bombing would seem to exclude the concept of "precision" or "pin point" bombing. Nevertheless throughout the Korea War the US Government and the Press repeatedly characterized the bombing as "precision" and "pin point."

In addition, the adoption of SAC's "area" bombing strategy, bombing whole areas in these cities to assure the destruction of industries and other targets situated within those areas, rendered moot the issue of using incendiaries. Though more runs and more explosive bombs would be necessary, most of the city would be blown to pieces anyway. General O'Donnell made this point when he testified: *"There were no compunctions on the part of our commanders to bomb legitimate military targets within those cities with high explosives."*

The tragic absurdities of this war, or perhaps any war, can be recognized in the case of the city of **Hamhung** and its nearby port city of **Hungnam**, a port, industrial and transportation center. In late July and early August we repeatedly bombed those cities with effects satisfactory to the military leaders.

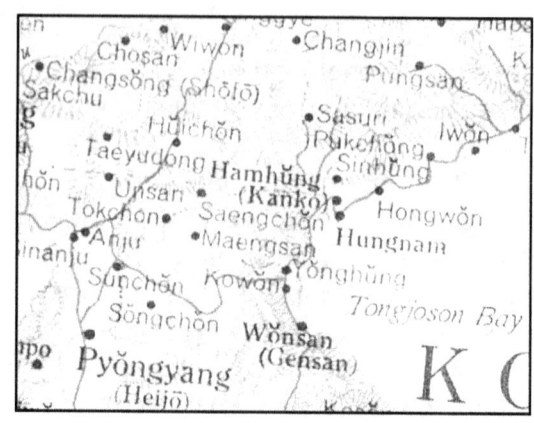

Stratemeyer, Sunday, 30 July 1950:

*"B-29's struck with 23 aircraft the Chosen Nitrogen Chemical Company plant at Konan (**Hungnam**) which is 50 miles north of Wonsan. Explosions rocked planes which were above 15,000 feet. Initial strike with radar; overcast cleared away, presumably by heat generated by ground fires, remainder bombing visual. Raid highly successful."*

Official Release 181 from MacArthur Headquarters, August 1, 1950:

*"The results of United State Air Force B-29 strike on the Chosen Nitrogen Chemical Company plant at Konan (**Hungnam**) on the North Korean east cast were described as 'excellent' by operations analysts of FEAF Bomber Command. . . . The mathematical determination of the results of the bombing Sunday, July 30, was that 85 per cent of the industrial target had been effectively damaged by the strategic bombers.. . . . The industrial center of the factory was picked up on the radar scope of the B-29's, and the bombing run, conducted high over a nearly solid-decked overcast, was directed by the radar operator. . . ."*

The Release further claimed that this high-altitude, radar directed bombing over *"nearly solid-decked overcast"* was so accurate that it did no damage to *"a housing and residential area located just outside the factory."*

Release 188, August 2, 1950:

> *"United States Far East Air Forces medium bombers staged their second major strike against the North Korean industrial complex at the east coast city of **Hamhung** . . . [It] was hit with more than 400 tons of bombs. Intense fires were seen and sharp explosions rocked the B-29's at an altitude of more than 15,000 feet. . . . Flames rising to an estimated 2000 feet and black smoke which mushroomed up to 12,000 feet cut off any view of the target shortly after the beginning of the attack. The last Superfortresses to make their bomb runs **found it necessary to use radar sighting."***

The Washington Post reported in its August 2, 1950 edition:

> *"United States B-29 Superfortresses made their second mass attack in three days on the North Korean war production center of **Hungnam** today and preliminary reports indicated **they almost blotted it out of existence**. . . . Jubilant bomber crews said they believe it was the most successful aerial attack since the Korean war began. . . . Today's target area was two miles east of that bombed Sunday. The first crews over said that the area hit in the first strike **looked pretty desolate and burned out**"* (emphasis added).

The center of Hungnam was already *"almost blotted . . . out of existence"* as of August 2nd, yet another major raid is sent out.

Official Release 197, August 4, 1950:

"The third major strike within five days against the North Korean chemical and munitions manufacturing complex [at **Hungnam**] *was made today when United States Far East Air Forces B-29 Superforts again dropped more than 400 tons of high explosive bombs. Today's target was . . . about three miles up the river from the explosives factory almost totally destroyed by B-29's on July 30. One-fourth of today's bombs was dropped visually and three-fourths by radar. . . . Bombing results were generally good, they reported, and fires were seen by some airmen through breaks in the clouds."*

A Stratemeyer statement quoted by the <u>Washington Post</u> on the 5th reported "the vital plant at Hungnam *'suffered such mortal damage in three large scale **precision** bombing attacks of the past five days that it can no longer be considered a major factor in the Korean war."*

Thus by early August the military seemed pleased with the amount of destruction they were able to wreak on Hungnam and Hamhung, though the bombing continued into October. Finally, the Army, having fought its way up the peninsula, accompanied by the usual carpet bombing to clear its path, arrived in late October to take physical possession of what was left of Hungnam. According to press releases from the Army they were greeted cheerfully by the inhabitants:

"LIBERATION CEREMONIES AT HAMHUNG"

"Major General Edward M. Almond, CG X Corps., and his staff officers receive flowers from the civilian population of Hamhung in token of their appreciation of liberation. General Almond addressed the people during the liberation ceremonies."

26 October 1950   US Army Signal Corps Photo.   Cpl. Alex Klein

---

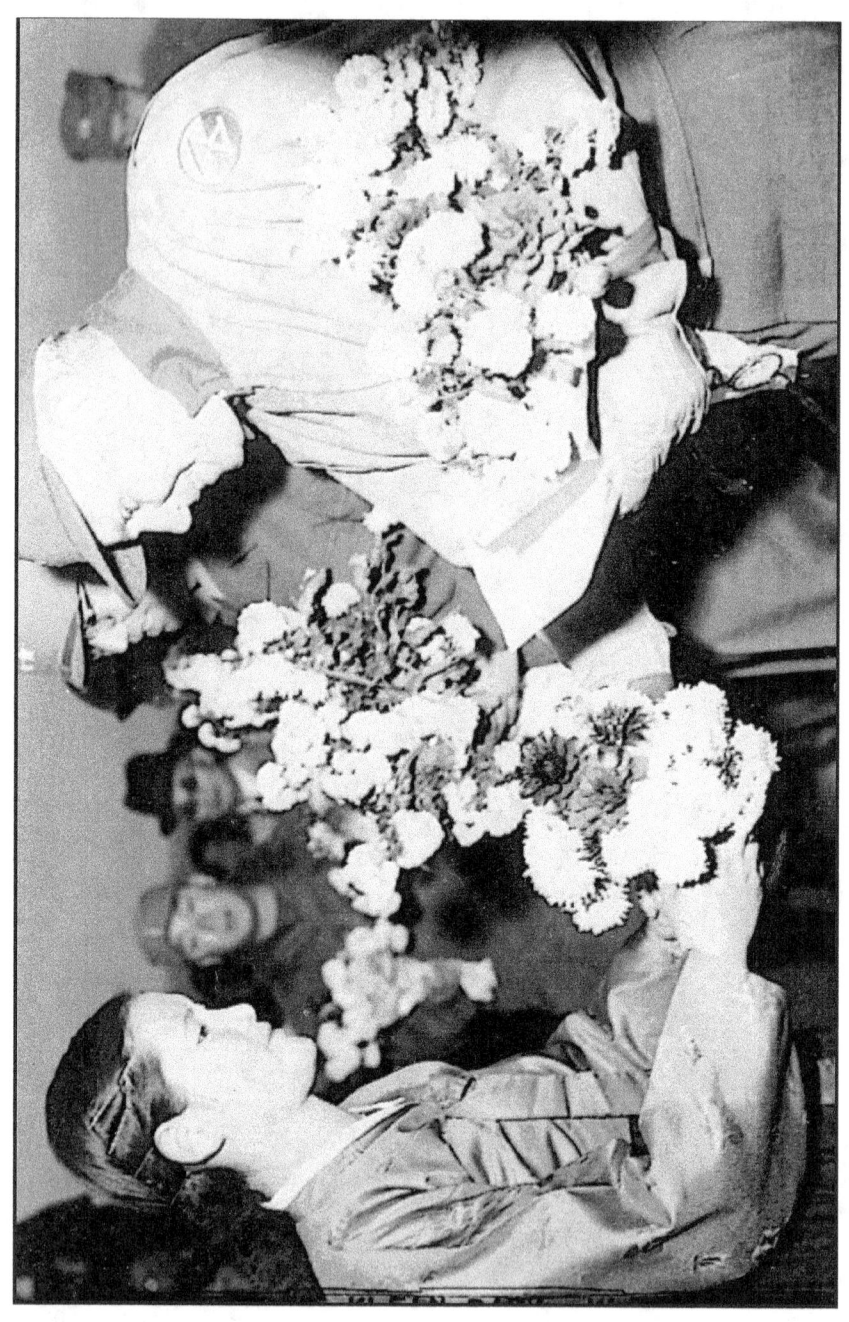

250

CHAPTER XIV

"HOME BY CHRISTMAS"

"[I]f the Chinese tried to get down to Pyongyang there would be the greatest slaughter."
General Douglas MacArthur, Wake Island, October 15, 1950

By September 3rd Stratemeyer could write in an official letter to General O'Donnell that *"practically all the Joint Chiefs of Staff targets have been destroyed."* The Joint Chiefs by mid-September saw no point in continuing to bomb rubble. O'Donnell's bombers were grounded as there were no strategic targets of any worth left. The bombing crews did practice runs while awaiting orders to return to the US.

On September 27th Stratemeyer wrote MacArthur:

"I consider the present status of the destruction of the enemy in Korea to be so much in our favor that I now consider it no longer necessary to retain all four (4) additional medium bomb groups in your command. The Joint Chiefs of Staff directive received [by] your headquarters direct cessation of all attacks on all strategic targets. . . ."

On Monday, 2 October 1950 General Stratemeyer's diary indicates that he was drafting his "forwarding endorsements" to the anticipated final reports of his four major commands regarding the Korean Conflict.

Seoul had been retaken by the Americans who promptly re-installed President Syngman Rhee in elaborate ceremonies on September 29th. MacArthur attended the cremonies during which Rhee was officially given back his capitol. Rhee was to keep his dictatorial control over Korea to 1960 with the backing of both the Truman and Eisenhouwer Admittatrations. He repeatedly got re-

251

elected by overwhelming majorities in what were generally considered to be rigged elections, which sometimes included the killing or jailing of opposition leaders, at one time even the arrest of a majority of the National Assembly. When the residents of Seoul rebelled in 1960 and got near to killing Rhee and his corrupt henchmen with their bare hands, the CIA airlifted him to Hawaii just before the crowds broke into the Presidential Blue House. But it was still not the promised democracy for the South Koreans just yet, though we kept on referring to it as a democracy, just as we do today with the similarly mislabeled State of Israel. The unfortunate people of South Korea would continue to suffer under

 successive US supported autocrats and military juntas for nearly 40 more years.

Sptember 29, 1950. Re-Instatement of Rhee . MacArthur at lectern; Rhee to the right. Photo from the Truman Library.

     MacArthur then sent South Korean, ROK, patrols over the 38th Parallel on September 30th; ROK army units entered North Korea on October 1st and 2nd. MacArthur publicly acknowledged the entry of ROK troops into North Korea on October 3rd. The US army followed on the 7th and Americans were engaged in their first battles in North Korea on October 9th. On the same day MacArthur issued a "surrender demand," previously prepared by the State Department as cover for advancing into North Korea, to the North Koreans. The American and ROK advances were swift as the North Koreans retreated, but of course did not surrender.

By the 17th of October General Walker was awarding medals to South Korean officers and attending victory celebrations in Seoul.

"Lt. Gen Walton H. Walker (foreground) C/G US 8/A, congratulates the ROK Army General Staff after presenting the Legion of Merit in ceremonies at Seoul, Korea. . . . ." US Army Photo by SFC Guyette   (KIP)   17 Oct. 1950

Planners in the Defense and State Departments, without consultation with any other country contributing to the U.N. Forces (though such contributions were miniscule and valued only for propaganda purposes so that the American action could be labeled as a "United Nations" matter) and without any input from the Koreans themselves, were devising detailed schemes for military and civil administration, occupation, for all of Korea once the remnants of the North Korean forces had been mopped up. State

Department officials were debating whether there should be War Crimes tribunals in Korea as there had been in Japan and Germany.

Rhee, to the consternation of American diplomats, kept announcing that he was the President of **all** of Korea; sending his police forces into towns newly occupied by ROK and American forces. Rhee's reputation as an authoritarian ruler running a police state was well established by then and he was an unpopular figure at the UN. State Department officials, Embassy Staff, and even MacArthur kept trying to reel him in, explaining that they would lose UN support for their operations north of the 38th parallel if it were known that Rhee's government would be extended into the North. But in fact no one stopped him from sending in his dreaded police agents behind the US and Korean Army as it moved up North Korea.

Even Stalin on October 12th is said to have recommended to Kim Il Sung that he evacuate Korea and retreat with the forces he had left into Manchuria to fight another day (Richard C. Thornton, Odd Man Out).

General Stratemeyer's and General Partridge's diaries at this time disclose that discussions and plans were being formulated for the "post-war" structure of the Fifth Air Force. Politicians in the US were taking positions and how tough to be at the expected coming negotiations for the end of the conflict. Perennial Republican Presidential candidate Harold E. Stassen on September 30th had already warned in a speech that any negotiations "not be used as a pawn in an appeasement deal with the Communist leadership of China or Russia." The US, he said, had won every war, but then had "lost every peace conference."

Commentators in the United States were already debating how the United States would deal with Korea in the approaching post-war. For example, an article in the October 22, 1950 issue of the New York Herald Tribune started with the sentence:

*"The war in Korea **drew to a close** in spectacular fashion **four months after it had begun**. United Nations forces captured the Communist capital, Pyongyang, a city of 700,000 population, on Thursday."* [Emphasis added.]

Similarly, on October 29th the <u>New York Times</u> reported that:

*"The United Nations **clean-up of all Korea** was advanced as Allied forces drove forward in the West and a United States Seventh Division amphibious landing on the east coast threw 27,000 infantrymen into a new attack toward the Manchurian border."* [Emphasis added.]

But there were also American casualties from this victory euphoria. Vito Marcantonio was finally defeated for re-election on November 7th. The <u>New York Times</u> in an extraordinary editorial on October 26th had for the first time in its history limited its recommendations for the New York Congressional Districts just one (there were 45): that of Marcantonio's East Harlem District. Calling his political positions over the years as *"remarkably compatible with the views of Moscow"* it also asked rhetorically:

"What were Mr. Marcantonio's views on our action in Korea? On June 25 North Korean Communists invaded South Korea, on June 27 President Truman announced United States aid to the South Korean people, and on June 28 the United Nations fully supported the United State position. But not Mr. Marcantonio. That night, at a "Hands Off Korea" rally at Madison Square Garden, Mr. Marcantonio called intervention in Korea 'Operation Desperation by Wall Street and the imperialists.'"

The <u>Times</u> had little influence in Marcantonio's primarily working class East Harlem District, but every other newspaper in the city (including the <u>Journal American</u>, <u>Daily Mirror</u>, Post, <u>Daily News</u>, <u>Herald Tribune</u> etc.), issued its own denunciation of Marcantonio, and with a lot more color.

There were even religious celebrations to give thanks to the Almighty for his/her obvious wisdom in supporting the right side.

"Lt. General Walton M. Walker, CG 8th Army; Col. Thomas Marnane, AG 8th Army; Lt. Col Sherry; Col. T.P. Finnegan, FEAF Chaplain; and Father Brian Geraghty, Superior of the Columban Mission followed By Bishop Paul Ro, Bishop of Seoul Diocese, enter the Catholic Cathedral at Seoul to celebrate **a Solemn Pontifical Mass of Thanks for UN Victory in Korea.**" 20 Oct 50   US Army Photo by SFC. A. Guyette   [Emphasis added.]

Even during the first retreat and before the landing at Inchon and the breakout at Pusan, God was expected to help us out.

> *"Victory is possible and probable, as I firmly believe that God marches at our side. . . . Perhaps it is HIS Will and His Way to test us, to try us for even greater things to come. He will not let us down. . . . In our will to win and in Him who can lead us to victory we place our trust.* (Congressman John Walsh, Indiana Dem.. On Floor of US House, July 19, 1950. Congressional Record, p. 10635.)

There was a great party going on in Korea, and the US newspapers were full of the victory celebrations. But the President was not at all happy, as he felt he had not been invited. After all, it was **his** idea in the first place to start this "police action" that had worked out so well. So, over the objections of some in the State Department who feared a dramatic meeting in the Pacific might make the Chinese think a plot to invade China was being hatched, Truman decided to give his own party and to invite General Douglas MacArthur to it. The General was to be a prop for photos suggesting that the President himself was also a war hero. This would help in the off-year elections coming up in a few weeks. On October 11th the New York Times had a headline on page one announcing a sudden decision by the White House: "TRUMAN TO FLY TO SEE M'ARTHUR; KOREAN REDS REFUSE SURRENDER; ALLIED FORCES CAPTURE WONSAN."

The whole story of the consequent Wake Island Conference between Truman and MacArthur is an embarrassment for all involved, and particularly for the institution of the Presidency. As some press reporters commented at the time, Truman was blatantly trying to capitalize on MacArthur's successes before it was all over. But things just did not work out as planned. MacArthur treated the President with obvious disdain from even before the beginning of the Conference; and then gave him the "bum's rush" at Wake. Truman, however, pretended not to notice, so hungry was he for pictures with the popular war hero MacArthur.

According to the "Log of President Truman's Trip to Wake Island" prepared by Lt. Comdr. William M. Rigdon of the USN, the President dispatched on October 9th a message to MacArthur informing him that *he urgently desired to meet with him.*" Since Mac was so busy in the middle of a war, the President offered to meet him in Honolulu, roughly as a half-way point for both of them. However, if the General felt that he could not travel even that far under the conditions of the war, the President suggested that they meet at Wake Island, much closer to Japan where MacArthur was located.

MacArthur, who had not been in the US since 1937, did not respond to the White House but instead the next day sent a message to the Pentagon for Chief of Staff Omar Bradley. In turn Bradley rushed over to the White House and delivered the message.

The General could not spare the time to travel to Honolulu but would meet the President at Wake, an island close to Japan.

Nevertheless the White House was delighted that Mac even agreed to the meeting and quickly issued a press release which resulted in the <u>NY Times</u> headline cited above, typical of those appearing in other US papers. The press release said he was going to meet Mac to *"discuss with him **the final phase** of United Nations action in Korea."* [Emphasis added.] Many skeptics wondered what there was to discuss.

How the White House had envisioned the Conference could be extrapolated from who went with the President on this long trip. Truman had with him a Presidential Party and Staff totaling *26* to fly in two planes. But then they were to be accompanied by a **Press Corps of *38***, flying along with them on a special press plane. Apparently the dominant element for this trip was the Press Corps, which would be sending pictures and stories all over America. At the same time the White House instructed MacArthur's headquarters that the General was **not** to take any of the "MacArthur-friendly" press corps stationed with him in Tokyo to Wake.

"President Harry S. Truman waves his exuberant presidential greeting upon his arrival in Hawaii. The President and his party are enrout to Wake Island to meet General of the Army Douglas MacArthur, Commander-in-Chief, UN Command, and stopped over for a day in Hawaii." US Army (Cordeiro) 13 October 1950

While stopping at Honolulu and visiting Pearl Harbor, Truman's advisors wrote up a proposed agenda for the meeting at Wake. The agenda included having a conference with MacArthur in the morning; then lunch; then a continuation of the conference and finally a dinner before both of them left Wake Island. Truman approved this agenda on the night of the 13th in Pearl Harbor.

Numerous obvious topics were listed for discussion, including the issue of trials for war criminals (an issue that Averill Harriman curiously kept raising -- subsequently blown off by MacArthur) and an emphasis was put on explaining to MacArthur that he should do nothing to provoke the Russians or Chinese from entering the war.

MacArthur's Headquarters across from The Imperial Palace in Tokyo.

At Wake MacArthur did meet the President as he landed. But with what seems a touch of disapproval the Presidential Log noted that Mac and his staff

"were all tie-less in open-throated khaki shirts. . . . [T]here were no military honors or ceremony."

Secluded residence of Douglas MacArthur in Tokyo. (Truman Library.)

261

So much for the American President from the American Emperor of the Far East. Truman would travel round trip on an airplane 54 hours for a total distance of 14,503 miles to meet Mac. For Mac, on the other hand, it was a just a hop and skip from Tokyo to Wake and back. The trip took 11 days for the President. Only hours for the Emperor. The entire period of time Tuman was on Wake from landing to takeoff was five hours and five minutes.

Will the Chinese come in? the President asked the General. Truman and his entourage in Washington had already decided that the Chinese would be insane to take on the mighty Americans. Even the CIA had weighed in with its considered opinion that the Chinese, though capable, would not be foolish enough to take on the Americans, particularly with all the problems they already had at hand.

In any event, Truman was not really interested in what MacArthur's thoughts were at this point, since he had already decided to take all of Korea up to the Manchurian border whether the Chinese came in or not. His Directives to MacArthur had already made that clear. But he and his people wanted to get MacArthur on record, just in case. As it turned out, The Truman Administration was able to make hay with these alleged comments during the MacArthur dismissal hearings the following year.

"What are the chances for Chinese or Soviet interference?" asked the President according to the transcript provided by General Bradley.

"Very little," responded MacArthur. *"The Chinese had 300,000 men in Manchuria. Of these probably not more than 100/125,000 are distributed along the Yalu River. Only 50/60,000 could be gotten across the Yalu River. They have no Air Force. Now that we have bases for our Air Force in Korea, **if the Chinese tried to get down to Pyongyang there would be the greatest slaughter.**"* [Emphasis added.]

As a matter of fact in a few days and seemingly unobserved the Chinese would begin moving up to 300,000 soldiers across the Yalu and indeed did try, and succeeded, *"to get down to Pyongyang."* The Chinese move, if detected by any of MacArthur's forces, was either discounted or simply not believed by the Commander and his aides in Tokyo. Perhaps it was arrogance, the same attitude shared by Truman and the policymakers in D.C. But later on Truman and his people were quick to blame MacArthur for the disastrous encounter with the Chinese troops.

However, it seems that we have to be somewhat cautious about Chief of Staff General Bradley's transcript of the Conference at Wake, since the Administration had made sure that only its own members would take notes at the meeting. Indeed when one of MacArthur's aides started to take notes, he was abruptly told that no notes were to be taken – and he stopped. But notes were taken. The transcript that has become the historic basis for what was said at Wake was compiled by General Bradley from notes taken only by the visitors from Washington.

Copies of this Top Secret transcript were later given to the Congressional Committee that was investigating the removal of MacArthur by Truman. This degree of control by DC seems to be in line with MacArthur's having been instructed not to take any of his press people with him to Wake. The story from Wake was to be the President's story. In return, MacArthur, utilizing only the passive resistance of a subordinate, did what he could to diminish the President.

The General in his Memoirs had a significantly different memory from Bradley's transcript of what he had said in response to the question of whether the Chinese would intervene. According to his recollection he responded to the President's question by first commenting that he was not in a position to determine what the Chinese and Soviet leaders in Peiping and Moscow would do, that it was up to the experts in the State Department and the CIA to analyze that question. He noted, however, that he had seen reports wherein those experts stated that in their opinion the Chinese would not be foolish enough to intervene.

However MacArthur did say, and this agreed with the Bradley transcript, that if the Chinese were foolish enough to come in, he would slaughter them. But MacArthur further explained in his <u>Memoirs</u> that his confidence was based on his ability to attack the Chinese in the most effective way, namely, those in the field in Korea but also at their bases in Manchuria. This he was not allowed to do.

Truman asked what there was left for the fighting in Korea. MacArthur said that there were about 100,000 North Koreans troops left and that *"it goes against my grain to have to destroy them. They are only fighting to save face. Orientals prefer to die rather than to lose face."* Nevertheless he expected the fighting to end by Thanksgiving and that he could return all the troops by Christmas.

He agreed to accept some more contributions of troops from our allies, even though they were worthless militarily, in order to keep a UN "flavor" on their operation. The participants then discussed the political advantage of making the US campaign look as much as possible as a UN effort, the "UN flavor."

Giving the US intervention a "UN flavor" seemed as important to MacArthur as it was to Truman. But there was some tension on this objective between Washington and the far distant Tokyo. The policymakers in Washington understood, though reluctantly, that they had to pay a certain price to secure this UN flavor; while the Commander in Tokyo seemed less aware of it.

The US Delegates to the UN and our embassy staffs across the world would be reminded daily that while they could count on the votes of most members of the UN, there were limits. One of those limits was represented by Sigmund Rhee. The US was

264

locked into him as its agent but his reputation as a despot running a brutal police state was well known by everyone else. Therefore the question of how to occupy North Korea and how much authority to give to Sigmund Rhee in that occupation was one of the issues that forced a focus on that tension between Tokyo and DC. The two sides were clumsy, or perhaps dishonest, in how they tried to ease their differences.

In order to get any sponsors or even votes for the October 7th UN Resolution which would clearly authorize going beyond the 38th Parallel and occupy North Korea, the State Department had to be vague about who had authority in North Korea and how elections were to be conducted. The British Delegate had warned the State Department that any attempt to suggest that Rhee would head a unified Korean government would be fatal to the Resolution. The eight sponsors, headed by Great Britain, that the US Delegation was ultimately able to obtain to front the Resolution would not touch Rhee with a ten foot pole.

So the ROK in the Resolution was recognized only as having authority in the South, and elections were to be held in the whole country to authorize a new unified government. The October 7th General Assembly Resolution and the subsequent resolutions of the UN Commission on Korea that had been created did not say anything about extending Rhee's control, and in fact stated that *the existing local officials in North Korea were to be respected and included in any plans for unification.* Exactly how the elections were to be conducted was purposely left vague, though they were to take place in the whole of Korea.

Rhee immediately and vehemently objected to the Resolution. In public he simply defied the UN and had his police forces, with MacArthur's approval, follow in the wake of the UN troops as they moved into North Korea. The local North Korean officials and their supporters who were supposed to be consulted about the unification of Korea simply disappeared in one way or another.

At the Wake Conference MacArthur expressed his own exasperation with the UN Resolution. When he read it he said he was "shaking in his boots" at the fear that it would disturb Rhee so much that it would turn him against the UN. The idea of treating North Korean officials the same as our allies who were fighting and dying with us was ridiculous, he said. His own idea of occupation, which of course as the Commander of UN Forces taking over this land by force of arms was perhaps the only one that really mattered, was summed up by him when he observed:

> *"North Korea will be under military* [that is, MacArthur's] *control. The U.N. resolution calls for the maintenance of local governments wherever possible. This will not be possible. We expect them to either **flee or be killed**. Local government will be maintained by* [his] *appointing local officials recommended by ROK officials."* [Emphasis added.]

It is not clear whether he meant that if the North Korean officials did not flee he would have them killed, or more likely, send in the ROK and Rhee's police, which would amount to the same sentence of execution for those officials. Without question then, even by Bradley's transcript, Macarthur announced at Wake that he would run North Korea together with Rhee. The President did not object.

No one at the Conference had the courage to tell MacArthur that the UN Resolution introduced by the UK and seven other countries which he so disdained had in fact been largely drafted by Acheson, Rusk and their aides with the President's approval.

Notwithstanding the reasons for the nuanced UN Resolution, everybody seemed in agreement that it would be ignored on the ground in Korea. It was a settled matter between Truman and MacArthur that the Rhee government should be fully supported and would be extended into the areas of North Korea being occupied by MacArthur's troops.

266

Dean Rusk, in attendance for Acheson, was in a better position than most to be fully aware of Rhee's autocratic and murderous behavior as he received reports from the embassy in Korea all the time. On Wake Island just before the meeting between MacArthur and the President, Ambassador Muccio had told Rusk that he had been thinking about a replacement for Rhee.

> *"He* [Muccio] *told me of his repeated efforts to keep Rhee moving in the right direction* [to avoid a confrontation with US allies at the UN], *that he had made repeated and strong representations to him. He said that he had **thought a great deal about an alternative to Rhee** but had thus far not been able to think of anyone who could do the job.* "(Rusk Memo, FRUS, 7:947. Emphasis added.)

It seemed everyone at State knew that Rhee as a leader was seriously flawed and they very much would have liked to replace him. However Rusk now found himself in the company of two ardent Rhee supporters, no less than the President of the US and the greatest General in US history. Would he have the courage to tell the Emperors that they had no clothes? Hardly. The most which the obsequious Rusk could get himself to do was to point out, somewhat meekly, that Rhee's Government was very unpopular. But even this he watered down by saying that this reputation was only according to vicious "propaganda" being spread about in the UN. Truman's immediate response was typical Truman:

> *"We must make it plain that we are supporting the Rhee Government and propaganda can '**go to hell**' "*. [Emphasis added.]

"Give them hell" Harry was at it again.

We have seen earlier how the US Occupation forces had made use of the refugees from the North in transforming the refugee youth groups into armed shock troops. Now at the

Conference this accomplishment was confirmed by Ambassador Muccio. He complimented the American mission as having *"done a great job training the young Koreans. They have pushed aside the old Chinese and Japanese trained Koreans. There is no hope in the old Koreans, but in the young ones there is great hope."*

On his way back to D.C. Truman gave a speech in San Francisco giving an account to the nation of his meeting with MacArthur. It was a particularly bellicose speech, demonizing the Soviets in the most violent terms and pitching his expensive containment program, though he also managed to use the word "peace" a total of 22 times. All in all it was a highly successful trip. The President had gotten himself to the head of the victory train and bathed in the company of America's greatest military hero. He even flaunted his Presidential prerogative to award MacArthur yet another medal.

President Truman, General MacArthur and Ambassador Muccio at Wake. Photos from the Truman Library.

CHAPTER XV

"BURN IT IF YOU SO DESIRE ."

With everyone celebrating the end of the conflict, Stratemeyer at this point, October 17, 1950, decided to engage in some one-upmanship with his competitors in the Army and the Navy. With his bombers and fighters no longer so urgently needed or just with nothing to do, it seems that he tried to come up with something spectacular for the FEAF to show off at the end of the war.

With no apparent military necessity at that time and while the US was on the verge of taking over all of Korea, he inexplicably recommended to MacArthur that not only should they totally burn down the city of Sinuiju on the Manchurian border but also to do so **without warning** to the population, a particularly high level of punishment. This city of 180,000 people was in the extreme north, on the Yalu border with China, a sister city of the Chinese city of Antung just across the river.

> *"It is requested that I be authorized to conduct an air attack on the city of Sinuiju with all available air means at the earliest practicable date on which the attack can be launched under visual flying conditions. The types of attack recommended are listed in order of priority, as follows: (a)* ***An attack over the widest area of the city, without warning, by burning and high explosives*** *. . . "*

General Stratemeyer had certainly evolved during the last four months. Recall how when Rosie O'Donnell was first assigned to his command Stratemeyer had been concerned about O'Donnell flamboyant reputation and his history of burning down towns and cities in Japan at the end of WWII. He therefore instructed O'Donnell that he was not even to bomb an urban center without

270

his prior approval. But now some months later Stratemeyer is asking his boss to annihilate tens of thousands of civilians just to send a message.

"Burning" of course meant napalm and other incendiaries. Stratemeyer in his memo to MacArthur of October 17th tried to give various reasons for this otherwise incomprehensible slaughter. His main reason was that he was concerned that it was the last city the retreating North Korean army would be going through and it might provide a foothold in Korea for the North Korean government to continue to claim some legitimacy.

> *"This city, with considerable industrial activity and an estimated population of over 60,000* [actually more like 180,000] *is a provincial capital and has the capability of becoming the capital of North Korea when Pyongyang is evacuated."*

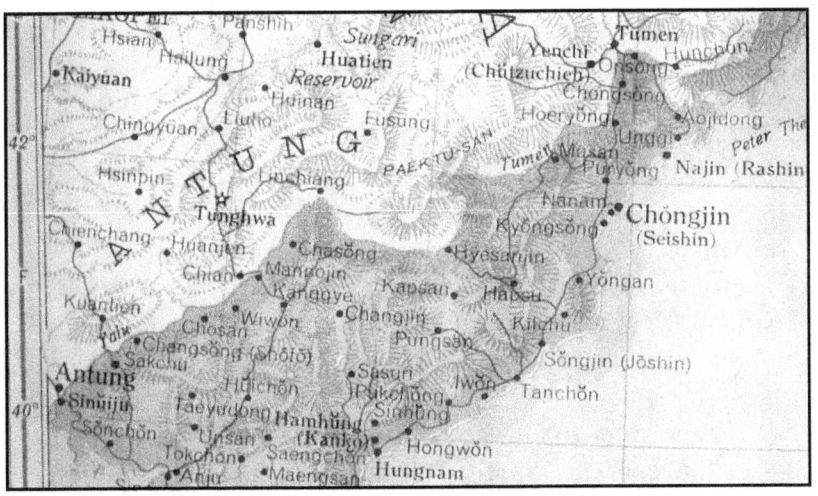

He also thought *"that **the psychological effect of a mass attack will be salutary to Chinese Communist observers across the river in Antung.**"*

Another "lesson" to the Reds – consume tens of thousands of men, women and children in a firestorm, just to show China and Russia how tough we could be. A monumental flaw in thinking, though shared with others in the military and the government. With all our firepower, let's give the Reds something to worry about. Four months earlier on the floor of the House of Representatives, Congressman Vito Marcantonio had warned that this whole frame of mind was wrong and would only backfire:

> "Remember one thing: A bomb was dropped on Hiroshima. It had terrible consequences, but it did not frighten the people of China and it did not frighten the people of Korea. For again, these people despite the terror of the atom bomb have refused to abandon their efforts for national liberation. They will no more abandon this objective that the American people did during the Revolution. . . ."

But as it turns out General Stratemeyer's big plans were put on hold, at least for the time being. Stratemeyer, Wednesday, 18 October 1950:

> "GHQ [MacArthur's Headquarters] returned my memorandum of yesterday, subject: Destruction of Sinuiju . . .: 'The general policy enunciated from Washington negates such an attack unless the military situation clearly requires it. Under present circumstances this is not the case'".

Were the story to end here, I think we would all say, "Thank God! There was somebody around with a little common sense." But, unfortunately, the story does not end here.

As of October 18, 1950, after Stratemeyer had initially asked for permission to start burning down cities and towns as "lessons" to the Reds, neither Stratemeyer nor MacArthur was aware that the Chinese had just begun heavy infiltration into Korea across the Yalu and indeed through the very city of Sinuiju. While they were debating "flaming it" as an example to the Reds, the Reds were moving through it. The Chinese, beginning on October 19th, according to Mao's letter to Stalin (Richard C. Thornton, <u>Odd Man Out</u>), moved skillfully by night and under heavy camouflage so that by the time of the eventual incendiary attack on Sinuiju on November 8th there were already 260,000 to 300,000 Chinese soldiers over the Yalu and in Korea. The first time that MacArthur admitted that the Chinese were taking a serious interest in Korea was on October 25th when Chinese troops decimated a ROK battalion near the Yalu. But when the Chinese as quickly disappeared, MacArthur and his intelligence chief, General Willoughby, discounted them merely as "volunteers" (Y'Blood Notes to Stratemeyer's November 3, 1950 Diary Entry).

Stratemeyer continued to press his case for the burning of Sinuiju. Stratemeyer's and his subordinate Partridge's diaries then indicate that they met personally a number of times in the next couple of weeks but neither specify why. One such meeting was on October 25th when they had a conference at Stratemeyer's office in Tokyo but Stratemeyer does not give the details of their discussion. But on November 3rd upon reaching his office that morning Stratemeyer fortuitously found a radio message on his desk from Partridge. Now General Partridge, who was the man on the ground in Korea, was requesting *"clearance to burn Sinuiju"* because there was *"heavy antiaircraft fire from city."* Stratemeyer conveniently was now able to comply with Washington's restriction; he had his *"military necessity"* reason for burning down Sinuiju straight from his operational man.

He immediately took this up again with MacArthur later that morning of the 3rd. But to Stratemeyer's frustration, MacArthur again said no. However, this time the reason given by MacArthur for the denial was entirely different. The Chief told Stratemeyer that he was thinking about using the town himself when they got there. They were not far from China's border now. MacArthur therefore *"did not want to burn it at this time. His*

273

intentions are to push the 24th Division to the Yalu River, taking Sinuiju. . . ."

However, MacArthur would not let his airmen feel unwanted. "*He* [MacArthur] *stated that he realized that there were not many targets left for the '29's but he wanted to get them back to business.*" Therefor MacArthur, during the same morning meeting on November 3rd, did agree to let Stratemeyer show off his pyrotechnics on some other towns. Stratemeyer suggested to MacArthur

> "*that* **as a lesson** *we could burn some other towns in North Korea and I indicated* **the town of Kanggye** *which* **I believe** *is occupied by enemy troops and is a communications center – both rail and road. He said,* '**Burn it if you so desire**,' *and then said, 'Not only that, Strat,* **but burn and destroy as a lesson any other of those towns that you consider of military value** *to the enemy.*"

Now the civilian populations of entire towns along the Chinese border could be designated as legitimate targets, provided Stratemeyer could fine some plausible reason to consider them to be "*of military value to the enemy,*" an easy enough hurdle, especially for a willing enough listener as MacArthur. No lieutenant could have asked for a more generous delegation of power. So even without Sinuiju, Stratemeyer was now satisfied. He again had targets for his idle planes -- whole cities and towns which he himself, with his own magic wand, could turn into legitimate "military targets" and so burn them down.

These were to be "lessons," presumably to the Chinese and Russians. It was as if we were saying: "If we are willing to cremate tens and hundreds of thousands of Koreans for no reason other than where they are living, just imagine what we would do to you if you gave us any reason." Did the fact that these Koreans lived in North Korean towns make them any more suitable candidates for

274

incineration? What was the difference between North and South Koreans? Ambassador Muccio did not think there was any.

> *"Koreans are Koreans. There is no basic difference between them. 80% of them are farmer, anyway. There is no basic schism between North and South Koreans except for a few politicos and intellectuals."*

General MacArthur agreed with that assessment:

> *"I believe there is no real split* [between North and South Koreans], *but their attitude is due only to the banner that flies over them. There is no difference in ideology and there are no North and South Korean blocs."* (Both quotes are from General Bradley's compilation of notes at the Wake Conference, October 15, 1950.)

It appears that the only sin committed by the tens of thousands of people living in these villages, towns and cities that were now OK to incinerate, was the fact that they lived close enough to the borders so that the Chinese and Russians could actually watch them go up in flames. Without question this decision to *"burn them if you so desire"* was an act of terror, either by Webster's definition, US Statutes or international treaties.

But this seemingly unnecessary burning down of cities now that the war had just about ended, as "lessons" being taught to the Chinese, only backfired, as Vito Marcantonio had predicted. The bombing only further convinced the Chinese that they had made the right decision to move into Korea. The Chinese passion to protect their homeland was not going to be smothered by bombs or the threats of bombs, even atomic bombs. Now American troops were actually at their borders.

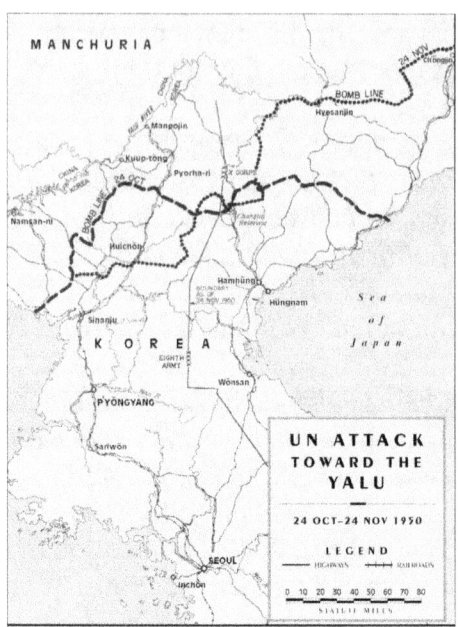

(Y'Blood, Stratemeyer)

The Chinese had utterly no trust in American assurances that they did not intend to cross the Yalu into China proper. The US Air Force's unrelenting and seemingly senseless bombing raids on Korea, plus the previous American policy reversals on having no interest in Korea or then again the false assurances about stopping at the 38th Parallel, convinced the Chinese that the Americans intended to reignite the Chinese civil war and invade China proper.

As if to highlight the seemingly capricious nature of this American campaign of annihilation, later that same day on November 3rd MacArthur abruptly changed his mind with respect to the city of Sinuiju itself. Even though he had just hours before told Stratemeyer that he wanted to preserve Sinuiju for his own use once they occupied it, he now gave the OK also to burn it to the ground.

"General Hickey [at that time MacArthur's Chief of Staff] *called at about 1900 hours and stated that General*

276

*MacArthur had approved the Partridge wire to burn Sinuiju by the Fifth Air Force. Hickey asked that I drop in tomorrow morning and **discuss other targets** with him as the Boss had asked that this be done."*

Stratemeyer does not give any explanation of why the Boss had made this 180 degree turn in a period of several hours. I can only speculate as to why MacArthur changed his mind during those hours. But there had been significant and ominous incidents on the ground between October 17th and November 3[rd,] though MacArthur was not yet ready to acknowledge what seemed to be happening.

When the Generals talked about "burning" a city or town, they were speaking literally. They would "*blow up*" something by destroying it with general purpose or high explosive bombs. But they would "*burn*" down a place with incendiary bombs. The primary incendiary cluster bomb used by the US in burning down the Japanese cities at the end of World War II was the M-69. "The M-69 was a simple weapon, shaped like a long tin can and weighing just 2.3 kg (6.2 lb). Since dropping quantities of individual bombs from high altitude would be wildly inaccurate – it was designed to be incorporated into an 'aimable cluster,' a type of cluster bomb that contained 38 of the M-69 firebombs" (Bombs Weapons Rockets Aircraft Ordnance, July 15, 2003 <http://www.danhistory.com/ww2/bombs.shtml>). The cluster bomb would break apart at about 2,000 ft altitude and scatter the thin-skinned incendiary containers which would rupture on impact and ignite the disbursing highly combustible chemicals (e.g., magnesium, phosphorus or petroleum jelly). The goal was to create a firestorm which would not only destroy property and people with flames at high temperatures but also would asphyxiate people by the resulting elimination of oxygen from the atmosphere.

This was not a pretty weapon. It obviously was by its nature "indiscriminate" in its destruction. The horrible purpose of using incendiaries on an entire defenseless city, to burn and suffocate civilians, could not be disguised. Naturally, therefore, Stratemeyer would be worried about the USAF's image when he later heard that there would be witnesses to this mission.

General Stratemeyer, 4 November 1950:

> *"I was a bit concerned this morning when I learned that ten (10) correspondents were accompanying the B-29's on their attack (burn) on Kanggye. . . . My statement will be generally, as follows: That wherever we find hostile troops and equipment that are being utilized to kill UN troops, we intend to use every means and weapon at our disposal to destroy them, that facility, or town. This will be the answer to the use of the incendiary-cluster type of bomb."*

Stratemeyer need not have worried. The exponential jump from incinerating troops and equipment to incinerating entire towns and cities, designating them as "military targets," was readily accepted by the American public as a regrettable but necessary event of war. There was no adverse reaction to his firebombing of Kanggye. Among other reasons, by coincidence his attack coincided with the first news accounts of serious Chinese involvement in Korea.

> Stratemeyer, Sunday, 5 November 1950:
> *"Redline Vandenberg from Stratemeyer. FEAF Bomber Command this afternoon bombed **the military supply center of Kanggye** with about 170 tons of incendiary bombs with flash report indicating all bombing done is usually with excellent results. Entire city of Kanggye was virtual arsenal and tremendously important communications center, hence decision to employ incendiary."*

There is no record that anyone laughed when the USAF called an entire city of 120,000 people a "military supply center."

278

Nor was the inconsistency between Stratemeyer's "belief" of two days earlier that the town contained troops with his belief now that it was an arsenal noted by anyone. A military necessity was a military necessity, even if you forgot which one it was. Stratemeyer's public relations effort worked. Or the American public just did not care about how many Korean civilians were needlessly killed.

The New York Times must have had a reporter among the correspondents Stratemeyer had mentioned who accompanied the B-29's. But the Times report on the raid only mentions it as one of an assortment of military activities that day and in fact gave it a Stratemeyer "spin:"

> *"The largest United Nations effort in the air* [today] *was made in a heavy attack on* **Kanggye** *by Superforts of the Far East Air Forces Bomber Command yesterday afternoon. Twenty B-29's plastered the Kanggye area with* **incendiary** *bombs. Observers said they saw large fires and columns of smoke rising from the* **neighborhood of the city**.

> *"Reconnaissance indicated,* **according to headquarters**, *that the* **whole area was being used as a supply base** *from which supplies and arms moved to Chinese divisions in the west coast area. Somewhere in the area the Communist High Command is believed to have its headquarters for the direction of the entire Korean campaign."*
> [Emphasis added.]

This raid on Kanggye produced very little publicity even though it had correspondents riding with the bombers, to the comfort of the nervous Stratemeyer. But the incendiary raid on the larger city of Sinuiju three days later received more attention in the Western press. Perhaps because it was located just across the Yalu River from China. Still, what would have been shocking news of a

279

doomsday incendiary attack on such a large population had to share the headlines with some other alarming news.

Suddenly, according to MacArthur, there were now approximately 70,000 Chinese soldiers in Korea. It was a new war, he declared. There were now "alien" forces who treacherously and without warning had attacked the UN forces. The cat was out of the bag. He no longer was able to hide the fact that he had provoked the Chinese into the war. MacArthur did not mention that only days before he had reported a total enemy force of about 20,000 Chinese soldiers. In fact, and only painfully learned just three weeks later, there were about 300,000 Chinese soldiers in Korea by this time. Nevertheless, because there had been no critical public reaction to his incendiary attacks on Kanggye and Sinuiju, Stratemeyer's diary entry and public statements thereafter suggest less anxiety about public reaction to the burning down of a city and its population. All is well that ends well.

Stratemeyer, Wednesday, 8 November 1950:

*"Reports on the bomb raid on the bridges and town of Sinuiju were made to me by General O'Donnell which I transmitted to General Hickey for General MacArthur. . . . The seventy (70) B-29's in squadron formations loaded with **thirty-two (32) incendiary cluster bombs; all results – excellent,** with first squadron receiving intense and inaccurate flak and all the remaining squadrons receiving meager and inaccurate flak.*

*"Each incendiary cluster is made up of 38 individual fire bombs; consequently, there were (32 x 38 x 70) 85, 120 fire bombs on Sinuiju. **General O'Donnell indicates that the town was gone.***

280

"There were no hostile fighter interception of our bombers. . .

"I reported to General Hickey that the missions for tomorrow would be with incendiary bombs, maximum effort of sixteen (16) B-29's would be over the towns of Sakchu and Puckchin. . . ."

There is no indication in the diary entries, the Official Releases or the related newspaper articles that the populations of Kanggye, Sinuiju, Sakchu or Puckchin were given any prior warnings so they could evacuate. As noted above, however, escape to shelters or indoors would have been fruitless in the face of an napalm attack as either the fire, carbon monoxide or the elimination of oxygen would have been fatal to those in the shelters.

The Official Release (627) described the target as *"the key communications and supply center of Sinuiju"* and detailed the various important military targets in the two and one-half square mile city.

Along the river front are many warehouses and factories. . . . an eleven track marshaling yard complete with roundhouses, locomotive shed, and maintenance shops. There is another five-line marshalling yard along the northeast boundary of the city. All were targets on today's attack.

Presumably the nature of the purely military targets in this city and the fact that they were at opposite ends of the city would justify to the public why it was necessary to destroy the **whole** city. An accompanying Summary of the air strike explained that the bomb runs were purposely aimed *"away from hospital area. All targets were of a military nature, with the principal objective being to eliminate Sinuiju as a future stronghold for supplies and communications needed by the Communists. . . ."*

There were **300 planes** in total involved in the strike on *Sinuiju* and over **630 tons of bombs** were dropped. Ten of Maj. Gen. Emmett O'Donnell's B-29's in the "air armada" dropped 1,000 pound bombs on two bridges while the other **69 B-29's "rained 85,000 incendiary bombs** *on the two and a half square miles of the built-up area on the southeast bank of the Yalu River,"* or, in plain language, on the City proper itself, as the City consisted primarily of that two and a half square mile of "built-up area" – residences, schools, temples, stores. One notes the ominous mention of an opening attack:

> *"Maj. Gen. Earle E. Partridge's Fifth Air Force F-80 jets and F-51 fighters raked the area prior to the attack with machine guns, rockets and napalm."*

It will be recalled that one of the methods of trapping the civilian population into self-made tombs is to chase them into shelters with preliminary attacks of regular explosive bombs and strafing. Then the firestorms created by the subsequent incendiary bombs would consume the oxygen in the shelters and the men, women and children in the shelters, however deep and however hidden, were dead meat.

The Press stories published on the 9th of November could have been written by Stratemeyer's public relations officer as they followed the Party Line. There was no discernible objection to this horrific form of warfare.

The first sentence of the New York <u>Daily News</u> read:

> *"U.S. Superforts smashed the Chinese Communists' main border base in northwest Korea Wednesday with a massive attack of fire and demolition bombs."*

The headline on page one of the <u>New York Herald Tribune</u> announced: *"MAIN CHINESE BASE IN KOREA RAZED BY RAID."* The <u>Herald</u> article helpfully pointed out that:

282

> *"Sinuiju, a city of over 100,000 . . . is on the main west coast highway in North Korea, leading to the industrial center of Mukden in Communist China. It has been the chief base through which Chinese Communist convoys have been passing."*

Notwithstanding the Official Release and the Summary's attempt to avoid saying it in so many words, the reporter for the <u>Herald Tribune</u> had no hesitancy in asserting that the *"B-29 Superfortresses and B-26 bombers set out to flatten the town with explosives."*

Describing Sinuiju as a *"stronghold for supplies and communications to Chinese communist troops fighting in Korea,"* the <u>Chicago Tribune</u> quoted an Air Force spokesman as saying that early damage reports indicated *"the town of 100,000 population was 'pretty well taken care of.'"* The headline in the <u>Washington Post</u> was *"80 B-29'S DESTROY 90 PERCENT OF CITY ON MANCHURIAN BORDER."* The <u>Post</u> reporter related that

> *"a jet pilot who watched the B-29s smash the city said that smoke pillars rose more than 50,000 feet after the attack and the entire city 'looked like it was on fire.'"*

The <u>Times</u> of London started its account of the attack by explaining that Sinuiju was *"the chief ferrying point through which Chinese Communist troops are brought from Manchuria into Korea. . . ."*

Fortune seemed to have been smiling on General Stratemeyer, or at least on history's image of the USAF. When he first sent his memo to MacArthur on October 17th entitled **"Destruction of Sinuiju"** and suggested the burning of the city, none of the five reasons he gave even mentioned that it was serving as a portal for Chinese troops and supplies, though he did think *"that the psychological effect of a mass attack will be salutary to Chinese Communist observers across the river in*

283

Antung." The Chinese began their movement in Korea on October 19th (Thornton), after finally giving up all hope that the Americans would stop their advance. At the time he wrote his memo General Stratemeyer had no idea that the Chinese Communists would be observing the annihilation of Sinuiju from the *same* side of the river as he was. So the main reason justifying the attack to the public *after* it actually occurred was not even part of Stratemeyer's original thinking.

As mentioned earlier, on November 3rd Stratemeyer's proposal to burn Sinuiju was at first denied by MacArthur because he was planning to use that town upon capturing it. Then MacArthur changed his mind that afternoon for reasons we do not know and gave the OK to burn Sinuiju. However, MacArthur had already approved an otherwise scorched earth policy.

> **"Strat,"** he had told the General, **"burn and destroy as a lesson any other of those towns that you consider of military value to the enemy."**

He had blessed the concept that an entire town or city in itself could now be "a "military target" justifying the killing of the entire population.

The next day Stratemeyer, as instructed, met with MacArthur's Chief of Staff, General Hickey, to *"discuss other targets."* He found the conference *"most satisfactory."* General Hickey had

> *"confirmed the instructions that he had given me the night before that General MacArthur wanted an all-out air effort against communications and facilities with every weapon available to stop and destroy the enemy in North Korea.* ***He reiterated the burning of towns and emphasized the importance of taking out Sinuiju.****"*
> [Emphasis added.]

MacArthur on November 3rd had approved "as a lesson" the burning of Kanggye and Sinuiju to the ground, both recommendations of Stratemeyer. Then he escalated that "lesson" to include "other towns," presumably as recommended from time to time by Stratemeyer who would make the decision that the town could be "of military value to the enemy." Even these extreme measures of destruction appear to have something of a rational veneer to it.

But then just two days later, with no apparent change in any circumstances, MacArthur geometrically escalated the parameters for wholesale destruction. He gave the following instructions to Stratemeyer:

"Every installation, facility, and village in North Korea now becomes a military and tactical target."

The Emperor-like CINCFE, by a simple nod of his head, had christened **everything** in North Korea as "military." Stratemeyer now didn't have to waste a second in dreaming up a specific reason. Exceptions were still being made for the major hydro-electric plants on the Manchurian border and the City of Rashin bordering Russia, in this minor way reflecting Washington's fear of provoking Russia into the conflict. Stratemeyer noted: *"General MacArthur reiterated his scorched earth policy to burn and destroy."*

General Stratemeyer immediately called his commanding Generals together and discussed with them MacArthur's new scorched earth program. His adrenalin was running at a high level.

*In discussing bridge crossings, one example that was shown to me indicated that **POW camp sites (reported)**, hospitals and prisons **would be vulnerable** to incendiary attack. **Whether vulnerable or not, our target was to take out** lines of communications and towns."*

So Stratemeyer was not only **with** the Program, but was with it **enthusiastically**. Everybody gets flamed, even American POW's if necessary!

285

That same day, November 5th, Stratemeyer composed and had MacArthur approve his formal orders "**Re the destruction of North Korea**" to Generals Partridge and O'Donnell. The orders read in part:

> *Except for Rashin, the Suiho Dam and other electric power plants in North Korea,* **to destroy every** *means of communications and every installation, factory,* **city and village.** *Under present circumstances all such have marked military potential and can only be regarded as military installations.*[The underlined sentence was added by MacArthur to Stratemeyer's draft order and Stratemeyer in his Diary underlined it [Y'Blood].] *This destruction is to start at the Korean-Manchurian border and progress south. . . . FEAF Bomber Command* [O'Donnell's B-29's] *will destroy the cities and large towns. Aircraft under Fifth Air Force control* [fighters, fighter-bombers and the lighter B-26's] *will destroy all other targets* **including all buildings capable of affording shelter.**

Desperation and panic at the highest levels had set in. These orders were to destroy **"all buildings capable of affording shelter."** It was now approaching winter in North Korea, with temperatures going to sub-freezing. If every building "affording shelter" were to be destroyed, how were the 10,000,000 people of North Korea going to survive? Did the decision of their leaders to unify their country justify another nation, 7,000 miles away, to come in and condemn them all to go on a death march in the winter storms, assuming they could first escape their burning homes?

Partridge and O'Donnell in the next two months dutifully unloaded tons and tons of general purpose bombs, napalm and other incendiary bombs on everything in North Korea.

Stratemeyer, Tuesday, 14 November 1950:

> *Went again to see MacArthur . . . . I told him that **I would continue to wash out all cities** and that 15 Nov we were concentrating our entire bomber effort on HOERYONG.*

Cities great and villages small were burned to the ground. O'Donnell knew what he was talking about when next June he testified before that Congressional Committee:

> *"I would say that the entire, almost the entire Korean Peninsula, is just a terrible mess. Everything is destroyed. **There is nothing standing worthy of the name.**"*

But surely Rosie was exaggerating.

Here is a Community Billboard for a town no longer in existence. But note in the background, there IS a building left standing, and in front of it there also appears to be the remnants of a church.

Yet the MacArthur "scorched earth" program did not work. The lesson to the Chinese Communists, who had been battling the Japanese for decades and at the same time engaged in a civil war with reactionaries, was not what MacArthur and Stratemeyer had intended. No one cried "Uncle." The Chinese resolve to defend their homeland was only strengthened. The Chinese soldiers, on foot and essentially armed only with their rifles, now drove the heavily armed Americans and South Koreans from their border.

CHAPTER XVI

LIBERATING KOREA FROM THE LIBERATING AMERICANS

The Chinese had been warning since the beginning of the conflict, in explicit and plain language, publicly and through diplomatic channels, that they would not tolerate an American Army on their border, no matter what explanations the Americans were now giving for their march up the peninsula. On August 28th Chinese Premier Chou En-lai in letters to the UN protested the repeated strafing by US and British planes of an airfield and rail yards in Manchuria on the Chinese side of the Yalu, killing three civilians and wounding at least 20 people. Chou in his note called the action criminal and one which "the Chinese people can by no means tolerate."

The charges were immediately denied by the UN Command in Tokyo, saying that their planes had not even flown over Manchuria. Newspapers gave prominent position to the Chinese protests. Commentators noted that already by late August the Chinese had massed at least 200,000 troops along the border in Manchuria and speculated as to what the Chinese would do. (See articles in New York Times on August 29, 1950.)

As a matter of fact the charges by Chou were true, but the pilots involved apparently had not reported what they had done, or at least their reports had not been forwarded by O'Donnell to Stratemeyer. Stratemeyer was surprised that he had to learn of the strafing from newspaper accounts and asked for an investigation. It was determined that we had indeed strafed an airport and rail yards in Manchuria. When MacArthur was told about his, he nonchalantly commented that it must have been a pretty poor pilot to have made such a mistake. He instructed Stratemeyer to conduct such disciplinary measures as he thought necessary, but to keep it

290

all within the Air Force and not to send any copies on the issue to MacArthur's Command. Obviously, no one was that worried about the Chinese. On getting the corrected report from Tokyo, our US ambassador to the UN then admitted that there may have been an unintentional violation of the Manchurian border. He disingenuously suggested that the US would pay compensation if the Chinese would allow a UN team into Manchuria to investigate the details. An offer, of course, that was not picked up.

This scenario was repeated again and again, till the Chinese gave up making specific complaints, but instead began seriously readying their forces for an expected American invasion. US newspapers speculated on both sides of the question of whether the Chinese would intervene. Indeed Henry Lieberman, a <u>New York Times</u> reporter based in the Far East did so himself in the same article . He called the Chinese buildup in Manchuria as well as Chou's repeated charges as threats which *"represent a propaganda offensive designed to further the Communist political aims already on the record rather than the augury of immediate Chinese Communist military action in Korea."* But then at the end of his article he comments: *"It is highly doubtful that the Chinese Communists will remain immobile on the Manchurian side of the Yalu River should the United Nations troops press on beyond the [38th] Parallel."* (September 3, 1950, <u>New York Times</u>.)

Embassy officials around the world reported back to the State Department their interpretations of Chinese intentions. Some were deeply worried that if the US crossed the 38th Parallel that it would provoke the Chinese to enter the war. One such was the more observant and intelligent State Department official, Livingston Merchant, then the Deputy Assistant Security of State for Far Eastern Affairs. On October 3rd Merchant wrote an urgent Secret Memo to his boss, Dean Rusk, expressing his belief that the reports of Chinese movement of troops should be taken *"with extreme seriousness and not be discounted as a bluff."* He asked that these reports be sent to MacArthur and the President. But even Merchant in the same memo noted that most of his colleagues at a

meeting on the subject "were inclined to regard it as a bluff."
Others dismissed the possibility of intervention because the
Chinese Communists had their hands full with battling 200,00 or
more Nationalist guerillas still in China proper. The Communists
had not yet consolidated their power in China and were just
beginning the rebuilding of a country devastated by decades of
warfare and the corrupt and inept Administration of Chiang.

US policy makers in DC were debating from July whether
to go beyond the 38th Parralel; whether the existing UN Resolution
permitted that and whether doing so would bring in the Chinese.
Ultimately the Americans and the British decided that crossing the
38th would not bring in the Chinese. On September 9th the National
Security Council sent NSC 81 to the President setting forth US
policy on the Korean War at that point. While it admitted the
possibility of Chinese or Soviet intervention, the Council
concluded that such was not probable. It concluded that MacArthur
should be authorized to proceed beyond the 38th provided there
was no Chinese or Soviet intervention at that point. But then it
provided that he was authorized to continue action only if he
believed that he had a reasonable chance of success. The Report
contained various caveats that suggested some hedging by US
policymakers, but it was approved by the President on the 11th.
Significantly in light of later events the NSC recommendations on
September 9th included giving MacArthur authorization to take
military action **outside** of Korea should the Chinese intervene and
MacArthur believed that such action would be necessary. Such
authorization of course was never given to MacArthur and it
became a major source of conflict between MacArthur and
Washington.

So while the US had already decided to go beyond the 38th
Parallel in early September, it continued to maintain in public that
it had not given the subject any serious thought as the battles were
still raging in South Korea. Meanwhile US Delegates to the UN
were being instructed to obtain a UN Resolution, preferably

introduced by some other nations, authorizing MacArthur to go beyond the 38th Parallel.

On the 27th of September with the President's approval MacArthur was sent a directive in accordance with the September 9th NSC 81 authorizing him to go beyond the 38th Parallel. This Directive, however, did not include the authorization already approved in NSC 81 to go outside of Korea or beyond the Manchurian border.

As noted MacArthur subsequently rolled past the 38th and proceeded up the peninsular. Long before that the Americans had begun a campaign to get world approval for the actual occupation of all of Korea and its unification. Careful negotiations proceeded among our allies and friends at the UN to get a resolution passed which would authorize the unification by force of the Korean peninsula and the establishment of a unified government. On the one hand the State Department was pressed by Rhee's people to support a Rhee-only government in all of Korea as the UN took it over. On the other hand the US delegates at the UN were told in no uncertain terms by our allies that if the US intended that Rhee would extend his government to the North, then the US should not expect *any* votes, much less sponsors, for its proposed resolution. American embassy officials also warned Rhee that if the issue of Rhee's extending his authority to the North were debated in the UN as he was demanding, then he could expect that the very existence of Rhee's authority even in South Korea itself would be brought into question by a number of allies and neutral states.

The efforts of the US in the UN proceeded with less speed than MacArthur's forces and MacArthur was north of the 38th Parralel just as the UN passed its Resolution in early October authorizing him to do so and to occupy and unify the entire country. At the same time Mao and the other Chinese leaders were coming to their own conclusions about the intentions of the US. Mao tried to get Stalin to agree to give Chinese troops air support if they entered Korea. Stalin steadfastly refused as he did not want any confrontation with the US, though he was eager that the Chinese have that confrontation. He offered them equipment and other material support, but not Soviet air support. Mao in the first two weeks of October finally decided that he had to intervene to prevent an invasion of China. The Chinese began their move into Korea just after the celebrations at Wake Island.

On September 30, 1950, before any serious infiltration into Korea, the Chinese had publicly announced that the Peiping regime "cannot stand by idly" while the United States troops crossed the thirty-eighth Parallel. The Chinese tried to make the US understand that it was serious about this threat. In a coordinated move the Soviet Press gave extensive coverage to his speech (Harrison E. Salisbury. "Soviet Plays Up Statement." New York Times, October 2, 1950). Premier and Foreign Minister Chou En-lai had stated in a that speech to a public assembly of Chinese officials which was broadcast nationwide that while the Chinese people desperately wanted a "peaceful environment" so they could rehabilitate their country, the United States should not mistake this for weakness (New York Times, October 1 and October 12, 1950).

MacArthur and the Truman Administration did just that. They brushed off these warnings as attempted "blackmail." The Americans assumed it would be foolish for the Chinese Communist, exhausted from their own long civil war and admittedly desperate for time and resources to consolidate their governing of China, to engage in a battle with the most powerful nation on earth. This was the nation which had only five years earlier dropped atomic bombs on another enemy. Indeed, according to Thornton, in the long internal debate among Mao and the other Chinese leaders about confronting the approaching Americans on their border, the damage that atomic bombs would do to China was discussed and the risk very reluctantly, but expressly accepted.

Marcantonio in his June address to Congress in opposing the intervention had foresaw that the Chinese would not shrink from protecting their country regardless of any threat of atomic bombing. It was obvious that we were threatening China itself by our wholesale involvement in neighboring Korea's own civil war. He pleaded with his colleagues to try to understand the power of the Korean passion for independence and for revolutionary change. If the Americans in 1860 were ready to kill each other on a massive scale to keep a nation united that had been in existence for just "four scores and seven years;" imagine the passion behind reunification for a people who had been a nation for over a thousand years.

The Chinese and North Korean soldiers, though grossly outgunned, entered Korea in the middle of October and began overrunning first the ROK forces and then the American forces. They kept right on marching down the peninsula notwithstanding Stratemeyer's carpet bombing. MacArthur had previously split his forces up and had on November 24th launched his "home for Christmas" offensive, as it turn out, just one day before the Chinese launched their own offensive, to the utter surprise of the Americans. Why MacArthur was again caught utterly by surprise is an issue that itself has produced books over the years. When the war began he had been looked upon by all political factions in the US as the one solid leader they all could count on. Editorials from the New York Daily News to the New York Times and the Washington Post had joined in a sigh of relief when Truman put General MacArthur in charge. Suffice it to say that he might have been another "wrong" for the period of many wrongs -- the wrong General for the wrong war.

General Stratemeyer was sensitive to the criticisms arising in the Press as to why we had been caught by such surprise. In the midst of planning a retreat, he had time to do a study which conveniently accused the Army as being at fault, not the Air Force. The following is from a discussion he recorded in his Diary entry of December 6, 1950 which was held in his office with a number of other Air Force officers:

Stratemeyer: *"Another thing, they are pointing the finger at us -- why we didn't see this build up, etc., and why with the tools we had, we didn't produce it. There are many reason, short distances, Yalu River, came over in driblets, crossed the ice. Etc. The finger is on us. I asked for a study be made – not an alibi – and sent it to Craigie* [General Laurence C. Craigie Vice Chief of Staff, FEAF] *this morning.*

Partridge: *"That is a perfect example of the Army's not producing enough photography interpreters. Thousands of pictures were taken and no one to sit down and evaluate them."*

General Walker in the west had been cautious and on the first appearance of the Chinese in late October had slowed his advance to the Yalu and regrouped. He had only "one day of fire" and his supply lines were stretched too thin to support any real fighting, as the Americans at that point had not expected any more fight from the demoralized North Koreans. When MacArthur ordered his general offensive on the 24th of November, unknown to him was that the Chinese were ready with their own offensive. On Walker's line they concentrated their first attacks on the ROK troops holding the middle and quickly overran them. Walker thought it best to make an orderly retreat without fighting to a better defensive position in order to avoid being outflanked and also to preserve all his equipment. His retreat continued for the entire month of December while making little contact with the advancing Chinese. His forces raced all the way down to below the 38th parallel, yet again abandoning Seoul, moving south now as quickly as they had moved north.

General Almond, on the other hand, with his X Corps. in the east had kept moving aggressively up to the border with China though his forces were also somewhat spread out in anticipation of supervising elections in the North. Consequently Almond's advanced units were met head on by the Chinese. The Xth fought bravely and fiercely in the bitter cold and took heavy casualties. Thorougly battered it escaped annihilation only by an unopposed mass evacuation at the North Korean port of Hungnam.

Lt. General Walton Walker unfortunately did not live to see the end of the retreat. He had been killed in a jeep accident on December 23, 1950 during the retreat. His replacement, General Matthew Ridgeway, found a demoralized, defeatist and retreat-oriented Army when he arrived a few days later, as well as a depressed General MacArthur. However it did not take him long to turn his men around, change their spirit and even go on the offensive. He soon recaptured again what was left of Seoul and set up a rational line of defense across the Peninsula. That line, approximately along the 38th parallel where it had all started, essentially remained the same in a stalemate that did not end until July, 1953.

General MacArthur with his 8th Army Commanders; General Walker (right) and then General Ridgeway.

But to get to that point, there had been a long retreat by Generals Walker and Almond. As Walker and Almond retreated, it was now the fate of what was left of the North Korean cities and villages to experience an American ***withdrawal***, having already suffered from the bombardments preceding the American ***advance*** shortly before. When the Americans withdrew in December before the advancing Chinese, they demolished whatever they could in

297

their hasty retreat. What they had not destroyed in their advance up the peninsula and in months of bombing, they now tried to destroy in their retreat.

"ABANDONED PYONGYANG EERILY QUIET UNDER SMOKE PALL FROM DEMOLITION" read the <u>New York Times</u> headline on page one of its December 5, 1950 edition.

> *"This former North Korean Red capital, eerily quiet under a pall of heavy black smoke, presented today the* **picture of desolation familiar to observers who had seen other cities being abandoned to an enemy. Fires were set by the retreating United Nations forces***. . . . In bewildered, sullen and sometimes uncomprehending knots, Pyongyang's residents peered at the endless retreating columns of the United Nations troops. . . . Fanned by freezing north winds, smoke sparks from flaming warehouses, supply dumps and gasoline stores whipped across the roads . . . stinging the eyes and nostrils of the troops riding away from this place. . . ."*

Another article in the <u>Times</u> is headlined: *"WITHDRAWAL A ROUT."*

> *"For the past few days installations at two of the landing fields in Pyongyang have been the scene of a 'scorched earth' policy. . . . Ammunition was not the only thing burning on the field. Large stocks of winter clothing that had been flown in for friendly troops were giving off acid smoke."*

The Chinese were reported to be 10 to 15 miles away. The people of Pyongyang had good reason to be "sullen" while they watched the UN forces retreat. Those forces had brought only devastation to them, including the round-ups and executions by Rhee's police. The Americans had to move carefully as they retreated, since the local population was seething with anger against them.

298

*"Little resistance from North Koreans could be
expected by the United Nation forces. [But] [t]he
retribution of the South Korean military authorities, and
the frequent hangings of alleged Communists ordered by its
summary courts, had alienated many people north of the
38th parallel. Aerial bombing had created a large homeless
population, sullen and resentful. . . . With this terrain and
in this political climate the United Nations mechanized
columns, helpless off the roads and alien among the local
population, were at a grave disadvantage. For the Chinese
the hills were a friendly, if a choppy, sea, on which their
troops would have the mobility of a fleet, a mobility which
would enable them to outflank these road-bound columns"*
(Times (London), December 11, 1950).

The population of North Korea, unfortunately, had not seen
the last of the destruction which the Americans and Rhee's police
could work. Another crop of political prisoners had been created
by Rhee's police during the short period they had swarmed over
the North Korean landscape. Now repeated stories of their
summary execution, along with their families, were reported. (e.g.,
a Reuters story headlined: "Seoul Executions Stir Westerners"
appeared in the New York Times on December 17th. A United
Press report headlined: "Seoul Halts Execution of Political
Prisoners" appeared in that newspaper on December 22nd.)

Then there was more destruction from the air. Stratemeyer
in his diary entries around this time routinely complained that the
Army in its hasty retreat was not destroying enough of the bridges
and buildings that could be used by the Chinese. Why is it always
up to the Air Force to do this work? he would ask.

When Partridge and O'Donnell began systematically
destroying North Korea's cities and towns and villages after
MacArthur's "destroy everything" orders, the UN troops were still
occupying the remnants of some of the cities. Portions of these
cities therefore survived in some measure. Now, even they were to
be leveled. There was work to be done.

Stratemeyer, Tuesday, 28 November, 1950:

"O'Donnell besides burning Taechon will burn and interdict respectively other villages and communication lines today. Weather is good."

Stratemeyer, Saturday, 30 December 1950:

> *"Dispatched the fol Stratline to CG Fifth Air Force . . . – **TOP SECRET** PERSONAL PARTRIDGE FROM STRATEMEYER. This radio in two parts: PART ONE (**TOP SECRET**) We have authority to destroy the following towns: Pyongyang, Wonsan, **Hamhung, and Hungnam. Attacks will be conducted without** psychological warfare **warnings** or publicity. At first opportunity . . . "* [Emphasis added.]

So now even those uneasy inhabitants who had so recently proffered flowers in "welcoming" General Almond to Hamhung were now to be incinerated, without warning.

Stratemeyer, Monday, 1 January 1951:

"Dispatched the fol ltr to General O'Donnell via courier:
*Dear Rosie – reference our authority to burn and destroy Pyongyang, Wonsan, **Hamhung, and Hungnam**, it is desired that **no publicity whatsoever** be given out as to these strikes. **No reporters** or personnel nor members of FEAF Bomber Command will be permitted to ride as observers on these strikes. Make sure that these instructions are strictly adhered to.*

It would be easy just to say that MacArthur had gone mad and it was all his fault. Indeed it does seem that *"the old general had lost his senses"* as Thomas B. Buell observes in his <u>Naval Leadership in Korea</u> published in 2002 by the Department of the Navy, Naval Historical Center. Buell was referring to MacArthur's proposals during the low point of the war to pull our troops out of Korea entirely and commence World War III by attacking China with atomic bombs. Likewise, Vandenberg's official biographer, Phillip Meilinger, writing under the auspices of the Air Force History Museums Program, had this to say about MacArthur's, and incidentally, Stratemeyer's, sanity:

> *"The FEAF commander* [Stratemeyer] *was coming increasingly under MacArthur's spell and also moving for a widening of the war. . . . When MacArthur began to go*

over the edge in April 1951 Stratemeyer followed, waxing rapturous in his diary concerning the brilliance and patriotism of the old general."

Now, in 2002, they tell us that we had insane people running the war back in 1950! Why didn't someone say that when it was happening? So much for the experts and the Press. And from what we have seen, perhaps the Generals had gone *"over the edge"* much earlier than Meilinger's date of April 1951.

But in my humble opinion, as they say, it was more than just MacArthur's doings. Or Stratemeyer's. Or the Military Establishment's. Or the Military-Industrial Complex. These were not rogue Generals or a military coup. It was American Policy set by "Give 'em Hell" Harry that had been enthusiastically supported by the country; at least until things got so bad that the enormous stupidity of Truman's adventure became obvious even to the stupid.

Congressman Tom Pickett of Texas:

> *"We have lost an unwanted fight in Korea. Many thousands of our soldiers are now evacuating from northeast Korea. . . . It would probably be the better part of wisdom to evacuate them all."*

Congressman Sikes of Florida:

> *"We can now more clearly evaluate the seeming disaster to our military forces in Korea. . . . I hope the lesson in Korea has taught us we can never afford to become involved in a land war with China."*

Congressman Johnson of California:

> *"While Korea may be a terrible mistake, I do not think the gentleman from New York* [Vito Marcantonio] *offers us a prescription to cure it."*

304

These comments were made while the House was considering an Administration bill for an additional 18 billion dollars for the defense budget. Marcantonio argued that additional armaments were not the way to go. He moved to defeat the Bill, but was voted down, 212 to 1.

But we need to note that during this whole debate about Korea Congressman Marcantonio was not alone in his opposition. For example, the right-leaning Congressman Robert Rich of Pennsylvania (Republican, 1930 – 43; 1945 – 51) had joined Marcantonio in his opposition to Truman's "containment" program -- a program that sought "peace" through warmongering. In January of 1951 Rich reminded the country that Truman had acted without the approval of Congress in going into Korea, a point that had been made by Marcantonio in June of 1950:

> *[W]e ought to do everything we possibly can to get them* [our troops] *out of   there, because this Truman war that we have had in Korea is just about one of the worst thing that ever happened to this country of ours. . . . "*

Yet, we did the same thing to another country in the Far East just 10 or 15 years later, almost exactly the same except perhaps for our introduction to the world of yet more diabolic weaponry, like Agent Orange.

Can one begin to doubt, after the national characteristics disclosed by the Korean War, and then in Vietnam and then again in Iraq, that any nation facing a hostile Administration in Washington had better have some bargaining chips for the game, like a plausible deterrent.

Perhaps it was Vito Marcantonio who had it all wrong. Perhaps this was no longer the America of George Washington and Abraham Lincoln that he had read about as a child and had so passionately absorbed. Nor was it now what his beloved Fiorello LaGuardia had led him to believe. Something happened along the way. It seemed to be a different country. What would he make of today's Trumanesque "War on Terror;" Obama's futile and horribly counterproductive "Drone War" (see, e.g., Walsh, Declan. "Drone War Spurs Militants to Deadly Reprisals." <u>New York Times</u> 30 December 2012: A1); or the Attorney General and the head of the CIA publicly arguing that the President had the right to summarily assassinate Americans on American soil (see Greenwald, Glenn. "Chilling legal memo from Obama DOJ justifies assassination of US citizens." <u>The Guardian</u> (London) 5 February, 2013.)

CHAPTER XVII

"MR. MALIK'S LATEST LINE"

If the American bombing in Korea was so horrendous, why didn't the world react?

It did, but it made no difference. The United States was able to bottle up the opposition and do what it wanted, curiously similar to what it has so far been able to do with its 2003 invasion of Iraq. In 1950 the United States had complete control over the United Nations -- many of the countries in the aftermath of WWII world were either being fed or re-armed by the United States. The Truman Administration had transformed the infant UN from Roosevelt's vision of a place where the great powers could talk out their differences, to a propaganda weapon to bludgeon the Soviets at every opportunity.

Back in 1950 the world was indeed being told what the Americans were doing to the Koreans. For example, reporting from India, Robert Trumbull in the New York Times wrote on August 8, 1950:

> *"Accounts of repeated bombings of Seoul* [at the time occupied by the North Koreans] *by United States aircraft and reports of villages left in flames as United States troops withdraw arouse indignation here* [India]. *Consideration of military necessity is overshadowed by the fact that an Asia people is 'getting it in the neck again.'*

> *"The Indians argue that killing Koreans and destroying property is not making friends for the United State in Korea, or in India"*

307

Could not be any clearer and sounds extraordinarily familiar even today.

Trumbull, reporting from the capital of India, New Delhi, and after trying to get a consensus of Indian opinion by talking to Indian legislators from all over the country gathered at the Capital, told the <u>New York Times</u> readers that

> *"with every day of the Korean war bringing more news of bombed cities and flaming villages, the unpopularity of the United States is growing."*

Indians thought it was pointless, according to what Trumbull could determine, for the United States to be killing people and destroying property in Korea. They did not see anything wrong with communism winning out in Korea or in Indo-China.

> *"[a]t this stage. They argue that if the United States system is better, it eventually will come to the top. . . ."*

But this type of common sense wisdom was not only absent in America at that time, but if expressed publicly by anyone would subject that person to popular claims of treason and of being a "fellow traveler." In addition, our Press was painting India with a certain hue of pink so anything from India was suspect in any event

A leader like Vito Marcantonio, who basically was beseeching his colleagues in Congress to adopt this same philosophy -- that our system was superior and would triumph in the end without all this unnecessary violence, was branded as a "Communist Stooge." This was no time to wait for the American Way of Life to win out over communism by simply being the better system. The newspapers were filled with belligerency, ranting and raving. They demanded that we immediately "draw the line"; that we instantly "contain" the poison of communism. Soon it would be too late – everything would be contaminated. The

308

subversives among us would undermine our morale and spirit; would confuse the public. If peaceful means like the natural forces of economic realities could not stop this venom from spreading, then we must knock the hell out of them with good, old, American Power. Certainly we would do it reluctantly, and with a heavy heart, since America is a land of peace and it is only peace that we seek with our armaments, but the communist enemy has left us with no other option ---- such was the thinking of those shaping public opinion.

Consequently, it seemed that anyone who even *seemed* to question the aggressive approach being taken by the Truman Administration would be colored with red or pink and be stripped of his or her humanity. This applied to individuals as well as to whole masses of people alike. Those in our country who did raise their voices in objection to the brutality and wantonness of it all, were chased from their jobs, harassed and called fellow-travelers, communists or worse.

Many churchmen in the United State had caught this spirit and were running with it. They called upon God to help them destroy the Devil, better known as the Communists. A good example of this is the florid and darkly threatening statements coning from Cardinal Francis Spellman, head of the Catholic New York archdiocese. On July 20, 1950, for example, a month after the war had begun and on the day after Vito Marcantonio's was the only vote in Congress against a military armaments bill, the Cardinal had this to say:

> *"This is a dire day for all America because* **there are some counted among her sons, who, by covert or overt acts of disloyalty,** *or treacherous acts of apathy,* **stand guilty of the murder of those American boys** *whose young, fear-frozen faces were filled with bullets as they surrendered, only to be slaughtered by* **bestial Communist enemies**.

"Entrusted with this peace [after World War II] *and the future of our youth – we have once again failed ourselves and them – beguiled, deceived, betrayed, defeated by Communists, fellow travelers, apathetic and guileful people and public servants. . . .*

"No words can describe the villainy of communistic acts. Yet we who had time and warning enough, warnings even from the Soviets themselves, to build ourselves spiritually and materially strong, fell victim to their vices as we fell victim to our own" (<u>New York Times</u>, July 20, 1950; see also <u>Daily Mirror</u> [New York], July 20, 1950).

As the military US Catholic vicar, or boss of Catholic chaplains, for decades, Spellman loved to fly about the world dressed in military attire with the soldiers to cheer on the wars, ANY war, from WWII to Vietnam. As the saying goes, there wasn't a war he didn't love.

(This last photo, taken from the internet, is from either the Chicago or <u>Herald Tribune</u>.)

The Cardinal condemned with equal and indiscriminate passion not only those Americans who were communists or fellow travelers, but also the vast amount of people whom he though were just *uninterested* in the whole messy business. He repeated a recurrent lament of the militant right wing when he bemoaned the fact that America had not used all of its strength effectively after World War II to shape things our way. America was the most powerful nation left standing after World War II, he would preach, and we should have used that power to impose our will on the rest of the world. God had entrusted America with a special providence.

This "man of peace" had been one of the first to rush over to the White House on August 11, 1945 to lend his moral support to President Truman after Truman had dropped atom bombs on Hiroshima and Nagasaki. *"ARCHBISHOP SPELLMAN PRAISED MR. TRUMAN'S LEADERSHIP OF THE NATION. . . ."* (<u>New York Herald Tribune</u>, August 12, 1945).

One can only imagine that meeting between these two diminutive men who would be able to see eye to eye both on a physical plane as well as on moral plane.

"Mr. President, I bring to you special Apostolic Blessings to thank you for annihilating more infidels in two days than any one of our great Crusader armies were able to do in a year."

Edward Sorel, Cartoon, 1967.

Spellman, who must have been presiding over a pedophile's paradise at the time, was later able to give himself a cheap thrill in 1954. With great relish he petulantly refused Vito Marcantonio's widow and mother's request to bury Marcantonio, who had just died from a stroke at the age of 52, in a Catholic cemetery.

It was the Soviets, ironically, on behalf of the Koreans, who did indeed loudly criticize America's bombing practices in Korea. But the US Government treated these grievances with ridicule and contempt. The Press followed suit and the US public, encased in a cartoonish world when it came to the Soviets, was deaf to these cries of anguish.

One of the forums for the Soviet protests was in the United Nations. The Russians had returned to attending UN Security Council meetings after having boycotted them from January. Jacob Malik, the Soviet Union's UN Representative, introduced a Resolution to condemn the bombing. From the Associated Press, September 7, 1950:

> *"Mr. Malik charged the United States airmen with the indiscriminate bombing of schools, hospitals and other non-military objectives. 'The American airmen in Korea are carrying out atrocious acts which have no military justification' he claimed.*

> *"Mr. Malik asked the council to 'force the United States' compliance with international law, and to put an end to the shameful bloody acts of the American interventionists, which are going on in Korea behind the mask of the United Nations.' "*

The Associated Press reported the response of the US Delegate to the UN, Ernest Gross:

*"He said the air **attacks were directed solely at troop concentrations, war dumps and military supply lines**. The North Koreans were forcing civilians to aid their operations, and were using private dwellings, hospitals and schools to house war supplies, but these crimes shrink into insignificance in the face of the shooting in cold blood of unarmed wounded prisoner, Mr. Gross said."*(Emphasis added.)

The US reply to the Soviet complaints about the bombing in Korea was that only military targets were being hit and that this was being done with "precision" bombing. In addition, the US was warning civilians to evacuate before the bombings. But the basic answer was that: "war is hell" and the aggressors were getting what they deserved. The "calamities" befalling the people of Korea were visited on them by the aggressors from the North who started the war. All the consequences, as regrettable as they may be, were the inevitable results of that aggression.

This was the reaction not just from the power elite in the United States, but from the Press and it seemed from the people of America as well. The slaughter in Korea did not seem to bother us Americans. Only accounts of our own soldiers' deaths or some new atrocity supposedly committed by the North Koreans could move us.

Secretary of State Acheson, on September 6th, and in anticipation of the Soviet's offering their resolution of condemnation in the UN on September 7th, issued a statement presenting the American side. Civilians regrettably were being killed, yes, but the fault was not that of the US. After repeating that only military targets were being bombed, he gave this explanation as to why civilians were being strafed in South Korea and why peasants in carts were being rocketed:

"It is well known that the Communist command has compelled helpless civilians to labor on these military sites.

314

Peaceful villages are used to cover the tanks of the invading army. Civilian dress is used to disguise soldiers of aggression."

This Party Line was put into an official report to the UN in General MacArthur's name, as the UN Commander, and read at a Security Council meeting the next day by the American delegate, Ernest A. Gross:

> *"Since the enemy is apparently **forcing civilian labor** to his use, problems of identification have become difficult. . . . On land, civilians are carrying supplies in **push-carts and donkey carts** which burn and explode when strafed. The enemy hides vast quantities of military equipment in civilian dwellings, resulting in the **necessity to fire and destroy such dwellings** when such information is firm. However, **the problem of avoiding the killing of innocent civilians and damages to the civilian economy is continually present and given my** [MacArthur] **personal attention.** "*[Emphasis added.]

At the UN Security Council meeting of September 7, 1950 Malik, already an object of ridicule in the US Press, presented a long list of facts based on diplomatic letters from the North Koreans as well as from US newspaper report. He urged support of his resolution to condemn the "barbarous" American bombing on "undefended Korean towns" that were killing innocent civilians and leaving others without "a roof over their heads" In addition to newspaper reports he also used an August 22, 1950 cablegram sent to the UN by Pak Hen En, Minister for Foreign Affairs of North Korea, to put together some of the facts supporting his resolution:

> *"The city of **Pyongyang** has been subjected to repeated bombings. . . . From 3 to 28 July, 18,203 dwelling houses in the city were completely destroyed. . . . More than 800 persons were killed and wounded. Ten plants and*

factories producing popular consumer goods, three hospitals, a teacher's training institute and several churches were destroyed. . . .

*"From 2 to 27 July the town of **Wonsan** suffered twelve attacks . . . in which 4,028 houses were destroyed, 1,647 persons -- including 739 women and 325 children – were killed . . . .*

*"From 2 July to 3 August the town of **Hungnam** was subjected to eight attacks, in which 200 airplanes took part, dropping 2,000 bombs. As a result of these attacks, three schools, a theatre, two polyclinics, a library, and other buildings were destroyed, 297 persons were killed and 446 were wounded.*

*"In a single air raid on the town of **Seoul** in the area of Yengsan on 16 July, fourteen hospitals, two educational institutions, a children's home and a Catholic church were destroyed. . . .*

"It should be added that the United States Command itself recognizes that its bombers meet with no resistance; this means that it subjects the undefended, peaceful towns and villages of Korea to barbarous terror attacks and thus commits its crimes against the peaceful population of that country with perfect impunity. . .

"According to Mr. Boyle, corresponded of the United States newagency, the Associated Press, another Korean town – Yongdong – was subjected to an equally barbarous bombing. He states:

'Yongdong, which only two weeks before had been the principal United States defence base in Korea, no longer exists. It looks like Nagasaki after the explosion of the atom bomb. It has suffered

*very heavily as a result of ceaseless attacks by
United States army and navy planes Only a thin
wisp of smoke rises above the ruins of the town; the
rest is a wilderness.'*

*"The correspondent Robert Martin wrote in an
<u>Overseas News Agency</u> report dated 7 August:*

*'A perpetual haze seems to hang over South
Korea these days . . . from the scores of little
villages which each day are reduced to smoking
ashes by jet fighters and the F-51 Mustangs. . . .'*

. . . .

*"Who will believe that arms were hidden in 18,203
dwelling houses in Pyongyang or in 4,028 houses in
Wonsan, hundreds of kilometers from the front . . ."*

*"Russian
Hospital
Building in
Pyongyang,
Korea,
where
advancing
US Soldiers
discovered
the bodies c
three North
Korean
civilians."*

25 Oct 50 U
Army Sgt.
Ennque
Marques

317

"Bomb damage to military area in center of city, Pyor Korea." 1 Nov 1950 FEAF of Information Services

This photo is credited to the US Air Force, and so would suggest that it was taken from the air. It appears that while one US airplane was taking photos, another bomber was still in action. Looking at the top left corner of this picture, I wonder if that plane is sending another bomb down, soon to surprise this lady into oblivion?

318

The representative from India, Sir Benegal N. Rau, during the debate on the Russian Resolution, felt compelled to state:

> *"I must confess that reports of large-scale bombings in Korea have been prevalent in India for some time and have greatly disturbed Indian public opinion. . . ."*

Yet the stranglehold of the US over the nations in the UN at that time was so complete that even the Indian delegate, though obviously disturbed by the reports of US bombing, voted against the Soviet Resolution, ostensibly because *"we cannot assume without investigation that all the allegations of bombing are true"* in the face of such adamant and detailed American denials that were being made.

Malik also charged that the United States Army and Marines were putting the torch to villages in front of their lines and behind their lines in order to deny hiding places to the enemy. The inhabitants, according to Malik, were first asked to evacuate and retreat with the US forces, but those who refused to leave were executed.

> *"Thus, in the burned down villages of Songjin and Nekwan over 3,000 Koreans have been shot; 600 have been shot in P'yongta'ek (Heitako) and about 1,000 in Taejon."*

These are our own Army pictures. Certainly looks like we are photographing homes that we are burning down.

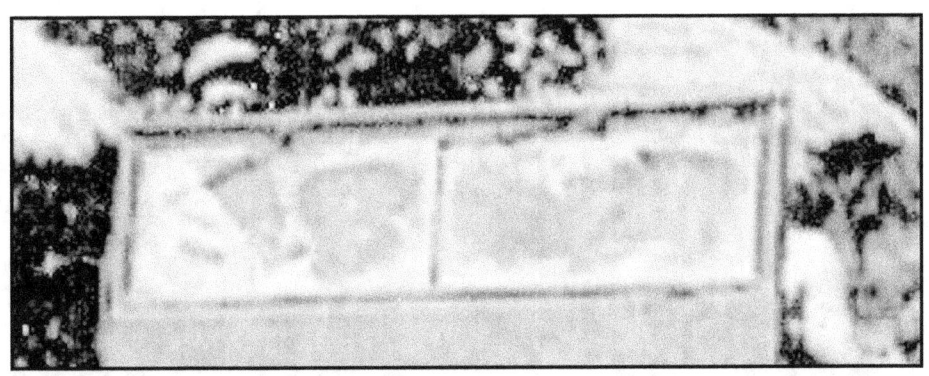

Later in the war, when the US and ROK forces recaptured these same towns, the ROK "discovered" thousands of murdered civilians and the world press was filled with headlines and pictures accusing the <u>North Koreans</u> of more atrocities. But, we have to ask, ere these the bodies of the same people allegedly killed in the US retreat by Rhee's police forces?

Malik, in his UN presentation in September, 1950, also reported cablegrams from the North Koreans condemning the American employment of **delayed-action** bombs. The North Koreans claimed that these snake-in-the-grass explosions had been killing civilians after they came out of their shelters to repair a bombing raid's damage, to get food when they thought the raid was over or to search for and bury their dead. Also reported by the North Koreans was repeated strafing of innocent people in the streets, travelers on roads and peasants in their fields.

The response to Malik's charges was uniformly dismissive: "sorry, but that's what you get." For example, from the comments of the Norwegian Delegate to the UN, Mr. Sunde:

*"I am not aware that the Soviet Union delegation
has presented any semblance of proof in support of its
contention that the air force of the United Nations has
carried out bombing in raids in Korea in violation of the
accepted rules of international law. War is always cruel
and a naturally destructive business, and it is a matter of
particular regret to all men of good will that it should be
accompanied by such harrowing suffering by the
defenceless civilian population; **but such is war**. The
responsibility always rests on the aggressors who are
willing to let loose the evil forces of war – in this case, the
North Koreans."*

The <u>New York Times</u>, one of the more moderate American
commentators on the Russian's charges, headlined its mocking
editorial: "MR. MALIK'S LATEST LINE." It too reiterated the
American "blaming the victim" position that

*"the responsibility for the unavoidable horrors of
war rests squarely on those who start it, and that, so far as
the air force is concerned, it attacks only military targets of
the invaders, though these often use churches, schools and
civilians to disguise such targets."*

These responses do not address the fundamental issue of
whether all the bombing was indeed "unavoidable;" whether the
bombing was an excessive reaction; or why almost as many of the
people we were trying to "save," those *south* of the 38th parallel,
were being killed by us as were their relatives who happen to live
north of that line drawn by Colonel Rusk late on that cursed night
in 1945.

What could justify what a correspondent for the news
agency, Hsin Hua, reported from Korea on 11 August as relayed
by Malik:

*"'Taejon [South Korea] was a large modern city
with a population of 200,000. Now practically nothing is*

324

left of it. There is nothing to bomb any more, but United States planes come here every day and bomb and strafe the city with unheard-of cruelty, trying to destroy every trace of its existence.' "

The terrifying shocks from the delayed-fuse bombs dropped by the Americans received special mention in a September 7th cablegram of complaint from Pak Hen En, Minister for Foreign Affairs for North Korea. As read in part by Malik to the Security Council on September 18, 1950:

> " *'In order to hinder relief work and increase the number of victims among the peaceful population, a considerable number of delayed-action bombs are dropped which explode just as the population are coming out of their shelters after a raid and beginning to look for the killed and wounded. . . .' "*

Malik further quoted from a cablegram of September 7th from the North Korean Minister for Foreign Affairs:

" 'On 19 August over 60 United States bombers bombed the city [of Chongjin], dropping upon it 1,012 bombs; as a result of that bombardment, 2,626 houses were destroyed, 1,034 persons were killed and 2,347 were injured; and hospitals, the industrial technical college, the girls' high school and other schools, the people's theatre and many other cultural institutions . . . were destroyed. Such bombardments take place repeatedly, as a result of which nine-tenths of the city of Chongjin, with a population of 120,000, has been destroyed. . . . On 20 August in the counties of Taedong, Sunchon . . . 68 United States dive-bombers carried out a raid and, flying low over the village, machine-gunned and dropped bombs on peasants working in the fields or gather in market places; as a result 33 peasants were killed and 54 persons injured on that day. . . .' "

The American Delegate, Warren Austin, during his indignant defense of American bombing practices before the Security Council on September 18th, read from a MacArthur report to the UN covering the period August 16 to 31. MacArthur after the war would recall that even though he was the "UN" commander, he <u>never</u> had direct contact with the UN. He took orders from the US Joint Chiefs of Staff. MacArthur also recalled that his reports "to the UN" were actually sent first to the State and Defense Departments who censored and even rewrote them before they were sent to the UN (LaFeber, Walter, <u>America, Russia and the Cold War</u>. 9th ed. Boston: McGraw Hill, 2003). So the report read by Austin as supposedly coming from MacArthur may actually have been written by someone in the State or Defense Department or by Austin himself, particularly so because a number of paragraphs seem to have been much too lawyerly crafted to counter the Soviet charges.

According to the supposed MacArthur report as read by Austin, MacArthur said:

" 'Our naval bombardment forces, both surface and air, are exercising every precaution to avoid harming the civil population, and are employing every possible means to identify and destroy military targets only.

. . . .

*'**Pin point** destruction of industrial and other military objectives in North Korea continues. Evaluation of photographs of these objectives after attacks shows remarkable accuracy has been obtained in striking the selected targets which in every instance have been of military significance. . . . The North Korean populace has been warned by radio and by leaflets to vacate their areas that contain military targets. They have been urged 'to leave these cities and **go to the country or to the mountains.' "***

Incidentally, I doubt very much that the lines in MacArthur's report to the UN about "pin-point" bombing or the regrettable necessity of killing South Korean men and women who

had been forced to work for the Northerners were really written by
MacArthur. He was in the process of nonchalantly ordering the
burning down of entire cities and he would have thought it utterly
foolish to be talking about "pin-point" bombing. He considered
himself a heroic and invincible figure; such petty lying would be
beneath him. Nor would he ever admit that he was allowing the
indiscriminate strafing of civilians behind enemy lines. Those lines
were more probably written by a nervous Defense Department
censor who was attempting to deal with the outcry being made in
the rest of the world, or at least in Asia, about the American
bombing.

"Pin Point bombing . . .":

Korean refugees were expected to be grateful to the
Americans for advising them to "... go to the country or to
the mountains."

329

330

". . . the fighters had standing "orders to strike the entire column [of refugees]. *The pilots did not like it, but most of us followed orders."*

Malik had repeated the North Koreans' complaint that:

> *"The United States interventionists are systematically destroying the industry of Korea in an attempt to condemn the Korean people to unemployment, destitution and famine."*

Indeed, that is exactly what the US was doing. Unwittingly, Malik had just given the standard American definition of "strategic" bombing.

Malik was taken aback that no one seemed moved by the fact that most of the towns and cities on the long list that the North Korean Foreign Minister complained had been indiscriminately bombed by the US was located below the 38th parallel and

331

supposedly friendly to the US. No one seemed disturbed that the American goal was admittedly the total destruction of a society.

This was the last time that the North Koreans complained to the UN about the barbarity of the bombing. They now understood that the Americans intended to lay their country waste and that the world did not care. These are the memories which Kim Jong-un and the other North Korean leaders have today. This is what guides their negotiations with Americans. This is why they know that only they themselves can prevent another American-made holocaust in their land.

CHAPTER XVIII

POW GENERAL WILLIAM DEAN TESTIFIES

General William Dean had a remarkable military life, filled with unusual contrasts and ironies. A Congressional Medal of Honor recipient and after whom schools and streets are named in honor of a real American hero. He served with distinction in World War II and was later appointed as military governor of Korea under General Hodge. During his tenure unfortunately tens of thousands of Koreans in the American Zone were killed by the South Korean police or constabulary who were at that time at least under the direct supervision of the American Occupying Forces.

Then he was one of the first American soldiers sent in from Japan to stop the advance of North Korean troops after June 25, 1950. Though a General he engaged in hand to hand battles with the North Koreans and even put out an enemy tank by himself.

General Walker (left) with General Dean at airfield near Taejon. July 7, 1950 (Wikipedia)

The T-34 tank knocked out by General Dean on July 20, 1950
(Wikipedia)

As noted above, Dean himself became a prisoner of the people he had been governing as Military Governor. While a POW he was even housed at one time in a prison he had inspected as Governor and found that the person in charge of the prison for the North Koreans, who treated him kindly, had himself been a political prisoner when Governor Dean had visited. Dean lived through an incredible experience as a POW which flames, torments and agonies seemed to have created a new person, or finally revealed the real William Dean.

His observations are contained in a biography written in 1954 with the assistance of a writer -- just a year after his release from captivity. It does not have the same sense of private and unvarnished thinking that Ward's diary does – it often enough echoes American anti-communist propaganda that was required of all public figures at that time – but it still contains many frank observations that are sometimes startling, all set forth by General Dean casually and gracefully. (Dean, William F.. General Dean's Story, New York: Viking Press, 1954.)

Dean had been separated from his men during the fighting and found himself alone, trying to escape capture by the North Koreans. He evaded them for weeks but eventually local South Koreans had seen him and turned him over to the North Korean Army.

If a US pilot went down in his parachute in Britain during World War II, anyone finding him would help him in any way possible. Britain was an ally. Even American pilots who survived being shot down in German-occupied France would feel safe if they were discovered by villagers. The occupied French people were allies even though under the gun of the Germans and were taking great risks in hiding an allied pilot. Even those pilots or soldiers who found themselves stranded in Italy, theoretically an enemy country, could often count on the Italian citizens to assist them if they could.

So why was it that in South Korea, our ally, an American General could not find a friend? Could it say that the Koreans in the South had not been happy with the American Occupation? Could it also say that the Koreans in the South felt more of an affinity and loyalty to their brother Koreans coming in from the North than they did for the occupying Americans, or even for their puppet Korean government. From this incident alone one has to ask what this makes of the Truman claim that we had gone into Korea for the defense of the Korean people? It might have been beneficial for those Koreans who were ruling the country under our supervision, but obviously not for the people as a whole in South Korea. In any event, this was one of the consequences of interfering in a civil war -- no matter how you sliced it, we were the outsiders.

Dean came across many work gangs during his travels in evading capture. He had referred to "impressed labor," South Korean men and women who were impressed to repair the roads and other facilities being destroyed by US airplanes. These laborers whom Dean observed were the very civilians that the Americans were "regrettably" strafing, and on whom they were "regrettably" dropping napalm and delayed-action bombs. Recall the explanation in the MacArthur UN Report – *"sorry, but we have to do it as they are helping the enemy who are killing our boys"* [paraphrased]. Never mind that these people we were killing were the ones we had come to save.

335

On the first day of his captivity, he had been put by the local police in the back of a jail and sat there in the background as an observer to the goings-on in the busy police station.

>"*Two North Korean Army paymasters . . . arrived shortly after I was brought in. They came with bundles of won notes and spent the whole night doling out piles of money to the local officials. Each <u>gun-soo</u> (corresponding to town or country officials) evidently had provided a hundred men for work on the roads, and this was the big pay-off. **The thing which struck me was that everybody was happy, and there was no resentment.** These officers were just **two Santa Clauses come to town, and nobody minded at all.** . . . I never saw the Inmun Gun* [North Korean Army] *steal anything outright . . . . When a soldier wanted a farmer's peach he always paid for it. He went out and bought it. So even when the currency turned out to be worthless, that individual solder was not the target of the farmers' wrath*" [emphasis added].

Neither the North Korean nor the local South Korean officials in that gathering had given the slightest attention to the bedraggled American prisoner sitting in the back of the jail. The next day he was to leave and his escort on this march

>"*consisted of one Korean youngster, in an Inmun Gun uniform and armed with a long rifle, and a civilian carrying a briefcase.*"

>"*The one thing I noticed especially was that **my guard was quite a hero to all the small children we met on the way.** Whenever we passed a group he would say a phrase to them and the children would reply in chorus. It sounded like 'Chosen-all,' which I assumed must be some **Communist slogan about a united Korea, because they all knew it and repeated it with enthusiasm.** Often the children would start singing a marching air, which I was to*

336

hear thousands of time – the Inmun Gun song" (emphasis added).

He arrived with his escort in Chinan and taken to a house which was being used by the military. In it he noticed that there were two women in uniform and that the soldiers gathered there were being given what looked to Dean like a course in politics. The course would be interrupted periodically by a series of rifle shots and a bell which was used as an air raid signal. Everybody would run for cover in doorways. *"I was moved to a seat in a closet doorway."* Later in the same town he was put into another building and had to sit in a corner for a long time. During his wait he heard what sounded like endless military drilling and counting from upstairs and it appeared that the local youths were being drilled all afternoon by instructors from the Inmun Gun in close order.

> *"Once again I was struck by the fact that if the people of South Korea resented the northern invaders, they certainly weren't showing it. To me, the civilian attitude appeared to veer between enthusiasm and passive acceptance. I saw no sign of resistance or any will to resist."*

This was not a Vito Marcantonio talking. It was a conservative military General who had earlier, as Military Governor, made every effort to suppress those South Koreans who had wanted any kind of liberal changes in their society. But Marcantonio's saying about the same thing as Dean in the United States Congress a month earlier got him lambasted as a Communist Stooge and a traitor.

The North Korean Army was now well into the South. There was an acceptance by the people. Could we have a more authentic survey than that of an American General given a front seat? There seemed to be no slaughtering or looting or raping. There was little death except what was being rained down by the American bombers and fighters.

337

What if we, as Vito Marcantonio and others had argued, had just left them alone? This passage from Dean's biography is the most eloquent and convincing argument against our intervention in Korea. By itself it eliminates the basic rationale which Truman gave for intervening, to save the people of South Korea from slavery, or some variation of that cliché. On the day that the prisoner Dean came to the conclusion that the people of the South were accepting union with their relatives from the North, he must have wondered about the politicians in DC and their game plans that had led to this.

General Dean's capture made clear that the people south of the 38th parallel preferred their own people to the Americans, or to the Rhee Government. Dean's survival as a POW, in addition, his treatment and then his release, gives lie to the reputation that the Western Press has given to the North Koreans fighters at that time. They did not put Dean on some kind of summary trial for war crimes, as they might well have been justified to do merely for his "scorched earth" eradication program on Cheju-do. They did not even make propaganda use of him, something that surprised Dean as he remembered how the Americans themselves had made propaganda use of captured German and Japanese high officials.

If the North Koreans did not execute this General Dean, whom nobody in the beginning knew was in their hands, then how much less could they have been guilty of many of the "atrocities" ascribed to them by the ROK and the American Military? It is evidence of character, even more compelling than alleged eye-witness accounts of those so-called atrocities that frequently found their way into the American Press. Certainly there were atrocities committed by North Korean troops in the treatment of American prisoners. But as MacArthur himself acknowledged at Wake it was not a pattern or a policy. Various units of the North Korean Army behaved differently.

If I should stop there, I believe I have already demonstrated that President Truman had been in serious error and made an

338

unfortunate mistake by intervening in Korea's civil war. It would just be a footnote in history.

But I am afraid that our history is much darker than that. Just think about it for a moment. General Dean could see in a few days on the ground in South Korea that the Koreans in the south were welcoming their northern brothers and were happy to be rid of the dictatorial Rhee and his American supporters. But during the Occupation and afterward, we had scores and scores of agents, spies and what not in North Korea, and hundreds of agents in South Korea. These agents were both Americans and Koreans. They were trained to pick up information; to determine the mood and desires of the people; to uncover any support the other side might have. I have to come to the sobering conclusion, therefore, that the American policymakers knew from before June 25th what General Dean learned, the hard way, in August. So if we knew that the South Koreans would prefer to be unified with the North Koreans, even by force of arms, then why did we interfere and make a holocaust of this little country? If it were not for the stated reason, to defend democracy (as there was no democracy under the dictator Rhee in any event) or save the southerners from slavery, then what was the reason?

Running through the entire American experience with Korea, from before Colonel Dean Rusk drew his line through the heart of Korea, to Stratemeyer's and MacArthur's burning down of cities to "teach them a lesson," is the suspicion that this was all a demonstration to terrorize the Soviets and the Chinese -- a convenient place for the Americans to "draw the line" without too much risk to themselves. There was no military reason to have the Americans take the Japanese surrender in a territory bordering Russia – we were just sticking it in their face. And so it continued – a "lesson", which in any event was not leaned, would cost the lives of at least 6,000,000 Koreans and Chinese and 35,000 Americans and destroy a country for generations.

339

This brings us to the lesson that the Korean War has for the leaders and people of North Korean today. If the "liberal" Administration of Harry S. Truman was willing to kill 6,000,000 people for the sake of teaching the Soviets a lesson, how many millions would the likes of Bush, Rumsfeld, Cheney, Rice, Wolfowitz, Bolton be willing to kill to teach their imagined enemies a lesson? Would they nuke Korea, all of it? I am afraid the answer is -- they certainly would. Thereafter the world will be truly at peace, an American-made peace as not a soul would question the will of the American people to fight for freedom, democracy and liberty.

Progressing on his journey under guard, the POW Dean arrived in the town of Chonju, *"just as a flight of our bombers unloaded on one end of the town near the railroad tracks."* He was rushed to the protection of an archway in a school in one of the mission compounds. Later when his guard brought him back they went *"past a mission hospital,* [where] *we met townspeople carrying two litters with a woman and child on them. Both were bloody masses."*

Why is General Dean reporting this in 1954? Why would an American General tell the world that American bombers killed women and children?

He continued his journey with his guard and

> *"drove through the other end of town, passing a group of houses still smoking from the bombs while civilians poked through the wreckage, looking for other victims.* **I don't know what the objective of this bombing was, but the railroad, a spur line, was unhurt.** *"*[Emphasis added.]

At one point early in his captivity he had been staying in Pyongyang when they suddenly moved out to a village 16 miles north. Later one of his guards, Lee, told him that the reason they moved was

> *"because of increased bombing of Pyongyang, including the use of anti-personnel, air-bursting bombs. . . . Lee told me . . . that the bombers were destroying the city. He was worried about his own family and friends, especially about his father, who was still living there."*

Bill Dean when he was writing this in 1954, during the McCarthy high days of Red-baiting and hysterical fear of Communism, wanted people to know certain things. He reports in his book a number of times how our bombers missed their targets, or apparently missed their targets, and hit and killed civilians. He was a witness, and his conscience would not allow him to be silent.

> *"During the next three years I had a true worm's eye view of our air war. . . .[But] I could see only what was right in front of me. . . . So when I say that bombers missed or hit an apparent target, or that bombing increased the hatred which one of a thousand Kims had for the United States, no over-all criticism of aerial warfare is meant or implied. . . . The fact that a bomber did miss, or a man did lose his wife and children, must be told, however, in order to understand what happened to the people around me, and how they thought."*

It was just a month later and after a lot more devastation, when the Americans in the UN were bragging about their "pin point" bombing which avoided damage to the civilian population.

On his way through the major South Korean town of Taejon, now in Communist hands, Bill Dean observed that

> *"the whole town was full of adults, apparently in labor gangs, moving in the direction of the railroad. There were hundreds and hundreds of men, marching in*

341

organized groups but with no weapons except occasional shovels."

In the South Korean town of Suwon which had served as an American and South Korean headquarters for a time and was now occupied by the northerners, he found that it

> *"was badly smashed by air attacks, and two more came while we were there. They both hit at the other end of town, and I was delighted to see air activity stepping up so much."*

After the attack Dean and his guards continued north and ran into a long line of waiting vehicles loaded with women and children.

"These looked like families, complete with all their household goods, going back to Seoul."

These are the people who would be bombed by the Americans continuously until the

"U.N. Forces, landing at Inchon, drove the Communists out of burning Seoul for the first time on September 26."

Time went by. He passed through some terrible bouts of suicidal despair, near death illnesses, periodically degrading treatment and sometimes glimmers of hope. But two years later he had become a celebrity among the North Korean soldiers and was being treated almost as a privileged guest, especially after discovered by a European reporter – though still a prisoner. On a trip to Manchuria, the reason for which he could not figure out, they were near the city of Kanggye in February, 1953, when Dean made these observations:

> *"I had my first real chance to see what the bombers had done while I was listening to them during the last two*

*years. . . . **most of the towns were just rubble or snowy open spaces, where buildings had been. . . . The little towns, once full of people, were unoccupied shells.** The villagers lived in entirely new temporary villages, hidden in canyons or in such positions that only a major bombing effort could reach them.*

"These people had been hurt by bombing and still were being hurt by it, but it looked to me as if their countermeasures were improving faster than our measures of destruction.

*"The town of **Huichon** amazed me. The city I'd seen before – two-storied buildings, a prominent main street – **wasn't there any more. . . . What few people remained lived in dugouts**, and what had been a city was snow-covered fields."*

Months later he was near Pyongyang where the armistice was signed in July.

"The very night of the cease-fire trains began running in and out of Pyongyang freely and at all hours. And with a speed remarkable when you consider the lack of communications, thousands of people suddenly surged out of the hills, leaving their caves and scattered shanties to pour back into the valleys, to their bomb-ruined homes."

This does not sound like a man who hated his captors or the people of Korea. It does not sound like someone who enjoyed seeing the damage done by his country's bombs. His book is interspersed with praise for the bombing and his joy at seeing aircraft coming over to do their destruction – but they read as pro-forma, obligatory sentences that had to be uttered in the America of 1954. One feels real emotion in him, however, when he tells of the guards who would quietly disclose to him the shocking news that they had lost their wives and children or parents in a bombing by the Americans of their village or town.

In the moments he had to wait for the final prisoner exchange he tells us about all the people who helped him while he was a prisoner, particularly the guards who both guarded him and took care of him. This is a different Dean than the Military Governor of the Occupation.

"A good many things happened to me [during captivity], *but nothing more important than my opportunity to know these people as I never could have done in a lifetime as an uncaptured general. It may almost have been worth the three years."*

CHAPTER XIX

THE ATOMIC BOMB IN KOREA

The United States did not use the Atomic Bomb in Korea. Though it seriously considered using the A-Bomb it was ultimately rejected because the military thought it would be ineffective in the war they were fighting and, more importantly, because it would pose serious risks of radiation fallout to our own troops.

The horror pictures of devastated Hiroshima and Nagasaki were still fresh in people's minds and the Truman Administration for the first few years after WWII had acted and thought that it was in a position to dictate terms to the world because of its Atomic monopoly. Much of American diplomacy after Truman first got into office was clumsily based on the explicit or implicit threat of using the A-Bomb.

We rejected sharing the Bomb's secrets with our allies, except for limited cooperation with Britain who was providing vital raw materials for the bomb. But Russia, also an ally in World War II, was deliberately frozen out -- with the consequent festering of paranoia on the part of Stalin. The proposals circulating in Washington to share the atomic secrets and somehow develop a worldwide cooperative to deny every nation use of the Bomb for the sake of preserving mankind were rejected by Truman and his advisors. Another fatal and historic lost opportunity for Truman and the ruling elite.

We were aware at that time not only of the immediate damage that an atomic explosion could create, but also something of its long term effects. Even before the war in Korea started, there had been very public discussions about these aftereffects, primarily what was unknown about them. For example, under the caption: "ATOMIC BLINDNESS," the Washington Post's editors, after commenting on the higher percentage of cataracts among Japanese survivors, noted:

> *"the steadily growing fear that the residual effects of atomic bombardment may be even more terrible than the immediate effects. One of the great anxieties is the possible hereditary consequences of radioactivity . . . . ."* (June 22, 1950.)

In 1949, however, the Truman Administration learned that it no long held a monopoly. Russia had exploded an atomic bomb. The reaction, however, was not cooperation and discussion, compromise or anything of that nature, but greater belligerence. Truman opted for escalation and confrontation. We speeded up efforts to jump into even greater instability, the hydrogen bomb -- a vastly more destructive weapon.

The sight of the mighty American forces being chased down the peninsula of Korea by "hordes" of Chinese foot soldiers armed just with rifles and without any artillery or tanks shocked the nation to its core during December of 1950. Notwithstanding our absolute control of the skies and our ability to bomb and napalm anyplace at will, unbelievably we were losing and it sent the nation into despair, anger and in some quarters even panic. Newspapers were full of debates, on the one hand, to give it all up and evacuate our troops, and on the other, to annihilate the Chinese with Atomic Bombs. The Military prepared backup plans for a total evacuation. Extra transport planes were sent in from other parts of the world.

Stratemeyer, Monday, December 4 1950:

> *"Was called to General MacArthur's office with Cabell* [Maj Gen Charles P. Cabell, Director of Intelligence, Headquarters USAF] *to hear a discussion . . . on the current Korean situation and General MacArthur's contemplated plans. . . . General MacArthur announced his*

contemplated plans which included not only retrograde movements, but, as a last resort . . . the later entire evacuation of UN forces. . . . There were other subject matters discussed that were of such a high classification that I dare not even put them in this document.. . . .

"During the conference . . . I made the following statement re evacuation from Korea [and then he gave the Air Force's capacity for airlifting the troops out of Korea] *. . . ."*

On the 6th Stratemeyer noted that "*I was depressed as hell at MacArthur's conference. I think MacArthur was too.*"

Partridge, who had just come to the Tokyo conference from the front lines in Korea, commented:

"You understand Walker has not been attacked; you understand Walker is not being pushed out of these positions, but is being outflanked. He does not know how many of them are there on his flanks. We strafe and kill 500 or 600 here and there all the time."

And later Partridge further comments:

"It is clear to me that General Walker is greatly depressed about being compressed in Seoul. Going into Seoul gave me the cold shivers."

A piece in the Washington Post on December 5th had headlined: "EVACUATION SEEN AS DIFFICULT; FEW SUITABLE PORTS AVAILABLE." The Post's editors further commented that:

"the situation is desperate . . . the cream of our Army is in Korea. We, and the non-Communist word, could ill afford to lose it or see it hacked to pieces.

347

Senator Harry F. Byrd of Virginia, an early enthusiastic supporter of the war just six months earlier, was quoted in a <u>New York Times</u> article of December 17, 1950 as saying that it had been "clearly obvious" for two weeks that American troops should be withdrawn from Korea because no reinforcements were available from any source.

> *"In simple language we are outnumbered and defeated in Korea. . . . [T]he military reverses . . . have brought about **national peril in a degree which we have never faced before in our history.**"* [Emphasis added.]

The <u>New York Times</u> military expert, Hanson W. Baldwin, had one of his articles captioned: "WESTERN CIVILIZATION FACES DESTRUCTION IF THREAT FROM EAST IS NOT MET BOLDLY" (December 1, 1950).

In this atmosphere "Give 'em Hell" and "The Buck Stops Here" Harry indeed gave everybody what they wanted. He responded "boldly."

At a press conference on November 30, 1950 after Truman said that he would take whatever steps were necessary to meet the deteriorating military situation, he was asked:

"Will that include the atomic bomb?"

His answer was:

"That includes every weapon that we have."

The exchange must have baffled or surprised the reporters. One reporter inquired further:

"Mr. President, you said 'every weapon that we have.' Does that mean that there is active consideration of the use of the atomic bomb?"

Truman replied:

"[T]here has always been active consideration of its use. I don't want to see it used. It is a terrible weapon . . . ."

The reporters apparently, could still not believe what they were hearing and perhaps were even frightened by what he had just said. The Atom bomb was an indiscriminately monstrous weapon -- with unpredictable and widespread radiation fallout and the unknown effects on humans even more feared than the known atrocities.. Was he even *kidding* about using it?

Q. Mr. President, I wonder if we could retrace that reference to the atom bomb? Did we understand you clearly that the use of the atomic bomb is under active consideration?

THE PRESIDENT. Always has been. It is one of our weapons.

*Q." Does that mean, Mr. President, **use against** military objectives, or **civilian** –"*

*THE PRESIDENT: "It's a matter that **the military people will have to decide**. I'm not a military authority that passes on those things."*

*THE PRESIDENT: "[**T**]**he military commander in the field will have charge of the use of the weapons, as he always has**."* [Emphasis added.]

Could "Give Them Hell" Harry, just five years after the horrors of Hiroshima and Nagasaki, be suggesting a repeat performance?

His language was quickly interpreted to mean that he had already given the aggressive warrior MacArthur authority to decide when to use the atomic bomb. Later that day, in reaction to a tornado of worldwide consternation, the White House issued a correction: the use of the bomb, it said, is always in the hands of the President and he had not yet delegated that authority. This, however, did little to stem the worldwide panic that immediately erupted from the press conference.

G. Hayden Raynor was an Advisor to the US Delegation to the UN General Assembly at the time. He wrote a Confidential Memo the next day, December 1, 1950, with a title: "President's Statement on Use of the Atomic Bomb" summarizing his conversations with representatives of some of the nations at the UN:

*"Many European and Commonwealth Delegates expressed to me yesterday general apprehension with respect to the President's statement and the hope that it **didn't mean what it seemed to mean**. The reaction was quite a serious one . . .*

350

[T]*here appeared to be* **great shock** *over the part* [of his statement] *which indicated that consideration was being given to its use. . . .*"

Eleanor Roosevelt, who was a US Delegate to one of the UN Committees at the time, recorded a conversation she had with Dr. Jamil M. Baroody, a Saudi delegate to the UN.

> "*Mr. Baroody spoke to me with deep emotion about the President's announcement of yesterday concerning the possible use of the atomic bomb in Korea. Dr. Baroody said that this matter had been discussed at great length among representatives of all the 'little countries" and that he would be grateful if I would transmit their views to the President.*
>
> "*Dr. Baroody said that the delegates representing the Near East and Asia were* **profoundly distressed and disturbed** *over the President's announcement that he was considering the possibility of using the atomic bomb against Chinese Communists . . . . The people of the whole Asiatic continent would never understand why the American people had decided to use the atomic bomb against them.* **They would regard it as an action of the white race against the colored races**. *. . . This fact* [that it had been used only against Japan and the Chinese] *would have a disastrous effect upon the relations of the United States with the rest of the world for years to come. . . .*"
> Volume I, 1950, Foreign Relations of the United States (FRUS), pages 115 and 116.

The editors of the New York Times also remarked on what leaders abroad were saying:

> "[T]*he very mention of the atom bomb sent an* **electric shock around the world** *. . . .* [T]*he world went through a* **veritable convulsion** *on Thursday at the mention*

351

of the possible use of the atomic bomb, and that is why Mr. Atlee [British Prime Minister] *is coming here.* (December 2, 1950.)

[All emphasis added]

Could Harry "The Buck Stops Here" Truman have just been bluffing in order to create all of this turmoil? Did he think it somehow would intimidate the Chinese or otherwise help our war efforts? It was a mystery to most observers. Could he be serious? Just five years later and he wanted a repeat of Hiroshima and Nagasaki?

Reporting on the feedback in India, a dispatch stated:

*"Certainly **the revulsion of feeling** in this country against any suggestion of using the atom bomb in Asia is great, and has caused an intensification of the latent anti-American sentiment among politically conscious people"* (Times [London]. December 4, 1950).

India's Prime Minister Nehru on December 3rd sent a message to his ambassador for delivery to the President which included this comment:

"Nehru believes that it is a matter of absolute necessity to avoid use of the atomic bomb. Such use would make war inevitable. There is wide-spread feeling in Asia that the atomic bomb is a weapon used only against Asiatics." (FRUS, 1950, VII, 1334.)

Our allies in Europe, who were still greatly dependent on us, e.g., the Marshall Plan, and were loath to be critical of the giant's moods, nevertheless could not restrain themselves at this potential apocalypse. They quickly unified behind British Prime Minister Atlee's decision to race to Washington the very next day for the purpose of urging caution on "Give Them Hell" Harry. The

352

Australian Foreign Minister, Spencer, thinking of some way to deflect this catastrophe, expressed the opinion that since it was United Nations' forces fighting in Korea, including a small contingent of Australians, that any resort to the atomic bomb should be a United Nations decision and not just a unilateral American decision (Times, [London], December 1, 1950).

That Truman actually was serious about using the atomic bomb in Korea, and that he would decide on his own whether or not to use it, became frightening clear during his talks with Atlee over the next few days.

The US from the beginning had had a limited sharing of information on the atomic bomb with the British primarily because it relied upon the British to supply some of the essential raw materials for manufacture of the bomb. At the Truman-Atlee conference the British kept trying to obtain Truman's promise to consult with them and other allies before any use of the bomb. Truman steadfastly refused, though at one point during the week long series of meetings he seemed to have given his word to Atlee, though he refused to put it in writing, that he would consult with the United Kingdom before its use. But even that meager assurance was watered down to meaningless ambiguities in the final communique issued by the two leaders after the conference.

> *"The President stated that it was his hope that would conditions would never call for the use of the atomic bomb. The President told the Prime Minister that it was also his desire to keep the Prime Minister at all times informed of developments which might bring about a change in the situation."* (FRUS, 1950, VII, 1435 - 1479.)

The was evident even in the sanitized records of his conversations with Atlee. That we in fact evaded a World War Three with such an inflexible and ideological leader must be considered a great a tribute to all the other people in Washington who made up our ultimate policies.

> *"The Prime Minister* [Atlee] *said opinions differ as to the extent to which Chinese Communists are satellites* [of Russia]. *He inquired when is it that you scratch a communist and find a nationalist."*

During their talks Atlee tried to nudge Truman towards a more realistic view of what was happening in the Far East. He tried in a delicate and diplomatic way to say the same thing that Marcantonio had said innumerable times in Congress and on the streets. The turmoil in the Far East was not being caused by the bogey man "communism," but by the deep-seated nationalism of indigenous peoples to rule themselves. That China was not a puppet of Russian. That their relations were complicated.

The reaction of Truman, as recorded by White House stenographers, was depressingly and fundamentally wrong, as well as stupid. It nakedly displayed the dangerously cartoonish view of the world held by the President of the United States:

> *"The President believes that they* [the Chinese] *are satellites of Russia and will be satellites so long as the present Peiping regime is in power. He thought they were complete satellites. The only way to meet communism is to eliminate it. After Korea, it would be Indochina, then Hong Kong, then Melaya. There was no chance to approach a solution without seeing clearly the course we should follow. He did not want war with China or anyone else, but the situation looks very dark to him . . . . He is not shutting the door to negotiations but does not think that they would be successful."*

Truman's simple minded and dangerously unintelligent view of what really was a complex relationship between China and Russia would shape American foreign policy for decades. It is a mystery how the President of the United States could be so profoundly wrong on such a fundamental issue. Nearly every other leader in the world, with the exception of Sigmund Rhee, understood that there were real differences between the interests of China and that of Russia. If every other leader knew, for instance, that Stalin had given almost no help to Mao during Mao's many years of warfare with Chiang, why did Harry Truman not know this? Where had he been for the past 20 years?

Even newspaper reporters knew that China was not a satellite of Russia. For example, in an October 29, 1950 <u>New York Times</u> Magazine article by Henry R. Lieberman, captioned: "Great Question Mark in Asia -- Mao. China's new leader is at once pro-Stalin but no yes-man, independent but no Titoist," the author noted:

> *"neither Mao's record nor his personality permits the conclusion that he is an automatics yes man."*

Well, there was at least one person in the United States who was not aware of that: Harry Truman.

Later on in his discussions with Atlee he further revealed his hopelessly tabloid-like worldview when he stated that:

> *"the Russians only understand the mailed fist and that is what we are preparing for them."*

Then after the reading of an American point for the group that any *"United Nations evacuation* [from Korea] *must be clearly the result of military necessity only"* and not a voluntary one, meaning that the US would not withdraw from Korea unless it was absolutely forced to do so:

> *"the President here interposed that we cannot get out voluntarily. All the Koreans left behind would be murdered.* **The communists care nothing about human life.***"* Volume III, <u>Foreign Relations of the US</u>, December 4, 1950, pages 1706 – 1716. [Emphasis added.]

This! . . . from Hiroshima Harry? **This!** . . . from Nagasaki Harry? And the Harry who at that very moment was refusing to say whether he would be dropping A-Bombs, the most indiscriminately destructive weapon known to mankind, over 10 or 20 cities in Korea and China.

What is it in the human spirit that could so deceive itself?

This was light years away from the flexible, nuanced and pragmatic way Roosevelt had handled international affairs or important decisions with our allies. The British were not happy with this, but they tried to put the best face on it as they trooped back to London with their tails between their legs. (See Times [London]. December 12 and 13, 1950.)

Two days after Truman's public threat to use the A-Bomb, Army Chief of Staff, General J. Lawton Collins, took off on a much publicized trip to speak to MacArthur in the Far East. The Press speculated that discussions would include possible total evacuation of American troops as well as the use of the atomic bomb. With Collins, significantly, traveled Major General Charles P. Cabell, director of Intelligence for the Air Force and Vice Admiral F.S. Lowe, the Deputy Chief of Naval Operation for logistics. General Stratemeyer's cryptic diary entries around this time give tantalizing clues but no full explanation as to American plans to use atomic bombs.

On December 1 Air Force Chief of Staff Vandenberg sent an "EYES ONLY" memo to Stratemeyer which quoted a news release from Washington about President Truman's threat to use the atomic bomb. Immediately upon receipt of this memo both MacArthur and Stratemeyer jumped into speculations.

Stratemeyer, Friday, 1 December, 1950:

> *"General MacArthur at 1400 hours today, in his office, stated that in a war with Communist China and if he was given the use of the atomic weapon, his targets in order of priority would be: ANTUNG, MUKDEN, PEIPING, TIENTSIN, SHANGHAI AND NANKING. [Capitalization in the original.]That if we get in the big one [war with Russia]. His targets would be VLADIVOSTOK, KHABAROVSK, KIRIN, and a further one which I believe was KUYVSHIEVKA."*

Later that day Stratemeyer sent a "TOP SECRET" radio to Air Force General Twining, Chief of Operations:

> *"Dr. Ellis A. Johnson, director ORO, DA [Operation Research Office, Department of the Army] has proposed to provide GHQ [MacArthur] within next week a critical evaluation of the possible use and effectiveness of atomic bombs in close support of ground forces in Korea. . . . It is understood that ORO analysts have been working on this project since September. . . ."*

Stratemeyer, Monday, 4 December, 1950:

> *"General Cabell with General Collis and Admiral F.S. Lowe arrived this AM . . . Was called to General MacArthur's office with Cabell to hear a discussion . . . . There were other subject matters discussed that were of such a high classification that I dare not even put them in this document."*

357

Stratemeyer, Thursday, 7 December, 1950:

> *"Attended conference in General MacArthur's conference room; present beside himself were Generals Collins, Hickey, Wright, Whitney, Willoughby, Cabell and myself: Admirals Joy and Lowe . . . . General Collins then posed this question – with the use of your present force, and the potential that might be made available, and a possible recommended us of the A bomb -- what would you do?"*

MacArthur speaking with the agreement of the others said that the issue should be put off for a month to see where they were at that time.

The British military staff that had been assigned to MacArthur's headquarters must have picked up the American excitement about the possible use of the A-bomb. Stratemeyer gives us their views in his diary. Saturday, 9 December 1950:

> *"1500 hours [British] Air Vice Marshal Bouchier gave me the following information. . . . British Chiefs of Staff view is that if the atom bomb was used in Korea it would **not be effective in holding up Chinese advance** -- but **make the situation more desperate** by inevitably bringing the Soviet Air Force into the war. The A bomb is our ultimate weapon and we should surely keep it in reserve as a deterrent, or for use in event of Russia launching a third world war. . . ."*

The British Chiefs of Staff also sent along their opinion that MacArthur's lobbying to cross the border into Manchuria with his forces or at least with bombing raids would also be counterproductive and would bring the Soviets into the war. Their sources warned about this eventuality, just as they had earlier warned about the Chinese entering the war if we crossed the 38th pararallel. Stratemeyer's diary for that day also detailed activities regarding evacuation, the continuing retreat on the ground and extensive messages to his commanders about Washington's concern that a general war could erupt at any moment. The commanders were instructed to prepare their forces for that event and take the necessary precautions, but without spreading a panic. Stratemeyer's final comment in his diary for that Saturday was: *"This was a tough day."*

Over a month later a decision to use the A-bomb in Korea and China does not seem to have been any further developed and was still under study.

Stratemeyer, Tuesday, 30 January, 1951:

> *"At 0800 hours I was briefed by General Banfill and Colonel Gould on the study that was sent to the Director of Intelligence, Washington, D.C. on the A bomb targets in the Far East. Every target selected by CINCFE and those selected by us were reviewed and complete data on each was submitted with our recommended list of targets."*

The Chinese had brushed off Truman's A-Bomb announcement as "saber rattling threats" that would not affect their actions. The Russians, on the other hand, began warning their people about the possibility of a general war with the United States.

The fears about long-term effects on mankind of the use of atomic bombs in Korea, while publicly discussed, do not seem to have played any role in American strategic thinking. The snatches of comments one catches among the Generals during the war give no hint of that concern -- the central question always was whether the A-bomb would help "win" the war. There had been little hesitancy about mass killings of the civilian population. As LeMay and O'Donnell readily acknowledged, they killed as many people using conventional explosives as they would have by using anything else. The answer as to why the A-bomb itself was not used in Korea or China during the Korean War is contained in the desperate arguments between the Joint Chiefs of Staff and MacArthur as revealed in part by their later testimony in Congress.

As much as they studied the subject the conclusion always was that the A-Bomb in Korea would not be an effective weapon. In 1950 the 300 atomic bombs held by the United States were blockbusters with a great deal of radioactive fallout. Their use in the confined battle area of Korea would endanger as many American soldiers as enemy soldiers.

This simple mathematical fact-on-the- ground, however, did not keep some of the more rambunctious Generals and politicians, as well as the increasingly unstable President Rhee, from constantly suggesting its use.

But even of greater concern to serious US policymakers was whether its use in Korea or in China might trigger a retaliatory attack by Russia. Were Russia to conclude from American use of the atomic bomb in Korea or China that America had decided to launch World War III, then Russia would have to move before it was extinguished. The Soviets at that time had retaliatory options which no power in the West could ignore or prevent. First, and most easily, it could overrun our Allies in Western Europe with its vast armies stationed in East Europe. Even more ominously for our side, our Generals could not guarantee that the Soviets could not deliver their own atomic bombs to the United States, even from their relatively small stockpile, estimated at about 30 at the time. Finally, the US simply did not have enough atomic bombs and airplanes to eliminate **both** China and Russia at the same time, so one of them might be able to survive the United States.

In other words, the Joint Chiefs of Staff at that time were concerned that in any all-out World War III, we might lose.

Hoyt S. Vandenberg, the Air Force Chief of Staff, testified as much before Congress during the hearings in 1951 on

MacArthur's ouster. MacArthur's insistent pushing to go into Manchuria and to bomb China in the view of the Joint Chiefs of Staff was leading us into a general war with Russia and China, and this was the last thing we could afford.

> *"The fact is that the United States is operating a shoestring air force in view of its global responsibilities . . . we cannot afford to peck at the periphery. . . . While we can lay the countryside* [of China] *waste, as well as the principal cities of China, we cannot do both."*

"Gen. Hoyt S. Vandenberg, US Air Force Chief of Staff, toured advanced air bases [in Korea] . . . [l. to r.] Jim Becker, AP war correspondent, Major Thomas D. Robertson, Lt. Col. Jack Dale, . . . Gen Vandenberg, Richard Cresswell and Lt. James F. Kirkendall . . . ." January, 1951 USAF

Vandenberg's biographer, Phillip S. Meilinger (Hoyt S. Vandenberg: The Life of a General, Air Force History and Museums Program), tells us that the portion of Vandenberg's testimony deleted by the censors stated that **80** percent of the USAF's tactical strength and **25** percent of its strategic forces were already tied up in Korea. An expansion of the war, in view of the known enormous Soviet air strength in the Far East which as yet had not stirred, would make the Air Force "extremely hard pressed." In other words, while we had more A-bombs, the Soviets had enough air power to eventually get around our defenses and into the US.

The realization that we might actually lose a war with Russia and China finally began to sink into even the densest heads on Capitol Hill. Thereafter the outrage over MacArthur's firing began to be muted and then faded entirely, except for fringe elements for which neither reason nor common sense played any role.

This testimony may have been given in secret, but it was nevertheless widely understood that we could not win a war against both China and Russia. General Omar Bradley, Chief of the Joint Chiefs of Staff, in arguing for extraordinary sums to rearm the United States and its allies, had

> *"bluntly emphasized the 'brushing and shocking' fact that as a result of our commitment in the Korean conflict this country is now without an adequate margin of military strength to meet a general enemy attack, must less defend our allies."* (Editorial, "Mr. Truman and the Crisis." New York Times, December 15, 1950).

As for our use of chemical and biological weapons in Korea, I cannot find anything definitive among the diaries, though I would not expect to find anything there. The Chinese and North Koreans at the time had accused the US of employing chemical and biological weapons, but nothing definitive has turned up in the Archives that I have searched. And no veteran has suggested that such was used. After 50 years, this absence of evidence should be enough to exclude the probability of their having been employed.

On the other hand, that they were being actively considered by some in the military and in Washington is clear from the diaries.

Stratemeyer, Thursday 22 March 1951:

> *"In Colonel Zimmerman's [Don Z. Zimmerman, Director; Plans and Policy, FEAF] report as of a result of his trip to Washington . . . two items disturbed me . . . . and*

362

(2) they (USAF) desired a request from FEAF for the use of chemicals and biological in the Korean war."

General Stratemeyer seems here to be saying that the Air Force planners in the US wanted the Far East Commanders to request chemical and biological weapons. The weapons apparently were already in stockpile and someone in Washington wanted the FEAF to ask for them. Stratemeyer is not happy with this, but does not explain why. No mention again is made of this subject in his diary.

General Partridge's diary, on the other hand, does not refer to employing chemical or biological weapons, except for napalm and other incendiaries. Partridge, however, was a lot more circumspect about what he put into his diary. Even so, there is one interesting discussion he relates about trying to destroy the Korean rice stockpiles and growing crops.

Partridge, Saturday 3 March 1951:

"This morning, Doctor Cohen came in response to my request for an Operations Analyst. While he is a statistician, and on his way up to Kimpo to analyze the bomber damage there, I took advantage of his presence to pitch him a problem regarding the destruction of rice supplies. We are currently locating rice in piles which are stacked in light straw bags without any cover from the elements other than the bags themselves. It seems to me that there should be some way of insuring that this can be made inedible. Presently, we are attacking it with Napalm in an effort to burn up the stacks themselves. We are not sure that this method is effective and I asked that the Operational Annalist study the problem.

*"In passing, I mentioned that there are now available in the States many **chemicals which might be utilized for spraying rice crops** to discourage the growth of*

the rice while still in the paddies. He mentioned the use of 24D weed killer as an example of the type chemical now coming available. We have no idea how much would be required per square mile nor would be strictly exploratory."

Partridge makes no further mention of the subject. *Agent Orange* was for another war.

A WORD ABOUT VITO MARCANTONIO

Vito Marcantonio represented East Harlem from 1935 to 1950, except for the years 1937 and 1938. He always ran as the candidate of the American Labor Party ("ALP"), a number of times also as the Republican or Fusion candidate, and twice (1942 and 1944) he was the candidate for the three major parties in his district, ALP, Republican and Democratic. The original base of his support was the first and second generation Italian voters in East Harlem; then they were joined by Puerto Ricans as they arrived into New York City and a significant segment of Blacks. His politics were left wing and even "radical" for his time, labor oriented and always on the side of the oppressed.

In Congress he led the decades long battle against the poll tax and for anti-lynching legislation; against discrimination in hiring in the federal government and by government contractors; and in desegregating Washington D.C. itself. Because of his politics the various leaderships over the years rarely gave him any committee assignments. The closest he ever got to an important committee position was when FRD and the Democratic Congressional leadership attempted to reward him in 1943 for getting a number of Democrats elected to the House so as to ensure the Party's majority. The Steering Committee recommended him for a seat on the House Judiciary Committee, where he could more effectively push his anti-lynching and anti-poll tax campaigns. However a solid Southern Block rebelled in the House and rejected his nomination -- a rare rebuke to Steering Committee. He subsequently refused to accept any substitute committee assignment.

By necessity then he became an expert in parliamentary procedure to make the most of his seat in Congress. He promoted his causes sometimes just as a single voice calling: "objection" or "point of order" or "point of personal privilege" from the back of the House floor. He would work with others where he could, for example in seeking to push bills like the poll tax bill onto the House floor by petition against the wishes of the leadership. On some issues, however, like the Korean War, he often found himself alone.

Paul Robeson, W.E.B. DuBois and Vito Marcantonio

His opponents tried everything to get rid of him. In 1944 they gerrymandered his district to include a large number of conservative German and Irish voters down the East Side to 59th Street, only to have him enter and win the primaries of all the three parties. Then they passed a law in Albany directed just against him, prohibiting a person from running in the primary of a party without that party's leadership's prior approval. But he kept winning anyway, as his devotion to his constituents and his endless hours of work for them were repaid at the ballot box each election day.

J. Edgar Hoover's FBI must have expended a vast amount of manpower to shadow this Congressman, as the minutia-laden but pointless file on him in the FBI would suggest. Most assuredly he was also one of the 12,000 Americans on Hoover's list of "potentially dangerous" individuals which he suggested be arrested and put into military jails in a report sent to the White House just after the start of the Korean War. (Time Weiner. "Hoover Planned Mass Jailing in 1950." <u>New York Times</u>, December 23, 2007).

The "Get Vito" crusade finally succeeded in 1950. The Republican and Democratic leaders agreed to join forces and field only one candidate against him. Meanwhile the more conservative labor leaders had broken away from the American Labor Party and established the "Liberal" party. That break-away right wing labor party also supported in 1950 the one candidate being fielded by the Republicans and Democrats. The numbers in his district now were against him. But he ran anyway.

It did not help that he was the lone dissenter that summer on the Korean War, nor that he took to the streets to oppose the war. Nor did it help that just before the November election some Puerto Rican extremists tried to shoot Truman in an outlandishly hopeless assassination attempt. Marcantonio had been closely tied in the public mind with the Nationalists and their cause of Puerto Rican independence. His enemies made the most of the guilt-by-association smear. The local papers promptly reprinted photos from 15 years earlier when he had gone to Puerto Rico to help defend the nationalist leader, Dr. Pedro Albizu Campos. Campos, the President of the Nationalist Party, had been convicted essentially for advocating the independence of Puerto Rico and subsequently served seven years in jail for his beliefs.

Every mainstream paper in New York, and in fact papers across the country, including the <u>Washington Post</u>, was calling for Marcantonio's head. The <u>New York Times</u>, for the first and last time in its history, limited its congressional ballot recommendations that November to one race, Marcantonio's. The <u>Times</u> strongly advocated the candidacy of the nonentity fielded by the three other parties in his District. The only common thread in all of this was the passion to defeat Marcantonio.

But he was not to be counted out until literally the last minute of that Congressional Session. We can catch a glimpse of the extraordinary measure of the man in two incidents in his last days in Congress. Both struck chords he had been sounding since his arrival in Washington in the mid-thirties.

On December 15, 1950 he moved to amend a Korean War military appropriations bill to add the following provision:

> *That none of the funds appropriated in this act shall be paid to any person, partnership, firm, or corporation which denies equality in employment because of race, color, or creed.*

He had been trying from his first day in office in 1935 to generate support for a national policy of non-discrimination in employment. He had some success during World War II with the Fair Employment Practices Commission and Executive Orders of FDR covering the defense industry. But things had gone backwards since the War. By this motion he was telling his colleagues: You hypocrites! Pretending to be rescuing the "little brown people" in the Orient when you are still sending segregated military forces to Korea and you won't give jobs to blacks or immigrants. Though he himself would not use these words. Until the very end he treated his colleagues with the greatest respect, and for the most part that respect was reciprocated. His motion, essentially symbolic, as expected was defeated 219 to 1. He had agreed with the leadership not to delay the bill provided they agreed to take a recorded vote. He wanted posterity to read the names of these people who were doing the wrong thing – for whatever it was worth.

Then on the very last day of that Congress, an extraordinary New Year's Day session on January 1, 1951, the leadership of the departing Congress was trying to get unanimous approval for a number of items to clean up its business. The most important was an amendment to the War Powers Act which would allow for the renegotiation of government contracts for the purchase of armaments and the like for the Korean War. Many companies had been complaining that the price of raw goods had gone up since they signed contracts with the government to produce the military clothing, the airplanes, the tanks, the armaments, and all the other products necessary for the war effort. Many now threatened bankruptcy and the consequent disruption of war production if they were not allowed to renegotiate the contracts and increase the prices. Industry's friends in Congress quickly got an emergency renegotiation bill, that is, a bill to raise the cost of the contracts, on the floor and the leadership urgently asked that it be passed unanimously.

But Marcantonio got up and objected.

He did not want to thwart the will of the Congress, he said, nor delay the production of goods necessary for the war, as much as he opposed the war. But he was not going to sit still while some people took advantage of the war to gouge on indecent profits.

I believe this bill is in the interest of increasing war profiteering and the men in Korea are being used as an excuse for war profiteering.

He moved to amend the bill so that all requests for renegotiation of prices had to be reviewed by the Comptroller General, an independent and trusted accounting arm of the Government, and not just by an official in the Defense Department's procuring office. This fundamental review procedure, which was a basic safeguard to all government contracts, should not be skipped by merely calling the situation an "emergency." The Comptroller had the resources and the know-how, Marcantonio argued, so the renegotiation process would not be delayed.

369

"I think every Member of this House," he said, *"will agree that the best guaranty against mulcting the Government and the people of these United States in using this emergency for war profiteering in this connection would be simply to add these words: 'Subject to the approval of the Comptroller General.'"*

Marcantonio's request was too simple and overwhelmingly compelling. No one could get up and argue against it. Emanuel Celler, the Brooklyn Congressman who was an old friend of Marcantonio's, was handling the bill on the House floor. Celler reluctantly agreed to add Marcantonio's words to the bill, since the Virginian sponsor of the bill himself was not objecting. But just as the House was about to add Marcantonio's amendment requiring Comptroller General review of all renegotiations, the Speaker, Sam Rayburn, intervened and put the bill aside, saying he would take it up tomorrow – with the new Congress, that is, without Marcantonio.

And so it went.

[For more on Marcantonio see Rubinstein, Annette T., ed. Vito Marcantonio: Debates, Speeches and Writings 1935 – 1950. Clifton: Augustus M. Kelley, 1973; Schaffer, Alan. Vito Marcantonio: Radical in Congress. Syracuse: Syracuse University Press, 1966; Meyer, Gerald. Vito Marcantonio: Radical Politician 1902 – 1954. Albany, State University of New York Press, 1989.]

The Author

Arthur J. Paone was born in Brooklyn, NY; graduated from Xavier High School in Manhattan; Georgetown College in D.C.; Cornell Law School, Ithaca, NY., and practiced the profession of law in New York and Dallas, Texas. He is now retired and lives in Belmar, NJ and Manhattan, NY.

Over the years he has written and self- published several books on different topics:

Wobby Wennedy, 1965, (under the name of Das Cellini), a satirical account of Robert Kennedy's 1964 race for the U.S. Senate from New York;

Conflicts of Interest, 1975, an analysis of the foundations of the Buckley family's wealth from aggressively promoted penny stocks based on ambiguous mineral leaseholds in environmentally sensitive Florida wetlands and Senator James Buckley's related activities in the US Senate;

Liberating Korea? , 2003, explains how wholesale American destruction during the Korean War has convinced North Korean Governments ever since that they must develop some type of doomsday deterrence to keep the Americans from doing it again, (revised in 2013 with new title: "Give 'em Hell" Harry's Liberation of Korea);

371

So Sue Me!, 2004, (under the names L. Meier and D. Cellini), a step by step roadmap of various legal theories under which the Palestinians could sue the State of Israel and its officials in U.S. Courts to obtain justice;

Hillary in Gilo, 2007, an account, with numerous photos, of Paone's 2007 visit to Palestine and the Israeli settlement of Gilo outside Bethlehem which then Senate Hillary Clinton had visited in 2005 to praise the Wall being constructed by Israel, all on confiscated Palestinian lands;

Israel, Our Frankenstein, 2010, written after Paone's 2009 journey to devastated Gaza and which debunks the Israel Lobby's deeply embedded myth that the theocratic and undemocratic State of Israel shares any common values with the people of the United States.

Along the way Paone has run for Congress twice (endorsed each time by the New York Times: 1974 and 1976); toyed with races for the US Senate; unsuccessfully sued the State of Israel in Federal Court to enjoin it from selling its Bonds in the US because the funds were being used by Israel to commit War Crimes as defined both under our laws and international law; and has obtained a US Patent (#8,156,580 issued April 17, 2012) for a modified sink.

He spends most of his time in Belmar, a "Jersey Shore" community, with his three dogs and cat, and with his wife who commutes weekly to Manhattan where she still works.

*[Personal note to the Reader. Sorry, but I do not have the energy or patience to do a decent **Index** nor to catalogue all the books and articles I have read and borrowed from to write this book. One of the downsides of being a self-publisher on a shoestring.]*